THE CULLING

First Edition
First Printing, 2013

Book design by Bob Gaul
Cover design by Lisa Novak
Cover illustration by Chris Nurse/Debut Art Ltd.

Flux, an imprint of Llewellyn Worldwide Ltd.

Library of Congress Cataloging-in-Publication Data
Dos Santos, Steven.
　The culling.—1st ed.
　　p. cm.—(The torch keeper; bk. 1)
　Summary: "In a futuristic world ruled by a totalitarian government called the Establishment, Lucian "Lucky" Spark and four other teenagers are recruited for the Trials. They must compete not only for survival but to save the lives of their Incentives, family members whose lives depend on how well they play the game"—Provided by publisher.
　ISBN 978-0-7387-3537-5
　[1. Survival—Fiction. 2. Contests—Fiction. 3. Brothers and sisters—Fiction. 4. Orphans—Fiction. 5. Government, Resistance to—Fiction. 6. Homosexuality—Fiction. 7. Science fiction.] I. Title.
　PZ7.D73673Cul 2013
　[Fic]—dc23

2012041699

Flux
Llewellyn Worldwide Ltd.
2143 Wooddale Drive
Woodbury, MN 55125-2989
www.fluxnow.com

Printed in the United States of America

THE CULLING

The Torch Keeper: Book One

STEVEN DOS SANTOS

flux
™
Woodbury, Minnesota

To my beloved mother, Gladys dos Santos, culled from this world way too soon. Not a day goes by that my heart doesn't ache for your warmth and encouragement, Mom. If I could have chosen, you'd be here with me now. Love you always...

PART I

THE RECRUITMENT

ONE

I've been chasing sleep for hours and finally accept the fact that I'm never going to catch it. Even if I could afford black-market meds and was willing to risk Cole's life, as well as my own, no amount of anti-anxiety drugs will quell the unease poisoning my blood.

Not on the eve of the Recruitment.

My palm presses against the cold windowpane of the box-like tenement we call home, wiping away a swatch of condensation. A spark of orange stains the dark sky, silhouetting the smokestacks from the Industrial Borough, hissing puffs of black death into the stars. That same lethal smoke birthed the cancers that devoured both of my parents' dignity before leaving two brothers with only each other.

And before this day is through, maybe not even that.

The floorboards creak. Probably another damn rat. That's three this week. I grope for the oil lamp on the nightstand, careful not to turn the flame too high, so as not to wake up Cole, asleep on the cot beside mine.

Too late. He's propped up on his elbows, his big chocolate eyes staring at me through the flickering light. "Did you have a scary dream too, Lucky?" he asks.

It used to bother me when Cole nicknamed me Lucky, instead of calling me Lucian, until I realized just how aptly it described the way I felt about having him in my life. And it's a hell of a lot better than *Lucy*.

I move to sit beside him, ruffling his hair. "What are you doing up, big guy? No school today, remember?" There's never school on this day. Or work for that matter. The Establishment makes sure that everyone participates in all Recruitment Day activities.

Cole reaches out a warm, pink hand and grasps one of my own. "I can't sleep, Lucky. The monsters'll get me."

Can he sense what's coming?

Leaning in close, I smile. "Nothing's going to hurt you, Cole. I won't let it."

He lets go of my hand and throws his small arms around my neck, burying his face in my chest. I enfold his trembling body in a tight embrace.

"Can you read me the story?" he whispers in my ear.

I pull away, staring at him. "I'll read it if you promise to go back to sleep."

He lights up. "Promise!"

I shake my head, rise, and walk over to the small dresser in the corner of the room, sliding it aside. I stoop and pry up one of the floorboards with my fingernails. Reaching into the dark crevice, I ease out a few sheets of blackened paper.

Cole's been fascinated with the story ever since I discovered it a few months ago, hidden in the basement archives of the Parish library, just after I started working with old Mr. Croakley. When anyone turns sixteen in the Parish, they're assigned an apprenticeship until they're drafted into the standard military—or recruited. I'd lucked out. I could have pulled sewer duty.

This particular tale was hidden inside a dusty book, part of a collection that ranged from astronomy to poetry. I must have devoured the entire compilation in a matter of weeks.

I sink into the creaking mattress beside Cole. "Now remember. You can't tell anyone about the story. I *mean* it. It would get us both into trouble and they could take you away from me. You don't want that, do you?"

His eyes widen. "No, Lucky. I won't never ever tell."

I hate to scare him like this, but it's the only way to protect him. The Establishment has very strict guidelines about what it deems appropriate reading in its schools, and fairy tales just don't make the cut. But I think a four-year-old deserves whatever happiness he can squeeze out of this life and I'll be damned if I'm not going to give Cole whatever I can.

Picking up the pages, I begin to read. Well, pretend to read actually. Most of the text is illegible, either burned or torn away. But it's the drawing that excites Cole.

So I've made up the tale, using a few of the key phrases that I can decipher. If Cole notices that the words vary with each reading, he never says. It's the ritual that seems to cast its spell—me reading, him listening.

And the drawing.

"There once was a beautiful queen that ruled over the land of Usofa," I begin.

For the next fifteen minutes, I go on and on about the benevolent Lady, how she reigns over the City of Sparkling Lights, tweaking this version here and there for dramatic effect. You'd think it was Cole's first time hearing this story, based on all his questions: Does the Lady protect the people from the monsters? From illness? Does she give them plenty of food, read to them?

Keep their parents alive?

As I patiently address each and every question, I know it's not answers he's looking for, but something far greater . . . something I'm not sure I can really give . . .

Reassurance.

"And they lived happily ever after," I finally finish, acting as if I'm going to put away the pages.

"The picture! The picture!"

I smile. "All right, buddy. Take it easy! Here it is."

His face is a mixture of awe and joy as he studies the drawing on the page I'm holding out to him. It's a regal woman, wearing a crown emitting the sun's rays, torch held high in her right hand, a large bound book in the other. Her face seems serene as she stares at the magical city before her, lit up like the constellations.

"She's almost as beautiful as Mommy was," Cole whispers.

I smile. How can he remember that? He was too young when she ...

An image of our mother floods my brain. The wheezing, gasping for breath, her eyes rolling up into their sockets—No. Not today. "Yep. She almost is." I pull the page away. "Now you promised you'd go back to sleep." I re-tuck him in, before he can protest.

He leans forward and kisses my cheek. "I love you, Lucky."

As I stare down at him, he suddenly becomes blurry. "I love you, too, Cole."

I plant a kiss on his forehead and snuff out the lamp's flame. In a few minutes I can hear the soft sounds of his rhythmic breathing. Hopefully, the dream monsters will be kept at bay, if only for a few hours. Why couldn't it be this simple with the real monsters?

Plopping down on my own bed, I can't get the image of the old sketch out of my mind. A beautiful city watched over by a noble Lady. A place where people were free. Free to express their ideas, live their lives without fear. No wonder Cole likes the story so much. A place like that would be paradise compared to our lives in the Parish.

Surely, it had to be a fairy tale. If such a place ever existed it's completely gone now, destroyed by the Ash Wars untold ages ago, replaced by the all-knowing, ever-present monster: the Establishment.

The monster that will decide in just a few hours whether or not I'll be responsible for my little brother's death.

TWO

The rusty key won't budge. I have to jiggle it a few times before the tumblers surrender and I'm rewarded with an anemic *click*. It stinks having to trust Cole's safety to a corroded piece of metal, but if I don't risk this outing, the thought of what could happen to him terrifies me even more. Hopefully I'll be back before he wakes up and finds me gone. Besides, he won't be totally alone.

Brushing away a few paint flurries that drift from the door onto my sleeve, I creep down the dim corridor, side-stepping mounds of trash, none of which is ever edible. Food, regardless of freshness level or olfactory appeal, is *never* thrown out. Period.

Something squishes beneath me. The heat of whatever it is soaks through my soles. I scrape the mystery onto the warped floorboards without bothering to look.

It's better not to know.

Finally, I'm at the end of the hallway, in front of Mrs. Bledsoe's apartment. It used to say No. 15 above the door, but the five had about all it could take years ago, just like Mr. Bledsoe had when their only daughter, Dahlia, was recruited. Now there's only the 1 left, both inside and out.

I'm about to knock when the sounds of a motor struggling to putter into existence on the other side cement me in place. Only it's not a motor. It's organic. The wheeze of tortured lungs repelling an invader, and only succeeding in hawking up tissue and darkness.

Reaper's Cough, as it's known in the Parish.

My eyes squeeze shut. Mrs. Bledsoe's always been there to help out. She was a rock for Mom when Dad passed. Then she'd practically adopted Cole and me when Mom couldn't hold on any longer. Now she'll be lucky if she sees another summer.

I open my eyes and take in the filth surrounding me, barely visible in the meager light, courtesy of the extra hour of electricity the Establishment so graciously provided us with on this oh-so-festive occasion.

Maybe Mrs. Bledsoe's the lucky one after all.

My knuckles meet the door.

The whooping becomes muffled, as if a hand is trying to suppress it before being betrayed by the next determined assault. Then the unmistakable sound of feet shuffling across the floor, pausing just beyond the door.

I tap softer now, leaning in close. "Mrs. Bledsoe, it's me, Lucian."

A long breath hisses free. No telltale phlegm this time. Relief, not Reaper.

The bolt squeaks its way across its housing, freeing the door, which creaks open about six inches. A set of eyes peers up at me, one bloodshot, the other encased in a grayish shroud. They find my own, and the wrinkles surrounding them relax. "Lucky? Oh, thank goodness it's only *you!*"

The door opens all the way, exposing a short, thin woman, gray hair matted around her skull, concave cheeks on a face the color of flour. Her hands are dry and cracked, like the walls.

Is this what I'll look like when *I* turn forty?

I tear my eyes away before she realizes I'm staring. "Sorry to bother you so early."

Her lips curve, showing as little of her yellowed teeth as she can get away with and technically call it a smile. "Like anyone could sleep, today of all days." Her words may be referring to today's event, but her liquid eyes are all about Dahlia on this loathsome anniversary. I can't help but feel guilty, intruding on her memories.

"Well, don't just stand there, boy." She steps aside and waves me in. "Come in and let me fix us some breakfast."

I almost chuckle at the lunacy of the idea that she'd have enough food to feed me, let alone the both of us, if it weren't for the sincerity swaddling her words. I stoop under the doorway and enter.

She cocks her head to peer behind me. "Where's my little Cole?"

"Mrs. Bledsoe, I can't stay. That's why I'm here. I need you to keep an eye on him while I'm out."

She shuts the door. The trenches dissecting her forehead deepen. "Where can you possibly be going at this hour of the morning? You know there's a curfew until Recruitment is underway. If you're caught by any of the Imposers without the proper authorizations..." She erupts into another hacking spell. Turning away, she pulls a ragged piece of cloth from a frayed pocket, clutching it to her mouth.

My hand finds her trembling shoulder, squeezing it until the convulsions peter out. "You need to see a doctor right away. Maybe I can barter for medical services in exchange for some labor until I can cover the rest of the fees."

I barely make enough money working at the library to feed Cole, with a few scraps left over for myself, but I'll find a way, even if I have to cut down on sleep and take a side job. No one should have to suffer like this. Especially Mrs. Bledsoe.

She shakes her head. "No need. I'm all right, dear. It's just a little hay fever. It'll pass."

The splattering of bright crimson on the rag she stuffs into her pocket says otherwise.

Why do we even bother to cling to this hell we breathe in, day after day?

Then I see Cole's shiny face in my mind's eye.

"Can you watch him for me, please? I promise I won't be long."

"Tell me you haven't gotten involved with..." Her voice drops to a whisper. "With *those people* and their crazy notions. I hear the word on the streets. And so does the Establishment. Rumor has it they're starting to make notes, take names ... there's even talk there was a raid down at the Roarkeshire Farm. I'm scared of what'll happen next."

It's more than just idle gossip. I watched it unfold, hidden in a tree in a neighboring field. The entire place burned to its foundation. No one ever came out. I can still smell the roasting flesh. But I can't worry her. "It's nothing like that." I shrug. "Besides, could it really get any worse than it already is?"

A hand shoots out and grabs my chin. "Oh, *yes*. It most definitely can. *Don't* you forget it."

Her intensity claws through me like icy talons. I shrink in her gaze. "I didn't mean any disrespect."

The grip on my chin relaxes, evolving into a pat on the cheek and then a mussing of my hair. "Forgive me, Lucky. I just worry about you and your brother. You're ... you're all I have left ... " She steps back, appraising me now, ice melted.

"Did you get a chance to see her yesterday during the Ascension Ceremony?"

She stifles another cough. "Just for a few moments. Right after the Prior gave the benediction. I can't believe she's been promoted to First Tier already."

Just one step away from becoming a full-fledged Imposer ...

"It seems like just yesterday she was recruited." Her good eye clouds over, too. "She looked so grown-up in her uniform. Not like my little Dahlia. I tried to get her attention as she left the dais, but... she must not have seen me." She wipes her eyes.

"I'm very sorry. I know it's been a long time."

"You're *so* like her. The same wavy dark hair... that olive skin she got from her father..." Her voice chokes off.

Being recruited tears families apart. That's why I have to risk what I'm about to do.

Clearing her throat, Mrs. Bledsoe places her hands on her hips. "Only *you're* too thin, boy! We need to feed you better. When you get back from your errand, I'll have some breakfast ready. And then the three of us will sit down and eat before heading off to the opening ceremonies. Like a proper family."

"Thanks, Mrs. Bledsoe." I turn before she can see the gratitude streaking from my eyes.

"And Lucky," her voice calls after me, "your mother and father would be very proud of you."

Without turning back, I walk out and shut the door, leaning against it to catch my breath. I wonder if she'd feel the same way if she knew that not only am I planning to break curfew, but I'm going to make sure I get caught by the Establishment in the process.

THREE

Pressed against the rear of the building, I slink down the alley, ignoring the soot and slime oozing onto my back. At least I remembered to wear my rattiest clothes, though considering the state of my wardrobe, it wasn't a difficult choice.

I barely escape a loud splash that spatters my boots with a strong stench of ammonia. Smothering a gag, I look up. A rusty basin disappears into a fifth-floor window, which slams shut with a rattle. Guess all those years of playing Dodge Piss in these very alleys with the rest of the neighborhood kids paid off. Or maybe it's just the universe hinting at the chances of my plan's success. Either way, I pick up the pace before I get the opportunity to relive another childhood fave: Shit Dash.

Overhead, a half-dozen gliders circle the dawn sky like predators. Their wooden wings beat courtesy of churning cylinders hidden in their bowels. Puffs of steam billow from two nostril-like exhaust ports on either side of their cockpits, resembling beastly breaths.

The craft are piloted by specially trained agents called Imposers. Imps, as us locals like to call them. The military's elite.

And today, five more of us will bypass the regular draft and be recruited for a chance to enter their ranks—at a terrible price.

Given the aircrafts' current flight formation, they must be on Recruitment Day recon patrol, no doubt surveying the quadrant for signs of what the Establishment considers *suspect activity*. The problem is, everything from three or more people enjoying the night air in public to someone just taking an early morning stroll, like I'm doing now, is considered suspect.

If these Squawkers spot a violator, they radio their findings to Establishment officials, and before you know it a team is dispatched to *apprehend the offending party for questioning*. Must be some pretty mind-scrambling questions, though, 'cause anyone who's been asked them never seems to remember their way home. Ever.

It would be so easy to let the Squawkers spot me and do their thing. Only there's no guarantee this particular unit will transport me where I want to go. Better to be detained by a ground patrol before the Recruitment gets underway. Then, with any luck, I'll be taken right inside the Citadel's detention area, taken before *him*, at last. Excitement and fear tangle in my veins.

What will it be like, seeing him after more than two years? Has he changed?

Just ahead, Liberty Boulevard slices through the alleyways. Crisscrossing wooden beams are set up at the intersection to cordon off the area for today's procession.

Creeping forward, I crouch beside one of the planks and stare up the street toward City Central. Tall, tarnished lampposts line either side of the boulevard, their flickering gas lights powered by the lungs of those unfortunate enough to slave away in the mines, like my parents and the Bledsoes. Under the veil of morning fog, the posts resemble grave markers, the muted light of each lost soul within winding and fading away under the shadow of the hulking stone mausoleum looming in the town's core, watching...listening...knowing all.

The Citadel of Truth. The nerve center of the Establishment's presence in the Parish. The place anyone in their right mind avoids.

I'm not feeling in my right mind this morning.

I spy my opportunity for an escort into the Citadel's walls in the form of two Imps clad in their signature black jumpsuits and helmets, patrolling the alley on the opposite side of the street. Something hanging on the rear wall of one of the buildings has them in a stir. The shorter of the two is pointing a rigid finger at it, then turns his head to mutter something to his companion.

The taller Imp, a female, reaches for the wall and rips some kind of poster from it. Then she unclips a radio from her belt and mutters something into its mic.

The response from the radio's speaker cuts through the quiet. **"Suspect activity confirmed** ... *crack* ... *hiss* ... **Sending in a Canid backup."**

They're sending in Canids? Looks like I'm not the only one teasing danger this morning.

Filling my lungs as if for the last time, I stand. Better to get it over with quick. For Cole's sake.

A dark blur soars over the barricade and plows into me, squeezing the air from my chest. Then I'm tumbling over hard cobblestones and slamming to a stop, pinned under the heavy weight of my attacker.

My mouth tries in vain to find some spit to swallow before giving up. Forcing my eyes open, I face my captor.

Maybe I hit my head harder than I thought. The figure straddling my chest is not an Imp, but ... just a guy ... a guy not much older than me. My eyes focus on long, tawny hair and chiseled features carved into a pale, smooth if somewhat smudged, face. His frame is large and muscled, the body of someone whose survival hinges on physical labor. No wonder I can't breathe with this giant pinning me down.

He glances up, reflecting the orange sky in the blue of his eyes. The heavens aren't the only thing dawning. I recognize this face, though it's been several years since I've seen it up close.

Digory Tycho, one of the two most popular and handsome boys in the Instructional Facility's recent history. The boy who everyone in the Parish says is a shining example of the core values of the Establishment, who will someday make a great Imposer and a fine husband to anyone lucky enough to catch his eye.

Yep, the great Digory Tycho himself, who never acknowledged my existence all through primary and secondary instructional levels, is sitting on top of me in a grimy alleyway, unkempt and reeking of Dumpster, in violation of Recruitment Day curfew no less.

Amusing, if not for the pain wracking my body... or the fear engraved on his face.

He leans in close. "You okay?" he whispers.

I squirm beneath him. "Can't... can't breathe... "

"Oh, sorry!" He shifts his weight off and squats beside me. "Let me help." He cradles me into a sitting position.

"Thanks," I mumble, massaging my still-throbbing right arm. Warmth trickles down my cheek. Sweat? I rub my hand against my face and raise my fingers, which are now coated a bright red. The alley starts to swim.

"Here, let me see that." Digory nestles me in the crook of his arm and fumbles in his tattered coat. I catch a glimpse of two rolled-up sheets with yellow ties stuffed into a pocket. He tugs his coat over them quickly, pulls out a handkerchief from the other side, and dabs it against my cheek. "What're you doing out during curfew?"

I crane my neck to look up at him. "You *do* realize that question works both ways, don't you?"

He half-smiles, a sparkle of white amidst all the gray. "Right, Lucian."

My name. He actually knows my name...

The sizzle and pop of radio static snuffs the twinkle

from his face. **"Proceeding to check for violators in Quadrant Seven."**

The Imps I'd spotted across the street are at the mouth of the alley. I need to get away from Digory now. No need to drag him into my mess.

But his arms tighten around me before I can move. He hauls me up. "We have to get out of here," he whispers in my ear. "If they find us, I'll be *shelved*."

I twist around to face him. "They wouldn't shelve you for curfew violation. Imprisonment, hard labor, yes, but not—"

He grabs my shoulders. "It's got nothing to do with curfew, Lucian. It's about treason. And there's only one punishment for that."

"Treason? What're you—?"

"Sssh!"

Before I realize what's happening, Digory drapes me over his shoulder as easily as if I were a scarf. Suddenly the alley is upside down and I catch a glimpse of two pairs of shiny black boots, then a patch of rusty metal, before the ground swallows me and I'm thrust into darkness.

FOUR

My nose tells me where I am before my eyes do. The cloying stench of human waste mingles with the stale air of rodent droppings. It's a combination I've smelled ever since I could crawl, especially on those muggy summer nights where you welcome any breeze that accidentally detours into an open window, no matter what scent it might carry. Digory's brought us into the sewers. Only now, so close to the source, the odor is overpowering, threatening to coax the stale roll of bread posing as last night's dinner ration from my stomach.

I wriggle out of Digory's hold, and he steadies me against the ladder he's clinging to until I'm securely perched on a rung opposite him. With our faces so close, his warm honey breath almost conquers the sewer's stink. I start to feel light-headed again. Must be all the blood rushing to and from my head. Forcing my gaze from him, I squint at the daylight tearing into the sewer's perpetual night through a slit in the manhole cover a foot above.

The Imposers are standing just where we were moments ago, stepping over the sewer entrance, pacing, searching. My heart sneaks in a few extra beats. All I'd have to do is reach up, slide the grate aside, and turn myself in.

Grasping the rung above, I hoist myself up . . . and freeze. My eyes pull back to Digory's. He could have left me lying in the alley and saved his own skin, but he didn't. Better for both of us if he had. His chivalry has definitely complicated things. If I crawl out of this hole, they'll nab Digory too. Who knows what they'll do to him?

No. I'll wait it out a few, until we've gone our own ways, before surrendering. I owe him that much at least.

"Any citizen harboring violators is asked to remand them to authorities at once!" a female voice bullhorns through the alley.

Looks like the Imps aren't giving up that easily. Once they lock onto the scent of their prey, they rarely let go, just like the Canids. And I'm sure we smell pretty ripe about now. It's only a matter of time before they stop searching the alley and start searching underneath it.

Digory shoots me a look, and I can tell he's thinking the same thing. He nudges his chin downward to the catacombs. Great. He wants to move into the maze beneath the city, hoping to lose them. How can he know that's the last thing I want to do right now? Guess I have no choice but to follow him down, conveniently separate myself from him in the dark, then backtrack once I'm sure he's in the clear.

A rumbling growl startles me, almost making me lose my grip on the ladder. Digory's arm is behind my back in a flash, holding me tight against the handrails. Something warm and wet drips onto my forehead and I look up ... and into a set of jaws crowded with glistening fangs, snapping and spraying drool through the gash in the manhole cover. The growls turn into a series of deep barks, which vibrate through my ears. As hideous as that muzzle is, it's not quite as unnerving as the eyes that take its place—cold, blood-shot pools of amber fury.

The Canid has arrived.

In seconds, a set of black boots appears by the hound. "Got something, boy?"

The male Imp's voice.

Digory pulls me against him, pressing us both close to the wall to avoid the angle of the grill's opening. He gently places a finger to my lips.

For what seems like forever, there's an eerie calm. The sound of the beast's panting commingles with the babbling of sewage slogging through the tunnels below, the skittering of roaches and other vermin creeping over pipes and into crevices, and the pounding of Digory's chest competing with my own. Maybe they won't see us.

The manhole cover begins to slide open, shattering that dream.

My eyes meet Digory's.

"Take him, please! We didn't know. I swear!" a voice shouts from above. It doesn't sound like one of the Imps.

The grate stops moving. The Canid and the boots have moved away from the opening. Could it be a trap?

Digory and I compete for who looks the most confused.

"No, let me go, please! I didn't do anything!" A different voice this time.

What's going on up there? Ignoring Digory's tug at my arm, I risk ascending another rung to get a better look.

Two men are gripping a struggling third between them. He looks to be about twenty, short and wiry, dressed in a dirty gray Sewage Plant jumpsuit. Tears stream from his eyes and onto quivering lips. I've seen that cornered look on more than a few Parish faces over the years, and each time it brings a lump to my throat. The old-timers say you eventually get numb to it.

I'm not sure I want to live that long.

Digory joins me on my rung. He doesn't look at me or say anything, just stares at the scene being played out. His hand touches mine and stays there.

The female Imp moves in closer to the terrified prisoner, the Canid now leashed at her side. She gives the beast's harness some slack and it lunges forward.

The young man shrieks. But the Canid stops just short of its mark, jaws snapping, spittle flying, each bark drawing another yelp from its potential prey.

The eyes of the disheveled men restraining the young guy are vacant, as if their minds have left the premises. The shorter, portly one is Fernando Frye, the foreman at the Sewage Plant. The tall lean one is Frye's son, Felix. It's probably not the first time they've turned in a friend and co-worker to the Imps. And certainly not the last.

"We found these in his locker, Captain Valerian." Avoiding her eyes, Frye senior hands the female Imp a stack of documents.

Valerian leafs through the bundle, handing them off to her partner one at a time. "Looks like we have ourselves a Worm, Arch."

Even from here I can see the telltale triangular symbol of the ID cards. The fact that there appear to be dozens of them, instead of just one, can only mean one thing.

I don't know what sickens me more, the fact that this poor guy's desperate enough to prostitute himself as a Worm or that potential Recruits would be driven to hire a Worm to impersonate one of their two Incentives—another of the Establishment's benign terms masking an unspeakable malignancy. *Family. Friend. Lover*—that's who they *really* mean when they say Incentive. Human beings reduced to mere choices, expendable collateral discarded round after round during a Recruit's ascension to hell.

Considering what I'd do for my little brother, I realize I'm not much different than this unfortunate young man or the people who might hire him, and that thought both comforts and repulses me.

The prisoner sinks to his knees. "You've got the wrong guy!"

"Black-market traitor," the male Imp called Arch grunts. "Don't you know it's an honor to serve as an Incentive for the Recruits? You and the other Worms pollute the process with your filthy impersonations."

"Please," the prisoner whimpers. "I just needed some extra cash for rations, I don't have enough—"

Arch's booted foot flies up. There's a loud crunch as it sideswipes the Worm's jaw, spraying blood.

I flinch.

The young man's head slumps over. He coughs, spitting out a couple of small white teeth onto the pavement.

Now I'm the one who's shaking, but not with fear. Digory's fingers entwine with mine, holding me in place. His other hand grips the rung, pulsing, as if he's trying to squeeze his fingers through the metal.

Valerian snatches the ID cards back from Arch, looking at the first one. "Well, *Tim Fremont*, or whatever your name really is. I'll Radio HQ. We have enough evidence here to start investigating these citizens and seeing which one of them was willing to pay off a Worm like you to commit fraud upon the Establishment." She turns to Frye senior. "We're going to hold you two for questioning."

"But—"

A growl from the Canid cuts the elder Frye off.

I can imagine scenes like this one taking place all over the Parish today. People being pulled out of their homes, dragged into the street, beaten, hauled away. All for daring to let people into their hearts.

All for daring to love.

Blinking the cold sweat from my eyes, I turn to Digory, motioning him to climb down into the tunnel. I need to get away from here, get to the Citadel, do whatever I can for Cole. That's all that matters.

Digory nods, then moves to follow me down.

"Just one more thing." Arch's voice dumps ice into my pores.

Digory and I stop and look back.

"Who is your cell leader?" Arch asks.

For the first time, the prisoner looks confused instead of afraid. "C-cell...what?"

"The *other* traitors," Valerian spits. "The ones that had you put these up all over town?" She holds out the poster I saw her tear from the alley wall across the street.

"Don't forget the one I found by the Dumpster." Arch is unrolling another poster, this one tied with a familiar yellow cord.

My eyes flash to Digory. He's searching his coat pocket, where there is now only one rolled sheet. The sun's angle has shifted, casting a shaft of light that slashes across his neck, which bobs in a silent swallow.

"I've never seen those before, I *swear!*" the young man pleads.

Arch clears his throat and reads from the poster. "*The Establishment is Lies. The Establishment is Death.*" He turns back to Tim. "Sound familiar, Worm scum?"

Digory's eyes are bulging. He looks like he's about to spring from the sewer. Now it's my turn to rest a hand on *his* shoulder and hold him steady.

Valerian strokes the Canid's head. "Perhaps all this Worm needs is a little persuasion."

The hound lifts its head and bays at the sun, a long painful cry that suggests it agrees.

Tim's face dissolves into madness. "I ate a worm once ... "

A dark stain appears on his trousers, spreading into a puddle of fear that soaks his shoes.

Valerian releases the Canid. It pounces on Tim in seconds. I turn away. But the sounds of screams, mixed with the squishing and chewing, paint a more vivid picture than my eyes ever could.

"Let's go." I risk a whisper into Digory's ear over the sound of nightmares.

And as I take his cold hand and pull him down into the city's entrails, I can't help but think that I now know what would have happened to Digory if I'd turned myself in.

FIVE

My feet sink ankle deep into the sludge marinating the sewer floor. I scan the gloom. "Which way now?"

We're standing at a juncture of three catacombs, which glow from a series of gaslights that disappear into the mazes of rusted pipes. It resembles the arterial system of some bio-mechanical beast.

Digory doesn't look at me. "This way," he commands, sloshing toward the tunnel on the right. "We'll skirt the alley and come up a few blocks west of the parade perimeter."

"You mean, in the middle of all those people in broad daylight?" I wade fast to keep up.

"Yeah, like I'd be stupid enough to hide us down here and make a grand entrance on the other side." I can hear his eyes rolling off his tongue as he splashes through the muck, oblivious to the septic wake he creates that's sprinkling me with slime.

"Digory! Hey! Wait up!" I slog up to him and grab his arm, twisting him to face me. "What's your problem?"

"Let go of me!" he snaps. "I'm trying to get us out of here."

I glance above us. "Look, if it's about that guy up there ... there's nothing you could have done. He was a Worm. You saw the IDs. They were going to take him no matter what."

He rips free of my grip. "You don't get it, Lucian. It's *my fault*. They wouldn't have been in that alley if it wasn't for me. *I'm* the one they wanted. That unlucky guy just happened to be in the wrong place at the wrong time. I might as well have sicced the Canid on him myself."

He slumps onto one of the pipes, burying his face in his hands.

For a second, I'm not sure what to say. The Digory I never really knew at the Instructional Facility always seemed cool, in control, as though nothing could ever faze him. Seeing him like this makes me feel like an intruder, as if I'm spying on him naked. Even the Establishment's idols aren't immune to its corrosive touch, I guess.

I settle down beside him, resting a hand on his arm. "You had no way of knowing what would happen. I'm sure whatever you were doing with those flyers was important to you."

He uncovers his eyes, which smolder in the tunnel's hazy light. "What I was doing is important to *everyone*, not just me." He pulls the crinkled poster from his coat and unrolls it. I sidle up to him, then take it and read:

RECRUITMENT IS FEAR.
RECRUITMENT IS CONTROL.
DOWN WITH THE ESTABLISHMENT.
PROTECT YOUR FAMILIES.

The words are accompanied by a silhouette drawing of Recruits, watching as a group of people, their Incentives no doubt, are being slaughtered by armed Imposers. One of the victims is the outline of a little boy. I shudder, but not from the draft stealing through the catacombs. Quickly rolling the poster up, I stuff it in my own jacket, against my heart.

"You really think you can stop them?" I whisper.

The spark on his face ignites. "Not by myself. But we can all stop them if we stand together. *We* can change it, make it better."

I remember what it was like to dream, once. Before my parents died. "It's not so simple, Digory. They're strong, organized. They've got weapons."

"We *have* to try." He grabs my hand. "Don't you care? Is this how you want to live the rest of your life? In a slum? Dead by forty, starvation and disease fighting it out for first dibs? Your little brother—"

"What about Cole?" My body stiffens.

"Is this the kind of life you want for Cole, assuming he gets the chance to grow older?"

"Stop it." I turn away.

But he persists, like an insect in my ear. "If he survives, he'll be drafted into the military—or worse. Recruited as a potential Imposer. Forced to undergo the Establishment's mind games." He squats on his haunches in front of me. "And you'll be standing by helpless as he's forced to choose whether you or any other person he dares to love dies."

"That's enough," I say, turning off the mental images. "I don't want to hear any more about it. Your insurrection, or the Establishment … I have to handle things *my* way so that Cole's neck isn't on the line."

Digory's grip tightens on my hand. "His neck's *already* on the line—as are all of ours. That's what Recruitment Day *is*. The Establishment's way of spreading fear and breaking us … by making us have to choose which one of our loved ones is the most worthy to continue living. If you call *this* living." The muscles in his jaw clench. "Do you know the Establishment's been manufacturing biological weapons, testing them on innocent civilians? Genetically re-engineering them? I even hear that Reaper's Cough is some kind of population-control experiment. There's no limit to what they're capable of."

My mouth goes dry. "I don't know how you know any of these things, and I don't *want* to know. I have to think about my brother—"

"Maybe *you'll* get recruited, Lucian."

"That can't happen … "

"Maybe *you'll* have to decide whether or not Cole lives or dies."

"Digory, please—"

"Unless you run out of options, and one of the other Recruits bests you during the Trials. Then Cole dies no matter what."

"No!" I shove him to the ground.

He just sits there in the putridness, staring at me, the fire in his eyes now embers.

"The fear controls us," he says softly. "Makes us weak. And choosing which one of our loved ones has to live or die—"

"Keeps us isolated ... *alone*," I finish.

He rises to bended knee and clasps both my hands in his. "It doesn't have to be this way."

"I'm sorry I pushed you. It's just ... Cole ... this day ... so much is riding on it."

Digory shakes his head. "I'm the one that's sorry for pushing you. You were right. What happened up there"—he cocks his head toward the surface—"it messed with my head."

"I understand. You don't have to be ashamed."

He looks confused. "*Ashamed?*"

"Yeah, you know. Not wanting to reveal yourself to the Imps, admit you were the one hanging these flyers instead of that poor guy. Anyone else would have been afraid too." Though if it'd been Cole, I wouldn't have hesitated an instant.

His eyes register shock and indignation. "I wasn't scared for *myself*, Lucian. If I'd have climbed out and accepted the blame, the Imps would have swarmed the sewer." His gaze pierces through me. "And I wouldn't have been the only one they found." He looks away. "I couldn't let that happen."

I stare at him through the flickering shadows, not saying a word.

Not knowing what to say.

"We should go." I stand, pulling him to his feet and

letting him go before I can become too conscious of the warmth radiating through his skin.

Digory clears his throat. "It's just up ahead." He walks past me, avoiding eye contact.

We tread through about a hundred feet of muck in silence before reaching another ladder.

He turns to me. "Once we get up there, it'll still be curfew. Even though they think they nabbed the conspirator, we can't take any chances."

"Got it."

He pulls himself up two rungs at a time.

I clamber up after him. As soon as we're topside and split up, I have to make sure the Imposers spot me. The only thing is, I conceived my crazy plan before I witnessed that Canid tear someone apart. My sweating palms almost slip off the next rung.

By the time I catch up to Digory, he's already sliding the manhole cover open, peering left and right just over the edge, and offering me his outstretched hand.

Gripping it, I scramble up the rest of the way and join him on the surface.

"This street's clear for the moment," he says. "I know some shortcuts we can use to double back, and from there I can get you home."

"I can find my own way back, thanks." From the look on his face, my words might as well be stingers.

"But it's dangerous. Let me just—"

"I'll be okay, *really*."

"Suit yourself." He kicks the manhole cover back into

place. "Besides, I can't waste any more time here, with the lives of so many others at stake." He storms into a side alley.

Damn it. "Digory, wait!" I race after him.

He stops and pivots toward me. "Yes?" The word strikes like hail.

"Thanks. Thanks for everything."

His expression softens. "One thing. You know what I was doing out here breaking curfew. You never told me what *you* were doing."

I can't tell him. Especially knowing how he feels about the Establishment. He'd never understand. I shrug. "Just making sure I get ringside seats for the procession."

Digory shakes his head. "I'm sure you'll take care of yourself, Lucian. Maybe someday you'll realize this is bigger than you."

He disappears into the maze of alleyways before I can say anything.

The only trace left of him is the rolled poster he's forgotten, nestled against my heart.

I reach inside my coat and trace it with my fingertips. Though it's made of paper, it feels more like lead. I need to get rid of it before—

"Halt. Hands where I can see them."

The blood frosts in my veins. My heart feels like it's going to burst through my rib cage. As much as I thought I prepared for this moment, the reality of it eclipses any notions I've deluded myself with. The terror is overwhelming, stifling my breaths.

I don't want to die.

"Turn around," a sharp baritone voice commands.

I can't move. It's as if I'm not in my body anymore. Digory. Why didn't I listen to him?

"I *said* turn around."

If I don't turn around, they'll shoot me from behind. And my brother will be all alone.

The signal from my brain finally reaches my feet, and I turn around to face my fate.

A squadron of Imposers is facing me, weapons drawn, a wall of black death.

Remember what Digory said... *the fear controls us, makes us weak.*

No. I won't be weak. I have to be strong for my brother. He's all that matters.

The lead Imp lumbers toward me, a tall, massive man with close-cropped pale yellow hair and winter-gray eyes. He shoves the barrel of his gun into my forehead.

"You're in violation of Government Statute F.4312— Observation of Ordinance Regarding Public Assembly. State your name, citizen."

"Spark," I manage, though my mouth is dry. "Lucian Spark."

"Mr. Lucian Spark. You will be detained and remanded into the Custody of the Citadel of Truth, where Honorable Prefect Cassius Thorn shall pronounce judgment and sentence you for this infraction. Do you understand?"

Not that they care if I do or not, but I play the game nonetheless. "Yes. I understand, Sir."

"Search him."

What little courage I've mustered dissipates in the crisp morning wind. Digory's poster. It's still hidden inside my coat pocket.

Two other Imps slither from the shadows and start to frisk me.

Getting detained for breaking curfew is one thing. Being arrested for an act of treason is *not* part of my plan.

I squirm at their touch. "Wait . . . please—"

It's no use. One of the Imps rips the poster from my pocket, unrolls it, and displays it to the commander.

His eyes look like silver gashes on his face. "Looks like we have us a traitor scum here," he hisses to his comrades.

"Please, it's not mine. I found it—"

He presses the gun harder against my head. "Shut up. I say we don't wait for the Prefect and carry out your sentence now."

Then there's a searing pain in my forehead, and—
Black.

SIX

I'm sprawled on a floor of sodden earth. It's barely bigger than a box. The air's heavy with dust and death, as if I'm breathing through a thin layer of rotting skin. There are no windows, no chair, no bed. Nothing. In the center of the floor, there's a small dark hole that reeks of human waste. There's only one way in or out—a rusty door that looks like it hasn't been used in years. From beneath it, a dim light squeezes through, my only source of illumination. At the bottom of the door is a slat, the kind that's supposed to slide open to slip the prisoners food.

My body's aching all over. I've been stripped to just my underwear. Aside from some cuts and bruises, I seem to be fine, except for the throbbing in my forehead. I touch my head, wincing at the jolt of pain. Apparently the only thing that connected with my head was the butt of that Imp's weapon.

Pulling myself to my feet despite the jabs of betrayal from my cramped legs, I stagger the two feet to the door, my palms slapping against the cold iron.

"Open up! I need to see the Prefect!"

My voice sounds like a stranger's, dry and hoarse. I rub my throat, willing the fear back into its nest.

When I get no response, terror drills into my pores and taps into a geyser of adrenaline that fuels my pounding fists against the door.

I've heard rumors over the years about how Imposers treat prisoners.

The skin on my hands is on fire. I can feel it growing raw, slick with blood.

A loud whine pierces my ear. The sound of a rusty bolt straining through its housing.

My hands drop to my sides. My breathing is heavy, competing with the sound of my heart pulsating in my ears. As the bolt completes its labored journey and the door gives an inch, I can't help but take a step back and brace myself.

The door pushes inward, unsettling dust and plaster. My eyes squint against the orange light now streaming into the cell. Probably just flickering gaslight lighting the prison corridor, but still bright to my light-deprived eyes. Then the light is eclipsed by a huge form in the doorway, which snuffs out the small flicker of hope before it can start to burn.

"Finally awake, huh?" This Imposer is the biggest I've seen yet—tall, broad-shouldered, legs like tree trunks. The name *Styles* is stenciled on the breast pocket of his uniform. Perhaps more unsettling than the rumble of his voice is the way his eyes slither over me, a mixture of contempt, hatred, and something else…something which makes me want to soak for hours, rubbing my flesh raw until it's clean again.

I clear my throat. "I need to see the Prefect."

The brute lets out a long laugh that almost sounds pleasant, except for the fact that I know he's mocking me.

Another shape appears at the door, shorter but just as hulking. His ID reads *Renquist*.

He leers at his companion. "What's going on here?"

Styles hikes a stubby thumb toward me. "Not too much. Pretty boy here is *demanding* to see the Prefect." He chuckles.

Renquist turns to me and snorts. "Is'e now? Would'ja like some tea an' biscuits first?"

This elicits another hoot and holler from Styles. His eyes flit to the hallway outside the cell, then to me, then back to his companion. "But first, don't'cha think we ought'a get him cleaned up real good?" I can't miss the unmistakable wink he gives his cohort.

Renquist squeezes into the room. With these two massive brutes in here, there's barely enough room to retreat. I can feel the heat of their bodies, sniff their sweat, which smothers what little circulation of air there is. They both turn to look at me, the laughter gone from their lips and eyes.

My mouth goes dry.

"Take me to the Prefect," I repeat.

Renquist ignores me and turns to Styles. "It's a shame to let this one go to waste. Has he been logged in yet?"

Styles nods, not taking his eyes off me. "We can always

do a little creative bookkeeping before it gets to HQ. This pretty boy will fetch a nice stash on the market."

My stomach tightens. The Emporiums. Hellholes run by traffickers in human flesh who peddle the poor like cattle to slake the decadent appetites of the elite. The slaves' bodies and minds are used until there's nothing left and then they're discarded without a second thought, leaving no trace of their existence. I grit my teeth. I'm not going to end up in some heap of crushed dreams.

The two move closer. Renquist leers at me, his tongue running across his lips. "Just as long as we get to sample the merchandise before we hand it over. I've been pulling double shifts for the past two weeks on account of this Recruitment and I need to blow off some steam."

Styles nods and takes another step. "Of course, partner. And I'm sure Pretty over here isn't going to tell a soul."

They close in on me.

I back away until the cold concrete of the cell wall presses against my spine.

I'll die before I submit.

"Styles! Renquist!" a new voice blares.

A female Imp is standing in the doorway, glaring at my captors. I recognize her from the alley.

Both Imps snap to attention.

"Captain Valerian," Styles barks. "We were just interrogating the perp."

"I *know* what you were doing." Her mouth and nose crinkle. Does she actually have some compassion flowing through her blood?

"Just give us a few more minutes," Renquist mutters.

"That's a negative, Officers. Your presence is requested in debriefing."

Styles's eyes dart between me and her. "But we can *break* him—"

"Stat!" There's no mistaking the authority in her voice. She obviously outranks them.

The two move away from me and skirt either side of her, practically bumping into each other as they exit the cell. I lean an arm against the wall and steady myself.

Valerian stares at me, her eyes cubes of ice. "Don't think for a minute I have any sympathy for a traitor. Your kind make me sick, spreading your poison. Filthy ingrates. You deserve the treatment you get, but we have laws, a system in place. Sometimes my colleagues let their ... *patriotism* ... get the best of them." She smirks. "I'd shoot you myself. Don't you forget that."

I nod. "I won't."

"You don't have to worry about that ... *yet*." She sneers at me. "Seems like you've gotten a reprieve, traitor."

She tosses me a dirty old blanket, which I drape over my body.

My vision is now sharply in focus. "What do you mean?"

"Retinal scan confirmed you as Lucian Spark. Seems when the custody manifest got circulated, the higher-ups requested you be taken up for a personal interrogation."

"You mean ... ?"

"That's right. I'm personally escorting you to the Prefect for questioning."

My knees almost give—a side effect of the exhaustion, relief, and anxiety swirling inside me.

She pulls out a triangular metallic device and points it at me. I've seen those in use before. Nerve stimulators. *Very* painful. Very *effective*.

"Move," she barks.

I shamble from the cell, squinting against the bright lights, with Valerian at my back.

The path to the Citadel's main tower leads me past the dungeon levels, where the anguished cries of those waiting for sentencing or questioning raise all the hairs on my body. From the festering prison, through the shiny metallic Imposer precinct, up spiraling staircases and through enormous iron doors, I travel higher and higher, Valerian's nerve stimulator pressing against the small of my back the entire way. If I were to make any move that she deemed suspect, a simple press of a button would do anything from frying all my nerve-endings to inducing instant cardiac arrest, depending on the device's setting and her mood. From what I've already experienced, I know I don't want to test either.

The closer I get to the Prefect's tower, the faster my heart beats and the shorter my breaths. It's been two years. Since just before my mother died. Other than a few smuggled communications, we've barely had any contact. If they find out we've interacted in any way, it could destroy him.

I'm not sure what to expect. Life in the service can change a person. I think about how I've changed since Mom died. How has *he* changed?

As Valerian prods my body up and around the winding

staircase leading to the Prefect's antechamber, my mind dances around the questions that I so desperately want answered, but so desperately fear the answers to.

Will he still feel the same way about me now that he's lived away from the Parish and been exposed to so much more, in two years, than I've been in my entire life? Or have I gambled Cole's life away in vain?

The stairs dead-end in front of a set of high, arched, paneled doors that are flanked by two other stone-faced Imps.

The answers to both my questions lie just beyond.

Valerian salutes the Imps. "Captain Valerian requesting permission to enter the Prefect's chamber with the prisoner."

The guards salute back. The one on the right presses a button on the panel by the doors. They move apart with a soft creak.

I gulp down the last of my spit, staring at the widening rift.

When Valerian nudges me inside, I almost risk the stimulator's wrath before my feet finally respond and propel their burden inside.

The room, if you can call it that, is the grandest I've ever seen. The ceiling towers overhead, culminating in a glass skylight that frames the noon sun in an oval, like it's an all-powerful eye. Tearing my eyes from the blinding light, I take in molded archways flanked by columns three times the width of my body. On one wall, marble busts of previous Prefects rest in alcoves a couple of feet apart, making you feel like dozens of eyes are scrutinizing your every move as you walk past them. Set into the opposite wall is a huge glass tank, displaying a couple of small trees sprouting every color of the rainbow. Bands of scaly black twist through their branches. My skin erupts into gooseflesh and I look away.

Across from this tank is a clear enclosure with two fluffy white rats pressed against the glass, their whiskers twitching as if they can smell me.

Ahead, a tall shape stands with its back to me, silhouetted on a balcony overlooking Town Square. I don't have to see the face to know who it is. My pulse quickens. Sure, he's taller now, but that outline is the same, imprinted in my brain. The last time I saw it was on the bank of Fortune's River. He was standing with his back to me then, too. Except we'd just said our goodbyes.

As much as I've played out this moment in my mind every day for the past two years, now that it's here, my mouth suddenly forgets to speak.

Valerian's hasn't. "Excuse me, Prefect Thorn. I've brought you the prisoner as requested."

He turns and faces me at last, but the brightness behind him masks his face in shadow.

"Leave us." His voice sounds deeper, more like a man's. He's eighteen now, I remind myself.

"But, Sir," Valerian responds. "The prisoner has exhibited signs of violent behavior. Is it wise to—"

"That will be all, Officer."

Valerian clicks her boots together. "Yes, Sir." She whirls and bumps into my arm, reigniting the bruise on her way out.

"And lock the door. I'm not to be disturbed."

"Yes, Sir!"

Then she's gone, the great doors swinging closed with a soft click.

He just stands there for a moment. Then he walks toward me. The sound of each step on the marble hammers into my head.

I'm breathing too fast. Trying to control it just makes it worse. I'm afraid I'll hyperventilate and collapse, not exactly the reunion I'd envisioned. But then again, it's not about us, it's about Cole. I take in a deep breath and tense my muscles to quash the trembling.

He stops a few feet away and just stares, not a hint of a word on his lips.

Despite all my efforts, I feel like I'm going to lose it right there. I can't take not knowing anymore. "Cassius," I murmur.

His thick eyebrows arch. He nods toward the door. "Do you think I was too hard on her?"

"Huh?" Of all the things I expected him to say, I'm not prepared for that question.

"I'm still working on my intimidating voice," he says, his tone dropping an octave. Then the seriousness evaporates from his face, leaving only a huge grin, brighter than the streaming sun.

My heart almost shuts down. He's adorned in a navy blue tunic trimmed with gold lace, attire befitting a Prefect. His wavy auburn hair is longer now, and each strand captures the sunlight. Sea-green eyes wash over me, carrying away the dread and pain. I'm trembling again, this time with emotions I'm not quite sure I understand and don't care if I ever do.

"I told you I'd come back for you, Lucky." His soft voice quavers at the end.

"So what took you so long, huh?" I choke on the words.

And then we're hugging each other so fiercely I can't breathe, but it doesn't matter because I can't think of a better place to die.

Cassius's chest muffles my sobs. I've tried to be strong for Cole, but everything that's happened today—meeting Digory, that horrible death in the alley, the looming Recruitment—it's all too much to hold in, and I welcome sharing this weight that's threatening to crush me with every breath I take.

All too soon, we pull apart, basking in each other.

The palm of his hand travels from his head to mine, measuring the difference in our height. "Look at you, my little Lucky, all grown up."

"And *you*, come back the youngest Prefect the Parish has ever known." My fingers trace the delicate embroidery on his lapels.

A cloud siphons the brightness from his face. "I'm sorry I didn't tell you myself." He enfolds my wrists with the warmth of his touch. "I couldn't risk anyone finding out ... that you ... "

My eyes drop to my filthy bare feet. I cross my arms over my chest, suddenly conscious of my near nakedness. "That you still associate with us peons?" I whisper.

His finger tilts my chin up until our eyes link. "No,

Lucky. It's not like that, I promise you. It's just that the Establishment has certain protocols when it comes to fraternization between government officials and citizens." He stuffs his hands into his vest pockets. "I figured I could do you and your family more good if our relationship was seen as a more neutral one, to dispel any claims of favoritism, that's all."

I bite my lower lip. "Yeah, I understand, Cass. It's not wise to show them you care about anyone in particular, especially if you're going to represent the Establishment's code of values." I don't intend to sound so harsh, but my conversation with Digory in the sewers still burns in my mind.

Cassius doesn't seem to notice. He's circling me, inspecting the flaps of the shoddy blanket that barely cover the cuts beneath. "As soon as I heard you were in custody I had them bring you right to me." He stops, brushing his forehead against mine. "How bad did they hurt you, Lucky?"

I shrug. "I'll be all right."

He wrinkles his nose. "What's that *smell*? Did you lose at Shit Dash or something?"

"Hey, I used to beat you at that every time, and you know it!" I give him a playful push away.

He shakes his head. "Faulty memory, Lucky. Come here." He leads me behind a red velvet partition that conceals a large clawfoot tub. "I had a bath drawn for you. You can get cleaned up."

"Thanks." I wince as he pulls the soiled mantle off my aching limbs.

He tosses it into a corner. "I think we can find you something that fits better."

Then I submerge my naked body into the water, bracing myself for the usual jolt of coldness, only to be shocked by how warm and soothing it feels, like a thousand toasty fingers kneading my sore muscles. People actually live like this? If I did, I'd bathe four or five times a day instead of the once-a-day ritual of enduring a freezing splash from a rusty spigot.

Cassius kneels beside the tub, using a sponge to gently scrub away the grime coating me, careful around my cuts and bruises. "Lucky, what about Cole? Your mother? How are they?"

My vocal chords twist tight. "Mom…she…she's gone. Reaper's Cough. About six months after you left." I blink, spilling a few drops into the bathwater.

He massages soap into my scalp. "I don't know what to say. I tried to make inquiries about your family, but you know—"

"Contact is forbidden. Yeah, I know." I sink deeper into the water.

"I'm so sorry I wasn't there for you. But I'm here *now*." He cups water in his hands and rinses out my hair, making sure it doesn't get in my eyes. "How's Cole handling things?"

I sit up. "Cole's a real champ. He's the best little brother a guy can have."

Cassius laughs. I've missed that sound. "I'm sure he doesn't even remember his Uncle Cass."

I turn and grip the tub's rim. "Of course he remembers you! I've only told him the stories of all our adventures, like a million times!" My mind floods with a stream of memories. "Well, *some* of our adventures, at least."

He winks at me. "Remember the time we snuck past that squad of Imposers into Old Man Roarkeshire's farm and got ahold of that Wanderer's Brew?"

"Just how much intoxicant was *in* that thing?"

Cassius stands, knuckles resting against his hips. "All I know is that Old Man Roarkeshire used it to polish the metal hinges in his barn."

I chuckle. "Great stuff!"

He grips one of the marble columns and swings completely around it. "We ought to take a ride out there sometime, see the old place!"

Visions of burning skin and its stench drains the remaining warmth from the bathwater. "We can't. It doesn't exist anymore."

A sigh escapes Cassius. "How stupid of me. I heard about… about *that*."

My eyes drop to a bubble forming a dome on my palm. A pair of eyes stares at me. Probably just my own reflection. But why are they sky blue and filled with accusation? I dunk my hand beneath the surface.

I've had enough. No matter how long I lie here, I'll never feel completely clean. Rising, I climb from the tub. Cassius picks up a towel draped over a pedestal and tosses it my way. With my back to him, I dry off. When I'm finished, he's holding a robe open and slips it around me. It's made of a lustrous black material that's softer than any I've ever felt before.

"It's called silk," he whispers in my ear. "Only the best for my Lucky." He reaches around me and cinches the robe's sash about my waist.

"Cole must be wondering where I am," I whisper back.

"So he hasn't been taken into a child assimilation program?"

Breaking from his embrace, I swerve to lock eyes. "Of course not. *I'm* his family. He belongs with me."

Genuine surprise darts from Cassius's eyes, like needles to my skin. "I only meant that I'm sure it's hard to take care of a—what is he now, four?—year-old on your own."

I back away on uncertain legs. "Mrs. Bledsoe helps out during my shift at the library. We don't need any outsiders." My heart gallops. I lean against the partition to steady myself.

Cassius moves closer, arms open wide. "But the Establishment's child care programs are a valuable—"

"I'm not going to give Cole to strangers, Cass. He's lost Mom and Dad. He's not going to lose *me*, too." A fog shrouds my brain.

Cassius reaches me and draws me close, a beacon in the mist. "I wasn't trying to offend you, Lucky."

Bringing my fingers to my temples, I try to massage away the throbbing. "It's just that—"

"Here! I know what you need!" He smiles, takes hold of my hand, and leads me to a table nestled in a small alcove. In its center rests a covered silver tray. Even before he lifts the lid, a mixed aroma of fresh sweetness and cooked meat overpowers my nostrils. My stomach growls. Saliva floods my mouth.

He raises the cover. "I thought you might be hun—"

I pounce on the tray. Grabbing the meat with my bare hands, I tear into it with my teeth, hardly savoring each morsel as it slides down my gullet. Then I'm stuffing cheese and fruits into my mouth, frenzied by the new tastes assaulting my tongue as I try to devour them all before someone steals them away.

When I finally look up, a monstrous beast stares back at me, teeth bared, a distorted face smeared with the blood of its latest kill. Then I realize it's my own face, reflected on the tray's silver cover. Disgust and shame overwhelm me.

"It's going to be all right, Lucky." Cassius leads me to one of the plush sofas, sets me down, and wipes my face with a handkerchief. We sit there in silence, his arm around me, my face buried in his shoulder. I'm not sure how much time passes before I find my voice again.

"Cole ... he's ... he's all I have left. That's why I risked coming here today—allowed myself to be taken into custody—it was the only way I could think of to see you face-to-face and ask you to protect him in case I get recruited."

"You took a big chance. If I hadn't seen your name on the prisoner roster ... " His arm squeezes me close.

I look into his eyes. "The Recruitment. Now that I'm sixteen, there's a chance I could be selected." My hands grab both of his. "You have to promise me that if that happens, you'll do whatever you can to keep Cole from being one of the Incentives. I'll never choose to ... I'll never choose him ... and you *know* what will happen."

He purses his lips. "You'll both be shelved."

"That's right, we'll be *murdered*, only they'll make Cole watch me get killed first. You were the one who told me how it worked, remember? How they make you choose between the people you love... what happened to your father... "

He brings my hands to his lips. "That's *not* going to happen to you and Cole. I'd never let it."

I scoot closer. "So you'll help us then?"

His arms envelop me. "Do you even have to ask? There's nothing I wouldn't do for you." He pulls away. "But Lucky, there's something you need to explain to me first." He springs from the couch and strides over to his desk.

When he turns back to me, he's holding up Digory's unfurled poster.

SEVEN

I can barely swallow. I clamber from my seat and limp over to him. "Cass, it isn't mine. I *swear* it. I ... I picked it up near the sewer. I'd never seen it before today." I look away. I hate the idea of dancing around the truth with Cass. But he wouldn't understand about Digory, would he? And the thought of Digory being slaughtered the way that guy in the alley was ...

Cassius nods. "I believe you. The Parish is going to be a real challenge for a new Prefect to administer. I'm going to need your help, your *support*, if I'm going to pull this off."

Gripping the edge of the desk, I brace myself against the cold granite. "What can I do to help you?"

He raises the poster higher. "This rebellion. It's got to be crushed. If it isn't, everyone loses."

"I don't know much about it, but ... " The stone edge of the desk digs into my lower back. "Is it so wrong for people to want a better life … something to look forward to?" My throat gulps dryness. "I know that's what I want for Cole. Does that mean I should be crushed, too?" I stand as straight as I can, forcing him to look up into my eyes.

He waves my question away. "It's not the same. You and Cole are different." The poster crumples in his grip. "You're not like these leeches who want to drain the government of its resources. Ingrates, all of them." He flings the banner on the floor, where it rolls up against the foot of the sofa.

My jaw plunges. "Leeches? Ingrates? It wasn't so long ago you used words like that to describe the Establishment, not its citizens."

His eyes dim. "I was young then. I didn't understand." He shakes his head. "Without order, civilizations whither and die. The Establishment's learned from the mistakes our ancestors made."

"And it's making even bigger ones." I stare into his eyes. "What's gotten into you? How can you think the Establishment *cares* about the good of all its people? I just saw someone not much older than we are get mauled to death by a Canid patrol. Have you taken a good look around you? Taken a good look at *me*?" I tug open the top of my robe, exposing the blue and purple blotches that contrast with my pasty flesh. Lacerations weave across my chest like the fancy lace pattern on his lapels, swirling downward to wrap around my jutting ribs.

He wraps me in his arms. "The guards who did this to you will be punished, I promise," he whispers.

I break the hug. "Don't you see? It's not about the guards or revenge. It's about having your dreams smothered, day after day, until there's nothing left."

"I used to think the same way." Taking my hand, he leads me out onto the balcony and points to the pockets of gatherers slowly filling the Square below. "The people need someone to look after their interests. They can't do it themselves." He turns the finger on himself. "*We* give them structure... a purpose."

I pull my arm free. "And just what is that purpose, Cass? Huh?" My hand sweeps the path leading from the onlookers up to the dais. "To be cattle in the slaughterhouse just waiting for their turn in the meat grinder? That's not living. You of all people should know that. Think of what happened to *your* family."

Hurt flickers in his emerald eyes. "But it's not going to happen to *me*, and it doesn't have to happen to you." He turns away and storms back inside, heading toward an elaborate wooden cabinet built into the alcove wall.

I'm at his heels, like a Canid at its master's side. "You say that, yet you serve the very government that recruited you and destroyed your family in the process."

Unlatching the cabinet doors, he pulls out a decanter of blood-red wine, sets it on the shelf beneath, and digs out two crystal goblets, handing me one.

I examine the glass, staring at him through a prism of haze before shaking my head and setting it down on the shelf. "These past few years I've told myself you were only doing what you had to do to survive, to come back to . . . the Parish. But now it sounds like—"

His thumb flicks the carafe's stopper off with a loud *pop*. "Like what?" His brows arch. "Like I've been *brainwashed*—is that what you're thinking?" Sighing, Cassius watches dark crimson gush from the carafe as he tilts it over his goblet. "I assure you I haven't been."

"I was going to say, it sounds like you've forgotten what life in the Parish is like."

The decanter clangs against my unused goblet as he puts the wine back on the shelf. "Of course I haven't forgotten. *I* survived Recruitment, remember?" Half his drink disappears in one gulp.

"And you shouldn't have *had* to. The whole Recruitment process is barbaric."

"The Recruitment is a training method, Lucky. Five candidates who fit a certain profile are chosen to bypass the standard draft and given the opportunity to serve in an accelerated Special Forces program. Facing the Trials fosters competitiveness in those candidates who have demonstrated exemplary strength and would be an asset to our military, while at the same time sending a very important message to our citizens."

"Yeah. Be careful who you love as it may cost you your life," I grumble. "Sounds like you've been memorizing the marketing manuals."

"No. It's a much more complex message than that. Don't value personal attachments *over* civic duty; doing so could cause our society to become fragile and susceptible to utter collapse, like it was before the Ash Wars. Is that so wrong, Lucky? And, if the effect of the Recruitment is to diminish the chance of the populace coming together and rebelling against the government—by neutralizing potential threats through recruitment and frightening people into avoiding emotional attachments—that's just an added *bonus*, right?"

He lets loose a sigh. "The Trials weed out the weak links. There are limitless opportunities for those who are resourceful, independent. Look at what I've achieved."

I throw up my hands. "Wow. If I didn't know any better, I'd swear I was listening to a public information broadcast on the wireless!" I head back to the couch and drop down, crossing my arms. "The Recruitment is state sanctioned *murder*."

He coughs, nearly choking on his second swig of wine. "It's *not* murder." He marches over and plunks down next to me. Scarlet droplets from his glass bleed onto the white marble floor. "Every Recruit is given an equal opportunity to advance to the next level of their training." He holds up his hand before I can protest. "Yes, it's unfortunate that the Recruit who achieves the lowest score after each round must undergo the Culling—"

"Stop sterilizing it!" I hug my knees. "The loser of each trial has to choose between the lives of two people they love, and if they can't do that, all three of them *die*. That's sick."

The color of Cassius's face matches what's left of his

drink. "Yes, they die. Is that what you want to hear, Lucky? Is that raw enough for you?"

"How can you defend the system? They made you choose your mother's life over your father's. What kind of people would make a kid do something like that?"

The glass drops from his hand, shattering into a million pieces. A ruby pool spreads at his feet, sliding toward the poster lying nearby. As he watches it, his face turns to stone.

"I tried to save them *both*, Lucky. I've replayed that last round in my head every night since." He turns to me. "You don't know how much I wanted to be the first Recruit to ever make it through every round with both of their Incentives intact and become an Imposer." Pools well in his eyes. "My father...he understood at the end. I...I saw it on his face. He wanted me to be strong, beat the others."

His expression melts and I see the Cassius I remember, a frightened sixteen-year-old selected during the Recruitment ceremony two years ago. "Oh, Lucky, why couldn't I save him too?"

I touch his shoulder. "I'm so sorry. You had to go through something no one should ever have to. Don't you see? That's how they break you."

He tears away. "But they haven't broken *me*. Don't you see? I can beat *them* at their own game. Now that I'm Prefect, I can change things, make a difference. And to do that, I need you."

"For what?" I lean back against the cushions.

He scoops up the poster. It unspools, the images now tainted red. "These insurgents. So far every attempt to infiltrate their nest has met with failure."

"I still don't understand what that has to do with—"

He rolls the poster back up. "This propaganda that was in your possession when you were taken into custody—"

"I already told you, it's not *mine*. You have to believe me." My pulse thrums in my ears.

Cassius smiles and squeezes my knee. "Of course I believe you. I know you of all people would never lie to me."

I shift my weight, but I can't get comfortable.

He leans in. "All I'm asking is that you seek these rebels out, ingratiate yourself to their cause."

"So you can go ahead and flush them out? They'll be *executed*. You know that." Digory's face haunts my mind. "I won't be a part of that, Cass. I don't want to get involved in this civil war. All I care about is my brother being safe."

He sighs and lets go of me. "You totally misunderstand my intentions. I want to put an end to the violence. There's no reason why both sides can't come to the table and work through these issues in peace."

I shift onto my knees. "You aren't going to arrest them?"

He swivels toward me, resting on his folded legs. "Things are going to be different, now that I'm Prefect, I swear it." His fingers tangle with mine. "I want what you want. Things to change. If these rebels continue to operate on their own, then they *will* incur the Establishment's wrath. Prime Minister Talon will wipe them out. I can prevent this, but to do so,

I need you to act as a conduit." His smile is soothing. "You're a Parish boy. Hardworking, well-liked. You fit the profile of what the rebels look for."

My eyes narrow. "And in return, you'll protect Cole by making sure I'm not recruited?"

He releases a long breath. "This isn't a quid pro quo, Lucky." He leans in, his eyes taking my own hostage. "I'd have prevented you from being recruited no matter what."

"You promise, all you want to do is talk to them, Cass? I mean, that's it? No interrogations? No torture?"

"None of that." He bounces off the sofa and pulls me to my feet. "I pledge to you on what we mean to each other, which is the one thing in this entire world that I value the most."

All my unease, my fears, evaporate with those words, and I feel ashamed for ever having doubted him. I feel myself glowing. He *does* still care. He's *still* my Cassius...

And the idea of a truce, of real change in the lives of the Parish's citizens, is too tempting. I can talk to Digory first and explain Cass's offer. He'll know what to do. And if he refuses, no one gets hurt. It's not like I'd be getting involved in anything.

I smile. "All right. I'll see what I can do. But it'll take time. I can't promise anything."

Cass grins, brushing the hair from my eyes. "Just knowing that you're going to make the effort means everything to me, Lucky." He hugs me tight. "It'll be just like old times. You and me against the world." His smile is infectious.

"Yep. You and me," I say.

"Which reminds me." He reaches into his pocket. "I have something for you." He pulls out a silver chain. Dangling from it is a pendant, bearing an engraving of two hands clasped together. He moves behind me and places it around my neck.

I hold up the medallion and marvel at every detail. "It's magnificent, Cass! I can't accept—"

"Nonsense! I had it molded from the silver pin I was awarded as the last Recruit left standing." He snaps the clasp together. "The thought of one day giving this to you has kept me going the last two years." He moves around in front of me, his eyes admiring. "Promise me you'll wear it always."

I grip the chain. "I promise."

A loud gong reverberates throughout the room, buzzing through my skin.

Cass groans. "Time to prepare for my Officiation duties."

My eyes travel longingly to the dining table. "Do you think I could take home some of that leftover food, for Cole and Mrs. Bledsoe?" I'm prepared to beg if I have to. Pride can't fill an empty stomach.

He claps his hands together. "I have a better idea! The Recruitment gets underway within the hour. I'll have a security detail escort you back to pick them up and return you to the Citadel. The three of you can watch the procession from my private box. There'll be plenty of food and refreshment for all."

Dampness smears his image. I blink him back into clarity. "I've missed you *so* much."

His smile is radiant. "Me too. This is going to be a new beginning, Lucky. A new beginning for the Parish. For the Establishment. But most importantly, a new beginning for *us*."

EIGHT

The lumbering steam coach transporting Cole, Mrs. Bledsoe, and myself back to the Citadel ebbs to a crawl about twenty feet in front of the tower's massive iron doors. Rods and pistons screech to a halt. Coughing up a final shroud of vapor, the vehicle stops dead. When the haze clears, I almost buckle under the weight of the stares coming from the crowd jammed into both sides of the street for today's ceremony. Fear and confusion as to why the three of us have been singled out for this special treatment is plastered on most of their faces. But it's the piercing glares scattered throughout the pack that force my eyes away in shame.

Cole springs from the cab. "Hurry, Lucky! We're gonna be late!" he cries over the clamor of the throng. He tugs my hand with both of his, urging me from the carriage.

"Take it easy, buddy. We're just on time. The parade's about to start. You haven't missed any of it." I hop to the ground. "Hey, what say you pretend I'm a caballus and ride me up to the observation box?"

He claps and jumps up and down a couple of times. "Can I, Lucky? *Please?*"

I scoop him up onto my shoulders, ignoring the pain. "Next stop, the Command Center, Sir!"

Cole tugs my ears. "Giddy-up!"

I turn to Mrs. Bledsoe, who's still sitting in the coach. She looks even paler in the bright afternoon sunshine. "You're so good with him," she says. "Reminds me of you and your father."

I take her hand and guide her out of the transport, into the hover chair that Cassius has so generously provided.

She fidgets in her seat, eyes suspicious. "I really don't need this contraption, dear. I can walk. I'm not an invalid."

"Nobody says you are." I tug the seat belt snug around her. "Think of it as being queen for the day. We're here to serve your every whim."

She coughs into her handkerchief. "If I fall off, you'd better catch me."

Our Imposer escort punches a button on one of the armrests. There's a puff of exhaust from the propulsion unit underneath the chair.

"Oh!" Mrs. Bledsoe exclaims. The chair rises a few feet off the ground.

"I wanna ride the flying chair!" Cole's heels tap against my chest.

My head twists up. "Hey. Behave yourself, or the ride ends now."

He buries his face in my hair.

I squeeze his foot. "If you're a good boy, you can ride it on the way back, deal?"

He bounces on my shoulders. "Deal!"

My eyes shift between Cole and Mrs. Bledsoe. "Everyone ready?"

"Yes!" Cole shouts.

Mrs. Bledsoe wheezes. Her gaze crawls up the tower. "Not really, but let's go." She fiddles with the controls of her chair and it swerves toward the Citadel.

"This way," the Imposer commands, then swivels on his heels and marches through the iron gates.

Taking a deep breath, I'm about to follow Mrs. Bledsoe across the threshold when a familiar figure in the crowd catches my eye.

Digory Tycho. His hair is hanging wildly about his face, framing his clenched jaw. The intensity in his eyes causes my heart to race.

I squeeze my passenger's ankles. "Cole, why don't you go inside? There's something I need to do first."

His heels dig into my chest. "Not fair! I wanna stay with you!"

I hunch down and pry him off me, setting him gently to the ground. "No whining. Mrs. Bledsoe will be with you. I'll follow right behind, I promise. Don't I always keep my promises?"

His lips thrust into a pout. "Yup."

"Okay then. Go on now."

I slap him on the butt and he runs toward Mrs. Bledsoe,

whose forehead has sprouted more creases as she stares first at me, then at Digory. I mouth the words *I'll be right there* and watch as Cole takes her hand, and then he and the hover chair are gobbled inside.

Before I even have the chance to fully turn around, Digory's tugging my arm, pulling me into an alcove on the side of the building under the scowl of a stone gargoyle. He eyes me up and down. "You're okay! I heard you'd been captured by the Imps. But that's impossible. You're here, *safe*."

I poke my head out of the niche and peer around the corner, scanning the crowd to make sure no one's listening. But they're all riveted on the procession winding down the boulevard. I melt back into the shadows. "Actually, you heard right. I was taken in for questioning. But everything's fine now. It was all a misunderstanding."

Digory's eyes taper into slits. "How's that possible? No one gets released on good behavior."

I shake my head. "It's a long story and I don't have time to explain right now."

There's a loud whinny from one of the caballuses in the procession, followed by a few screams. One of the bystanders is barely pulled out of the beast's path by the crowd. Its rider, Prior Delvecchio, gallops ahead without even a look back. I huddle closer to Digory so he can hear me above the commotion. "There's something more important I need to talk to you about. Remember when you asked me why I was breaking curfew?"

He nods, still looking at me funny.

"There was someone here I had to see. Someone I needed to ask for help."

His eyes brush the Citadel's walls, painting them with contempt. "There's no one inside this … this *place* … who would help anyone." When he looks back at me, understanding dawns on his face, mixed with fear. "But if you got released, it must mean you're cozy with one of the higher-ups. And the only person with that kind of authority is the new Prefect, Cassius Thorn." He slaps his forehead. "Of course! *You* two! I remember. You were always together before he left the Parish …"

My pulse sprints. "How did you know—?"

He grabs my hands. "Believe me, Lucian. He's *not* the same anymore. No one who could rise to that position so quickly could ever be."

I pull away. "He's *not* like the others. He wants to help."

Digory backs away. "What are you talking about? What did you tell him?"

"Relax. I didn't tell him anything. It's what *he* told *me*. He wants to change things. He really does care about the citizens of the Parish."

Digory sighs. "And you *believe* that?"

"It's true. He wants to meet with the leaders of the rebellion, have a face-to-face, hear their grievances, reach a compromise."

Digory crosses his arms. "How exactly does he plan to accomplish this?"

"Through …" I clear my throat. "Through *me*."

"You mean through *me*, don't you?"

"What?"

He moves close again, squeezing my arms. "You didn't tell him about what we talked about, did you?"

"Of course not!" I shake myself loose. I notice several onlookers giving us the eye and lower my voice. "All he did was ask me to pave the way. I didn't promise him anything. That's why I'm telling you now. I wanted to run it by you before—"

"Before you report back to *him*?" Digory's face is on fire. "Have you forgotten what they did to that kid in the alley?"

It's a memory I'll never forget, no matter how many dams my brain wedges against it. "That wasn't Cass. It was *the Establishment*."

Digory clenches his fists. "He *is* the Establishment."

Now it's my turn to get angry. "You're *wrong*."

His gaze softens. He reaches out and lifts the pendant Cassius gave me, studying the clasping hands before letting it drop back down against my heart. "Lucian. I saw your brother and Mrs. Bledsoe entering the Citadel. If you love them as much as I know you do, you'll get them out as soon as possible."

I'm genuinely touched, even if his fears are unfounded. "Digory, I didn't mean to just spring this on you. I thought you'd be happy there was someone on your side, willing to listen. Someone that could *do* something. I can't risk anymore. I have what's left of my family to think of."

He nods. "It means a lot to me that you thought you were helping, but you're not. I don't want any part of Cassius's deal." He stuffs his hands into his pockets and looks away.

Seeing the disappointment in his eyes sends guilt coursing through me. "If you're worried I'm going to tell Cass—anyone—about you, don't be. It was a bad idea to mention it."

"Probably worse than you realize." His eyes dart through the crowd before returning to me, filled with sadness. "Besides, I'm more worried about *you*. Be careful, Lucian. If Cassius Thorn promised to protect you and your brother from the Recruitment, you can bet there's a price. Just be sure you're prepared to pay it."

He turns and walks away, swallowed by the crowd.

"Digory! Where're you going? Come back! I didn't tell him anything! I swear it!" I shout, not caring who hears me.

But he's gone, vanished as though he never existed, leaving me surrounded by thousands and feeling utterly alone.

NINE

The palatial Ceremonial Suite is nearly twice the size of Cassius's private quarters. I hurry past two Imposers flanking the archway that leads to an open-air observation platform.

"What took you so long? Is anything the matter?" Cassius asks. He's seated at the head of an oblong table with Cole and Mrs. Bledsoe, shrouded in shadows created by the awnings of the suite's massive Palladian windows. Just beyond them, glaring sunlight beats down on the panoramic balcony roosting over town square.

I smile and sit in the empty chair. "Nope. It was hell getting past the mob out there." I avoid his gaze. "Did I miss anything?"

He sips from his goblet. "Just breaking bread and getting reacquainted with the charming Mrs. Bledsoe and little Cole here."

Mrs. Bledsoe pushes her empty plate aside. "Charming?

Me? I don't think anyone's ever referred to me as such!" Her attempt at laughing degenerates into a bout of coughing. She clasps the handkerchief to her mouth.

I go over to her, kneeling by her chair. "Are you all right?"

She waves me away. "Yes, yes, don't mind me. It's all the excitement."

"You should relax, Mrs. Bledsoe," Cassius says. "After the ceremony, I'll have my personal physician take a look at you."

"Why, I couldn't possibly—"

"I *insist*," Cassius interrupts her. "You are the mother of a Recruit who prevailed during her Trials. You've also been like a mother to Lucky." He smiles at me. "That makes us family."

"Lucky!" Cole runs over and pulls me to my feet. "You can see the *whole* Parish from up here!" He giggles. "Uncle Cass says everyone looks like itty bitty ants!"

I turn to Cassius, who's beaming. "Oh, he did, huh?" But suddenly the image of the townspeople as insects makes me very uncomfortable.

A familiar Imp stops at the threshold, clicks her boots, and salutes. It's Captain Valerian. "Sir."

Cassius rises. "Did you get the itinerary I requested, Captain?"

"Yes, Sir. It's ready for your approval."

"Very good." He turns to us. "Please excuse me for a second. This won't take long."

"Sure, don't worry about us," I say.

His eyes penetrate deep. "But I do worry about you.

Very much so." He stands and crosses to the archway leading back into the suite, huddling with Valerian as a half-dozen government aides clad in stiff gray suits bustle about, checking hovering mics in anticipation of Cassius's speech and lighting the torches on either side of the podium erected on the balcony.

I turn to Cole and Mrs. Bledsoe. "So what do you think of him, guys?"

She cranes her neck to stare at him. "He certainly *looks* all grown up."

I take in the sight of Cassius in his uniform and pride fills my heart. "He *is*."

Mrs. Bledsoe shakes her head. "I can still see that little boy cowering behind those eyes. Shy and angry all at once."

Unease settles over me. "I don't know what you mean. Cass was always kind to me. Protective."

"There's a very thin line that separates being protective and being possessive."

"I'm not sure I know what you're saying," I respond, feeling a little annoyed.

She smiles. "No, I don't suppose you'd be able to see it."

Cole's busy stuffing his mouth with chunks of chocolate cake he's lifted off the dessert tray. His mouth and fingers are coated with frosting, which he smears against the fine linen tablecloth, totally oblivious. I'm about to scold him but decide against it. For once in his life let him get sick of eating too much, even if he pukes it all up. It'll probably be the last time he ever has the chance to. Besides, after the way I gorged myself in Cassius's suite, who am I to judge?

Cass returns to the table. His face is flushed, probably from nerves. "We're ready to begin now."

I smile at him. "You'll do great."

He just nods without saying a word and walks past us.

As soon as he steps onto the balcony, his presence smothers the hubbub of the spectators below. The mic hovering over him activates with a low hum. The glare of spotlights brush over him, painting his body into a dark silhouette.

"Citizens of the Parish," he begins. "It is an honor to stand before you as your new Prefect, as one who has lived amongst you, on this Day of Recruitment, a time-honored tradition of service and dedication to the pinnacle of justice. The Establishment."

At first, the applause is lukewarm, but as the spotlights caress the crowd with their telltale beams, the momentum builds to a never-ending rumble of thunder.

My eyes strain to catch an improbable glimpse of Digory in that multitude. I can't help but think of the loneliness etched in his face. I know I need to make things right between us.

After what seems like hours, Cassius holds out his hands. The din dulls into a murmur, and then to utter silence. "In addition to the mandatory military service required of all our youths on their seventeenth year, five individuals have been selected today, based on a combination of IQ, psychological, and physical aptitude tests administered during their final year at the Instructional Facilities. These Recruits shall be given the opportunity to train with the best and prove their mettle in the Trials, where the Recruit that excels above the others shall join the elite Imposer Task Force."

He turns to Valerian, who hands him a box covered in a mechanism made of ornate gold. Cassius enters a code into the digital display on its lid. The gears on the outside of the box begin turning, engaging each other like a jigsaw puzzle. Each twist and turn of a tumbler is broadcast over the Parish's speaker system, amplified so much that it feels like the heavens are pounding down their fury on us.

Mrs. Bledsoe is hunched over, trembling, her eyes wide sheets of glass. She gets to her feet and moves close to us. I have no doubt she's remembering that day years ago when she stood in that very crowd, with her husband and her daughter, and listened as her life was damned to hell.

Cole's giddiness has drained away. He presses against my leg, saying nothing. His fingers find mine and clamp on.

The last tumbler falls into place with a loud *gong* that echoes through the square.

Cole lets go of my hand and covers his ears. I scoop him up into my arms, trying to shield him from so much more than the power of that melancholy note.

The lid springs open with a drawn-out hiss.

"Lucky, I'm scared," Cole confesses to my ears alone.

"Me too." Why deny it, when my trembling embrace would betray me anyway?

Cassius's tongue traces his lips. He reaches into the box and pulls out a large envelope bearing the seal of the Establishment. The seal depicts a lone fist clenching the hilt of a sword; the tip of the sword is jagged and broken, the missing piece presumably resting in the heart of the past. Cassius then trades the box for a golden letter opener Valerian hands him, which looks more like a dagger. He nods and wedges the blade's point into the envelope's edge, then tears straight through.

Mrs. Bledsoe winces. One hand clutches her chest. I wrap my free arm around her, pulling her close. No one should have to experience this terrible feeling once in their lifetime, let alone twice.

Cassius tilts the envelope and pours five small computer chips into the palm of his hand—five lives that will change forever in just a few moments, along with those of the ones they hold most dear.

The chips momentarily disappear from view when he clenches them in his fist and strides toward a pedestal known as the Revelation Terminal.

"Citizens of the Parish," he announces. "I now give you this year's Recruits. May they serve the Establishment and its people with all the courage of those that have come before them."

He inserts the discs into the terminal. Outside, the jumbotrons surrounding the Citadel come to life, flashing bright colors from all over the spectrum, interspersed with fragments of faces compiled from the town's records of all the eligible candidates in the Parish. A drum roll builds to a crescendo as the crowd waits in a mixture of excitement and dread for the first name to be revealed.

The whole thing is pretty theatrical, as Cassius could just rattle the names off and be done with it. But this is what the Establishment does best—prey on the fears and sanity of its citizens.

The screens explode with a graphic of shattered glass, revealing the image of the first Recruit.

A girl with long curly red hair. Then the still image morphs into a live feed, where her bright blue eyes are opened so wide it looks like she doesn't have any eyelids. She's looking around frantically, as if she's not exactly sure what's going on. A hand comes into view and points her toward one of the viewing screens. My stomach sinks when I see the fear soak her eyes, as she realizes in front of thousands that she's been selected.

"Ophelia Juniper!" Cass announces. "Come forth to serve your country!"

Ophelia looks dazed. Behind her, I catch a glimpse of two cloaked figures holding on to her before she's prodded away by an Imposer working the crowd.

"What's going on?" I can read her lips until the directional mic picks up her audio like a sniper's target. "Where do I go?" The surveillance feed tracks Ophelia's movements through the crowd, which parts to give her a wide berth as she makes her way toward the reception area. She attempts to go left, scratches her head, turns right, then left again. "I'm so sorry. I'm a little confused." She teeters in a circle a bit until an Imp grips her by the arm and guides her up the stairs.

"Why is she crying?" Cole's lower lip quivers.

I shift my stance to try and block the screen, but it's pointless as the image is visible from everywhere. In all the excitement, I've forgotten that this is the first Recruitment

Cole has actually witnessed. "She's just sad because she has to go away from her family a little while, that's all."

"You mean like when Mommy and Daddy had to go away?"

My mouth goes dry. "No, not like that at all."

"You're right," Mrs. Bledsoe blurts out, her voice heavy with emotion. Her eyes are glued to the screen. "This is very different."

Cole's arms wrap tighter around my neck, his cheek like ice against mine.

The jumbotrons are doing their thing again, flashing a collage of desperate faces. This time there's a graphic of an explosion, replaced by an image of the second Recruit—a spectacled face I recognize from the Instructional Facility.

"Gideon Warrick!" Cass's voice booms through the plaza. "The time has come for you to take your place and serve. Come join your fellow Recruit!"

The cameras scan the crowd before homing in on Gideon's face. Unlike Ophelia, Gideon doesn't look confused, just resolute, as if this is exactly what he's been expecting all along. It doesn't surprise me. I remember him being an outsider at school, always the butt of one joke or another just because he was smart and withdrawn, not fitting in with the rest of us. But he was never afraid. He stood up to anyone who gave him a hard time, even if it resulted in a beating. It's this same determination I see etched on his face now. He turns and hugs some indiscernible figures behind him, then marches forward and up to the platform next to Ophelia as if he's making his way past the snickers in the school corridors.

The crowd stares at him in awe, and in relief that he's spared one of them, I'm sure.

Cole twists and turns in my arms. "I wanna go home!"

"*Behave yourself.* It'll all be over soon." But a chill courses through me as I realize that for Ophelia, Gideon, and their loved ones, it's just beginning. Just like it was for Cass on that terrible day two years ago, when the sound of his name being announced ground my heart to pulp.

I look at him now. His back's still to me. I fight the urge to rush up to him, turn him around so I can look into his eyes, make sure I can find the hint of disgust that I know *has* to be there. He wants to change all this. He *will* change all this.

Won't he?

The jumbotrons go dark and the images flash faster. You can feel the crowd's anxiety like a chilly film coating everything.

A clash of cymbals reveals the likeness of the third Recruit, a beautiful girl with long raven hair and green gems for eyes.

"She's pretty," Cole says to me.

"Yes, she sure is."

"Cypress Goslin," Cassius announces. "Your opportunity to attain the highest level of citizenship awaits you. Come and begin your new life!"

The feeds cut from the photo to a live shot of Cypress staring directly into the monitors, cold, fearless. When the Imposer arrives to pull her away, she rips her arm out of his grip and marches forward and up the stairs to take her place besides the statue-like Gideon and the quivering Ophelia.

Cassius clears his throat. "Here you have the first three of our brave new Recruits. Only two slots left. Two more opportunities to be a part of the greater good that is the Establishment. And just who will join them now? Who will step up to the podium without fear and assume their responsibility as a citizen of this noble society?"

The screens go crazy this time, flickering faster and faster, creating a disorienting strobe effect. Around me, I catch a series of snapshots of Cole's frightened face, Mrs. Bledsoe with tears streaming from her eyes, and Cassius's profile as he turns his head—the flare of his nostrils, the twitch in his cheek—and in that instant I know something's wrong.

The jumbotrons explode with color, and then everything goes dark before an image appears.

There's a disconnect between my eyes and my brain. The face I'm seeing…it's not possible. It's too much of a coincidence. We were just talking. Things like this don't happen to people you were just talking to. They happen to strangers, or people you barely know. Not *him*. One look at Mrs. Bledsoe's grief-stained face hammers home that it can happen to anyone.

"Digory Tycho!" Cassius announces.

But hearing it has no more impact than seeing that face plastered five-stories high on the surrounding screens. It can't be true. I can't *let it* be true.

Mrs. Bledsoe squeezes my arm. "What is it? What's

wrong?" Her voice sounds as if it's echoing down a long tunnel.

I can only stare ahead, suddenly forgetting how to speak.

"Are you okay, Lucky?" Cole this time.

His soft voice penetrates the numbness. I have to keep calm, if only for him. "I'm fine, buddy." I bury my chin in his hair, my eyes never leaving the image of Digory's face.

"Digory Tycho," Cassius repeats. "Come forward and join your comrades!"

At first, the cameras pan the crowd wildly, searching for their target but not finding it. The murmuring in the crowd builds like a simmering kettle. Where is he? Has he fled? If so, he'll be hunted down and killed on sight, not to mention what will happen to whatever family he's left behind. Family. Does he even have any? In that instant I realize how little I really know about Digory, and how dismal the chances are of ever learning more.

"I'm here!" a voice shouts over the buzzing of the masses swarming the plaza.

Digory.

The thumping in my chest turns to a spring, until it sinks in just what's waiting to greet him. He's just traded in the firing squad for a slow death of body and soul.

"It's that boy from the Square. Is he a friend of yours?" Mrs. Bledsoe whispers.

"H-he ... no ... "

"It's better for you both." Then she's hacking into her rag, sounding more terrible than I've heard until now.

Digory reaches the podium and trots up the stairs two

at a time, taking his place next to Cypress. If she looked fearless, he looks defiant. And even though his face fills the sky, it feels like he's a million miles away.

Cassius leans forward on the railing, still giving me his back.

Why won't he look at me?

"Excellent!" Cassius's voice booms. "That's the kind of spirit I'm talking about. So confident. So courageous. I'm sure I speak for the entire Establishment when I say, I can't wait to see what *you* are made of, Digory Tycho!" Though the words are intended for all, they're targeted to one.

He knows. Somehow, he *knows*.

Before an Imposer can stop him, Digory steps up to the microphone. "I appreciate your confidence in my abilities, Prefect Thorn, and I look forward to doing my people proud by showing *you* just exactly what *I'm* capable of!"

The crowd erupts into applause, only this time it feels natural, not coerced. Next to me, Mrs. Bledsoe is clapping, mindless of the blood-stained handkerchief smearing her hands. Even Cole joins in, not knowing why he's clapping, I'm sure, but sensing the surge of emotion around him.

My hands burn, and I look down to see my palms colliding, over and over again.

Cassius swipes his own hands in the air as if he's trying to erase the crowd's existence. Eventually, it has the desired effect. The applause flows to a trickle, then to a couple of drops before fading a few uncomfortable beats later.

Cassius's hands drop to his sides. "It is truly wonderful to behold the enthusiasm of the civic-minded. It appears we may have our first fan favorite." He laughs. "But I caution you that stockpiling one's faith in the guise of an individual will certainly lead to disappointment. The only entity one can truly depend on is the Establishment. To think otherwise, well … is not very prudent."

His words cast a pall over the spark Digory had ignited. On the monitors, shoulders that only moments ago stood tall and proud return to their ingrained slouches. Faces turn toward the ground, feet take a few steps back. Cassius's time away from the Parish has served him well. He knows how to play the game, preserve the status quo.

But Cass, my wonderful Cass, surely he still occupies a room inside this stranger's body? It's all for show. Remember what he said. He wants to change things. I have faith that he'll do the right thing.

"And now," he continues, "I present to you the final plebe on this year's Recruitment Day!"

For the last time, the displays come alive with sounds and color. My muscles tense. I find Mrs. Bledsoe's hand and entwine my fingers with hers, squeezing so hard I'm afraid I'm going to crack some bone. My forehead slumps into Cole's.

He smiles. "Maybe they'll pick *you* to win this time, 'cause you're so *lucky*!"

"Maybe." My voice is hoarse; my stomach muscles twist.

I have faith in Cass. I have faith in Cass. I have faith in Cass.

I'm not sure if it's on purpose, but this time the shuffling of faces on the screens seems to go on forever. I can't stand it anymore. All I want to do is grab Cole and Mrs. Bledsoe, bolt out of this room, and forget this place, forget this day…

But I can't get Digory's face out of my mind, and I feel ashamed. He's standing on that platform probably more frightened than he's ever been, but you'd never tell by looking at him. And here I am, being a coward when I have Cole and Mrs. Bledsoe depending on me.

The flashing stops and a face appears. I shut my eyes before I can make out who it is, holding on to normalcy for one more desperate moment. My teeth dig into my lower lip.

I pry my eyelids open to face my worst fears.

TEN

My captive breath bursts free. The face that fills the square isn't mine. It's not even male.

"Desiree Morningside!" Cassius's voice echoes through the square. "You have been chosen! Join your fellow Recruits on the podium!"

It takes a few moments for the words to sink in. Then relief washes over me like the first spring shower, whisking away the anxiety that racks my body. My knees buckle and I lean into Mrs. Bledsoe to steady myself.

"They couldn't have *you*, too," she says. Her eyes mist over and she clutches me.

Cole nudges my cheek with his nose. "Don't be sad you didn't get picked," he whispers in my ear.

I choke back my emotions and squeeze them both.

A live shot of the faces of the first four Recruits to be selected occupies the four corners of one of the screens.

Ophelia, twisting her head to and fro as if she's still not sure where she is. Gideon, stern, his eyes shifting around him as if he's studying every minute detail and committing it to memory. Cypress, looking bored, as if she has more important things she'd rather be doing with her time. And finally, Digory, his mouth curved into a huge, dimpled grin, his eyes staring right at me, through me.

I guess it's just the front he's putting up, the bravado in standing up to Cassius and the Establishment.

Because otherwise I can't think why this last selection would make him so happy.

And then the stream of relief I've been feeling is contaminated by the dread of what I know lies before him, emphasizing how fleeting true bliss is in the Parish. I look at the empty space in the center of the screen where the live shot of the fifth and final Recruit should be plastered. It seems what little happiness one can wring free of life always comes at someone else's expense.

"Desiree Morningside." Cassius's voice knifes through my brain. "Come forward and take your place at once."

I set Cole on the ground. My eyes connect with Mrs. Bledsoe's, now drained of any traces of joy.

"What's going on? Where is she?" Mrs. Bledsoe asks.

"I don't know," I whisper.

The cameras swoosh through the square and the restless crowd in search of a live shot of Desiree. But she eludes the spotlight. Her still image is superimposed on the lower right corner of the jumbotrons' live feed. I stare at the short banged hair, sad brown eyes, thin lips—it's hard to picture her as a deserter, on the lam for openly defying the draft. My chest tightens. What's happened to her? And what effect will her absence have on this ceremony?

I lean into Cole and Mrs. Bledsoe. "Stay here."

Forcing myself to move, I walk toward Cass. Before I can get more than a couple of feet, Valerian and another Imp block my path.

I clear my throat. "Ca...uh...Prefect Thorn? Is everything all right?"

His only response is the raising of his hand, signaling me to stay back. Valerian sidles up to him and whispers in his ear.

Movement on the jumbotrons distracts me. There seems to be some commotion going on in the plaza. Someone screams. The camera swoops around and zooms into the alcove underneath the sentinel gargoyle where I'd met with Digory. Bystanders swarm the spot. Through the pall cast by the gargoyle's shadow, a pale hand on the ground weeps a trail of darkness which forms into a murky puddle on the cobblestones. The feed flickers and cuts to black, replaced by the official government seal.

"We should go now," Mrs. Bledsoe whispers, behind me.

I can't take my eyes off Cassius. Valerian is doing all the talking and he's just nodding. Finally, she clicks her boots together, salutes, and exits the balcony. The aides move in for few more minutes of conferring before they, too, fade into the background.

Cassius leans into the podium, raising his arms. "Citizens of the Parish, it appears an unfortunate situation has arisen. It has come to my attention that our final candidate will be unable to perform her obligation as a Recruit. Regrettably, she has exhibited a deficiency of character and has decided to take the coward's way out, rather than accept the penalty for not fulfilling her responsibilities."

Coward's way out? The hand lying in that pool of blood... Desiree Morningside ended her own life, rather than take part in the Recruitment.

Or *did* she?

Cassius clears his throat. "As Parish Prefect, it now falls to me to delegate a replacement candidate to assume the vacated slot." He lowers his head. "Believe me when I say this is a decision that I do not make lightly. Since coming back to the Parish, the place where I grew up and experienced my fondest memories, I've had the opportunity to reconnect with old friends, friends who have been more like family to me over the years."

Hearing him speak this way, I can almost believe his aloof recounting of Desiree's tragic demise is all for the benefit of his superiors. It has to be. The Cassius that I know would never be so cold and indifferent to the loss of an innocent girl's life. But is this all just a memory I'm desperately holding on to?

Cassius finally turns to me. There's a trace of a smile on his face, but it's tainted by the glistening reflections in his eyes. The last time he looked at me like this was when he left two years ago to join the Service.

When he thought we'd never see each other again.

He stretches out his hand, beckoning me. "Perhaps my

dearest friends of all are here today with me now … Lucian Spark and his family."

I'm stunned, frozen in place. Government officials in particular are discouraged from fraternizing with the rest of us common folk. For Cassius, a newly appointed Prefect, to recognize our relationship publicly like this, and risk damaging his fragile reputation, is a bold move.

Too bold.

As he motions me forward again, his hand hangs in the air, palm open …

… just like Desiree Morningside's.

I lock my joints against the tremors.

Stop it. This is *Cassius.*

Before I lose my nerve, I stride over to him, Mrs. Bledsoe and I holding Cole's hands between us. Cassius edges up to me and places an arm around my shoulders. I catch a glimpse of the Recruits' faces still plastered on the screens. All but Digory are staring up at Cassius.

"Lucian and I have been friends, *best* friends, since we were children. We always told each other everything, shared all our secrets, as children do." He gives my shoulder a hard squeeze.

Cole points to one of the screens. "Look, Lucky! That's *us!*"

"Sssh!" His hand feels warm against my icy one.

"Upon returning to the Parish," Cassius continues, " I made the sad discovery that as children do indeed grow up, regrettably, so do the magnitude of their secrets, stretching the bonds of friendship tighter than they were meant to without inevitably tearing."

My eyes open wide. The thumping in my chest tries to drown out his words, but can't stop each one from puncturing my heart. "Cass, what are you doing?" I whisper through stone lips.

His eyes turn to cold glass mirrors. "Imagine my utter devastation when I discovered that the person whom I loved most in the entire world is in league with the insurrectionists threatening to unweave the very fabric of our entire society." He whips out Digory's poster and unfurls it in one quick motion, displaying its message for all the Parish to see:

RECRUITMENT IS FEAR.
RECRUITMENT IS CONTROL.
DOWN WITH THE ESTABLISHMENT.
PROTECT YOUR FAMILIES.

Gasps and murmurs erupt from the crowd, and from right beside me.

"What's he talking about, Lucian? What have you done?" Mrs. Bledsoe's questions are more of a plea.

I open my mouth to speak, but the words can't seem to make it past the heart lodged in my throat.

Setting the flyer aside, Cassius resumes the dismantling of our friendship. "I tried pleading with him, tried to make him see the error of his ways, appealed to the sacredness of our duty to the Establishment, but it was all for naught.

The poison injected into him by those infidels amongst us is quite virulent, infecting the love for country until all is destroyed ... unless we, as One People, can seek it out and crush it before it can spread!"

There is a smattering of applause that multiplies exponentially, drowning everything else, including my sanity, in its wake.

On the jumbotrons, Digory's eyes seem to penetrate mine across the vast chasm that separates us. Any trace of cockiness is gone, crowded out with concern and fear. He's been right all along. He warned me against trusting Cassius, and I didn't listen.

All I want to do is crawl into a hole, away from Cassius and Digory both. Away from their causes, their rebellions, the Establishment ... none of that matters to me. The only thing that does is standing right beside me looking afraid. My little brother. I tried to protect him from all of this. Now I've only succeeded in thrusting him right into the middle of this nightmare.

I stoop and bury him in my arms. "I'm so, so sorry."

"Can we all go home now?" Cole asks.

Cassius sighs. "Don't let this touching little scene fool you."

Glancing up, I'm shocked to see a close-up of Cole and me on every single screen. The numbness I've been feeling simmers and heats to anger. How dare they intrude on such a personal moment? I hate them. I hate them *all*.

Cassius points to us. "The truth is, this is a terrifying

example of how our children are being indoctrinated into the fringe element seeking to corrupt the morals and values that are the cornerstone of our society."

"I wanna go home, *now*!" Cole cries into my ear.

I pat his back, whispering, "It's going to be okay. Don't be scared."

"I'll take him." Mrs. Bledsoe reaches out for him.

"Thanks." Our eyes meet for a moment as I hand him over to her. Then I turn and focus my glare on Cassius. "Whatever problem you have with me, leave Cole out of it. He's only a kid. He doesn't understand any of this and you're scaring him. He has nothing to do with whatever you *think* I did."

He reaches into his pocket and pulls out a cluster of familiar-looking, yellowed parchment papers.

"Oh, but you are so wrong, Lucian. He has *everything* to do with it. You have already begun to corrupt him with your arcane literature—stolen, I might add, from the very library where you are apprenticed, and which you are entrusted to protect."

The old pages I'd brought home from the library.

Cole's story.

"The Lady." Cole squirms out of Mrs. Bledsoe's grasp and runs to Cassius.

I lunge to intercept him, but two Imps aim their weapons at my head and I freeze.

Cassius has already scooped Cole into his arms. He smiles at him and I feel shards of ice pierce my flesh. "You know this Lady, Cole?"

"I ... " Cole's eyes dart to the pages in Cassius's hand, then to me, then back to Cassius. His face trembles with confusion and fear. "I'm not supposed to tell." His voice is barely above a whisper.

Cassius shakes his head. "Of course you aren't supposed to tell." His eyes find mine. "Your brother taught you to lie very well."

He tosses the pages into a nearby torch. Instantly, the paper curls into crisp blackness, extinguishing the lights of the Lady's city forever.

Cole wriggles free of Cassius's clutches but doesn't say a word. Instead, he just stands there, his eyes transfixed on the flames eating away at his dreams.

I try to run to him, but a heavy boot slams into my ribs. The pain is agonizing. I curl into a ball, wrapping my arms around my midsection, yet that only seems to make it worse. My throat floods with bile.

Cassius pats Cole's head and shakes his own in mock sorrow. "There you have it, my Good People. This poor, innocent child's mind has been subverted by his very own brother, who, instead of protecting him and raising him to be a law-abiding citizen, is inculcating him into the ways of treason and sedition."

"You should be ashamed of yourself!" Mrs. Bledsoe shouts at Cassius, her voice filled with more strength than I've heard in forever. "After all you've meant to each other, all his parents did for you. You're all he's talked about for the past couple of years—"

"Mrs. Bledsoe, no. *Please*," I call out.

"Of course," Cassius sneers. "The self-appointed mother speaks out. The one that instead of providing guidance and morality to these two lost youths has enabled them on their path to destruction. From where I'm standing, that makes you an accessory to their crimes. Is it any wonder your own daughter refuses to have anything to do with you?"

I pull myself up to my knees, fingers clasped. "Leave *them* alone."

"You're right," Mrs. Bledsoe continues. "I've been like family to the Spark boys. I'm older. I should have known better. I failed in looking after them when their folks died. *I'm* the one that should be punished, not them."

My eyes bounce between them. "Stop this! This is insane. Cass, for the love of—"

"There *is* no love when our society is threatened!" Cassius bellows. "You are each guilty of acts of subversion against our government. As Prefect, the onus is on me to mete out a suitable punishment."

Then it all clicks. Desiree Morningside's convenient suicide, the empty slot in the Recruitment. My trial and conviction before all.

My worst nightmare's coming true...

I spring to my feet. "Just execute *me*. Let *them* go."

Pity fills his eyes. "The Establishment is not a heartless entity. Like a parent, we must be stern and deal harshly with our children, even though we still love them. In the spirit of compassion and the possibility of redemption, I hereby name Lucian Spark as the final Recruit, with Cole Spark and Edwina Bledsoe as his two Incentives. As you battle for the lives of those you love, Lucian, may it give you time to reflect on your errors in judgment and reignite the flame of patriotism you so obviously lack." He turns to the Imposers. "Take them."

"Lucky!" Cole screams.

I tear away from the Imps and stagger to my brother, folding him up in my arms and squeezing him as tight as I can. "I'm so sorry, buddy... I'm so sorry..." The moment seems frozen in time, as if nothing has come before it and nothing will come after it.

Hands dig into my shoulders and rip us apart.

I strain against my captors, reaching out my fingers, which graze Cole's. Trails of heat stream down my cheeks. "Don't be scared. I promise I'll take you home. And I'll find you a new story to read, over and over again. And it will be the best story ever, 'cause it'll never end, just like us. I love you, Cole."

Then I'm dragged inside the Ceremonial Suite, away from my sobbing brother and Mrs. Bledsoe, leaving my heart behind.

"Wait!" Cassius calls. The Imps drop me to the ground. Cassius steps through the archway and kneels beside me.

"Why?" I ask, a short question to fill a gigantic void.

Though I'm surprised by the tears in his eyes, I'm not moved. Not anymore. Not by anything.

"You broke my heart, Lucky. I came to you for help, and you chose *him* over me."

I'm too dazed to immediately register what he's talking about. Until I catch a glimpse of a face on the jumbotrons behind him.

Digory. Another non-coincidence in this never-ending chain of events.

Cassius reaches down and caresses the silver chain around my neck. "A simple transmitter. When I found that poster on you, I thought you'd lead me to the rebels eventually, though I had no idea how soon. Imagine my shock to discover that you went right to him and agreed to keep his activities a secret from *me*, the person you claimed to care so much about. The person who would have done anything for *you*." He rips the chain from my neck, cutting into the skin.

But nothing can hurt me anymore.

"Digory's a good person. More of a man than you'll ever be, Cassius."

A flicker of hurt in his eyes flames into a glare. He signals the Imps, who jerk me to my feet to face him.

"I hope you enjoy your time with this Digory. Especially since you'll be competing against each other to save the ones you love from the Culling." He leans in closer, his hot breath like irons on my cheeks. "Tell me, Lucky, is he worth Cole's life to you?"

I spit in his face.

His eyes are green skewers. Nostrils flare. He flicks away the foamy trail trickling off his chin.

Valerian slings a metal collar around my neck and clamps it tight. I gasp. Then the other Imps hook a leash to it.

The last thing I glimpse, as I'm hauled away from the archway, is my face plastered on the jumbotrons right next to Digory's.

PART II

ORIENTATION

ELEVEN

The freighter bulldozes through the black sea, smashing against the crisscrossing whitecaps.

"Attention," a voice blares from the ship's com system. **"We have arrived at the Infiernos training installation. Prepare to disembark."**

My joints are stiff from days of solitary confinement in a cramped stateroom; the Recruits were separated right after we boarded the ship. Steadying myself against the railing, I take in a lungful of salty sea air and peer over the bow, searching through the patches of early morning mist.

An island looms directly ahead. A huge, steel, domed structure squats on the horizon, pockets of smaller buildings and turrets spreading away from it. One tower rises hundreds of feet above the rest, its peak an oval of clear glass that observes all. Jutting pillars, resembling horns and lined with teeth-like spires, form a perimeter around the complex, which stretches from the shoreline to what appears to be miles deep inland.

"Let's go." A tall, thick Imp shoves his weapon into my back and I double over. Clutching the railing, I regain my balance and trudge on as he prods me the rest of the way.

The freighter deck is a whirlwind of activity as the crew bustles about, guiding the vessel into the shadows of a huge hangar-bay hewn out of a natural cave formation. Overhead, stalactites mix with gleaming steel girders and cat-walks, resembling a massive set of fanged jaws that swallow us whole.

Once we're moored, I get a glimpse of the other Recruits as a squad of soldiers hustles us down the gangway. The girl with the raven hair—Cypress—is followed by my former IF mate Gideon, and then Digory.

He smiles at me, but I look away and brush past him.

When the time comes to vie against the other Recruits for my Incentives' lives, Digory's the last person I want to compete against. After all, he's probably the strongest and most skilled Recruit. But that's not the only reason. I can't even imagine what it would be like if by some insane miracle I best him in one of the Trials and have to stand by while he's forced to choose which of the people he loves must die. It would be like I'd murdered his kin myself, even though it was to save my own. How could we ever look each other in the eye after something so horrid?

No. I can't do that. I won't. Let someone else bear that horrible burden.

The only Recruit missing from our group is Ophelia. Not sure where she is.

But there's no time to speculate.

We're herded through a maze of corridors that take us past a crowded mess hall, an indoor stadium where soldiers are engaged in a slew of hand-to-hand combat exercises, and a vast parade ground where squads march and run in formation. From the color and cut of their uniforms, it's apparent these soldiers have been separated into distinct groups: the black-clad Imps, the blue hues of standard infantry, and the more recent, inexperienced draftees clad in telling green. Should we have any doubts which way to go during this *tour*, Imps stand sentinel, station after station, graciously pointing the way with the barrel of their weapons.

I'm almost out of breath by the time we emerge into an oval-shaped chamber filled with half a dozen personnel clad in stark white medical uniforms, hovering over shiny metallic instruments and data screens.

The medic who appears to be in charge sweeps us all with a contemptuous look. "Strip," he says, stifling a yawn.

Once we're all naked, I make sure to keep my eyes glued straight ahead as we're subjected to bio-scans and all sorts of physical examinations. I feel like every inch of me is being poked and prodded. They check pulse, blood pressure, brain wave patterns, and vision, and then extract blood samples. At least they let us go behind a partition to provide them with a urine specimen.

After the invasive med exam is over, we're issued black

jumpsuit uniforms and duffel bags, and given "physical assessment" tests.

"Drop and give me twenty push-ups," the Chief Medic says when it's my turn. He holds up a digital chronometer displaying one minute and activates it.

I drop to the ground and begin. But my best effort proves to be pathetic. By the fifth rep, my arms are buckling so much I feel like my joints are going to pop free of their sockets. By the sixth, I've collapsed on my chest and I'm rasping for breath—humiliated at first, and then terrified by what it bodes for my chances of making it through the Trials.

The medic shakes his head and jots something down on his clipboard.

The push-ups are only the beginning of the ordeal. These are followed by sit-ups and a one-mile run, both of which I fail at miserably. At least most of the others aren't much better, with the exception of Digory, who not only completes each task but manages to elicit a grunt of "Not bad" from the doc.

I look away before Digory can catch me staring at him.

When the physical examinations come to a merciful end, we're escorted to the next station, where each of the guys is strapped in a chair while hovering spheres use laser tech to shear our hair until it's neatly cropped. Only Gideon opts for a full buzz cut. Cypress is allowed to keep her hair pinned back.

"Time to meet your drill sergeant," one of our armed escorts barks.

The Imps lead us down another corridor and take

flanking positions by the door as we file into the briefing hall, with me bringing up the rear. By the time I'm through, Digory's already standing on a long red line between Cypress (and her intimidating eyes) and Gideon. Still no sign of Ophelia Juniper.

As I walk past her, Cypress eyes me as if I'm some annoying insect just out of reach, which she'll allow to exist as long as I don't get too close. I really don't see *that* happening.

"Traitor scum," she mutters through perfect rose lips.

The words sting, but I try not to break my stride and give her the satisfaction. Unfortunately, I'm not smooth enough, and the falter in my step spawns a smirk on her face.

Crossing Digory's path, I can't help but send a quick glimpse his way. But his eyes stare blankly ahead as if I don't even exist. That bothers me more than Cypress's contempt. Can't say I'm surprised, though, after the way I snubbed him when we got off the freighter. It's still sending a pang through me, no matter how much my brain screams it's for the best.

I step into the spot next to Gideon, and I'm finally rewarded with a half smile. At least *someone* doesn't want to swat me and knows I'm alive … for now, anyway. I extend a hand, but Gideon just stares at it as if he's not sure what it means.

"I *thought* it was you they called last, Spark. How've you been?" he whispers.

My hand drops back down to my side. "You just thought it was me, Warrick?" I whisper back. "What? I thought you were smarter than that. My Recruitment too subtle for you?" I punctuate the last with a wink.

He taps his temple. "I can be a little dense sometimes."

I nod. "I remember." I mean it as a joke, but hurt flashes through his eyes and I instantly regret saying it. "To answer your question with the obvious response, I've been better."

Gideon's index finger straightens the glasses on his nose. They look grafted together from several different pairs, held together by heavy black tape. Being from the Industrial Borough means you don't throw things away, cause you never know if you'll ever have enough money for a replacement. Still, I'm not sure how he tolerates seeing through the fracture in one of his lenses. This world is cracked enough without adding to it.

He cocks his head. "Did she give you the look, too, Spark?" He nudges his head in Cypress's direction.

"You mean Black Widow over there?" I mutter under my breath. "What's her story?"

"I don't know all the details, just that she and her people are Aggies," he volunteers, as if that explains everything.

"She's a farmer? I'd have pegged her as a butcher."

He shakes his head. "It seems like this new Prefect is going for variety. I heard he wants fresh blood for the pool, has all these new ideas. Who knows? It may be for the better."

I swallow a geyser of acid scorching my throat. "I doubt that."

"Careful." He looks around. "These bulkheads have ears."

"Gotcha."

Gideon bumps my shoulder with his. He cocks his head, whispering lower than before. "What d'ya think about this Digory Tycho? Guess he's not better than the rest of us, like he thought back at the IF. He still looks pretty strong, but I think I can take Mr. Popularity down when the time comes."

My eyes dart to and from the still stone-faced Digory. "I don't really know much about him. We were never friends."

Gideon nods. "I say you and I stick together. I mean, for as long as we can. Us against them until the end." He stares down the line at the others.

My eyes wander over to Digory once more. Still no change.

I turn back to Gideon. "Yep. Us against them."

I grab his hand before he can stop me and shake it a few times, sealing the deal, before releasing it.

His eyes go from terror-filled to grateful. He studies his hand as if it's some new appendage that's sprouted from his arm.

"Attention Recruits! Officer on has the floor!" bellows one of the Imps guarding our corral.

The power of that voice snaps us all to attention. A tall woman, over six foot at least, strides into the room, flanked by two hulking males even taller. She stands a few feet in front of us, scanning us with twin cold slits passing for eyes. When she grins, her teeth look small and sharp, like the mouth of a predator savoring its next meal.

She licks her lips, as if she's read my mind. "Welcome to Infiernos. I'm Sergeant Slade. I must say, in all my years of overseeing new Recruits, this has got to be the most pathetic collection that's ever stood before me." Her grin turns into a smirk. "Then again, I do so enjoy a challenge. And *you'd* better, too. Not that whatever pleases you makes one iota of difference to me." She nudges her chin in the direction of the banks of monitors embedded in the wall. "In any event, should any of you entertain the notion of deserting your posts, I'd seriously rethink that strategy."

As if on cue, the screens come to life with images of the giant pylons positioned around the entire perimeter of the base. The blinking green lights on them change to yellow, then red. Slade turns to the nearest display. "Infiernos is protected by a highly sophisticated defense grid which includes sensors that detect body-heat signatures. Anyone attempting to cross the barriers while the fences are active will trigger a sonic pulse powerful enough to implode the brain and make it leak out your ears." She glances back at us and shrugs. "But you don't have to take *my* word for it."

The next thirty seconds are a grisly montage of prisoners being pushed and thrown into the armed barriers, complete with piercing screams of agony as their insides turn to mush. When the monitors finally, mercifully, go dark, Slade turns around to face us again. "Any questions?"

We all shake our heads.

"Who are we missing?" she barks.

I risk a glance down the line. Ophelia and her curly red hair are still a no-show.

That can't be good.

The sergeant steps forward and stands nose-to-nose with Cypress. "Identify yourself, Recruit!"

"Cypress Goslin, ma'am."

"*Sir!*" Slade barks.

A twitch exposes a chink in the armor of Cypress's composure. "E-excuse me?"

Slade widens her stance and leans in, her forehead practically touching Cypress's. "What's the matter, does the Aggie in the group have crops growing out of her ears? You will address me as *Sir*, not *Ma'am*, not *Miss*, not whatever other term of endearment you so choose. Understood, Recruit?"

"Yes, Sir," Cypress mutters.

"I can assure you, Recruit Goslin, that if you're having trouble enunciating, I have a repertoire of techniques available at my disposal that will ensure you scream at the top of your lungs."

"Yes, Sir!"

"Much better. Pity. I was so looking forward to motivating you." She steps back. "I'm sure I'll have that opportunity very shortly. You're bound to make a stupid mistake. Don't you agree, Goslin?"

"Yes ... Sir!"

"Very good. You learn quickly. I can see the hatred burning in your eyes, but you're capable of controlling it. Hold on to that emotion. Let it nurture you. Draw strength from it. It can prove quite useful as you prepare for the Trials."

"I will, Sir!"

But Slade has already moved on, stationing herself in front of Digory. "Identity, Recruit?"

"Digory Tycho, Sir!"

"Tycho? Hmmm. I've heard a lot about you, Recruit.

It seems you have quite the reputation, as one of the most promising candidates at your Instructional Facility."

"Yes, Sir!"

Apparently Digory's not about to make the same mistake Cypress did in her initial responses.

Slade eyes him up and down. "I see. Unfortunately, this isn't some popularity contest where you can charm your way past instructors and your fellow students to the top of the class with the minimum effort you are used to."

Digory's face remains stoic. "Understood, Sir."

Her eyes continue to appraise him. "You're obviously quite strong, Tycho. But physical prowess alone is not enough to emerge triumphant during the Trials. A good Recruit will possess an exceptional acumen, acute cunning and guile which I'm not sure your all-star school-boy status has prepared you for."

Gideon lowers his head and I can tell he's holding back a chuckle, which makes me want to dissolve our newly born alliance before it's taken its first steps—until I think it's probably the first time he's stood and watched while someone *else* was being bullied.

His attempt at subtlety doesn't escape the eye in the back of Slade's head. "Do you find me amusing, Recruit?" She strides over and plants herself smack-dab in his personal space.

His body stiffens. The familiar fear reappears in his eyes. "No, Sir!"

"Too bad. I'm known for possessing one of the keenest senses of humor in the entire battalion." Her words are as dry as sun-baked sand. "So if you're not laughing at my wit, you must be laughing at my person. Do you find me odd-looking, Recruit?"

"No, Sir!"

"Foolish then?"

"Not at all, Sir!"

"I see. Then you must be mad, Recruit. Simply laughing at things for no reason at all. Are you mentally deficient, Recruit?"

"Yes ... I mean ... no ... Sir!" Sweat gathers on Gideon's brow.

Despite his slight toward Digory, I can't help feeling sorry for Gideon and angry at myself. I never stood up and defended him against his tormentors at school, and I can't do it now.

Slade sucks in her cheeks. "You are just incapable of formulating your own thoughts and standing by the strength of your convictions, Recruit."

"Yes, Sir!" Gideon squeals.

Slade claps her hands. "At last, an honest answer. How refreshing! And to whom do I owe this kernel of truth in this granary of deception?"

"Pardon me, Sir?"

She sighs. "You were doing so well for a moment. Your *name*, Recruit. What is it? Or should I just call you Recruit Dense?"

"Oh, Gideon Warrick, Sir! But you can call me whatever you please."

"Recruit Dense it is, then. And nothing about you will *ever* please me."

She moves away without another word. My heart goes into overdrive as she hovers into view, her shadow moving across me and eclipsing the overhead fluorescents.

"Lucian Spark, Sir!" I volunteer, figuring I'll save her the trouble and speed up the ritual.

The frost in her eyes tells me I might have exercised a severe lapse in judgment.

Her brows stretch toward each other. "It surely has been a grueling day. I must be tired. There's no other explanation for why I imagined this Recruit speaking to me without first being addressed."

"I'm sorry, Sir!"

She palm-slaps her forehead. "It just happened again! I need to get myself checked out by Medical as soon as possible to ascertain whether or not I'm having some kind of breakdown."

I'm about to respond, but my teeth decide to prevent my tongue from making the situation worse. Just relax, stare straight ahead but avoid eye contact. Breathe deeper, slower … imagine Cole's face, not the visage of this scaly reptile in front of me ready to sink its fangs into my self-respect and spit it out.

"Actually, Recruit," she drones on, "now that the voices in my head seem to have cleared, I see you aren't really in need of an introduction after all, considering your memorable performance during the Induction Ceremony."

Again my teeth come to my tongue's rescue. I didn't

hear a question or a direct address, so I continue to stare past this moment to some imagined, undetermined future time when Cole and Mrs. Bledsoe are miraculously waiting for me at home.

"What's the matter, Lucian Spark? Does being involved in a plot to overthrow our government render one incapable of forming a complex and cohesive sentence?"

"Don't know, Sir."

"You don't know how to form a complex and cohesive sentence?"

"No, Sir. I was referring to your insinuation that I'm involved in any type of treasonous actions against the Establishment. On this topic, I possess no knowledge whatsoever and can say nothing to help further your assertions except that they are completely invalid."

The only rebel around appears to be my tongue. I can't help myself. It's worth whatever degradation she plans on inflicting on me if it'll wipe that smug look off her face, even for just one moment.

But instead, my little rant just seems to have dangled a slab of meat to her starving sadism. Her lips peel back even further from her glistening teeth, and for a second it looks like her jaw's about to unhinge to swallow me whole.

"How arrogant, for someone who barely dodged execution but for the rank sentimentality of our new Prefect. It appears he believes that the scum of society should be given the chance to reform." She leans in, close to my ear. "I assure you, we Imposers are not quite as gullible."

My gut explodes in a burst of anguish generated by her

powerful fist. I double over in agony and drop to my knees, waves of nausea and pain alternately slamming into my body. Clutching my burning stomach, I open my mouth, convulsing but only retching up air.

When I open my flooded eyes, it takes a moment to focus. Why are there two Slades glowering down at me? I shift my gaze to the six Recruits besides her. A few blinks and six become three. But only one isn't staring straight ahead. Only one is looking directly at me.

Digory.

Slade has her back to him and she misses the flash of tenderness on his face—the same look I remember when he nursed me back in that alley, a lifetime ago it seems. Then Digory's eyes dart to Slade, transforming into angry orbs. I catch a glimpse of a curling fist. He's about to make another monumental mistake with grave consequences for his life, second only to meeting and befriending me. If he attempts to strike her, the Imp sentries will cut him down before he can get within a few feet of her.

I force a palm up. "*Please…*"

Though the words are meant for Digory, the satisfied sneer on Slade's face indicate she thinks they're a gift to her. Let her relish her false victory, as long as it keeps Digory breathing.

He stares back at me. I try to channel the power of my words into that soothing blueness, willing him to under-stand just how much I need him to listen to me right now.

I'm rewarded with a barely perceptible nod and an un-furling hand.

My head slumps down in relief this time.

"So, the traitor has learned a little humility," Slade croaks. "The first of many lessons to be learned during the Trials. Though I confess, Spark, I'm rooting for your early elimination. The rest of these incompetent Recruits may be an embarrassment to the Establishment, but your ascension and assimilation into the ranks would be nothing short of a travesty."

Then Digory starts to move, and I cringe when I think of him throttling her and paying the price. But he moves past her in a flash, instead stooping beside me.

"What are you doing, Recruit Tycho? No one gave you permission—"

"He's hurt, Sir!"

And without waiting for her to continue, he takes me in his arms and lifts me to my feet, making sure I can stand on my own before he lets go.

The loud clicks of the sentries' weapons being locked and loaded shatters the tense quiet. In a flash, their guns are trained on us, ready to fire.

TWELVE

The longest seconds of my life pass, without any blinks or breaths...

Despite my lingering nausea, I shift my stance and lock my feet firmly in place. My whole body is tense, waiting for the impact of the bullets to rip me apart. I wonder if it'll be over quick, or if I'll feel the burning in my guts as I'm torn inside out?

Digory moves from behind to stand beside me, one of his shoulders shielding half my body.

Finally, Slade gestures to the sentinels. "Stand down."

The Imps lower their weapons but hold their position. Digory gives my shoulders a final squeeze, then resumes his place in the formation.

I set the breath I've been holding free.

Slade stares Digory down. "Thank you, Recruit Tycho.

Your generous assistance has provided me and the other Recruits with much valuable insight."

A test. It was all a test designed to expose any attachments among the Recruits, affecting everyone's strategies and alliances in the upcoming Trials. Digory and I might as well have paraded naked for everyone to see.

Gideon shoots me a suspicious *what was that all about* look and turns away. Perhaps he's already rethinking our deal. From what I can see of Cypress, her cocky expression would suggest she's already emerged first at the Trials and is preparing her acceptance speech. As for Slade, you can see the wheels and gears turning on her face, measuring just how long it's going to take to twist this rare glimpse of compassion to her own ends.

That settles it. I'm going to have to work doubly hard to convince everyone that Digory and I mean nothing to each other. We can't. Not if either of us stands a chance of making it through this thing with as little scathing as possible.

Slade resumes her place front and center. "*Five* Recruits selected for the Trials, but only *four* present." She pulls a printed form out of her jacket pocket and eyes it eagerly. "That would make our deserter—"

"Ophelia Juniper here! I mean, present!" calls a voice that seems more suited to a squealing child. She practically skips, then trots, to the spot next to Cypress. Cypress doesn't bother to conceal a snort.

Thinking better of her decision, Ophelia dashes past Cypress to my end of the line, her hair bouncing all the way, her eyes wide. One look at Slade and I can't help but think that Ophelia reminds me of the prospective mate of a black widow spider, trembling from excitement over the empty promise of married life.

"Ophelia Juniper reporting for duty!" she proclaims. "Oh, you *already* know *that*. I mean that my name's Ophelia." She giggles, her hand pressed to her chest. "I'm sooo sorry I'm late. I have this habit of getting lost all the time. I must have taken a couple of wrong turns and ended up in the mess hall. Terrible sense of direction, ever since I was five. Mother thinks it's that bout of … " Her hand twists one of her curls over her ear. "Well, I was ill, you see, and my inner ear … my balance was very much affected … but here I am. I made it!"

Slade lets the quiet linger like a no-longer-welcomed guest. She wants us to squirm at the oblivious Ophelia's expense. Despite my resolve to stay strong, I can't help but feel sorry for this innocent girl and fear for what penalty the sergeant will inflict on her.

Slade approaches Ophelia with a smile. "You *did* make it. How fortunate for all of us here. We were so worried about you." She reaches out and caresses Ophelia's curls. "You have such pretty hair. I trust the accommodations have been to your liking?"

Ophelia's laugh is coated in nerves. "Well, my cabin on the boat we came on was a lot bigger than my room back home."

It's the first time I've seen her hold still. Her eyes go vacant for a moment, as if she's searching for a memory to warm the emptiness, a look that's reflected on the faces of the rest of the Recruits. If anyone ever told me I'd long for the rat-infested hovel I share with Cole, I'd have thought they'd inhaled too many toxic fumes... I guess a home isn't really measured by the flaking plaster or invading rodents, but rather if there's someone there who actually gives a damn if you return each day *in spite* of those things.

Slade's tongues slithers across her lips. "Recruit Juniper?"

I lean toward Ophelia. "You okay?" I whisper, which has got to be the most inept question ever.

Ophelia returns from whatever refuge beckoned beyond her eyes. It's like someone has switched on an automaton. She blinks a few times, her lips forming into a smile. "Too bad I didn't have one of those porthole things in my cabin to see where we were going, though." She cocks her head toward me and a conspiring hand cups the side of her mouth. "Not that I'd have any idea anyway." Another anxious giggle. "But it was nice having some stew. I can't remember the last time I ate something other than a ration bar. Thank you so much!"

The grin on Slade's face stretches so wide I'm expecting her lips to tear apart. "Actually, I wanted to thank *you*!"

My stomach muscles clench.

Ophelia presses the tips of her fingers to her chest. "Thank *me*? For what?"

An invisible hand wipes away the grin on Slade's face. "For providing a lesson on the importance of *punctuality*."

The hand caressing Ophelia's curls balls into a fist.

"Owwww!!" Ophelia's hands reach up to grasp Slade's,

but the Imp is too strong for her. "Please, stop! You're *hurting* me! Ah!"

"Am I, dear? I've got just the remedy to ease your pain." Slade's free hand digs into her tunic pocket, producing a flash of silver.

The sight of the blade glues me in place. This can't be happening. This pathetic girl hasn't done a thing except get lost.

Slade holds the knife directly in front of Ophelia's horrified face, allowing her to memorize every single notch on its cutting edge. Then, dragging Ophelia by the hair, Slade dumps her at Cypress's feet. "Will you try to prevent me from teaching this slacker a lesson, Recruit Goslin?"

Ophelia reaches out and wraps a hand around Cypress's ankle. "Please! Don't let her ... please ... help ...!"

Cypress never looks at her. Instead, she just kicks Ophelia's hand away as if she's a pesky rat. "I will not try and help her, Sir!" Her reply is almost drowned out by Ophelia's shrieks.

Slade smiles. "Very good, Goslin!" Then she grips Ophelia's hair once again, yanks her to her feet, and pulls her in front of Digory. "What about you, Tycho? Are you going to try and help her?"

Digory stares straight ahead, but unlike Cypress, his face is twitching. His forehead looks slick, his eyes squeezing shut with each piercing shriek.

"I ... I ... " He bows his head.

"*Help ... me ...* " Ophelia is squealing now.

"Speak up, Tycho!" Slade hisses. "Are you going to try to stop me from meting out justice, or not?"

His looks up, taking her in.

Ophelia reaches out to him. "*Please...*"

"I...I...*can't.*" He turns away.

"I'll take that as a *no*, Recruit." Slade grins. "Interesting that you had no qualms about coming to Spark's assistance." Ignoring the bloody claw marks on her hand, Slade heaves Ophelia to Gideon's feet.

"I won't help her, Sir!" Gideon practically screams before Slade can even pose the question. He's obviously trying to get this torment over with as soon as possible, not that I blame him. Except now it shifts the terrible burden onto me.

Slade hauls Ophelia right in front of me. Her feet drop out from under her, but Slade still holds her aloft by the hair. "No! Please...no!" Her legs flail, her body racked by sobs. Her eyes meet mine, pleading. "Help me. Please don't let her kill me!"

Then it's not her face but the guy in that alley, screaming as he was being torn apart while I did nothing. Nothing except turn away and flee.

My foot inches forward.

"Are you going to help her, Recruit Spark?" Slade bellows at the top of her lungs.

Ophelia reaches out a bloodied hand. "I know you won't let me die. You're not like the others. You're good..."

"Please. Don't say that," I whisper, more to myself.

Slade presses the glistening blade to the girl's throat. "Answer, Recruit Spark! Help or not?"

My eyes trace the tears streaming down Ophelia's face. "Don't make me do this . . . "

The point of the blade pricks the girl's skin, drawing a drop of blood that knits like a poisoned thread across her throat.

"I beg you!" Ophelia's voice quivers.

Spasms wrack my body. Could I be quick enough to knock the knife out of Slade's hand before it finds its mark?

The blade digs in deeper . . .

"I don't want to die," Ophelia blubbers. "I want to see my mama . . . "

And now it's Cole's face I see, reaching out to me, crying, begging me to save his life . . .

There's only one thing I can do.

"No!" I shriek, drowning out Ophelia's screams. "I won't help you! I won't help you!" I scream the words over and over again, my hands over my ears, my eyes closed, snuffing out any trace of this girl before she tempts me into sending my brother to his doom.

My throat starts to burn, and I think Slade's blade has turned on me until I realize it's just the strain I've inflicted on my vocal cords. I stop yelling, clearing my throat. Before I can stop myself, my eyes flicker open.

Just in time to see Slade's hand slicing the blade—across Ophelia's hair. She saws into the curls, pulling, ripping the hair away, hacking away at the girl's scalp until there's nothing left but ragged patches clumped unevenly around the skull. When she's done with the last cluster, she throws Ophelia to the ground.

The girl's cheek smacks the floor, her face buried in a cushion of her former curls that barely deadened the sound of the impact. She reaches out a blood-smeared hand, groping the deforestation of hair surrounding her. Grabbing a cluster, she examines it with her one visible eye, as if trying to make sense of why it's no longer on her head. Then that eye turns to me. But it might as well be an index finger pointing right at me, rigid, unforgiving.

I try to look away but I can't, held captive by the unspoken questions that Ophelia stares at me. There's one that hammers into my brain, over and over again, as if her lips are pressed to my ear and she's screaming it at the top of her lungs.

Why?

"Cole," I whisper. I can't tell if she hears me, but if she does, it's an answer that doesn't satisfy that unblinking eye. *Stop staring at me. There was nothing I could do*, I think at her desperately. My fists curl, but I still can't break contact with that loathsome eye. All I want to do is gouge it out of its socket and grind it to pulp beneath my boot, anything to make it stop. Anything to smother the evidence of my cowardice.

I breathe in deep. I have to keep myself together. If this is how unraveled I'm feeling now, *before* the Trials have even begun, I can't imagine what it'll be like when we're forced— when we have to choose which one of the people we love—

Slade stoops and pulls Ophelia to her feet, breaking the eye's hold on me. She's not as brutal as she was a few minutes ago, brushing some strands from Ophelia's face and shoulders.

Does the monster have an ounce of compassion? No. This must be just another one of her sick games, designed to keep us off balance.

"A valuable lesson has been learned here," Slade says smoothly. She prods Ophelia toward the center of the line so she can get a better look at all of us. "Take a good look at these four faces, Recruit Juniper. Not *one* chose to come to your aid. During the Trials, remember that when the time comes—these four are all prepared to let you and your kin die."

After how I fared under the scrutiny of the one eye, I know I'll be completely defenseless against two. My gaze drops to the floor.

"And you four Recruits," Slade continues. "Take a good look at Recruit Juniper. Remember that she could be any one of *you*."

My eyes dart to Gideon, who meets mine for a second before he shifts his stance and looks at the dark monitor. Cypress is staring at Slade, her gaze unflinching, not caring about the rest of us. I can't bring myself to look Digory's way, not sure if I'm more concerned about whether or not he's looking my way than what I'll see there if he is.

Slade lets go of Ophelia. "Rejoin your fellow Recruits."

Ophelia obeys without a word, moving back to her position beside me. As she passes in front of me, I no longer see fear reflected in that eye, but something even more unsettling.

Hatred.

"Now that you know what brand of loyalty you can expect of the others," Slade continues, "I suggest you get a good night's rest. Tomorrow morning you begin Initial Entry Training. First Call is at oh five hundred hours, followed by Physical Training at oh five hundred thirty, Breakfast at oh six hundred thirty, and your first day of Basic Pre-Trial Prep Exercises at oh eight hundred thirty." She walks down the line again, glaring at each one of us. "You have been selected to become Imposers, the best of the best. I don't tolerate failure. For the next ten weeks until the Trials begin, all of you belong to *me*. Dismissed!"

As we scramble out of the briefing hall, I can't help but think the next two and a half months are going to be the worst of my entire life.

THIRTEEN

The first night in the barracks seems endless.

All of us Recruits are crammed into the same small quarters, barely large enough to fit five beds. Cypress and Ophelia's cots are on the opposite wall from mine, which is sandwiched between Digory's and Gideon's. Through the gloom, I can make out the peaceful expression on Digory's sleeping face, hear the gentle purr of his breath escaping his slightly parted lips in time with the rise and fall of his chiseled bare chest.

Can I *really* trust him?

I force myself to turn my back on him.

Despite surrendering to exhaustion, I end up tossing and turning for hours, waking up several times bathed in sweat, my mind filled with nightmare images that haunt long after I've opened my eyes.

The Culling. Before I was recruited, the phrase had little

meaning—two words shrouded in vague foreboding, like a half-remembered dream. Now, the term's sharp as crystal, stabbing me deep, shocking each nerve ending as I fight to control the spasms. What horrible trials can they have in store for us, worthy of such an unthinkable decision? And how will I be able to pass them all? We were told there are at least six rounds... *SIX* whole rounds to make it through. Just *one* mistake and Cole... Mrs. Bledsoe... My eyes squeeze shut, but the *what ifs* just batter through my brain, pounding against my skull... screaming... crushing...

Moaning from the other side of the barracks.

I snap back to the now.

Gideon writhes, half out of his cot. Like me, he's covered in sweat. It seems I'm not the only one who can't get any shut-eye. I slip out of my own bed and kneel down beside his, grateful to focus on someone else's tortured mind.

During his thrashing, I catch flashes of something snaking up his bare back—a thick band of knotted flesh.

Scar tissue?

Then he rolls over and it's gone.

I reach out and tap his shoulder. "Gideon, it's just a bad dream," I say softly.

He's mumbling something. I lean in closer so I can hear.

"I didn't mean it," he murmurs. "Please don't... I promise... I'll be good... "

I slump on my haunches.

His thrashing ebbs and dies. I pull the threadbare blanket over his still form. I'm not sure how long I stay there, but I watch him, listening until his breathing becomes a light snore.

Eventually, the door to the barracks bursts open and the lights flare on in a blinding burst.

"Rise and shine, maggots!" Slade's blurry silhouette calls from the doorway. "Time to get your lazy asses out of bed."

Ophelia moans. "Five more minutes, *please*."

Slade rips the blanket off her. "Move it!"

The five of us practically fall all over each other, scrambling to hit the communal showers in the adjacent building. Ophelia, especially, makes sure to give Slade a wide berth.

Digory catches my eye as he jogs alongside me. "Mornin'."

I nod and pull ahead of him into the showers, picking a spot at the opposite end.

If Slade's gentle wake-up call didn't do the trick, the ice-cold water jetting from the spigots sure does.

"Holy crap!" Gideon wails from under his showerhead. He's trying to keep his back to the wall so no one will see what I saw last night. "This is colder than the water back home."

Cypress snorts. "You don't know what *cold* is."

Fortunately, the shower's mercifully short. In a matter of minutes, we're dressed in our uniforms and lined up in the Company area, a paved rotunda just outside the barracks.

Slade's waiting for us with a reptilian grin. "Welcome to your first day at Infiernos."

"Doesn't that mean *hell*?" Gideon mutters under his breath.

Cypress smirks. "You got that right."

Ophelia raises her hand. "Excuse me, but what time do we eat breakfast, again?"

Slade's grin widens. "Why, right now." Her eyes ignite with fury. "Drop and eat the pavement. All of you. Twenty push-ups. *Now*."

The next hour is a grueling workout, starting with an upper body warm-up consisting of push-ups and jumping jacks. This is followed by a lower-body regimen of squats, and then an upper and lower body cardio-combo featuring pull-ups, squats, lunges, crunches, and running, with barely any resting time in between.

Slade's shrill whistle pierces my ears, signaling the end of morning calisthenics. I've never heard such a beautiful sound. "That has got to be the most pathetic display of Recruit performances I've ever seen," she bellows. Her face wrinkles in disgust. "Hit the DEE-Fak."

"DEE-Fak?" I grumble, trying to push up from a kneeling position.

"Short for Dining Facility." Digory's holding out a hand to me. If it weren't for the sweat glistening on the muscles barely contained by his tank top, you'd never guess he'd participated.

I shake my head and wave him away. "That's okay. I can manage."

He sighs. "Suit yourself." Then he stomps away after the others.

After a couple of tries, I finally get my bearings and limp after them.

The breakfast spread is more food than I've seen in my

entire life. The five of us sit at a small metal table in the mess hall, segregated from the other Imps, barely talking while we gorge ourselves on eggs, sausages, grits, oatmeal, toast, juices, milk, and coffee. Chewing and slurping. All too soon the spread starts to dwindle and I find myself shamelessly picking crumbs off my plate, staring at the empty surface longingly.

Digory's arm grazes my own and I involuntarily shudder.

He's holding out the last two pieces of singed bacon, one slice slightly bigger than the other. He grins. "Saved you a piece."

My eyes bob between the two. "Any preference?"

"You take the bigger slice."

"But—"

He doesn't give me a chance to finish. He stuffs the smaller slice into his mouth and holds the larger piece to my lips. He chews quietly, his square jaw pistoning his portion into a bulge on his left cheek. Twin oceans of blue stare at me, looking almost amused.

My hand breaks free of its paralysis and reaches up to grab the other piece he's offering. Our fingers brush. A jolt-like static zips through my skin. For a moment, his hand engulfs mine as I take a bite, our eyes never breaking contact.

Then guilt overwhelms me.

"What's the matter?" Digory's eyes are now turbulent seas. "You thinking of your brother?"

I nod and push my plate away.

"Oh, sweetie, don't fret," Ophelia coos. "I'm sure they wouldn't hurt your little brother. He's just a baby."

"You'd be surprised what some people will do to their babies," Gideon says in a flatline. He chews off a piece of cornbread. "You know what they call the Complex, where they keep the Incentives stashed?"

"Purgatorium." Cypress stabs at her eggs with a fork, her eyes glassy.

"That's right." Gideon's lips curve into a vacant smile. "Pretty intense sounding, huh?"

I fight the sudden urge to lunge across the table.

Digory glares at him. "Shut it, Warrick."

When Gideon looks up from his own plate, he seems genuinely surprised. His eyes flit between Digory and me. "Oh, I'm sorry. I didn't mean—no. They wouldn't hurt him…"

"Uh…this is the Establishment we're talking about, right?" Cypress asks. She takes a last swig of juice and looks around to make sure none of the other Imps sitting nearby are listening. "The Recruitment…killing our loved ones…ring any bells?"

"Thanks for making my point." Digory sighs.

Confusion elbows the sarcasm out of her expression.

Digory grips my hands. "Goslin's right. It's *because* of the Establishment's cruelty that you can guarantee they're making sure all of our families are being well-nourished and taken care of. They'd never risk anything happening to them and spoiling their sadistic psychological torture." He leans in closer, drowning me in his eyes. "Cole's fine right now, Lucian. If you trust anything, trust *that*."

I squeeze his hands back. "Thanks," I whisper.

Ophelia rests a hand on my shoulder. "During the Recruitment. That woman up there with you and your brother, Spark ... that wasn't your mama, was it?"

I shake my head. "Mrs. Bledsoe. She's *like* a mother to me. To me and my brother. She's looked after us ever since ... " I swallow. "For a while now ... "

Ophelia smiles. "Mamas are so important." Her eyes pool. "Heck, mine's sacrificed everything for me." The pools dry up. Her eyes are somewhere else again, just like during Slade's "welcome." "Mama's made me who I am today."

And just who are you? I wonder.

She laughs, almost as if she's read my mind. "Me and my sister, both."

"The two of them, your mother and your sister ... they're your people, I take it?" I ask.

"They sure are! I'd do anything for them!" She giggles. "So you see, Spark. We have a lot in common. I have my mama and sister. And you have your brother and that darling that's like a mama to you." She gives me a hug and leans into my ear. "I'm sure you'd just be totally crushed if something happened to that sweet little brother of yours."

A chill slithers down my spine. I break free of her embrace and stare her down. "I guess I'll just have to make sure that doesn't happen."

She beams. "One can only hope."

Then she turns to Gideon. "As long as we're talking about family, who are *you* making a stand for?"

Gideon mumbles something unintelligible.

"What did you say, Giddy?" she squeaks.

He swallows the last of his cornbread. "My parents."

"Parents?" Cypress grumbles. "I would have thought you sprang from a test tube or something."

I'm expecting Gideon to fire back, both barrels blazing. But he doesn't. Instead he just looks at her. "Nah. I'm one of the ones lucky enough to have both a mother and a father."

"You must be *so* excited!" Ophelia squeals. "Have you thought about what you're going to say to them when you see them again?"

He smiles. "I've thought of nothing else ever since I heard my name get called in Town Square." He shrugs. "Guess I won't know exactly what I'm going to say until the time comes."

For the first time, I realize that there's so much about them I don't really know.

Including Digory.

I opt for the easier target. "What about you, Goslin?"

Cypress looks up from picking at her teeth. "Me? What about me?"

I roll my eyes. "Who are your Incent—*family*? Who are you fighting for?"

She bolts upright. "None of your business!" She grabs her duffel bag. "You guys are really annoying with all your prying. Besides, tactically, it makes no sense to give away all your weaknesses." She shoves her empty chair against the table. "Morons."

I shake my head. "Maybe we're just trying to get to know each other bet—"

"Get to know each other better for *what*?" she snaps.

"So we can say, *I really like that girl or that guy, even though they forced me to pull the plug on my mother?* Sheesh!"

Ophelia's eyes supernova. "So one of them's your mama, too!"

"No. Neither one is my *mama*." Cypress walks a few steps away, then turns. "If it makes all of you feel any better, I've never even laid eyes on the ones I'm fighting for."

All too soon, Slade appears at our table licking her lips. "Hope you enjoyed your breakfast. Now's when the fun begins."

With the exception of an hour lunch break, the rest of the day consists of nonstop training exercises, including Drill and Ceremony training, where we're issued fake weapons so we can get familiar with their feel and added weight while being instructed on the proper procedures for marching, standing at attention, facing right or left, and standing at ease.

After all that, Slade lectures us, and I have to bite my tongue as she drones on and on about the Establishment's *values* and code of conduct. Then it's on to Basic Weapons Marksmanship, including disassembling, cleaning, and reassembling our weapons, with Slade sneering and shouting at us the entire time.

"Not *that* way, Spark! It looks like you're handling a mop!" she barks.

By the time dinner rolls around, everyone's looking pretty somber, including Digory.

"Hope you enjoyed your first day of training," Slade announces back at the barracks. "Tomorrow I won't be so easy on you."

We're all too exhausted to take advantage of the one free hour of personal time we have until lights out, so we crash early. Gideon's tossing and turning again, and Cypress and Ophelia are already snoring lightly. I strip to my underwear and plop onto my cot.

I glance at Digory. The perfectly symmetrical contours of his body ripple as he takes off his uniform, folds it neatly, and stuffs his gear into his locker.

He never did say who *he* was fighting for. He knows all about me and Cole, but he's never spoken about his people. And part of me's been afraid to ask. Though I'm not quite sure why…

He slips into bed. "G'night, Lucian."

"Digory," I whisper. "About the Culling. Who are your —?"

"Get some sleep. We have another busy day tomorrow." Then he rolls over, and I'm staring at his broad muscled back in the shard of moonlight that cuts through the small window of the barracks.

Is he really that tired or is it part of some strategy, like Cypress suggested?

After all that talk about trust, Digory obviously doesn't trust *me*.

There's too much at stake to let my guard down. Cole and Mrs. Bledsoe are the only people I can afford to think about.

I can't afford to trust anything anyone says anymore.

The last thought I have before my aching body drifts into unconsciousness is that I'm not sure how I'm going to make it through the rest of basic training, let alone the Trials.

FOURTEEN

I never get the chance to press Digory on his Incentives. The next three weeks are even more grueling, with Slade piling more and more on us each day. The morning calisthenics become more intense, and there's added instruction on Ground Fighting Techniques, Map Reading, Land Navigation, Compass Use, First Aid Training, and Dressing Wounds.

During Basic Combat Training, we're deposited by a Squawker onto a circular training platform, about twenty-five feet in diameter, that hovers high above the steel dome of Infiernos. We've been placed under the tutelage of Styles and Renquist, the two burly Imps who roughed me up in my cell at the Citadel.

"Whatever you do," Styles grunts, indicating a yellow line running the circumference of the platform about a foot away from the edge, "don't attempt to cross the energy field."

I stare over the edge of the platform and immediately look away, overcome with vertigo.

Gideon lets loose a nervous chuckle. He traces the yellow line with the toe of his boot. "I wonder what happens if we do?" he whispers. Without hesitating he kicks a small pebble past the stripe.

POP!

The rock sparks and shatters into a dusty cloud.

He removes his glasses and wipes the lenses clean. "Guess falling over the edge is the least of our worries."

"Let's go, people!" Renquist barks.

Styles and Renquist instruct us in unarmed hand-to-hand combat techniques, flinging us around the exercise mats as if we were rag dolls. Then they pit us against each other in bout after bout, the winner of each round taking on the next Recruit.

Of course, Digory takes Gideon down easily. "Sorry," he mutters as he lifts Gideon to his feet as if he were a small child.

Cypress gives Digory a heated tussle, both of them swinging, spinning, and kicking until their breathing's ragged. But in the end, she pounds her fist on the ground in surrender once he manages to straddle her in a chokehold. "Good job," he says, offering to help her to her feet, but she just glares at him.

When it's my turn, Digory looks pained. "Don't worry," he whispers.

A flash of anger hits me. Does he really think I'm not capable of handling myself?

I charge at him, but he hooks his foot underneath mine and we both tumble to the ground, rolling across the platform. Before he can get a grip on me, I slither from his grasp, roll onto his back, and pin his arm behind him.

"Good job, Spark!" Cypress shouts.

Digory chuckles. "Not bad."

"Thanks."

Before I have a moment to bask in my victory, Digory wrenches free of my hold and rolls on top of me, pinning my hands above my head. I struggle underneath the weight of his body, but his grip's like iron. Then he's staring down at me, breathing hard, his glistening torso heaving from his efforts. He grins. "You're welcome."

I can't help but grin back. "Next time."

When I give the surrender signal, he takes my hand and pulls me to my feet. The smile's disappeared. "You okay? Did I hurt you?"

I sigh. "You *wish*."

Cypress shoots me a look of disgust.

Finally, it's Digory against the only remaining Recruit, Ophelia. He leans in to her just as their match is about to start. "Don't worry. I won't hurt you."

As soon as Renquist gives the signal, Ophelia hooks a foot around Digory's ankle, grabs his arm, and flips him over. He crashes to the ground, his head barely contained within the yellow perimeter line.

Digory twists his head and ogles the line, mere centimeters away. His eyes bulge. The sound of crackling and the stench of singed hair fills the air . . .

Ophelia's boot presses into Digory's chin, pushing him closer to the yellow barrier. Her eyes have that same vacant expression I saw in them before.

"Ophelia..." Digory groans through the pressure on his windpipe. "I give up." His hand slaps the platform's surface.

"Good job, Recruit Juniper," Styles grunts.

Ophelia lifts her boot from Digory's throat and steps back, her eyes glowing with satisfaction. "I did *good*?" Then she's giggling, a sound that pours down my back like ice cubes.

I rush past her and crouch beside Digory. "Are *you* hurt?"

He sits up, rubbing the red welt on his throat. "I'm fine." He musters a smile. "She just caught me off guard." His shakes his head. "Won't happen again."

As exhausting as the training is, I find that each day my endurance increases bit by bit, the soreness in my body easing off a tad as it becomes more solid and toned.

Maybe I'll make it to the Trials after all.

If anything, channeling all the physical energy has kept the nightmares at bay—at least for now.

After a particularly arduous day of training, as I'm just about to slip into sleep after lights out, the barracks door crashes open. Half a dozen hulking Imps clad all in black, wearing masks that cover everything but their eyes, swarm inside, carrying flashlights.

I bolt up in bed. "What's going—?"

"On your feet!" the lead figure shouts.

The next thing I know, the five of us are being dragged from our bunks by these brutes.

"You're hurting me!" Ophelia squeals.

I exchange anxious looks with Digory just before a hood is pulled over my face. With no eye slits, I can't see a thing. Panic surges through me like an electrical current. The coarse material feels like it's smothering me. I can't breathe.

"Wait! I need my glasses!" Gideon cries.

Then I'm being dragged and shoved outside, I think. "Is everyone okay?"

"Lucian!" Digory's voice, a few feet away.

"Keep your mouths shut!" my captor hisses into my ear. "Inside!" A large hand shoves me. I trip over my own feet and land on my knees.

"Strap them in," another voice calls to my right.

I'm yanked to my feet and shoved into a seat. A harness comes down over me and locks into place.

My heart's thumping out of control. What are they going to do us? What if they've decided we're not working out and they're going to kill us?

"Cole…" I whisper to the dark.

"Lucian?" Digory whispers back, right beside me.

His fingers grope for mine and his touch is just enough to keep me from going over the edge.

A metal door clangs shut. "Let's move!" one of the Imps shouts.

There's the grind and whir of engines and then a deep vibration as whatever vehicle we're in begins to move.

The next hour is agonizing. We're jostled to and fro for what seems like forever. Then at one point we stop and are transferred to some other vehicle. This time it feels like we're airborne.

"Hang tight!" an unknown voice calls through a loudspeaker. "We're in for some chop!"

The craft is buffeted by turbulence and I lean closer to Digory to steady myself.

I can hear muted sobs coming from close by. Ophelia? Gideon?

When it's finally over, the craft comes to a rocky stop and the engines cut out with a long whine. A loud clank like the opening of a door—a hatch?—then the harnesses click open and we're pulled from our seats and prodded down a slope, some kind of ramp I imagine.

The first thing I notice is a biting cold wind that sets my half-naked body shivering. The last time I felt like this was when—

My hands are uncuffed and the hood is ripped off my face.

Of course. We're standing on the deck of a ship, much larger than the freighter that brought us to Infiernos. An aircraft carrier, by the looks of it. Before us, Sergeant Slade stands alongside the goons who kidnapped us from the barracks. They've removed their masks and I recognize Styles and Renquist among them, grins plastered on their faces.

"Welcome to your first impromptu FTX, Field Training Exercise," Slade announces. "For the past several weeks, your training has concentrated on increasing your fitness and endurance, as well as learning basic survival and combat skills. Now the time has come to put your newly acquired proficiencies into play."

There's an audible shift in our stances. Our eyes dart to each other, and then back to Slade and the Imps.

Slade gestures to the dark horizon. "Out there is a communications station." She points to the rear of the platform we're standing on. "The life raft behind you contains a map with coordinates to the radio tower, along with a compass and emergency supplies. Your mission is simple. Arrive at the station in one piece." Her tongue traces her lips. "But I do suggest you spend as little time in the water as possible, what with the hypothermia factor, not to mention the aquatic predators that roam these seas."

Digory clears his throat. "Excuse me, Sergeant, Sir. Permission to speak?"

Slade's eyes slash him from head to toe. "Permission granted, Recruit."

"What if we aren't able to reach the radio tower?"

Malice edges out the contempt in her face. "Failure is not an option in *my* platoon, Recruit Tycho." She pulls out a sleek palm-sized device topped with buttons.

In that instant, my eyes have just enough time to connect her words with the hinges on the platform floor, which separate us from Slade and the Imps.

Slade's mouth twists into a sneer. "Good luck." Her finger jabs at the black box's top button.

The floor disappears, sending the five of us tumbling into the roaring abyss yawning below.

The icy water hits me like a thousand syringes plunging into my body.

Something tugs at me, pulling me upward. Then I'm breaking through a barrier. Sounds rip through my ears, muffled at first. I'm not sure where I am. Deep cold slices through the numbness of my skin.

A high-pitched siren unclogs my ears. It blares again, only this time I realize it's not a siren, but a scream.

I cough up a mouthful of salt water, just in time to swallow another one.

"Lucian! I gotcha!" Digory calls in my ear. He squeezes me tight.

"I'm okay." I spit ocean.

"Gideon! You got her?" he calls to my right.

I manage to turn my head enough to see Gideon treading water. He paddles toward us, Ophelia clinging to his side.

"She's good." Gideon responds through puffs of frosty breath. "But we need to get out of this wa-wa-wat-er fast before we fr—"

"I *know* that!" Digory shoots back. "Where do you suggest we go? The raft's gone…"

During their exchange, I've been looking past them at a rectangular shape drifting steadily away from our position. The raft. And in it, the silhouette of a girl, her long hair whipping about in the wind.

Cypress has stolen our only chance of survival.

The thought of what will happen to the rest of us jump-starts my heart. Sucking in a lungful of ice, I break free of Digory and dive into the water after her.

"Lucian! Wait!"

But Digory's voice is drowned out by the splashing of my flailing limbs and the sound of my heart battering my ears. Every breath is a battle. I can't feel my arms and legs as they carve into the water. My only focus is reaching that raft. I take in another gulp of frosty air and catch a glimpse of Cypress. I'm almost there.

My strokes are short and fast. Arms dig up the sea. Feet gyrate as rapidly as propellers. Ironically, it's Cassius I have to thank for becoming such a good swimmer. All those times when we were kids, racing each other in the swamps behind the electrical plant, swimming through all that muck, having to hold our breath to avoid the awful stink infesting our nostrils as we tried to push each other's heads beneath the surface. And now, years later, he's holding my head down again. Only this time, he's not playing, and he's not going to let me come up for air.

The flash of fury fuels my strokes, faster and faster, until at last I reach the raft. I grab on to the side of the boat, leaning against it as I struggle to fill my aching lungs with air. I'm panting like a Canid. Slower. Breathe slower. I have to stop gulping air or I'll hyperventilate. Everything's hazy, and for a moment I feel like I'm going to pass out and slide back into the ocean for good this time.

The panic jolts me into action. Digging my fingers into the rubber rim, I hoist myself up and over the raft's edge. My left hip slams onto the bottom before I roll onto my back.

I'm so numb, my body doesn't even ache after that marathon swim. If it weren't for the pain in my lungs, I might just be taking a little rest, sprawled out on this raft gazing up at the night sky.

The starfield is shattered by a wooden oar that appears out of nowhere. It gleams in the moonlight for a split-second, then it slices in a downward arc toward my head. My paralysis evaporates like a puff of frosty breath. I roll out of the way.

Thwack! The blade's edge grazes my left ear and *whomps* into the raft's floor.

Cypress raises the oar again. But this time I'm ready for her. The toe of my boot hammers into her shin.

"Ah!" She stumbles backward, trips over a backpack, and crashes against the equipment canisters strapped into the corner of the raft. Her hand loses its grip on the oar's handle. She lies there stunned. Her other hand rubs the back of her head.

Chills rattle my body. I force myself to sit up. "Are you *crazy?*"

She doesn't respond, just continues to squirm. A few moans escape her opened lips. Did she strike her head too hard? I didn't mean to hurt her. It all happened so fast, with that damn oar coming right at me.

My knees creak their protest. Pulling myself to my feet, I stagger over and squat beside her.

"Cypress," I barely manage. The wet clothes are taking their toll on me. "I didn't mean to hurt you. But why did you . . . ?" I reach out to touch her cheek, but I'm so numb I can't tell where my fingers end and she begins.

Her open palm clamps around the oar's handle. She springs up and knocks me aside, holding the oar's tip to my throat. Her eyes are colder than the black sea.

This time it's anger that energizes me. Every second Digory and the others stay in that freezing water is a stroke of the pen on their death certificates.

"I don't know what your problem is, but we have to go back and get the others *now*!"

She shakes her head. "It's nothing personal. There's something I need to do on my own."

"But they'll freeze to death if we don't get them out of the water!"

"I don't really care."

"You'd just let them die like that, without another thought?"

"They would do the same to me."

"Are you so sure? I wouldn't." I grip the oar's tip. "Go ahead then. Bash in my skull. Open up my throat." It's hard to differentiate now between the shivers of terror and cold.

The oar digs deeper into my neck. The blade is shaking. Wooden splinters pierce my skin. The muscles in her face twitch, but her eyes remain glacial. Still, she hesitates.

"It's a lot easier to paddle away and leave people in the dark than outright butcher them, isn't it, Cypress? The thing is, they're both pretty much murder, and I don't think you're capable of that."

"Not yet, anyway," she grunts. She pulls the oar away and bends over me.

I take in a deep breath, bracing myself. But she just offers her arm and pulls me to my feet.

"Thanks." I rub my neck.

Her eyes narrow. "For what?"

"I don't know. For not killing me, I guess." I grab a second oar and plunk down on one side of the raft. The tip of my paddle sinks into the sea.

"Don't press your luck." She mimics my actions on the craft's other side.

"Right. Let's move."

It's slow going for the first minute or so, but our rowing falls into synch. Soon we're speeding back to where I left the others behind. But the closer each stroke brings us, the more I fear that we're too late.

"Digory! Gideon! Ophelia!" I call out into the gloom. "Can you hear me?"

The only reply is the crash of waves breaking against the raft.

I paddle faster, my oar stabbing the water. A tide of panic rises over me.

Cypress matches me, row for row. "It's too late. They're gone."

"No, they're *not!*" I shout the words, as if the louder I make them the more they'll be true.

Dropping my oar, I stand up, cupping my hands around my frozen lips. "Can anyone hear me? Digory! Are you out there?"

My eyes scan the ocean. Nothing... only the hungry dark scarfing down everything in its path...

"Over here!" a voice calls. The two greatest words I've ever heard.

I drop and plunge my oar back into the water. "It came from *that* direction!" I point just off to our starboard side.

She's already rowing. "I see them."

As we draw nearer to the voice, I can't help wonder who it was that called out. Between the thrashing of our oars in the water and the stutters and weakness in that cry, it's impossible to be sure. It doesn't matter. The three of them are still alive. They *have* to be.

"Look!" Cypress shouts.

A clump of tangled limbs floats listless in the water. My heart sinks.

"Watch your oar!" I shout back to Cypress. I struggle to maneuver the raft around so I won't hit them with the oars. I throw my oar down and lean over the edge, gripping an icy arm.

Cypress is at my side in a flash, helping me haul the three of them up and over onto the raft. First Ophelia, shaking uncontrollably. Then Gideon, who looks like all the blood's been drained from him. And finally, it takes all of our strength to drag Digory aboard. Even in the pale moonlight, I can see the gray taint to his skin.

Cypress grabs my shoulder. "There may be thermal blankets in that supply container over—"

"Check it!"

Then she's gone, ripping through the gear stowed in the corner.

I lean in close to Digory, looking for signs of life. "Digory!" I slap his cheek lightly. But there's no response. I hold my hand in front of his nose. Not a hint of warmth from his nostrils.

Nothing.

This is *not* happening! I grab his shoulders, shake him. "Digory! Wake up! Listen to me, damn it! *Wake up!*"

"Wrap yourselves in these." Cypress throws a couple of thermal blankets at Ophelia and Gideon, and plops down next to me.

"I don't think he's breathing," I say.

"Cover him in this." Cypress pulls the thermal blanket close and I help her wrap it around his bare chest. There's a click and an orange glow, and the blanket begins to heat.

Cypress hands me another blanket. "You too."

Dazed, I offer no resistance as she cloaks me in the therm's comforting warmth. But even that's not enough to douse the icy fear creeping through me. I pull myself close to Digory and wrap myself around him. Maybe my added warmth will be enough to spark life back into his veins.

"Listen to me, Digory," I whisper in his ear. "You're going to be okay. I *promise.*" I press my head against his chest. Shivers rock me, despite the heat radiating from the blanket.

Gideon stands over us, wrapped in his own thermal blanket. He's colorless. "He tried going after you, but I started to drown while trying to help Juniper here, so he came back. He saved our lives." He looks away. "I'm sorry."

A flash of anger sears through me. "Don't eulogize him,

Warrick. He's *not* dead!" I turn to Digory, whose face now has a blue hue.

The resuscitation exercises we learned in first aid training. Damn it. What if I've wasted too much time already?

I squat beside Digory and Ophelia. "Tilt his head back!"

Her eyes go wide. "What?"

"Just do it!" As Ophelia tilts Digory's head back on her lap, I place both my hands on top of each other in the middle of his chest and start pushing, over and over again. Then I pinch his nose and blow two breaths into his lips before returning to pumping his chest.

"This is all *your* fault!" Gideon yells at Cypress. "You took the raft and left us to die. You killed him." He grabs her shoulder. "Maybe you ought to spend a few minutes in that freezing water and see how it feels?"

She glares at the fingers clutching her. "Unless you're planning on reliving the experience, I suggest you take your hand off me."

Ophelia shakes her head. "It isn't working!"

With each thrust of my hands, an image flashes into my mind. The first time I saw Digory at the Instructional Facility. Meeting him in that alley years later. His defiant look during the Recruitment.

I lean forward and pinch his nostrils closed again, press my lips to his, and blow in more air. I think about all those times he stole my breath away. Why doesn't he use it now?

His eyes remain closed. His body still.

Ophelia touches my hand. "I'm really sorry, Spark. He's gone."

I yank my hand away. "No!" My fists pound his chest. "Come back!" *Whomp!* "Open your eyes!" *Thwack!* "Don't"— slap—"Give"—slap—"Up!" *Smack!*

"Spark! *Let him go!*" Gideon grabs one of my fists in mid-swing.

Digory's eyes snap open. Icy water spews from his mouth. He leans forward, coughing and gasping for air.

"You did it, Spark!" Ophelia holds up the back of Digory's head, steadying him against her.

Relief floods me. Pushing Gideon aside, I squat beside Digory, pull the thermal blanket over him, and pat his back. "It's okay. You're okay now."

He continues to cough. But eventually it peters out, as does the trembling. Little by little, the pink returns to his skin. Finally, his breathing eases into a normal rhythm.

His eyes wander around the raft, taking us all in.

"I feel like a Squawker ran into me," he says at last. His voice sounds a little weak, but at least it's not laced with chill. "What happened?" He looks right at me. "The last thing I remember, you took off after..." His eyes narrow at Cypress. "*Her.*" He bolts upright. "Warrick! You were drowning—!"

"Take it easy, Tycho," Gideon says. "At least *you* came back." He glares at Cypress. "Quicker than some *other* people." He looks back at Digory. The hint of a smile appears on his face. "You helped us out." His head swings to Ophelia. "*Both* of us. We owe you one."

Ophelia nods.

"Don't worry about it, Warrick." Digory smiles. "So, what happened to me?"

"You just passed out," I say before anyone else can respond. My eyes sweep Ophelia, Gideon, and finally Cypress before relaxing on Digory. "But the therm's doing its job and you're better now. And we have a Radio Tower to find."

Cypress just stares at me with a crooked smile painted on her face. Her eyes shift between Digory and me. "So much selflessness tonight is gonna make for a much more interesting competition during the actual Trials."

Gideon pulls out the map and rattles off the coordinates while I grab the compass, Ophelia and Cypress take the oars, and Digory trains the binoculars toward our destination.

Behind us, the carrier is just a few specks of flickering light on the horizon. We're all alone now, adrift in the engulfing blackness.

I study the faces around me. Digory. Gideon. Ophelia. Cypress.

No. Not alone.

We have each other.

"I see it!" Digory points into the distance.

Before us, a tiny island looms, with a triangular tower at its center.

We can barely contain our whoops and hollers. We did it. *Together.*

As we approach the shoreline, the island flickers. At first I think it's lightning from an approaching storm. Then the radio tower shimmers—and vanishes, along with the island, sky, and stars.

Harsh lights come on. When my eyes adjust, I see that

we're actually indoors, in a vast domed tank, surrounded by huge empty walls.

Screens.

Congratulations, Recruits, Slade's voice booms from the loudspeakers. **You have successfully navigated through your first training Simulation without any casualties. This concludes Phase One of your training. Only two more phases to go. But I warn you. No more coddling. Now get your butts to bed. We start bright and early tomorrow.**

The elation on our faces evaporates like the virtual horizon.

FIFTEEN

"We've got three minutes before this thing blows sky high!"

Cypress's warning ricochets through the circle of fifty-gallon steel drums marked *Toxic Waste*, which surround us on all sides.

"I *know* how to tell time," Gideon hisses at her.

Cypress scowls. "Based on your performance the last few weeks, I've learned not to assume anything where you're concerned."

I shove past Ophelia to get between them. "C'mon, knock it off, people."

Gideon reaches an arm across the nearest cylinder, his glasses reflecting the blinking red light of the timer that's keeping pace with the rhythm of my heart. "I think I got it."

"Careful," Ophelia whispers. She hands him a pair of wire cutters as if they were a delicate piece of glass.

"No sudden movements," Digory says, right behind me.

The sound of his voice ignites something inside me. He's barely spoken to me these past two weeks—ever since I revived him during that Sim.

I turn to him. Flashes of crimson dance in his eyes, thawing the ice into fluid blue. As our eyes meet we spark for a second, but then he looks away and the moment dies like a fading ember.

As Gideon struggles to access the control panel, no one makes a sound.

Finally, he turns and shakes his head, not looking any of us in the eye. "No use. I can't reach it."

A sigh escapes Cypress's lips. "Surprise."

Gideon thrusts the wire cutters at her. "I'm sure these'll work on vocal chords."

She smirks. "It'd be fun to see you try, anyway."

I grip the drum myself. "There's a lot riding on this. This bomb's not going to diffuse itself." I try to twist it around as carefully as I can, but it must weigh a ton.

Without saying a word, Digory pulls me aside and grips the metal cylinder himself, lifting it a couple of inches off the ground. Thick cords bulge from the sides of his neck. His biceps threaten to burst through the sleeves of his damp T-shirt, which clings to his body like a second skin.

"You're going to set it off, Tycho," Cypress growls through clenched teeth.

Ignoring her, he pulls the drum out and away from the other ones, turning it enough to expose a silver box attached to its side.

He's been exerting himself way too much since we started

Phase Two, especially given what almost happened to him on that raft, but I've learned it's pointless to try and talk him out of anything.

"Easy..." Gideon mutters under his breath.

Digory sets the drum back down with a low thump, which still manages to stir up a gritty shroud of dust that prickles my skin.

"Two minutes..." Ophelia's hands are clasped in front of her mouth and she's bouncing on her boot heels.

"I know. I *know*." Gideon's already on his knees with the screwdriver, fiddling with the control panel. In seconds, he's unscrewed it from its moorings and detached it from the drum. He stands, cradling the bomb's canister like a baby.

We all back away, giving him plenty of room to maneuver.

One of his feet tangles in some cables and he lurches—

Our collective gasp drowns out the steady bleeping of the countdown clock as Gideon teeters for a few agonizing seconds—

Before Cypress reaches out to steady him.

"*Don't drop it,*" she whispers.

His only response is the wisp of his breath, which fogs up the clear display of the bomb's throbbing innards as he pries the panel open with the screwdriver, exposing several black cubes connected by red, blue, and yellow wires.

"That's it, Warrick. You got this." I'm already warming to the idea that we may just make it through this latest ordeal of Slade's.

Digory and I crowd together, avoiding each other's faces.

The frigid air pumping through the overhead vents pecks at my flesh and gives me the shakes. There's an awkward second when our shoulders graze. I steal a quick, shallow breath. Part of me wants to stare him down, ask him how he's feeling, both physically and otherwise. But I trash the impulse and bury it deep. I can't let him know how I really feel.

Especially since I don't know myself.

Gideon's eyes are bouncing from one wire to another, the wire cutters trembling in his hand.

"You're wasting too much time. Let *me* do it." Cypress reaches out for the explosive canister.

"Let him alone, Goslin." Digory blocks her. "He knows what he's doing."

Ophelia tugs my arm. "Only thirty seconds to go!"

Cypress looks like she wants to strangle her. "*Thanks for the update.*"

My heart's a drum roll. "Gently … Warrick … yeah … nice and slow … "

Gideon hesitates, closes his eyes for a moment, then snips the blue wire.

Nothing happens.

Peals of nervous laughter fill the air. We're still in this.

"Ten seconds!" Ophelia squeals.

With only two options remaining, Gideon grins and shifts the wire cutter over to the red wire—

That *can't* be right. He's supposed to cut the reactor wire *before* he cuts the ignition feed. I spring forward and wrench the tool from his hand.

"Spark!" he yells. "What the hell are you—?"

Snip!

I cut through the yellow wire instead—

An alarm blares through the room, cleaving my eardrums. The overhead florescent lights blink out, replaced by the swirling reds and yellows of twirling emergency beacons engulfing the chamber like wildfire.

The intercom crackles to life with a burst of static: **"Detonation Activated. Mission Failure. Repeat. Mission Failure."**

But I don't need any warning announcement to tell me how badly I screwed up. The glares in everyone's eyes are much more potent. The wire cutters slip from my fingers and clatter to the floor, disappearing along with the steel drums when the ground beneath opens up and swallows them whole before resealing.

Wish that were me.

Gideon shakes his head at me. "What's *wrong* with you? I had everything under control. All I had to do was clip that red wire..."

A wide grin stretches across the canvas of Ophelia's face. "So what if Spark messed up. We all know *you* knew what you were doing." She moves toward Gideon with open arms, but he backs away.

"I'm real sorry." I grab his shoulder from behind.

He whirls on me, fist raised.

Digory squeezes between us, palms thrust outward. "Whoa! Easy, Warrick."

Gideon's eyes are feral, the look of a cornered animal ready to fight to the death.

No one says a word, not even Cypress. We just stare, listening to this stranger's panting breaths, wondering if he'll strike.

He finally blinks. In that instant, he's Gideon again. He lowers his fist, looking confused as to why it was in the air to begin with. His index finger nudges his glasses back up his nose.

"Forgive me." His face is redder than the light's glare. "I guess you just spooked me."

Cypress snorts. "*We* spooked *you*?"

Digory lowers his own hands. "It's all right. We've all been on edge. And with good reason."

I step from behind him. "Digory's right. You did a great job, Warrick. Sorry I screwed things up."

He stuffs his hands into his pockets. His eyes drop to his fidgeting feet. "Thanks. Any of you could have done it."

"Agreed." Cypress sighs.

Ophelia glares at her. "But none of *us* did." Her face softens and she takes a tentative step closer to Gideon. "I think you're the best!" She lifts her hands so he can see them, and slowly wraps them around him.

Gideon awkwardly pats her back. He doesn't seem to know where to look and chooses the exact moment to look down at her that she looks up at him.

Their lips meet and she gives him a quick peck.

Cypress looks away, suddenly more interested in her boots than making some snide remark.

Digory erupts into whooping and laughter, relieving

the tension. "Ladies and Gentlemen, I believe we have another explosion."

Ophelia giggles.

I get the sense that somehow this is a real special moment for Gideon, and when I think about all the teasing he endured during our years at the Instructional Facility, I'm glad for him.

His glasses fog up. He removes them and lifts the end of his shirt to wipe the lenses. With his shirt riding up his back, I catch another glimpse of that ugly scar.

He must feel the weight of my eyes crushing him. He grabs a fistful of shirttail and tugs it down. Our eyes connect for a second, and I glimpse naked fear before he shoves his glasses back down like a barrier to his soul.

What could have hurt him like that?

I'm not sure how long I'm standing there squirming, avoiding everyone's faces, when the sirens finally fade and the lights return to normal.

The last thing I'm expecting to hear is the sound of clapping from across the room.

Slade's staring at us, hands now crossed behind her back.

"Congratulations." Her face is a mask of disgust. "You are now all officially *dead*, thanks to the recklessness of Recruit Spark. "It appears *someone* hasn't been paying attention to his instructors." Despite Slade's usual condescending manner, there's something different about her today. She looks...tired. Her usually pristine uniform is kind of wrinkled, as if she slept in it. Something other than my screw-up is pissing her off.

I stand at attention and salute her. "I'm sorry, Sir. But I thought—"

"*That* was your first mistake, Recruit, and, given the failure of your mission, your *last*." Slade's eyes reflect the light like molten steel. "If this had been an actual Op instead of a training Sim you could have been responsible for not only the loss of countless personnel, but inflicted devastating consequences on the foundation of the Establishment itself. As such, there must be consequences."

"Agreed, Sir." I step forward. "The failure was all my fault and any punishment should be mine alone."

This time she grins. "How noble of you, Spark. Unfortunately, you undertook this mission as a *team*. The failure of one is the failure of all. As of this moment, all leisure time before lights out has been cancelled for the duration of Phase Two."

I cringe at the audible groan from the others behind me.

"Instead," Slade continues, "you are all assigned to Fire Guard and Charge of Quarters duties when you aren't involved in training exercises, including nightly patrol shifts, cleaning the barracks from top to bottom for my inspection—including the latrines as well as the lockers—and running personal errands for me on a twenty-four-hour on-call basis. What this pathetic platoon lacks in resourcefulness it will make up in diligence, until you are the most efficient squad in all of Infiernos." She pauses. "Oh, and how could I forget the extra hour of morning calisthenics?"

Even I join in the moans this time.

Slade's glee turns into a scowl. "Now get out of my sight."

As we scramble out of her way, I'm shocked when I catch a glimpse of the last expression I'd expect to see on her face.

Fear.

SIXTEEN

True to her word, Slade makes the last week of Phase Two even more of a nightmare by introducing visits to the Tank. During our instructions on Bio Warfare, we're issued protective gas masks and forced into a sealed chamber while Slade pumps it full of experimental toxins. It's terrifying enough to be trapped in a coffin-like room, with nothing but the sound of hissing death for company, but we're forced to take off our masks a few seconds before we're allowed to leave the Tank, just so we can briefly experience the effects of the toxins firsthand as Slade forces us to recite our name, rank, and ID number to test how well we can focus under the drugs' effect. Once we all figure out that wrong answers earn you another go around, we *really* try to focus. The last thing any of us wants is to experience more of those brain-splitting migraines and violent shakes.

In addition to our already crowded daily training and

instruction, we're also forced to tackle the Teamwork Tower protocol, a series of obstacle courses located on rotating platforms hovering hundreds of feet above the ground. We're forced to depend on one another at these dizzying heights to navigate simulated landscapes of rocky terrain, snow-capped peaks, and desert regions, climbing rope ladders and bridges before rappelling down hundred-foot walls.

Our next FTX, however, takes place on the ground. It's an overnighter in the Southwest Quadrant of Infiernos, away from the coast, deep in the interior of the island. In this vast, isolated area of dense undergrowth, we will fend for ourselves, building shelters and hunting for our own food.

After going the whole day of the FTX without eating, Digory, Cypress, Gideon, and I leave Ophelia behind at the camp to finish setting up the shelters while we spend the evening racing through thick brushwood in search of food. Clutching makeshift spears we whittled from branches, the four of us pursue a floppy-eared lepus. But as sunset approaches we have nothing to show for our efforts, except for the bloody signatures of thorns and branches inscribed on the exposed skin of our sweat-drenched bodies.

I collapse to the ground with the others, too hungry and tired to swat at a mosquito feasting on the back of my hand. Then a smiling Ophelia steps into the clearing—carrying the lepus in her arms!

"There, there," she coos, stroking the creature's head. The animal squirms, but she holds it by its hind legs and head. "You are just *too* cute!" She nuzzles its nose with hers.

"I finished with the shelters early, so I figured I'd join the fun."

Before any of us can say anything, her smile disappears and her eyes turn to glass. She locks her grip around the animal's ears and tugs, snapping its head backward.

CRACK! The sound of splintered bone ricochets through the clearing.

The lepus thrashes in her grasp for a few seconds and then hangs limp.

Ophelia turns to us, beaming. "I'm *so* starved. Let's eat!" She giggles.

After watching her expertly decapitate the animal, slice into its back legs, rip the skin off, plunge the blade deep into its lower abdomen, and carve up to the rib cage and pelvis with the precision of a surgeon, I'm suddenly not too hungry anymore.

Instead, I help Cypress gather a mixed bundle of grass, twigs, and bark. Digory and Gideon ignite it by using a sharp rock as a flint, until the kindle becomes a roaring blaze that we can cook the meat over.

We splay out around the campfire, and I'm just about to grab a piece of meat when a movement in the thicket catches my eye.

I freeze.

Someone's standing no more than a couple of yards away, peering out from behind a large, dead tree. A dark silhouette but for twin pools of firelight swirling in the eyes.

My heart jams up my throat.

"What's the matter?" Digory asks.

I jab a finger toward the tree. "There's someone over there!"

I spring to my feet and make a run for it, but Digory races after me and grabs my arm. "Careful! Look at the pylons. We're at the sonic fence perimeter, remember?"

He's right.

The tree's barren limbs continue to sway, casting shadows on the massive columns like skeletal fingers, curling and beckoning.

The figure's gone.

"There *was* someone there..." I whisper.

Digory's hand squeezes my shoulder. "It's okay. We're all very tired and stressed—"

I grab his hand and tear it away. "*Don't...patronize...me!*"

"Lucian—"

But I whirl before he can finish and tromp back to the campfire, kicking up flurries of earth in my wake before dropping cross-legged near Cypress. I can't even tell the difference between the heat generated from the roaring blaze and that which boils my blood.

He feels *sorry* for me...

Gideon leans forward. "I'm sure you did see something, Spark. This place is crawling with Imps watching our every move, keeping tallies on our progress, making sure we don't try and desert."

"I'm sure that's exactly all it was," Ophelia squeaks, linking an arm around Gideon's and squeezing.

Cypress clears her throat. "I think Spark saw something else."

Of all the things I thought she'd say, that wasn't one of them. "You do?"

Green fire dances in her eyes. "I think it was one of the Lost Recruits."

"Excuse me?" Ophelia interrupts. "Did one of the Recruits get lost?" Her index finger bobs at each one of us in turn. "Hmmm. I counted five. I think we're all accounted—"

"She's referring to the Fallen Five," Digory announces. He plunks down on the opposite side of the circle from me.

"But they're just a myth, right?" I cast my eyes around the campfire. "I mean, they're not *real* . . . are they?"

Cypress bites her lip. "Oh, they're real."

I remember hearing the story of the Fallen Five from Cassius when I wasn't much older than Cole. He used to say that they'd come for us in the middle of the night and whisk us away from our beds if we weren't careful. The thing is, on many of those endless nights, while my folks slaved away in the mines, I cowered in my cot, hungry and cold, and prayed that they would.

Is Cole thinking the same thing now?

Ophelia's eyes twinkle. "Looks like I'm the only one who's never heard of these Falling Five."

"*Fallen*," Gideon corrects her. "The *Fallen* Five."

She giggles. "Sorry. So where exactly did they fall from?"

Digory tosses a twig in the flames. "The Fallen Five

were a quintet of Recruits drafted on Recruitment Day, just like we were. Ten years ago."

Ophelia bounces on the sand. "So by *fallen* you mean that they all *fell*, as in *failed,* during the Trials, and no one was promoted that year, is that right?"

"Partially," Digory responds. "No one was promoted that year because no one ever made it *to* the Trials."

Ophelia frowns. "I don't understand. What happened to them?"

"They vanished," I say. "All five of them. Without a trace. Shortly after arriving at Infiernos."

She glances at the tree, then hugs her knees. "M-maybe they had an accident and were lost—"

"They were on an FTX just like we are now," Digory continues. "Their packs and supplies were found. Everything was intact... except for them."

She shakes her head. "It's just a story meant to frighten children! That's all!"

"It seems to be working," Cypress mutters.

Gideon folds his arms. "You know, I just thought about something that hasn't crossed my mind in years. When I was six, my folks and I lived next door to a family whose daughter was recruited. Tasha Gillespie, her name was. I was pretty young at the time, but I remember being scared when she just disappeared and never came home. I thought she'd done something terrible and her parents had sent her away. I couldn't sleep for weeks, afraid the same thing was going to happen to me. That was *ten years* ago. Maybe she was one of the Fallen Five..."

"I think the Establishment murdered them," Digory says. His words are a needle that weaves an icy thread around the ring. "They probably found out one of the Establishment's many secrets and were silenced before they could expose it, like everyone always is."

I lean in. "Sssh! Careful, Digory,"

Cypress yawns. "I think you're all giving the Fallen Five too much credit." Her gaze pierces Ophelia. "They weren't lost in some pathetic Field Training Exercise." Next she fixes on Gideon with a glaze of contempt. "Nor was it some terrible punishment by their parents." Finally, she turns to skewer Digory with her eyes. "And they weren't *martyrs*, sacrificing their lives to the Establishment for the good of our society."

"Then what happened to them?" I challenge her.

She turns to me and I brace for what's coming. But instead of dripping with mockery, her eyes are pools of emerald bitterness. "They were deserters, cowards, nothing more."

Her words stun me. I can't conceive of the implications of what she's saying. Any notions of fleeing I've ever had are quashed when I think about Cole and how he's depending on me to come through.

"Cypress, deserters aren't just risking their *own* lives," I say. "Their Incentives . . . anyone they leave behind . . . they're all subject to punishment. That's why we're all here. How could anyone do what you're suggesting?"

Her eyes drop to her lap. "How could *he*?" she whispers. A shaky hand swipes across her face. Then she bolts to her feet and marches into one of the shelters, throwing the flaps open and disappearing inside.

For a few minutes, nobody says anything. We just stare at each other across the crackling flames, watching the shadows dance across the orange glow on our faces.

Who is she talking about?

"Do you really think the Fallen Five were murdered?" I finally ask Digory. "Cypress seems certain they're alive. But if they *are* alive and hiding out, why haven't any of the Recruits over the last nine years caught a glimpse of them?"

"Yes, I do believe the Establishment killed them," Digory answers. "But if by some miracle Cypress is right, there's a very good reason none of the other Recruits has ever seen them."

Adrenaline revs my heart.

"What is it?" Gideon asks.

Digory tosses more twigs into the fire. "After they disappeared, the Establishment moved the Trials to another base—whether this was done to cover up evidence or prevent it from happening again, that's open to debate."

"But the location of the Trials has always been kept secret! How would you know—?" I stop myself. His connections within the rebellion … "I understand."

He nods. "If Cypress *is* right, we may get our chance to solve the mystery of the Fallen Five."

Ophelia rubs her arms. "Why's that?"

He looks around. "This year"—he lowers his voice—"the Establishment decided to return the Trials to the original venue."

My eyes open wide. "You mean—?"

"We're the first to return. That's why they installed those

pylons around Infiernos. Whatever happened to the Fallen Five, it happened right outside that sonic fence."

I glance back at the narrow path creeping into the jungle. It's framed by a canopy of interlocking branches that resemble gnarled fingers clasped together in dark prayer. A wisp of mist curls forth like a dying breath. I hug myself, trying to rub some feeling back into my marble skin.

SEVENTEEN

It's the last night before we're set to begin Phase Three, the final stage of our training before the Trials begin. I'm on adrenaline overload and can't sleep.

A groggy Gideon trudges into the barracks in the middle of the night and taps me on the shoulder. "You're up," he grunts before collapsing onto his cot. For the first time, I'm grateful to be on CQ duty.

In no time at all, I've slipped into my uniform and out the door, briskly walking the perimeter of the barracks, trying to burn up the anxiety churning through me. I plow through my rounds in record time. Along the way I encounter pockets of soldiers making supply runs, performing maintenance checks on vehicles, packing up equipment. In each instance, they look haggard, as if they've been pulling double shifts. A couple of times they drop their voices to a whisper as I walk by, as if I cared what secrets they harbor.

When I'm done, I'm still jumpy with nervous energy and decide to jog up the three-hundred-plus steps to the top of the circular Observation Tower.

Even though I'm breathing heavily by the time I arrive at the top, I can't help but think how much more stamina I've built up during my training. Six weeks ago I'd have probably passed out after about a hundred steps.

Six weeks. Seems like a lifetime.

From up here, I have a moonlit view of all of Infiernos. About fifty yards ahead of me, at the base's front perimeter, the sea crashes against the shoreline. Further down the beach, I can just make out the cove hiding the bay where the freighter docked on our arrival. Behind me and on either side, the complex stretches several miles inland—the giant dome, the other barracks, the training fields, the landing strips, the officers' quarters—all surrounded by the massive pillars of the sonic fences, which occasionally spark when some unfortunate animal veers too close.

I strain my eyes, trying to make out what lies beyond the base, but even in the moonlight I can't see anything through the darkness and haze. For a moment I wonder if we're actually on an island at all...maybe we're on a peninsula, and, if so, what is it connected to?

I turn my head back toward the ocean and lean over the railing, gulping a lungful of salty air from the rippling black sea, allowing it to wash away the mustiness of the barracks. I haven't felt this invigorated in months—ever since Cassius's betrayal.

Above, millions of stars blanket the night sky. Back

home at the Parish, I don't remember ever seeing so many of them, what with the smog from the Industrial Borough clogging up our skies. It's beautiful and mysterious all at once. If I tilt my head at just the right angle, to block out my surroundings, it's as though I'm floating in space, which seems about right.

I've never felt so far away from everything I've ever known.

Movement behind me.

Despite the roaring of the wind, I can hear my heartbeat. My grip tightens on the railing. Maybe I won't live to compete in the trials after all. Maybe Cassius is planning to assassinate me before I get the chance to have my revenge.

I whip around.

Digory's lips are curved in a dazzling smile, reflecting the moon's gleam that surrounds him in a halo. His hair shimmers like liquid gold.

My muscles relax.

He holds his palms up, his eyes mirroring my surprise. "I didn't mean to sneak up on you. I called out your name, but I guess you didn't hear me."

I smile back. "Why aren't you in bed?"

He stuffs his hands in his pockets. "Couldn't sleep. Just like you."

I nod. "It seems everyone's been tense lately. And not only about the Trials. Have you noticed all the anxious looks, and the whispering? I'm not just talking Slade and the other officers—the enlisted are looking pretty wired, especially those recon units."

"I've noticed. And we're not the only ones—Cypress mentioned it too, and so did Gideon. Something's definitely up."

The black jumpsuit I'm wearing is made of thin material, hardly protection against the chilly night biting into my flesh and making my teeth chatter.

"Here, take this." Digory removes the jacket he's wearing and wraps it around me.

I try to give it back to him, but his hands hold it firmly on my shoulders. "What about *you*?" I ask.

His grin captures the starlight. "I'll be all right. I'm pretty cold-blooded."

He means it as a joke, but I can't help but wonder what he's capable of when the time comes to defend his people during the trials.

What *I'm* capable of.

Silent minutes flutter away into the night. This is the first time we've really been alone since arriving at Infiernos. I brace myself for some well-meaning questions or comments about stuff I really don't want to talk about.

Instead, Digory tugs up the jacket's collar around my neck and nudges his face toward the sky. "I can't believe how many stars there are up there."

I inhale cool saltiness. "I've never been away from all that cloud cover in the Parish. This is the first time I've ever gotten a really good look at the constellations." I lean forward on the railing and point toward a particular cluster. "See there, I think that's the one the ancients called Taurus."

His shoulder grazes my own, his eyes following my

finger as I trace an invisible pattern in the night. "*Tau-rus?* What's that mean?"

"The legend goes that Taurus was a god disguised as some kind of animal—not sure what it's called—a *bull*, I think. You see that outline that looks like a beast?"

He nods.

"Anyway, this Taurus fell in love with a beautiful princess while she was playing on the seashore and literally swept her off her feet, carrying her away and making her his lover."

Digory turns and his eyes penetrate mine. "Leaving their symbol for all to see until the end of time. I like that." He smiles again. "I don't think I ever heard anything like that at the Instructional Facility. It's one of those banned fairy tales the Establishment's always going on about, isn't it?"

I shrug, expecting him to bring up Cole's story of the Lady, the story that Cassius used to damn us. He doesn't. I exhale, plunging ahead before thoughts of Cole's plight shut me down. "Apprenticing at the library and sneaking into the restricted section does have *some* advantages. The funny thing is, no matter how hard the Establishment tries to hide literature it doesn't approve of from the world, the sky's full of stories for all to see."

Digory steps onto the lower railing, hikes a leg over the upper railing, and raises himself into a sitting position. "Like what else?" He holds out a hand to me. "Show me another story, Lucian."

It's as if one of those gods of the constellations is beckoning me, ready to sweep me away from the earth to live out the rest of my existence in the heavens.

I take his hand and allow him to haul me up beside him. "Let's see." My eyes scan the sky. "Ah, yep. *That's* Orion."

"Who's Orion?" Digory's face is lit up like Cole's when I tell him about the Lady.

"Orion was a hunter." I connect a group of stars with my finger. "You see how you can make out his bow and arrow?"

Digory laughs. "Yeah, I can see it. That's incredible."

"According to the restricted books," I continue, "Orion hunted with two faithful beasts ... now let's see if I can ... oh yeah ... *there's* one." I trace another pattern in the sky.

Digory's eyes squint. "I'm not sure I can make that out."

"Of course you can. Here." I take hold of his hand in mine and make the outline again.

"Oh, yeah. Now I see it, Lucian." His smile fades. "Wait a minute. That looks like a Canid."

"Very good, Mr. Tycho. You're looking at Canis Major. And that"—our hands map out another cluster—"is Canis Minor." I wink at him now. "Or the smaller Canid, as you'd call it. These two aren't as visible this time of year as their master."

"Hmm." His brows knit in mock annoyance. "I'm not sure I like this guy Orion so much if he hangs out with Canids. Are you sure his name's not really *the Imposer*?"

I actually laugh out loud this time. "It's not like that at all. The hunter was actually in love with one of seven sisters known as the Pleiades." Once again I guide his warm hand in mine, indicating six bright lights.

"That's only six," he says, his breath hot in my ear. "What happened to the seventh?"

I purse my lips. "Alas, she didn't return his love and went far away, never to be seen again."

He shakes his head. "Poor guy."

"That's not the worst of it, though."

He scoots closer. "What could be worse than having the person you love not want to have anything to do with you?"

My pulse gallops. "The poor, heartbroken Orion, wandering around in search of his lost love, stepped on Scorpius" —I guide Digory's hand toward another distinct pattern— "and died."

Digory flinches. "Ouch! Not the ending I was hoping for." He chuckles. "I think I like the Taurus story better."

The salt air stings my eyes. "Not every story has a happy ending, but that doesn't mean it's not worth telling." I turn away. Concentrating on the brightest star I can find, I hope he won't notice I'm doing everything possible not to give in to the ache I feel for my brother.

"I wonder what it would be like, Lucian, to love someone so totally, so ... you know, so *powerfully*, that even the stars can't contain themselves from proclaiming that love for everyone to see," he says softly. "It must be the grandest feeling in the world."

I shrug. "They're only fairy tales. You said so yourself, Digory. "

His eyes return to the sky. "They don't have to be." He squeezes my hand.

Neither of us says anything for the next few minutes.

We just stare out to sea, listening to the waves crash in the distance, harmonized by the mourning wail of the wind.

"So tell me," Digory says at last. "What story are you looking at now?"

I'm losing the fight against my emotions. "I'm not looking at a story. I'm just thinking how far away these stars really are. By the time their light reaches us, the stars could have been dead thousands of years."

He brings my hand to his knee and holds it there. "Don't worry. Cole's all right, Lucian. I *know* he is. You have to keep believing that."

My eyes burn. "But he's a prisoner in that awful place—what did Cypress call it? Purgatorium." I swipe at my eyes but the wind has already dried them. "He may as well be one of those stars."

"But he's not alone, Lucian. Look. Look up there." Now it's his turn to guide my hand in the sky. "You see that bright star up there?"

"Mmm-hmm."

"Let's just say that's Cole for a minute. Well, look around, Lucky. He's *not* alone. There are millions of other bright lights out there, and one of them is you." He moves my hand to another star twinkling in a different area of the sky. "And as you just showed me, they're all connected." He begins moving my hand from star to star. "Sooner or later you'll find the path that connects you to each other again." He traces the final point until it interconnects with the bright star representing Cole. "I promise you." He adds his other hand and completely envelops mine in his.

My sadness boils over into liquid heat stinging its way down my cheeks. I wrench my hand away. "How can you promise me something like that? You know what we're up against, what's about to happen. It's an impossible situation, barring some unlikely miracle. The only way Cole and I can both survive this is if I can somehow make it through to the final round and win the Trials. In order for *that* to happen, everyone else's loved ones will have to die in the Culling. Do you get that, Digory? Including the people *you* love, who, by the way, you've never told me a thing about. So unless you and the others are prepared to sacrifice your own just so I can see my little brother again, I'd refrain from making promises that will be impossible to keep."

"I know how hopeless it seems, Lucian. Trust me. And I'm sure the other Recruits do too. But the moment you stop believing that it's *possible* ... well ... that's the moment that it's not."

Waves of confusion rock me. It's hard enough living and training with Digory. But being *alone* with him—it stirs up too many conflicting emotions.

All that time at the Instructional Facility, he hardly ever spoke to me—barely even *looked* at me. What if all this new-found concern during our training is part of his strategy, making me ... *like* him, rely on him ... just so he can crush me when I least expect it, the way Cassius did?

There's too much at stake.

Swinging my legs back over the railing, I spring back down to the platform. "Sorry. I know you're only trying to make me feel better. But I think it's best if we each go it alone from this point on."

"You do, huh?"

If he's only been turning up the charm to lull me into a false sense of security, he's got the aching expression down pat.

I take off the jacket and hold it out to him. "Here. Take it."

He dismisses me with a wave of the hand. "Keep it. You need it more than I do."

I'm tempted to look away from the blossoming hurt on his face, tell him I don't mean a word of what I'm saying, but it has to be done, for his sake as well as my own.

"Good luck during the Trials, Lucian. I guess we're going to find out what we're both truly made of." His voice is quiet, barely above a whisper. But the air of finality about it catches me off guard like an unexpected crash of thunder.

He bolts from the Observation Tower without another word.

Leaving me to wonder if I've just made one of the biggest mistakes of my life.

By the time I make it back down to the ground, exhaustion is finally starting to catch up to me. But before I can round the corner leading to the barracks, I spot a figure darting through the shadows from one equipment bunker to the next. A fresh wave of energy takes hold of me. Recalling all my recent stealth training, I slink into pursuit, partially from curiosity and a sense of duty...

Mostly to avoid having to face Digory back at our barracks.

When the figure ducks behind a supply crate, I catch a glimpse of pale skin and raven hair in the moonlight.

Cypress.

What the hell is she doing skulking around?

But she's already on the move again and I continue my tail, shadowing her as we dodge one ground patrol after another until she stops behind an electrical shed that overlooks two of the perimeter pylons.

She turns in my direction, but I duck behind the bunker that's diagonal to her, before she can see me. Then I crawl to the edge and peer around the corner.

Styles and Renquist are talking to the pilot of a troop carrier—an oblong transport vehicle, with an open-air bed, that looks like a floating coffin without the lid. The craft is hovering a few feet off the ground, just on the other side of the invisible sonic barrier.

"—After all your recon, you'd think you guys would've turned up something already." Renquist's voice carries in the wind.

"Maybe they don't show up on infrared at all," the pilot's voice crackles. "Look, just open the shield and let us back inside."

Styles belts out a raucous chuckle. "Don't get your skivvies in a wad, Corporal." He holds his walkie to his mouth. "This is Sector Seven. Deactivate field for squad re-entry."

Cypress crawls to the edge of the shed. By the looks of her posture, she's ready to spring.

She's going to make a break for it.

The hum between the two pylons winds down and the lights dim.

Renquist motions the vehicle forward. "You're clear!"

The carrier soars through the gap, just as I dash to the shed and tackle Cypress before she can bolt. We tumble to the ground and roll back behind the shed, my hand clamped over her mouth. She jams her elbow into my gut and I see a different variety of stars as she squirms free.

"Don't do it," I whisper.

But my warning's moot. The hum of the sonic pulse vibrates through the air once again and the field flickers, having been re-energized.

"Let's pack it in, people!" Styles shouts as both he and Renquist are hoisted into the cab by the other soldiers and the carrier speeds off into the distance, leaving Cypress and me alone in the dark.

She kicks gravel into my face. "You idiot! I've been monitoring the recon patrol schedules for weeks. This was my *one* chance to get outside the fence before the next rotation, and you screwed it up!"

Her boot hauls back to kick me, but I grab hold of her foot before it makes contact and twist. She yelps as her body slams into the ground.

"I've had a really long day and I'm not in the mood." I grab her hand and yank her to her feet. "*Talk* to me. What's so important that you'd risk your Incentives' lives by going

AWOL? You know what they'd do to your family if you deserted, don't you?"

"They'd probably be better off getting it over with quickly than where they are now." She turns away. "You wouldn't understand."

I clear my throat. "Maybe I understand better than you think."

She flashes me a look laced with anger and panic. "What are you getting at?"

"Back on the raft, during the first training Sim. The way you were so desperate to strike out on your own—away from everyone else. None of the others saw the look on your face— the desperation. You said there was something you *had* to do."

She turns away again, and my words keep coming in a rush.

"And your knowledge of the Fallen Five, and how sure you were that I saw something in those woods in the Southwest Quadrant. Just now, you were willing to risk everything to venture out beyond the perimeter, with no map to guide you. You also seem very familiar with the living conditions of the Incentives—it's almost like you've been here before. And since this is a military installation, and you're too young to have ever served, there's only one other reason I can think of for you to have ever been here."

I brace myself for a hostile outburst, but none comes. Instead, her eyes grow moist.

I swallow hard. "You were one of the Fallen Five's Incentives, weren't you?"

This time she doesn't bother to wipe the wetness that

spills from her eyes and traces its way down her cheeks. "Yes. I know what it's like, Spark. Being dragged away from your family and locked in that hellhole Purgatorium. Wondering if someone loves you enough … enough to … *choose* … "

"But you survived. That means there's hope."

Her eyes fill with venom. She leans in close until we're practically nose to nose and jabs her finger in the center of my chest. "If you tell anyone else what you've seen and what I've told you, I'll kill you myself."

She shoves me out of her way and heads back toward the barracks without ever looking back.

Alone, I stare into the darkness long after she's gone.

EIGHTEEN

The only good thing about Phase Three training is that it keeps me too stressed and exhausted to dwell on the fact that both Digory and Cypress have been virtually ignoring me for the past couple of weeks. Whenever I cross their paths and they give me the silent treatment, I keep telling myself that it's fine, because I can't afford to lose sight of what's at stake here.

But every time Digory turns his back on me, it takes a bit to shake the dull ache inside.

In between waking up at the crack of dawn for target practice with actual Pulsator guns firing live ammo and spending the entire day under the scorching sun enduring our final physical training tests, there's not much time to dwell on anything else—*anyone* else—and I slump into bed exhausted every night, too tired to even scrounge up a mild nightmare for a change.

But this morning's different.

Right after breakfast, the five of us are herded by Styles and Renquist to the East Landing Platform as a hovering Squawker touches down.

My pulse quickens. Today's the day basic training comes to an end with the last of our Field Training Exercises. Earlier this week, they had us facing a mock group of rioting insurrectionists during nighttime combat operations. "Urban Terrain Crowd Control," they called it. I couldn't help notice the wince on Digory's face as we were forced to fend them off with shields and jolt sticks.

He catches me staring at him now, and I look away.

"I wonder what they have in store for us this time?" Gideon mutters into my ear, over the hum of the craft's engines.

The Squawker's hatch springs open and Slade is standing there, smirking. "What the hell are you sorry lot waiting for? Get your asses on board."

No sooner do we finish scrambling aboard and strapping ourselves in than the Squawker takes off again. I'm practicing my deep breathing techniques, trying to get a grip on my nerves while my mind races with the possibilities of what today's final exercise will be.

"There's no reason to get bent out of shape," Digory whispers to the Recruits, as if reading my mind. He shoots a look my way. "It'll probably be just another Sim."

I'm just starting to relax when, instead of landing at the main compound, the Squawker soars over the sonic fences that protect Infiernos and heads deeper inland, further and further away from the coast.

"Where the hell are they taking us?" I mutter, more to myself.

I can't help but remember the conversation I overheard between Styles, Renquist, and the pilot of that troop carrier. Whatever's out here beyond the perimeter fence, it has the entire base on edge. From the day of the bomb diffusion Sim, when I noticed the look of worry on Slade's face, it's been spreading. The furtive glances among the officers, the tense, weary expressions of the enlisted whenever they return from perimeter patrol...those that *do* return, that is.

What is it they're not telling us?

Ophelia and Gideon look nervous as they gaze at the barren landscape whizzing past the windows. Even Digory looks ill at ease.

Only Cypress's face burns with excitement. Our eyes meet and she smirks at me before pressing her face back against the glass.

This is what she's wanted, all along. To be outside the safety perimeter.

But why?

Slade emerges from the door of the cockpit, and everyone turns away from the window and snaps to attention.

"Now listen up!" she growls. "A situation has arisen. It seems we've lost contact with one of the recon patrol units led by Commander Cordoba. Your mission is a search and rescue Op." She holds up a small handheld screen and tosses it to Gideon. "Using the team's last known coordinates, you're to track them, ascertain their whereabouts, and bring any survivors back to base."

"Excuse me, Sergeant," Digory says. "Will we be provided any ground backup? Any supplies? MREs?"

As awful as those pre-packaged Meals Ready to Eat taste, they'll sure beat an empty stomach after a long day of being out on the field.

"No ground transport shall be provided, Recruit. You'll be traveling on foot with no survival packs or med kits, and only a limited supply of drinking water. Anything you eat you'll have to pick or kill. Among other things, an important part of this mission is for you put the skills you've hopefully acquired during your training to the test." Her expression softens. "I advise you not to dawdle, and to make your best effort to get back to the barracks before sundown." She gazes out the window. "If you aren't afraid of the dark *now*, you *will* be ... "

A look of stark terror settles on Gideon's face.

As much as I've grown accustomed to Slade's melodramatic embellishments during our training exercises, there's an edge to her tone now, and a hardness to her expression, that sends a chill through me.

Just how much of this exercise *is* a Simulation?

"Drop point ETA thirty seconds," a voice blares from the cockpit speakers.

"Get your chutes on!" Slade commands. "This is your stop."

As we strap into our jetsail harnesses, Slade grips the handlebar overhead with one hand and presses the hatch release with the other. Wind rips through the open cabin. "Good luck!" she shouts.

One by one we leap through the hatchway and into the sky—first Digory, then Cypress, Gideon, and Ophelia, and finally me.

Adrenaline rushes through my veins as I free-fall after them. The ground's coming up fast and I resist the urge to kick in the thrusters.

Remember the training. It's not time yet.

"One ... two ... three ... four ... five," I mutter to the wind before jamming my thumb onto the button that activates the jetsail's steam propulsors. Using the toggles on my handgrips, I maneuver the steering lines of my pack's sail until I'm knifing down in a reasonably smooth arc. Before I hit the surface I catch one last glimpse of the Squawker, disappearing into the morning fog. Then I hit the surface, rolling on the ground alongside the others.

————

After eight hours of tracking the missing recon patrol's troop carrier signal through sparse, rocky terrain, we finally clear the last of the trees and emerge into a clearing—and what little breath I have left is torn away.

The bowl-shaped crater in the earth must be at least a mile in circumference. Just below us is the battered hull of the troop carrier we've been searching for. And scattered throughout this canyon, as far as the eye can see, are large mounds about twenty feet high, shimmering under the dying sun. They remind me of giant versions of the ant hills behind the old power plant in the Industrial Borough. But instead of being composites of sludge and weeds, these symmetrically perfect knolls are made up of hundreds of pale faces—staring back at us, eyes black, mouths agape ...

Skulls.

My own mouth drops open. But before I can make a sound, a collective moan erupts from the leering faces.

I stumble backward into Digory. The groans build in intensity until each skull's shrieking its fury into the sky in a maelstrom of despair.

Ophelia clamps her hands over her ears. "What's that terrible sound?"

"It's only the wind whipping through the eye sockets." Cypress's voice is just as haunting.

Gideon steps forward. "We gotta get a closer look."

Using the trunk of a dead tree, the five of us manage to roll it into place, at an angle from the rim of the canyon to the floor, so we can shimmy down it for ten feet until we hop off it at the bottom.

Even though we don't find any survivors in the carrier, a quick survey of the grid yields rust-colored stains throughout, a grim indication of what must have happened here.

"So where are the bodies that go with these skulls?" I finally ask the question that no one else dares to.

Gideon's staring right into a pair of dark sockets on a skull in the nearest mound. "I'm more disturbed by why someone took the time to arrange these in neat little piles ..."

Digory's nose wrinkles. "Maybe it's some kind of burial rite."

I hear Cypress slam something closed inside the cockpit of the troop carrier. "Even though this baby's pretty banged up, she'll still fly," she says as she climbs out.

I nod. "At least we won't have to walk home."

"I found something!" Ophelia's squeal breaks the tension. We all turn to see something glistening in her open palm.

Gideon's eyes grow wide. "Let me *see* that." He stumbles over to where she's waiting and scoops it from her. One hand holds the wobbly frame of his glasses in place while he inspects a dangling chain.

"What is it?" I call.

Gideon's jaw drops. "It's an identification tag. A *Recruit* ID tag."

Cypress lunges for it, but he rips it away.

"You sure?" Digory asks.

Gideon pulls out his own tag from around his neck and compares them. "Same size, same shape. *You* tell *me*."

I clutch my own chain, the one that's holding me hostage for my brother's life. "Is there a name on it?"

Holding the tag up to his face with one hand, Gideon rubs the surface. "Nothing I can make out. Looks corroded. But there *is* part of a serial number."

Everyone else's attention is fixed on the chain, and I don't think they notice the pained look on Cypress's face as she massages her forehead.

Digory shoots me a look. "A Recruit ID tag way out here? Are you thinking what I'm thinking?"

"If you're thinking Fallen Five, yeah, me too."

Cypress's eyes are riveted on the tarnished silver swaying from Gideon's fingers. "They must have come right through here."

Ophelia wipes sweat off her brow. "So is this whole mission a Sim, or not? I'm confused."

"I've been wondering the same thing," Gideon mutters.

I shrug. "No way to be sure. Slade and the others are definitely worried about *something*, though."

Digory clears his throat. "If something's got Slade of all people worked up, then we should be, too."

The sun hovers noticeably lower on the horizon. In a matter of minutes, the temperature's dropped enough to dry the perspiration on my forehead.

A tortured moan stretches across the canyon like a soul being pulled apart.

My eyes ricochet around the crater's remains. "What *was* that?"

Ophelia's face is as pale as the skulls. "We need to get going."

Gideon shakes his head. "We can't abort the mission until we find proof, one way or another, of what happened to that patrol. I don't know. An identifiable corpse. A message. Anything." He looks around. "I suggest we split into teams and search the area before reporting in. Juniper and I will take the south quadrant, and Tycho, Spark, and Goslin—"

But Cypress is already tromping through the site, her eyes desperately searching as she disappears behind one of the mounds.

Gideon shrugs. "Keep in touch through your walkies." Then he and Ophelia head off in the opposite direction, leaving Digory and me to explore on our own.

After almost an hour of sifting through the site and finding no evidence of the missing patrol's whereabouts, I run my fingertips along the surface of the nearest gruesome mound. Interspersed between the skulls are thigh bones, femurs, sternums, clavicles—all jammed against rib cages and all manner of vertebrae. If there's one thing we learn quickly in the Parish when dealing with Imps, it's the names and locations of each bone in the human body.

The whole macabre assemblage is held together by a slimy, thick resin. I bring my fingertips to my nose and sniff, then wince. Whatever it is, it reeks of ammonia. I wipe the gunk on my fingers against my pants.

Thwack!

A skeletal hand springs from behind the mound and latches onto my wrist—

I try to wrench free but the grip is strong, frenzied.

"Let…go…of…me…!" I pull with all my might and a figure comes crashing through the mound. Bones scatter everywhere. A heavy weight drives me into the ground, knocking the wind from me.

"You're dead!" I pummel the figure on top of me as its stone-cold hands grip my throat, squeezing. The light dims. My head swims. I start to float away…

"Get off of him!" Digory's voice. Far away.

The pressure around my neck is gone. The canyon

comes into focus once again. Air cascades through me like a waterfall.

I bolt into a sitting position. A hand touches my shoulder, and I flinch.

"Are you okay?" Digory is crouched beside me.

My fingers knead my sore neck. "I'll ... live. What happened?"

Digory nudges his chin toward a figure lying in a skeletal pile. "*He* did."

I spring to my feet. "They're nothing but bones—they *can't* be—"

Digory stands beside me. "This one's very much alive. Trust me, Lucian."

I creep closer to get a look at my assailant.

It's just a guy. Mid-twenties, maybe ... hard to tell. He's covered in filth and coated in the same goo that holds the bones in place. Scraggly black hair juts from his scalp in long strips, tangling with his patchy beard. Thin red slashes crisscross his prominent cheekbones, and his murky-green eyes are stretched into wide ovals. There's madness there.

Despite the creepiness of the way his gaze seeps into my pores, there's something else about him that sends a shudder through my own bones.

"Digory. *Look* what he's wearing."

Even though this stranger's clothes are ripped and flapping in shredded tatters, there's no mistaking the familiar jumpsuit design and the ID tag that hangs from his scrawny neck.

"A Recruit uniform," Digory whispers.

I snatch the ID tag loose. The man yelps as if I've struck him and curls into a fetal position.

I dangle the silver chain in front of Digory's face. "He's one of *us*."

NINETEEN

The Recruit just lies there, still as a corpse. The only sign of life is the tide of soft whimpers that rises from him.

My brain spirals. "He *has* to be one of the Fallen Five." I squat close to him. "It all fits. His age ... clothes ... where we've found him." My eyes pierce Digory's.

"He's definitely about the right age." Digory plucks the ID tag from my hand. He twists it in his fingers, examining the front and back. "Name's covered in gunk. Can't make it out."

"What's your name?" I ask the stranger.

He just shakes his head as if he doesn't know the answer.

Realization dawns on me. "It must have been *him* that I saw ... behind the tree—" I glance at Digory, not bothering to conceal my *I told you so* expression.

Digory counters with a *sorry I doubted you look* and stoops beside the stranger. "It's gonna be okay. How have you survived out here all on your own? What do you do for food?" He cushions each word as if it's made of delicate porcelain.

The Recruit's breathing shifts to a slower tempo. His whimpers become a sigh, then a purr. He looks away. "I get by."

I edge in closer to him. "Don't worry. We're gonna get you out of here. Take you home."

The unknown Recruit springs up. His eyes boomerang between Digory and me.

"It's too late," he rasps. He's trembling all over. He leans into my ear. "The Fleshers will get you too," he whispers.

Fleshers. I'm not sure what he's talking about, but something about the word and the way it quavers in his throat causes my skin to break out into thousands of tiny bumps, swelling to burst free like hungry larvae feeding off fear.

The man's eyes flood. "They... they ambushed us... there were too many of 'em... they just kept coming... and coming... but *I* got away..." He buries his face in his hands. "Never saw the others again." He looks up. "I looked for so long, but I never found 'em." His eyes cloud over in a swirling haze of memory. "There was a little girl... I forget her name now. So pretty... such nice hair..." Tears stream down his cheeks. "Why can't I remember her name?" His head snaps to the left and he looks up, as if he's heard something we can't. He clamps his hands over his ears.

"What's wrong?" I ask.

"That sound... that *terrible* sound. It's them! The Fleshers. They're all around us! Make it stop! Make it stop!"

Digory stoops and pries the Recruit's hands from his ears. "What are ... the Fleshers?"

The man smiles for the first time, revealing a full set of grimy teeth, all intact except for the jagged center tooth. "The Establishment wasn't the only thing that survived the Ash Wars. There are others ... *things* that prefer the dark ... " His snorts become cackles until his entire body is convulsing with laughter, despite the stark terror in his eyes.

I rub my arms, trying in vain to warm my body. "We're looking for a missing recon patrol from that wrecked troop carrier," I tell him. "Do you know where they are?"

Drool seeps from the corner of his lips. "They're right *here*," he whispers. "All around us ... listening to everything we say ... "

Digory and I crane our necks in every direction.

"There's no one else here," Digory says.

"There sure as hell is!" the man snaps. He digs into the mound he was hiding behind and pulls something out, thrusting it in front of our faces.

A severed arm.

I stare in revulsion at the pale flesh, which seems to be relatively intact. Fresh. At least in appearance if not in odor. The fingers are curled inward, clutching something gold—a pin, from the looks of it. Clamping a hand over my nose and mouth, I lean in and yank the object free.

It's an Imposer badge. I can't read the first name because it's coated in something dark and sticky. But the last name hits me like a sonic pulse.

"*Cordoba*. The commander of the missing recon patrol."

I force the words through clenched teeth and look up as I hand the badge to Digory.

"Looks like we have our proof." His eyes are somber as he tucks the badge into his pocket. "Whoever or *whatever* did this has Slade and the others running scared."

"It isn't a Sim," I whisper. "It *isn't* a Sim…"

Just above the grisly wrist the Recruit is still holding out to me, there's a semicircle of indentations separated by small spaces. The pattern is almost perfect, except for a jagged slash at its center.

Bite marks.

I look back up. The fallen Recruit's staring at me, licking his lips, mouth once again upturned in a foam-coated grin… proudly displaying his chipped front tooth.

The crackle of my walkie nearly gives me a heart attack.

"There's something coming!" I hear Gideon shriek through the speaker. "We gotta go. *Now!*"

"The Fleshers," I whisper.

A tremor rocks the basin.

"Let's get the hell out of here." Digory grabs my hand and pulls me away from the mound.

In the distance, dark shadows flit among the hives of bone like marauding insects, nibbling their way toward our position as we scramble toward the carrier.

Another powerful rumble rocks the ground, the deep bass of a siren that vibrates through the canyon like the cry of some prehistoric beast, followed by a series of clanks and grinds from some poorly oiled machine, mixed with sickening wet squishes and a clatter… like snapping teeth.

We run nearly smack into Gideon and Ophelia.

"Where's Cypress?" I gasp out.

"Probably already at the ship, getting ready to take off without us." Gideon jabs a finger past us. "What the hell are those things?"

Ophelia's eyes bulge. "The Five."

I shake my head. "Sounds more like five *thousand*."

Digory pushes us forward. "We're not sticking around long enough to find out!"

That siren blasts louder than ever and a big blur of creepy bursts through the hives just ahead, cutting us off from the carrier.

"Take cover!" Digory shouts.

I dive to the ground and roll behind the nearest mound, pressing close to it so whoever or *whatever* it is can't spot me. Jagged bones pierce the skin on my back. My heart punches the walls of my chest. A drought hits my mouth. I try to slow my breathing so I won't pass out.

The mechanical noise putters throughout the canyon. Rusty gears clink together, screeching in protest. At first it seems further away; then it gets closer and closer. I hug my almost bare torso against the chill. The thing must be making a sweep. What is it about that sound that gnaws at my memory?

Then it hits me. Back at the Parish. Walking home from school past the Borough's processing plants—

It's the sound the meat grinders make during a particularly sparse season.

The sound creeps nearer. It's just on the other side of the mound I'm curled behind. My eyes squeeze shut.

Whirrrrrrrrrrr...

Clackclackclackclackclack...

My body's clenched so tight it feels like my own bones are about to pop from their sockets.

Why won't it go away?

It *knows* I'm here...

The grinding noise clacks off, replaced by a nauseating sloshing.

Slopslopslop...

A light flicks on, bathing my peripheral vision in a sickly yellow glow.

Another loud *click* adds a new sound to the assault on my senses.

Buzz!

The vibration is so strong, it hurts my teeth and I have to gnash them tight to prevent a telltale chatter. Not daring to breathe, I slink further around the mound, before the thing can reach me. I'm not sure how big it is, but if I can keep moving out of sight I just might be able to—

My belt loop snags on a piece of bone.

The yellow beam creeps around the bend. Silhouetted in the shadow of its glow are twisted shapes that look like they've been ripped free of a nightmare.

I claw at the loop, trying to jerk it free, but it won't budge.

The amber light burns a path toward me, just inches from my boots...

I twist my body out of its path, curling my legs beneath

me just as the glow sweeps the spot my feet occupied moments ago. My fingers grope the jagged bone holding me hostage, scraping against it and drawing blood, which just makes it slick and harder to grip.

Snapsnapsnapsnapsnap …

I tug as hard as I can—

Pop!

The loop rips away. I'm free! I scuttle further around the bend on hands and knees, ignoring sharp rocks digging into my skin. In my panic, my boot kicks out behind me and crashes through the mound.

A loud rattle of bone rains down all around me.

A very loud rattle.

A mechanized shriek pierces my eardrums. The grotesque confirmation that the Fleshers are on to me. I clamp my hands to my ears.

Whir …

Clacketyclacketyclacketyclacketyclackety …

The rhythm of the sounds is much quicker now, and loud enough to penetrate the ringing in my ears.

Something grabs me—

"Run!" Digory hauls me to my feet and then we're racing after Gideon and Ophelia.

We tear through the canyon, careening past the rest of the mounds, zigzagging over rocks, leaping over fissures. Swirls of blinding yellow and twisting black haunt the corners of my vision. They're all around us, swarming over the mounds like locusts, but I'm too afraid to turn and get a better look, too afraid to see what kind of monsters would be responsible for this hell, would make a fallen Recruit crave flesh …

Too afraid to find out if what happened to the lost Recruits could happen to me.

I stumble down a slope after Digory and Ophelia, rolling, my flesh scraping against rock and bone. But I'm running on pure adrenaline now, impervious to pain.

I skirt the next mound—

Just in time to see the troop carrier taking off without us.

"The bitch is leaving us behind!" Gideon cries.

The dark shadows close in on us from all sides.

It's over.

Then the carrier banks, swinging in a wide arc until it's hovering just overhead. The hatchway springs open and a familiar silhouette stares down at us, long raven hair whipping in the wind.

Cypress tosses down a rope ladder, which wriggles down like a long snake, grazing my skin as it sways against my nose. I recoil.

"Don't just stand there like idiots!" Cypress shrieks. "Get your butts up here now!"

"Ophelia!" Gideon cries.

But Digory's already scampering up the rope and towing him along. "She's in good hands with Spark." He pauses and shoots me a desperate look. "Lucian! Move! Now!" Then the two of them disappear inside the carrier's open hatch.

Just as I grab the lower rung, a heavy weight slams into me, knocking me to the ground, smothering me.

My eyes snap open.

But it's not a Flesher.

It's the fallen Recruit.

There's something different about him. I search his eyes but don't find madness. Only fear, and sadness.

The monstrous chorus of the Fleshers approaches all around us...

The Recruit looks behind, then back at me. Liquid fills his eyes. "My name's Orestes..." he whispers. "Please take me... *home*..."

His words are a vise to my throat. My heart crumples. No matter what he's done, he's still a human being, broken by the Establishment like so many others before him.

"Yes. Come with us," I say, barely squeezing the words past a sob. "You'll be safe. We'll take care of you."

He smiles—

His throat bursts open. Dark crimson sprays onto my face, into my eyes, and runs down my cheeks in hot rivulets.

Metallic gore fills my mouth. I spit it out. Every nerve-ending sizzles with shock.

The young man stares at me. He doesn't look like he's in pain. More like he's confused. Soft gurgling noises purr from his lips. He convulses, choking on his own blood, still staring as it fountains from the ragged hole in his neck, dousing me in its warmth. His eyes flutter and roll back into his head. Then he pitches forward onto me, each shudder pumping more blood over me until he's still at last.

The chain of his ID tag snaps off his neck as I clench it in my fist.

Then I push him off me and he rolls onto his back with a thud. I wipe the mixture of tears and blood from my eyes. A blurry figure comes into focus.

It's Ophelia, standing over me, still clutching a sharpened bone fragment in her hand. The white bone is coated in red. Its sharp end still drips chunks of the Recruit's throat onto the ground, *plop, plop, plop*. Her face is spattered with red flecks that stream from her eyes down her cheeks like bloody tears.

She grins, chilling the blood flowing both inside and outside my body.

"I wasn't going to let him hurt you," she giggles. Her voice sounds muffled, as if I'm listening to it underwater, slow, warped. The dark fires of dusk blazes in her eyes.

"Lucian, come on!" Digory's muffled voice shouts down from the carrier's hatchway as it hovers above.

The next few seconds feel like a dream as I somehow haul my numb body up the ladder, after Ophelia and into the aircraft.

The hatch seals.

"There's just enough juice to make it back to base," Cypress grunts from the pilot's chair.

"Punch it!" Gideon yells.

Then Cypress is gunning the ship toward Infiernos. Below us, the Fleshers are a vague blur of nightmares carving a dusty path right toward our base.

Digory grabs me by the shoulders, his eyes wide as he stares at my blood-soaked body. "Where are you hurt?"

"It's not mine," I hear myself say.

The cockpit speakers crackle to life.

"Attention! Red alert! All troops return to base STAT. The perimeter fences will be activated in T-minus one minute," a computerized voice blares through the encroaching night.

On the cabin monitors, we see the pillars of the closest fence blinking yellow, signaling that they're preparing to power up and seal off the base.

If we don't make it to the fences in time, we'll be trapped outside in the open ... with *them*.

The only sounds in the cabin are the thrum of the engines mingled with our breathing and the blaring of the alarms.

The emergency lights blink faster and faster until they're a solid yellow. There's not much time left and we're still about a mile away ...

I clench my fist, feeling the Recruit's ID tag digging into my skin as Cypress banks the carrier in between two of the sonic pylons, just as the lights go from amber to bright red—

"Perimeter fences activated. The base has been sealed."

Turbulence rocks the cabin and, for a split second I brace myself to be torn apart. But then we're gliding down and landing on the roof of our barracks, roughly, but all in one piece.

Once the hatch is opened, we limp down the gangway. The faces around me are a mixture of tears and relief. We cling to each other, hugging, squeezing. We did it. We made it through. Staring at the bloodied ID tag still clutched in my hand, I find it hard to feel anything.

I'm not sure how long we stand like that, but when we

finally pull apart, we're ringed by Slade and a dozen other Imps.

Her eyes look anxious. "Did you find anything?"

Digory pulls out Cordoba's blood-stained badge and thrust it into her hand. "He didn't make it. None of them did. But *we're* fine, thank you, *Sir*."

The Sergeant swallows hard and hands the badge off to one of her subordinates. "Congratulations, Recruits." Her usual disdain is replaced by a cross between disappointment and surprise.

She never expected to see us again.

Alive.

Slade's smile is devoid of mirth, malice, or any emotion whatsoever. "You've successfully completed your orientation period and survived Basic Pre-Trial Prep. Tomorrow you graduate—and, as a reward, you will have the opportunity to visit with your Incentives one last time before the Trials begin."

TWENTY

Graduation Day. On this last day before the Trials, the Establishment has moved us from our cramped and sparse barracks to the Officer's Lodge. Each of us has been provided with a private luxury suite—in honor of our *accomplishment*.

I barely recognize myself in the floor-length mirror. I'm not used to seeing such a crisp reflection, especially one that's decked out in fancy clothes I'd never expect to wear in a million years. My dress uniform is made up of a stark-white, long-sleeved shirt; cobalt-blue pants with a complementing vest; and a long-tailed coat that's embroidered with silver brocade the same color as the buckle on my leather belt. A white silk scarf is neatly coiled around my neck, matching the gloves on my hands. I shift my weight in a pair of gleaming black boots.

The garments feel strange, constricting yet cushy against my skin. I sigh. When I first arrived at Infiernos, I wouldn't have had any idea how to put this stuff on. I turn my head from side to side. Whatever was in those cleansers in that biometric voice-activated shower I just took has left my hair a shiny, wavy black. My skin seems healthy and tanned, not burned. I actually look … well … not *too* shabby. A wide grin spreads across my face.

After what's seemed like forever, the moment I've been longing for these past few months is here.

I'm finally going to *see* Cole and Mrs. Bledsoe again!

I let loose a chuckle. They probably won't even recognize me.

Neither will Digory.

My elation evaporates, along with my saliva.

This isn't just a graduation ceremony. It could very well be the last moment I share with the people I love most in this entire world.

By the time the bullet-shaped Trans-Cab shuttles me over to the steel-domed Academy Pavilion, there's already a procession filing into the building in full military regalia, complete with marching band. But despite the legion of soldiers, the only sound I can hear is my heart thudding in my ears.

My eyes scan the troops as I pass them. They've stopped marching and are frozen like statues. Hundreds of eyes creep over me, like a swarm of cockroaches devouring a piece of bread, as I make my way up the steps and through the front doors of the Pavilion. Even the trumpeters have stopped playing their procession march, the last notes trapped by the atrium's vaulted ceiling and bouncing back in discordant echoes.

Even though I've completed Orientation and successfully made it all the way to graduation, these soldiers still see me, Lucian Spark, as a traitor to the Establishment. They'd never accept me into their ranks. The contempt they feel for me now is just as potent as it was on the day I stepped off the freighter ten weeks ago. If not more so.

I want to shout at them at the top of my lungs, tell them I don't give a damn, that the last thing on earth I want is to be one of them. But I can't make a scene. Not with so much at stake. And they know that.

The only thing I care about is seeing Cole at last.

Inhaling deeply, I raise my head high and match their stares until they start to fidget and look away. Then I dash up marble steps two at a time to the balcony, my eyes searching the crowd for the others.

Cypress is standing not more than ten feet away, peering over the railing at the crowd below. She looks stunning in her uniform. Her raven hair's been washed and combed to a lustrous sheen, plaited at the sides and joined in a long braid that hangs down her back. Her skin looks like it's been polished to a smooth creamy finish, with just the right hint of pink on her cheeks to complement her wine-colored lips.

She could almost pass for one of those princesses pictured in the Establishment's banned fairy tales—except for her eyes, which are vacant and puffy. In the three months that I've known her, I've never seen her look so ... *defeated*.

I walk over to her. "What's wrong? Why haven't you gone into the auditorium?"

She barely glances at me. "Not sure I can face them. Don't know what to say."

"*Them*? You mean your Incentives?" I sit down beside her.

She nods. I can feel her shoulder trembling against mine.

I sense that now's the time she'll be the most receptive. I can't help her unless I know exactly what's troubling her, even though there's probably nothing I can do. Reaching out, I hesitate a moment, then take her hand, expecting her to rip it away and shove me. But she does neither.

"Cypress. I know it's none of my business, but after the Fallen Five disappeared, how did you ... I mean ... ?"

"How did I *survive*?" Her smile is laced with bitterness. "Believe me, I've asked myself that question many times over the years. When my brother was recruited, his only options were my mother and me. Two out of the ten Incentives who had no one to fight for us after the Recruits disappeared. Since it couldn't be proven one way or another that the Fallen Five had deserted, the Establishment decided that rather than shelve us, the adults would be taken to the mines." She pauses. "I never saw my mother again."

She looks away as if she's reliving that painful memory. I can see the anguish etched into her face as if by a powerful chisel.

"I'm so sorry, Cypress. I know what losing a mom feels like."

"She was one of the lucky ones. Probably died within a year or two." She shakes her head. "Us children weren't as fortunate. We were forced into servitude at the Emporiums. Harmony House."

The Emporiums. Centers of unspeakable perversions, where every depravity can be purchased by sick minds in possession of enough currency.

Her eyes squeeze shut. "I was only six at the time. Unfortunately, I was a very pretty child..."

"I'm so sorry." I squeeze her hand. "But with your brother missing and your mother dead, who are *your* Incentives?"

She takes a deep breath and stares at me, her eyes hollow, empty wells. "My two children."

I can barely contain my rage. "Those *animals*. They took an innocent young girl and—"

She sneers. "*I'm* the animal, Lucian. I wanted to have a child, replenish the stock. Though I didn't bargain on twins."

I grab both her wrists. "But *why*—?"

"So I'd be deemed tainted and decommissioned. Nothing spoils the mood more in the pleasure pits than a girl who's in the breeding stage." Her eyes meet mine. "Boys have a longer shelf life."

I grip Cypress tighter, this time to steady myself.

"So you see, I used my own children—gave them up as ransom—to get transferred from that hell hole to a work farm without ever once laying eyes on them." A chuckle dies in her throat. "And now it's all come full circle and I'm getting exactly what I deserve. No wonder my brother abandoned me. He could sense what kind of terrible, selfish person I am."

"Cypress, don't..."

Her eyes grow soft. "I never told you this, and I'll deny it if you ever repeat it, but I *really* admire you, Lucian.

The way you love your little brother … the way you'll do anything to be with him again, unlike my brother. Maybe that's why a part of me still hates you."

"Maybe you're wrong about your brother. Don't you think it's possible that something could have prevented him from coming after you, something beyond his control?" Thoughts of our experience with the Fleshers turn my blood cold. I block them out as best I can. "I mean, you have no way of knowing that he abandoned you."

"Maybe someday I'll find him and I'll be able to hear the explanation from his own lips. Until then, the Orestes I knew is dead to me."

A jolt rips through my body. My brain bobs in my skull. How do I tell her what became of her brother?

"Spark? Are you okay? What's wrong?"

I shake my head. "We'd better get inside."

————

Every time the door to the small reception room swings open my heart surges—then deflates like an old tire at the sight of yet another stranger crossing the threshold. It's been over thirty minutes already—the Graduation Ceremony is about to start—and still no sign of Cole or Mrs. Bledsoe.

And Digory's still a no-show, too. I'm finally going to find out who his Incentives are, find out how who is so important to him.

Who it is that he loves …

A high-pitched giggle echoes across the room. Ophelia's

jumping up and down, embracing a woman and a little girl. She reminds me of that naïve girl who bounced into Slade's welcoming-committee speech on the first day we arrived at Infiernos, so long ago it seems now. The sight of their tender family reunion causes sadness to cluster in my throat, making it hard to swallow.

What's taking Cole and Mrs. Bledsoe so long? I'm about to rip through my skin.

"Don't panic, Spark," Gideon says, as if reading my mind. "I'm sure your family will be here any minute."

He's standing alongside two other people, a man and a woman with shell-shocked eyes, their drab, plain clothes in stark contrast to his neatly pressed uniform. The woman's graying hair is twisted into a bun, resembling a wrung-out washcloth. Even though the skin under her eyes is dark and puffy, her stare is strikingly similar to Gideon's.

The man has his arms folded. His salt-and-pepper hair recedes from his forehead like an outgoing tide, draining what's left of its color. The tip of his aquiline nose veers sharply to the left as if it's been broken.

"These must be your folks," I say, trying to draw them in with a smile. But it's as though I'm not even there.

Gideon fidgets, his eyes bouncing back and forth between the couple and me. "Mom, Dad, this is—" He looks at me pointedly. "This is my friend, Lucian Spark."

Friends. Yes. After Cassius, I never thought I'd be able to call anyone else that ever again. But with everything we Recruits have been through, we're bonded now for the rest of our lives, however short that might turn out to be.

I hold out my hand. "It's an honor to meet you, Mr. and Mrs. Warrick."

Mrs. Warrick stares at my hand as if it's covered in manure. "We *know* who *you* are."

Gideon's eyes swell. "Mother!"

My extended hand drops to my side.

Deep fissures burrow into the corners of Mr. Warrick's eyes. "This is a family discussion. You're not welcome here." His voice is gruff.

"No, Dad! Please!" Gideon steps between us.

I clap Gideon's back and can't help notice his wince. "It's okay. *Really.*" I turn and nod at the Warricks, then look back at Gideon. "You should be very proud of your son. Enjoy your evening."

As I walk away, I catch a few of Mrs. Warrick's hushed words. "An enemy of the state! You don't want to be mixed up with *him.* You know I always do what's best for you—"

But her voice is drowned out by the thumping of blood ringing in my ears.

Something must be wrong...

Pushing my way toward the tall glass doors at the rear of the hall, I almost crash into Ophelia and her family.

"I'm so sorry," I mumble.

Ophelia is beaming. "It's okay. I was coming over to introduce you to Mama and Maddie."

The girl's a couple of years younger than Ophelia. Whereas Ophelia's hair is—*was*—a tangle of curls, her sister's hangs limp and lifeless. It matches the blankness of her narrow eyes, which are hammocked by pronounced folds of flesh. Her forehead is broad on her small head. Her tattered dress drapes her body with all the finesse of rumpled laundry on a clothesline.

Ophelia hugs her close. "This is my little sister Madeleine."

Madeleine drops her eyes and ducks behind her sibling, peeking up at me from the shield of Ophelia's shoulder.

I wink at her. "Hello, Madeleine. My name's Lucian."

"She's a little shy around new people." Ophelia squeezes her again. "It's all right, Maddie," she coos. "You don't have to be afraid."

I peer around Ophelia and stare into the child's eyes, smiling. "What a *pretty* dress."

She cups a hand over her smile and looks down at her shoes. "Nife to meetchu," she mumbles.

Her mother sighs. "For goodness sakes, Ophelia. Don't let *her*"—she glares at Madeleine—"cling to you like that. It's embarrassing enough we have to parade her around in front of everyone without worrying about her wrinkling your uniform."

Madeleine's eyes puddle. Her smile fades and she shrinks into the background like Ophelia's shadow.

Despite their mother's warnings, Ophelia kneels in front of her sister and wraps her in a hug. "Don't worry, sweetie. Mama's just nervous. You look *sooo* beautiful tonight. That's why everyone's staring at you instead of ugly ol' me!" She plants a kiss on her forehead.

Mrs. Juniper rolls her eyes and smiles at me, exposing pointy teeth. Her resemblance to Ophelia is uncanny. Sure, there are a few more creases the cheap cosmetics can't conceal, but it's like looking at Ophelia fifteen years from now. Despite the worn fabric of her dress, she wears it with an elite air over her hourglass figure.

Her eyes twinkle. "You're Spark, aren't you?"

I nod, bracing myself for the same disdain I received from Gideon's folks. Instead, she surprises me by clamping her arms around me in a tight hug and planting wet kisses on both my cheeks. A hand slithers across the back of my neck. "Such a bright boy. And handsome, too." Her lips brush against my ear. "Pity we had to meet under such ... *trying* ... circumstances. Perhaps we can work out an arrangement that will be mutually beneficial to both you *and* my daughter ... "

She rambles on and on, something about working with Ophelia to eliminate the competition during the Trials, but her words become an insect's drone as I focus on the scene taking place just behind her.

Two sets of bright green eyes are peering up at Cypress, belonging to a little boy and girl not much older than Cole. Her twins. Their hair is shiny black, just like Cypress's; their cheeks are flushed with pink. Both are dressed in neatly pressed matching amber jumpsuits. Their little hands are entwined.

Cypress turns away from them. Her eyes meet mine. She's trembling—rage or pain, I can't be sure. Tears stream down her face.

A crushing weight squeezes all the air free of my lungs.

I have to get out of this room.

Nodding as politely as I can, I pull away from Mrs.

Juniper. "It was a pleasure meeting you. But I really have to find my family."

Before she can protest, I barrel past her and push open the terrace doors with such force I can feel them rattling in their hinges.

Under the blanket of a thousand stars, Digory leans against the railing, gazing out at the coastline that's just beyond the entrance to Infiernos. The sparkling ocean is kissed by the shimmering rays of the full moon. Digory's uniform seems painted on over his broad shoulders and narrow waist; his hair is combed back and glistens like spun gold.

When he notices me, blue dawn blooms in his eyes. His mouth melts into a smile that almost blinds me with its brilliance.

I simmer in his warmth, which is as comforting as a pot of broth on a cold wintry night.

"You clean up nice, Recruit," he whispers.

"You don't look too shabby either, Tycho," I whisper back. "Guess you made a full recovery after our encounter with those Fleshers."

"Feeling much better ... like I could fly right now ... "

I chuckle. "Probably all those enhancers they loaded your blood with in the Bio-Pool."

He closes the gap between us. His smile disappears, replaced with a look of burning intensity, like comets ripping through the atmosphere. "I don't think that's the reason at all."

The radiance of his eyes ... the moon ... the stars ... overwhelm my senses. I feel lightheaded. "I didn't see you inside ... was wondering where you were ... "

"Sorry. I got tied up. My Incentive ... we had a lot to talk about."

My eyes risk blindness and find his again. "Your *family*? You've seen them?"

He seems surprised. "Why, yes. Haven't you seen your brother and Mrs. Bledsoe yet?"

The simmer in my blood starts to bubble into panic. The Warricks. The Junipers. Cypress's twins. And now Digory. Everyone accounted for except Cole and Mrs. Bledsoe. "No. I haven't seen either of them." I can feel the color draining away from my face.

"I'm sure they're okay." His hands grip my waist and pull me into him. "Don't worry. Everything's fine."

I nestle my head against his chest. My ears are filled with the deep sounds of our pounding hearts, beating like a hailstorm until they synch into one strong, steady rhythm.

"I'm scared, Digory. And not just for them ... the others too. Cypress, Gideon, Ophelia. I saw them inside, with their families ... it hit me just how real this all is ... how much they've all suffered ... *everyone* ... it's just like you told me when we first met, but I was too wrapped up in my own situation to see it ... it has to end ... "

"It will. But we have to be strong." He tilts my head up with a delicate touch of a finger on my chin. "No matter what."

My heartbeat ratchets ahead, leaving his trailing like its shadow. "What do you mean?"

"*Please*. Let's just have this one moment, just you and me, no one else … one moment where we don't talk about any of that … where none of it exists." He pulls me close again and nuzzles his head against my collar. "Where we can pretend tomorrow is a lifetime away … " His voice is burdened with a deep emotion that I haven't heard before, and it makes me wonder just how much he's been bottling up inside.

For the first time, I feel that it's *him* who needs *me*.

I clasp my hands around his back. We start to sway.

He sighs against me. "Our first dance … " His breath is warm and soothing against my neck.

I laugh. "All that's missing is the music."

His lips graze my ear and it's like fireflies are buzzing around my heart. "If you close your mind to everything else and listen, you can hear it."

My eyelids sag, giving way to the hypnotic lilt of his voice. The only time that exists is now. Nothing before, nothing after.

Soon the night's a symphony: our hearts beating like percussion in time with the chirping crickets, the wind whistling through the trees, the branches twanging as they bend in the wind's wake, the pounding surf crashing onto the shore like powerful cymbals …

We spin around the terrace, our cheeks pressed against each other, holding onto each other so tight I can't tell where I end and he begins. Soon I've lost track of how much time's passed. All I know is that I don't want it to ever end …

But it has to. This is much bigger than Digory and me.

Bigger than our families. It's about the right to live … the right to dream … the right to hope …

To have a future to look forward to.

Our dance slows to barely a sway, and finally we're just standing still. When I open my eyes, he's staring at me, his face a mask of sadness as if he's read my mind. We stay like that for a few minutes, drinking each other in like men dying of thirst, not knowing when or if another sip will ever come.

He caresses my cheek. "Thank you."

"What're you doing out here with me? Shouldn't you be inside with your family?"

Now it's him that looks away. "I needed a few minutes to myself. To clear my head." His eyes connect with mine again. "There's so much I wanted to say to you … I *needed* to say to you … before … "

"Before *what?*"

"Before the Trials."

My blood cools to lukewarm. All this time Digory's avoided talking about his family, who his Incentives even *are*, although he risked everything in being open with me about his involvement with the resistance—to the point where it put him in this mess right alongside me. My muscles twitch. As curious as I am to know what he's been holding back, there's a part of me that's afraid to know what secret could possibly be darker than treason against the Establishment. I'm not sure I can handle whatever it is he has to say, especially when I'm running out of things and people to believe in.

His fingers interlace with mine and he leans in close. "You're going to hear certain things tonight, but you *have* to trust me."

The sound of my heart spatters through my ears like raindrops *kerplunking* off the gutters back home. Every second of wondering is a prolonged agony.

"*Just tell me,*" I whisper.

The doors to the terrace burst open. "You two. Get inside," Slade grumbles from the threshold. "Ceremony's about to start."

"But I haven't seen my brother or Mrs. Bledsoe yet." I take a step toward her. "Where are they?"

"You'll find out soon enough." She avoids my gaze, fixing her eyes on Digory instead. "Your husband's been looking for you." Then she pivots on her boots and disappears inside.

Husband?

TWENTY-ONE

Digory *has* someone already? Of course he does. Yet how could he let me think... make me *feel*...? You'd think after everything that's happened, I'd be numb to anything else by now. But between my missing family and this latest reveal, why does it feel like my heart's been shoved into a grinder and sliced into thousands of bloody clumps?

My fingers slip away from Digory's. "Your spouse is one of your Incentives." My voice sounds foreign, as if it doesn't belong to me.

He reaches for me, but I pull away. "Lucian, you don't understand—"

I swipe a hand across my eyes. I'm boiling over with pain and I want to scald him, too. "You don't owe me an explanation. Especially after what *I* did to you."

Confusion clouds the stars from his eyes. "What you did to me?"

"You honestly don't believe it's a coincidence that we both got recruited, do you?"

He takes a step toward me and I back away. "What are you talking about?"

"Cassius had you recruited because he heard about what you were involved in back at the Parish—from my own lips."

And though it's technically true, my not mentioning the part where Cassius planted the transmitting device on me paints a whole different picture.

My words are like a brand that sears his face. Instantly, I regret what I've said, but the damage is done. His stance goes rigid. The muscles in his jaw and cheeks stiffen. "I *trusted* you."

"I have to find my brother." I turn and fling open the doors.

The reception room is empty. Everyone must be inside the hall by now. I stride past the two soldiers standing sentry by the doorway, trying to keep my expression neutral so they can't see I'm dying inside. I pick up the pace when I hear the footsteps behind me. I need to get as far away from Digory as possible. I need to find Cole. That's the only thing that matters. Everything else is a distraction, and I deserve to feel gutted for giving in to weakness and allowing myself to dream my life could be any different than it has been until now.

It never will be.

The auditorium's packed with enlisted personnel and officers. My trek to the first row, which has been cordoned off for the graduating Recruits, is a stinging, wet blur. I squeeze past Cypress, Ophelia, and Gideon. Fortunately, when Digory arrives, he's forced to sit in the only remaining seat at the opposite end.

Standing off to the side of the stage, flanked by a squad of Imps, are the Incentives—Gideon's parents, Ophelia's mother and sister, Cypress's twins, and a handsome, carmel-skinned guy about Digory's age. That must be *him*. But where's his second Incentive?

I scan the crowd, looking for my own Incentives, blinking the moisture away.

My heart sags. I don't see them anywhere.

There's a buzz of static on the intercom system that settles into a flatline hum, mimicking the feel of my heart. The lights dim, along with my remaining hope, as Trumpets blare and Sergeant Slade takes the stage.

"Welcome," she announces, as soon as the fanfare has died out. "On this occasion we gather to honor five exemplary cadets. They have proven they possess the necessary attributes to partake in the Trials, for the opportunity to enter the ranks of our military's elite."

The applause echoes through the amphitheater like rumbling thunder.

When it fades, Slade rambles on about the Establishment's principles and values, but her words barely register as I obsess about the only thing that matters.

Where is my family?

There's more applause, and then Cypress has to nudge

me as, one by one, we're called to the stage to receive our graduation pin and shake hands with Slade.

"Congratulations, Spark." Slade forces the words through clenched teeth. She jams the badge against the left breast pocket of my uniform, almost piercing my skin.

Then I'm moving in a daze to the end of the stage away from the Incentives and taking a seat, where I'm soon joined by the others.

Slade fades into the background as the beam of a spotlight appears center stage, illuminating a familiar silhouette that seeps deep into my eyes like a terminal sickness.

Cassius.

He's blinding, in a coat as stark white as a violent blizzard. His reddish-brown hair is slicked back, reminding me of the color of dead leaves covered in sleet.

When he raises his hands, every sound in the ballroom dies. "Distinguished members of our armed forces and Trials Committee, I'm honored to be a part of this Recruitment Graduation."

More applause.

Cassius folds his arms behind his back. "I stand before you as the Parish's most recently appointed Prefect, a fellow patriot, not only to join in honoring these five courageous military volunteers, but to apprise you of an unprecedented development in the history of the Trials."

A murmur zips through the crowd like an electrical current, sizzling and popping along the way. My chest tightens. *Unprecedented development?* In my gut I know it's tied to Cole and Mrs. Bledsoe. I grip the sides of my chair with sweaty palms.

"Most of the Recruits are gathered here with two of their Incentives, representing those they care most about and who will aid in motivating them through this arduous but necessary duty to our beloved government." He sweeps a hand in the direction of the Incentives. One by one, Cypress's, Gideon's, Ophelia's, and Digory's family members are illuminated in the beams of spotlights.

Cassius points to them. "As you can see, two of our Recruits have not been joined by both of their Incentives. The first is Digory Tycho..." He gestures and a split-screen image appears behind him: Digory's stoic face on one side, his husband's anxious one on the other. The camera pans to the empty space on the stage where his missing Incentive should be and freeze-frames.

"The other Recruit who is not yet joined by his Incentives," Cassius continues, "is Lucian Spark." The screen divides again, this time with a shot of the empty space on the stage where Cole and Mrs. Bledsoe should be standing.

A blinding spotlight blasts my eyes. I shield my face with an arm as my image fills the screen behind Cassius.

"Where *are* they?" My question, amplified by the directional mics, echoes through the hall.

Cassius stares at me, his murky green eyes like tufts of moss overgrowing the stone of his face, etched with lines of contempt and something else.

Hurt?

How dare he feel anything but shame and guilt after all

that he's done to me and my family? My blood steams in my veins. I want to lunge at him, wrap my hands around his throat—

He clicks his tongue several times. "Unfortunately, Recruit Spark, the Trials are all about exploring the strengths and resourcefulness of our prospects from the moment of inception. Everything that has transpired since Recruitment Day has been a part of this process, and all of your performances have been evaluated and scored accordingly."

My vision is a dark tunnel with only Cassius visible on the other end. "*Scored*? I don't care how many *points* we got for barely escaping with our lives from those things— those *Fleshers*—that killed your scouts and have you all in a tizzy. All I care about is my family. Why aren't they here?"

Slade marches toward me with Styles and Renquist in tow, but Cassius waves them off.

He sighs. "All the tests you have endured since you began your training at Infiernos were designed to assess your skills and weed out the weak amongst you. Surprisingly, you all passed. But unfortunately, one of you just barely made it through, and, as with every part of the Trials, consequences must be addressed."

My mouth goes dry. It feels as if my heart's trying to punch through my rib cage. "Where *are* they … ?"

"According to the code," Cassius continues, "the penalty for being the lowest-scoring Recruit to complete Basic Pre-Trial Prep is the forfeiture of Incentive visitation privileges. And you, Recruit Spark, regrettably graduated in last place."

At first, it's like he's speaking some other language, gibberish ... then the weight of his words settles in, crashing through like an anchor into the depths of my brain. The prospect of seeing Cole and Mrs. Bledsoe is the glue that's held me together. Without that ...

I spring to my feet. "You *can't* do that. *Please*, Cassius. I'll do anything you ask ... *anything*." I stagger from my seat and drop to my knees at his feet. "Just let me see them ... Cole ... even if it's only for a few minutes ... I—I *beg* you ... "

He shakes his head. "No need to supplicate, Lucian. The Establishment isn't totally heartless. We do realize that from time to time, small exceptions can be made." His voice is so convincing. I can almost believe him. *Almost.* He extends a hand and pulls me to my feet.

"*Thank you*," I whisper.

The leaves of his eyes glisten with dew. He gestures to someone offstage. "I'm afraid you can only see *one* of them."

His words are a punch to the gut. "Don't make me choose. Not now ... not *yet* ... "

He purses his lips. "You won't have to."

Styles and Renquist march onto the dais. Renquist is holding a shiny black vase. They flank Cassius and click their boots against the hard marble in attention. Renquist holds the vase out to me.

A growing sense of dread overcomes me. I try to peer around them. "Where are Cole and Mrs. Bledsoe?"

"Take it," Cassius orders.

I take the container from the Imp. It's colder than my trembling fingers. "What *is* this, Cassius?"

A long sigh hisses from his lips. "It's Mrs. Bledsoe—or rather, what's left of her. The poor thing had Reaper's, as you know. Awful business. She wasn't strong enough to endure all the excitement, and unfortunately succumbed to her illness last night."

I feel like I'm disconnected from my body, hovering overhead, observing the events rather than experiencing them. None of this is real. I'm just having a nightmare. That's all. I clutch the urn to my body. The porcelain's like ice against my chest. I can feel the rapid-fire thumps vibrating through it, as if trying to compensate for the lifelessness within.

It's *real*.

All I can do is stand there, rocking the urn back and forth, blinded by the flood pouring down my cheeks.

"My *brother*..." I try to run past the Imps, but they grab me. I twist in their clutches. "I want to see my brother!" I won't believe he's still alive until I see him myself.

Cassius shakes his head. "I'm sorry, Recruit. No more exceptions for you."

All that pent-up fury bubbles over and explodes. I rip free of the Imps and lunge at him. We crash to the floor. The urn topples from my grasp and smashes with a loud crash, engulfing Cassius and me in a cloud of Mrs. Bledsoe. I straddle him. He looks up, his eyes daring me to strike. I raise my fists to pummel him—

The air is torn from me as something slams into my lower back, sending jolts of pain through my body. I fall over, curling into a ball. Cassius slides out from under me. A flash of a boot and another kick sends fire into my kidneys. My eyes grow dim...

"Don't hurt him! Let him go!" Digory's voice echoes through the hall.

"Bring Tycho over here." Cassius's voice penetrates the painful fog clouding my brain.

Style's rough hands grab me on both sides. He drags me to my feet. I manage to open my eyes. Everything's a blur, but Cassius's face comes into focus. He smirks at me and leans in to whisper in my ear. "You should thank me. When the time came, you'd have chosen to end the Bledsoe witch's life yourself before your precious little brother's. I just expedited the process and took the decision out of your hands. Now you can go into the Trials guilt-free."

"*Murderer...*" I hiss at him.

Renquist and another Imp shove Digory toward me, his arms pinned behind his back. His eyes are choppy blue rivers. "Lucian, are you hurt?"

There's not a part of me that doesn't hurt, both inside and out, including the parts of me that he's touched. I drop my gaze to the broken urn and the scattered ashes.

Cassius clears his throat and raises his hand to silence the crowd's stirring. "I apologize to all of you who had to witness that. But it will help you to understand the dynamic that sets these Trials apart from any others we've ever held." He holds a hand out, indicating Digory. "Here we have one Recruit, who aside from his husband, has no other discernible family or close friends our research was able to discover. Of course, as in rare cases such as this, Tycho could be assigned an orphan as one of his other Recruits. But…" He points to *me* now. "Here we have another Recruit, who through no fault of his own has lost one of his Incentives before the Trials have even begun." He shakes his head. "What to do?" A smile flashes across his face. "Observe."

3-D holograms appear throughout the chamber, the largest of which towers right behind Cassius on the dais, all projecting the identical images.

Digory and me.

It's footage of us on the Observation Tower, sitting on the railing, gazing at the stars.

I wonder what it would be like, Lucian, to love someone so totally, so… you know, so powerfully, that even the stars can't contain themselves from proclaiming that love for everyone to see. Digory's voice blares through the audio system.

The image switches to the raft during our first Sim exercise, me slung over Digory's body, both of us half-naked, me whispering into his ear.

Listen to me, Digory. You're going to be okay. I promise.

Other images flash by in quick succession—Digory defying Slade and standing up for me when we first arrived at Infiernos… him feeding me breakfast at the mess hall during our first day of training…

The images fade into our moment earlier tonight. Digory and me on the terrace, his head nuzzled against my neck.

Let's just have this one moment, just you and me, no one else… one moment where we don't talk about any of that… where none of it exists... where we can pretend tomorrow is a lifetime away...

Footage of us dancing, swirling in each other's arms...

All the holograms fade. The lights come up.

The crowd is silent. And then the murmuring begins.

"May I have your attention, please." Cassius calls out above the clamor. The muttering fades. "As you can see, Digory Tycho has demonstrated strong emotional ties toward Lucian Spark. All of you witnessed yourselves his concern for Spark just a moment ago, casting protocol aside to try and protect him despite the fact that he's already married to another. And Lucian Spark, likewise, has strong feelings for Digory Tycho, stronger than any other living person other than his own brother, now that his poor unfortunate surrogate mother is no longer with us."

The audience begins buzzing again. Cassius allows it to continue for a moment before raising a finger. A hush falls through the hall. "So, for the first time ever, two of the Recruits shall *also* serve as each other's Incentives. Both their lives now hinge on each other's progress during the Trials. Should one falter, he will have to choose between his competitor's life and the life of his regular Incentive. Note that if he chooses his competitor, this decision will also have repercussions on his *competitor's* regular Incentive. Without anyone to fight for him, that Incentive's life will be forfeit as well." Cassius nods. "As of tomorrow morning, you will be witnesses to one of the most interesting Trials ever, where the question of self-indulgent love versus love of country will take on an even more significant meaning. Let the Trials begin!"

The applause swells into a thunderstorm.

"No! You can't do this!" I shout over the roar.

"Lucian!" Digory calls. The Imps are already hauling him off stage.

Cassius signals the Imposers and they drag me past him. "I'll *kill* you for this," I hiss at him.

Soldiers point at me, some laughing, others waving their fists, as I'm towed by, down the aisle and out of the hall.

I guess I gave them their little scene after all.

PART III

THE TRIALS

TWENTY-TWO

I've spent the entire sleepless night locked in solitary, thanks to my outburst at the Graduation Ceremony. Flight risk or suicide watch? Not that the outcome of either would be any different.

It's the first time at Infiernos that I've craved the sagging mattress of my bunk, back at the barracks. I don't know how many hours I've done nothing but stare into the suffocating darkness, wondering when the night will end—and dreading the moment when it will.

My cell door wooshes open.

Captain Valerian, the female Imp I haven't seen much of since she sicced the Canid on the kid in the alley, stands there, weapon aimed at me.

"It's time, Recruit." She tosses a bundle at my feet.

Black combat fatigues and boots.

This is it. The moment that everything's led to, ever since

my ill-fated reunion with Cassius on Recruitment Day. The point at which all of our fates converge, for better or worse—Digory's, Cypress's, Gideon's, Ophelia's, mine, and those of everyone we love. For months I've forged new friendships, only to have to tear those bonds apart now for Cole's sake.

I tear off my formal wear, still smudged with Mrs. Bledsoe's ashes, and slip into my new skin. Without waiting for a verbal prompt or the butt of Valerian's weapon, I take a deep breath and stride past her. Styles and Renquist are waiting out in the barren steel hallway.

"This way," Renquist grunts.

I march down the corridor after them, toward a bright opening on the far end. An elevator, by the looks of it. Gritting my teeth, I step in, past two more Imps flanking the doors.

The others are already waiting inside. Digory tries to make eye contact, but I drop my gaze. I can't. Not now. Instead I concentrate on the others. But none of them seem to notice me. While they all look a little more kempt in their identical combat fatigues than I'm sure I do, the one thing they all share in common is the look of dread splattered across their faces.

The elevator doors slam shut.

It's difficult to swallow as the car plunges. I almost reach out and grab Digory's arm to steady myself, but catch myself at the last second, opting for one of the handrails against the wall.

The floor vibrates with the speed of our descent.

Welcome Recruits!

Sergeant Slade's voice startles me, seeming to come from every direction.

Congratulations on being inducted and honored with the opportunity to join the Imposer Task Force.

Honored?

The Trials will take place on the lowest level of Infiernos, in a facility known as the Skein, an intricate series of connected corridors and doorways, each leading you to one of the challenges you will face.

My body tightens with a surge of claustrophobia.

At the completion of each mission, the Recruit who places last will make his or her selection during the Culling. You will all then be given variable rest periods at one of the holding stations before you proceed along the accessways to the next Trial, and so on and so forth until the final mission.

Yeah … we move on after effectively murdering one of our own …

Once both of your Incentives have expired, you will be eliminated from consideration and immediately shipped off to the work camps in the western provinces until your services are no longer required.

Unless you drop dead from exhaustion or disease first.

The Trials shall continue until there is only *one* remaining Recruit with at least *one* viable Incentive. That Recruit shall earn a place in the elite Imposer training program.

If you're fortunate enough to have any surviving family when this is all over, you'll live out the rest of your days in servitude to the monster.

Any questions?

The sounds in the elevator are a mix of clearing throats, grunts, and muttered nays.

Another jolt and the car grinds to a halt.

I can't swallow.

A slot by the doors springs open to reveal five black bands, each encompassing some kind of metal device.

You will each take a locator and place it around your wrist before exiting and awaiting further instructions.

One by one, we reach in without saying a word or making eye contact and pull out a locator, clamping them around our wrists like manacles.

The doors tear open—

And my eyes nearly leap from their sockets.

A vast field spreads out before us, strewn with smoking debris and collapsed buildings, simulating a war zone. Countless bodies litter the horizon, sprawled out in contorted poses—just more gritty scenery in this horrific mock-up.

It *can't* be real.

Except these bodies are twitching and writhing, filling the air with a chorus of moans that no actor or automaton could ever imitate so convincingly. The wails penetrate deep and cover every inch of my skin with goose flesh.

Where did all these people come from?

But I know the answer without having to be told: they're our friends and neighbors from the Parish, the innocents dragged from their homes in the dead of night to be questioned under the flimsiest of evidence, never to be seen nor heard from again. People with families just like ours, reduced to grisly props.

You will now take your places at the edge of the battle zone, just behind the energy barrier at the amber starting line.

Following Slade's instructions, I trudge toward the starting line just outside the crackling energy barrier. Filing after Gideon, Cypress, and Ophelia, I take my place beside Digory at the far end.

Cypress sighs. "All those people..."

"*Them*?" Ophelia whimpers. "What about *us*? I mean they're just lying around. Why haven't we started yet?" She's bouncing from one foot to the other. "I can't take much more of this waiting! Mama and Maddie are counting on me. If I don't come home soon, Mama'll get all flustered with Maddie and—"

"*Shut up*, Ophelia," Digory mutters.

Her jaw drops.

"Digory's right," I say. "It's not all about you."

Ophelia glares at us, then whirls on Cypress and Gideon. "You two were there last night. You *saw*. You *heard*." Her finger stabs at Digory and me. "These two are in this *together*."

"That's not true," I hurl back.

"Don't let her get to you," Digory says.

Ophelia's eyes pounce on him. "Interesting, but the fact is, you are *not* to be trusted. You'll turn on anyone—*use* anyone—to get what you want. After all, for someone who's married, you seem a lot more concerned with the welfare of Lucian Spark."

Her words sting. Last night floods my brain. She's right. He *is* married.

I move aside, leaving a wider gap between myself and Digory.

Ophelia's eyes dart between Gideon and Cypress like a predator's. "Tycho and Spark have each other's backs and will sabotage *our* chances while we're forced to fend for ourselves ... unless we band together and stop them. It's our only chance. *We* have the majority."

Gideon and Cypress glance at each other. They don't say a word, but I can already see the gears spinning in their eyes. She's getting to them.

The Trials have barely gotten underway and the paranoia's already poisoning everyone's minds.

Attention Recruits. At the end of the countdown, the first leg of the Trials shall commence.

On a screen on the far side of the carnage, a digital clock's already hacking away at the precious seconds before this nightmare gets underway.

One minute and thirty seconds ... twenty-nine seconds ... twenty-eight seconds ...

Your task is simple. You must proceed across the battle zone to the safety zone on the other side.

Across the way, a yellow beacon flashes in time with my ragged breaths.

Scattered throughout this containment area, random collaterals have been fitted with beacon bracelets that match the individual frequencies of the locator wristlets you all now wear.

I study the locator that's snug around my wrist. *Random collaterals?* What the hell does Slade mean by random col—?

A few feet ahead of me, just past the starting line, a glint of metal on the wrist of one of the writhing bodies catches my eye. My eyes dart through the field. From what I can see, they all are wearing beacon bracelets—the wounded, the sick, the dying...

The Establishment's random collaterals.

My own locator feels like it's cutting off the circulation in my hand.

If you come across one that's a match, a green signal will confirm it and you must transport that beacon to the safety zone on the other side.

In unison, our five wrists blink green.

If you come across a beacon that's not a match, you will receive a red signal and must continue your search.

Our wrists flash bright red before going dark again.

You are free to utilize any tools or equipment you find along the way to accomplish this goal, but we caution that you may encounter certain variables in your mission, such as taser mines, nerve scramblers, stun rifles, pain inducers...

Variables. Slade's sterile word for booby traps and who knows what else...

The object of this Search and Retrieve Trial is to collect your one matching beacon and transport it to the safety zone. You will commence the next Trial in the order you finish this one. The last Recruit to collect his

or her beacon must partake in the Culling and choose between his or her Incentives.

Incentives. Cole—and now Digory. I glance at him. He's as pale as stone. Even the tide in his sea-blue eyes has ebbed. His eyes meet mine and I look away. There's no question who I'd choose first. But despite everything that's happened between us, I can't even think of letting it get to that point. And I have to make sure Digory doesn't falter either, or Cole's as good as gone. Cassius has really linked our fates with his chains.

Good Luck, Recruits. Until we reconvene at the next launch point.

Slade's voice fades and the lights grow dim . . .

The starting siren blasts away.

TWENTY-THREE

Air rushes around me. Someone slams into my shoulder, knocking me across the starting line. My eyes saucer as I brace myself for the blast of the energy barrier. But the only impact is my face thudding against the hard earth. I look up in time to see Ophelia smirk before sprinting off into the fray.

I spit blood and spring to my feet, ignoring the spasms in my wobbly legs.

A hand grabs my shoulder.

I whirl into Digory's gaze. "You okay?" he asks.

I tear away from his grasp. "I'm *fine*."

Then I'm off, wading through a sea of bodies. I gag at the stench. The entire place reeks of blood, festering wounds, and death.

Clenching a palm over my nose and mouth, I squat over the first body I come across, a teenaged guy not more than a year or two younger than I am. His scraggly dark hair is matted to his ashen face. The whites of his eyes are visible through half-opened lids. The beacon's draped over the wrist of a bony hand, which is pressed against a gurgling wound in his abdomen as if trying to keep something from spilling out.

Shooing away the buzzing flies swarming over his lesion, I press my locator next to his beacon.

There's a harsh *buzz* and the locator's light turns the same color as his soaked shirt.

Not a match. What a horrible way to die, out here, alone in such filth.

His icy hand locks around my wrist. Bloodshot eyes spring open the rest of the way.

My heart nearly erupts through my gullet.

"*Please ...*" The word flows from his lips through a gout of blood. "*Help ... me ...*"

I pull my arm from his wrist and clasp his hand. "I'm *sorry*," I whisper.

Then we're torn apart. Cypress shoves me out of the way so hard that a bolt of pain jolts through my arm. Her dark hair's pasted wildly across her dirt-streaked face like poisoned veins.

One look at her eyes snuffs out my anger. Stark naked desperation, the kind bordering on crazy. She eyes the boy's tracker and grabs it with muddy hands that smell of rot. This isn't the first body she's come across.

The moment her locator connects with his bracelet, there's another harsh buzz and red flash.

She flings his hand down as if it's shocked her. Her engorged eyes turn on me. "Not *him* either."

Then she's bounding off, crouching over another victim.

The boy coughs up another mouthful of blood. "*Please*... don't leave me. I don't want to die... alone... "

The weight of what's at stake crushes the air from my lungs.

I can't help him.

Fog shrouds my brain, as if I'm in the throes of some terrible nightmare my mind's trying to filter so I won't break. This *can't* be real. I back away...

My eyes sweep the field. Everything looks fragmented. Digory hunches over a clump of tangled limbs about ten yards to my right. Lifting wrist after wrist. Holding his locator to them. Hands reach out to touch him back. He bows his head. Pity-soaked eyes. Mutters unintelligible words...

To my left, Ophelia digs through heaps. Flings aside body after body as if she can't figure out what to wear...

Only Gideon appears to be taking his time, strolling through the battle zone and occasionally stooping to check a beacon as if he were in a field searching for a particular flower to pick.

All around them, fireflies flit about, filling the air with their incessant buzzing even as they dot the landscape with bloody pinpricks of light...

Not fireflies—*beacons*. The thought burns through the mist clouding my head.

Then it's like my brain's launched into overdrive, careening forward until it synchs into real time. My breath comes in short, shallow bursts through my dry mouth. I squeeze slower breaths through my nostrils until the landscape stops spinning and the dizziness passes.

I sprint over the unnamed boy without even a glance back.

Beyond him lies a pale middle-aged woman, crumpled like a wad of paper.

The faces.

Don't look at their faces.

I grip the beacon, trying not to touch skin. But the hair on my body prickles when my little finger grazes icy flesh.

Buzz. Red light.

Letting go of her, I scurry through the human wreckage, dodging past Digory, skirting Gideon, leaping over a crouched Cypress, knocking into Ophelia, scavenging through body after body, groping through torn rib cages and steaming piles of entrails until I'm covered in gore and reek of the living dead myself.

But still I push on and on, gulping down the bile and vomit. A part of me dies with every body I desecrate. And through it all, the moans and wails sear into my brain.

I'll never stop hearing them until I fester in my own grave.

Soon, I've lost count of the running tab of bodies I'm keeping in my head. Why haven't I found anything yet? I risk a fleeting glance around at the others. They're all still searching, too. Could the Establishment be cruel enough to not have fitted any of the bodies with matching beacons?

Then a worse thought hits my brain, with the same

ferocity as the inner fist trying to beat its way out my chest. What if Cassius deliberately disabled just *my* locator? It wouldn't be the first time he's tampered with the Trials. After all, didn't he have Digory recruited and Desiree Morningside murdered just so I could take her place and provide him with two pawns to play his sick little game with?

I grab another wrist lying in the rubble. It's so small the beacon nearly slides off the bony hand.

A child's hand.

"It hurts," a tiny voice moans over and over again.

My eyes squeeze shut against the molten river about to burst free. I clamp my free hand against my ear, trying to muffle as much of the agony as I can. If I can't *see* them, they're not real.

Bleep.

The sound startles me.

I *finally* found one.

Scooping the child in my arms, I hug its head against me.

But when I look down, the tracker's still blinking red, sending a vibrating pulse burning into my chest.

I spin.

Digory's a few yards away, cradling a frail-looking woman in his arms as if she were a newborn.

"Don't worry, ma'am. You're going to be okay," he coos. The green lights of the flashing locator and beacon reflect on both their skin like the hushed lightning of a distant storm, illuminating their faces with a shared gratitude and relief.

Skeletal fingers clutch his collar. "My daughter ... *please* ... you have to find her ... "

"Let's get you out of here first."

Then he's scrambling off toward the safety zone with her.

My heart swells—then bursts with the realization of what Digory's heroism means to the four of us still struggling to make it through this.

A flash of green to my right blinds me, accompanied by a steady *bleeping* that matches the rhythm of the blood battering the arteries in my brain. For a second I'm disoriented.

Someone else found their beacon.

Obscured by a veil of smoke, Gideon's silhouette props the green-flashing arm of a stick-figured woman over his shoulder and stumbles with her through the battlefield, disappearing in the same direction that Digory took off in.

Two down and only three to go.

I hunch my head and bury my face against the small head nestled against me. Whatever I'm going to do it has to be done fast. "Please forgive me," I whisper into a tiny ear.

Bleep.

What the—?

Cypress's eyes lock with mine. Her locator and the kid's beacon are both flashing green. She tries to pry the child from my arms.

"*Don't* let Goslin have the girl, Spark!" Ophelia kicks a body out of her way and scrambles toward us, eyes flickering like wildfire. "If she takes her, we'll both be tied for *last* place."

My arms tighten around the faceless girl. She's right ...

Cypress tugs harder. "*Give* her to me." Her words are drowned out by the wailing child held hostage between us.

An invisible force slams Ophelia to the ground. "Ungh!" She doubles over, clutching her side.

It was a taser mine.

I lurch toward her, dragging Cypress and the child along with me. "Ophelia! You okay?"

Cypress's fingers dig into my arm. "There's *no* time."

Ophelia stirs, rising to rest on her hands and knees like a crouching beast. "We can *both* save our families, Spark. You hold Goslin here while I hide the girl."

She lurches to her feet and sprints closer. In that instant I know that if she reaches us, she'll stop at nothing to make sure Cypress doesn't rescue the child.

I can't bear the weight of any more blood. Even if I made it all the way through this, I'd never be able to look in Cole's eyes again.

I release my grip and the child slips into Cypress's arms. "Take her, and make sure she's tended to right away."

"Thanks," Cypress whispers.

"*What* are you doing?" Ophelia lunges at them.

I shove my body in front of Cypress and the girl. Ophelia rams into me, fingers raking my back like talons. Her bloody claws reach out and clamp onto the frail little shoulder.

The child screams.

Cypress's fingers dig into Ophelia's hand, ripping, pulling, but Ophelia won't let go. Her head plunges down and her teeth sink into Cypress's wrist.

"Ah!" Cypress's face contorts in agony.

With every ounce of strength I can muster, I try to pry Ophelia loose. I twist and lock my arms around her, but it's like trying to hug fire. Finally, I wrench her free. But her body bucks and kicks, jaws snapping like a rabid Canid, spraying me with a mixture of burning spittle and Cypress's blood, which is dripping from the bits of flesh lodged between her teeth.

Cypress's face is drained of color. Dark blood oozes from the missing chunk on her hand. As she whisks the child away, large dark eyes peer over her shoulder at me like shards of guilt impaling me where I stand.

Ophelia's arm squirms free of my hold, and she jams a thumb into my eye.

Blinding pain shoots through my socket. I swing her away from me, hurling her into the ground. I clutch a palm against my eye, half expecting to feel the molten gore of a shattered eyeball squeezing through my fingers. But the throbbing and blurred vision confirm there's still something there.

There's a flash of her boot. Then a searing pain in my groin. I curl up into a ball, knees pressed against my stomach. Tears stream from my eyes, seeping down my cheeks and between my lips. The salty taste mixes with the blood where my teeth have bitten into my upper lip.

She looms over me, a dark blur. "Guess we're about to find out who you love more, your brother or Tycho." She hunches down. "Personally," she whispers, "I'm counting on it being your brother. After all, he looks so sweet and adorable." Her smile is laced with blood-stained teeth. Then she takes off.

Adrenaline surges through me, mixed in a whirlpool of anger, desperation, and fear that propels me up. The months of intense training kick in. I tear after her, leaping over the bodies I've already rummaged through, dodging the taser mines, holding my breath as I pass through the clouds of smoke, avoiding the fire of the automatic stun rifles. Faster and faster. Everything's a blur.

Soon, I'm gaining on Ophelia. She's reached the far end of the battle zone and is digging through the last cache of victims, a tangled heap of arms and legs about ten yards away from the safety zone. When she glances up at me, I can see the beads of sweat trickling down her forehead.

Good. She's scared.

She'd *better* be.

I dash up to the opposite side of this miserable pile of humanity and start pulling out arm after arm, pressing my locator against them, ignoring the blood, the smell, the countless moans that rise upward and fill the air with a chorus of doom. Flashes of red and the crackling buzzers from the locators bombard us with light and sound, giving the entire scene the appearance of a human bonfire.

Despite the din, one small sound rings through my ears like a clap of thunder, accompanied by a flash of green lightning.

Bleep.

Ophelia's found her beacon before I have.

I can't feel my fingers as they fumble from one beacon

to the next, rewarded with one sharp buzz after another. I chance a look through the wailing mound. Ophelia's bathed in green strobes that fragment her face as if I'm flipping through hundreds of images of different people. Her eyes connect with mine, conveying one clear message:

I've beat you. Now you get to watch Cole or Digory die.

Something's wrong. Her triumphant expression scrunches into frustration. She tugs on the arm she's clutching, trying to pull it free of the writhing mound.

"No! Let go of me!" A girl's voice. Her wail pierces the air, a sobering reminder that these aren't just *things* we're digging through. I drop the wrist I'm holding and grab the next one, trying not to squeeze too hard in my panic.

Ignoring the screams, Ophelia continues to yank. But despite the sound of unsettling *squishes*, the girl won't budge. The thought of what she might be stuck in makes my stomach heave and I stifle a gag, reaching for the next beacon.

Ophelia cups the pale face. "Hush now." She runs her fingers through the girl's gore-matted blonde head.

But the moans continue.

A long sigh escapes Ophelia's lips. "You know, this whole thing might go a little easier if you just SHUT UP!" She grabs a fistful of hair and slams the girl's head down into a protruding leg, over and over until the cries degenerate into garbled whimpers.

Ophelia shakes her head. "Much better." She giggles. "*Now* I can concentrate."

A flash of green and a loud *bleep* nearly stop my heart mid-pump. I stare at the locator pulsing in my hand as if it's some strange artifact. Then it sinks in. I *found* it. I found my beacon.

I dare to stare at the face of my lifeline to Cole and Digory, a burly, middle-aged man covered in pustules who gazes at me through yellow-tinged eyes. He's wearing the gray uniform of a miner, with the name Martino stitched into the breast pocket.

"It's going to be okay, Martino," I lie to him through a forced smile.

His mouth opens. "M-my … w-wife … "

Dark green and brownish phlegm oozes from his mouth, choking off the rest of his words. My father's face flashes before me, but I allow that mental tunnel to collapse and seal off that painful memory.

"C'mon, I have to get you outta here!" Gripping both his arms, I heave with what little strength I have left. Inch by inch, his huge frame slides from the tangled mass until he's free and clear.

I wipe my brow and glance up to check Ophelia's progress. Her glee has turned to pure venom. She tugs on the girl, her teeth clenched, her face burning like a vibrant sunset. She's trembling from the effort. One of her feet is braced against some poor soul's face for leverage. Suddenly, the body gives and the girl slides out to her waist. Ophelia lets out a sound that's half sob, half laughter. Then she's pulling again.

My knees wobble as I haul the heavy man to his feet. He must outweigh me by at least a hundred pounds. Something in my lower back *pops*. "Uuuunh!" Electricity sizzles every nerve-ending. I inhale deep. Placing one of Martino's arms around my neck, I stagger against his weight, lumbering toward the safety zone.

In the distance, I can see someone waving.

Digory?

Not that much further to go. If I can just hold it together a little longer, I'll make it through this round and Cole and Digory will be safe.

"Don't worry," I rasp to the miner. "We're almost *there*."

He grumbles a reply that consists more of hot drool trickling onto my neck. I should be disgusted, but for some reason I'm elated. I'm going to get through this. And maybe this poor guy'll be able to rebuild some kind of life for himself after all this is done.

Despite the aches, the hammering in my chest, my starving lungs and dry mouth, I speed up.

Digory and Cypress are waiting. It's hard to tell, with my hair obstructing one eye and the still-throbbing blurriness in the other, but I think that's Gideon kneeling beside several figures lying prostrate on the ground.

"See?" I huff to my silent companion. "Just…a…little… further…"

I get no response. For a moment I'm afraid he's no longer with me, that I'm lugging around a mere shell of what was once a vital living being. My legs buckle from the dead weight. I stumble but somehow manage to stay on my feet, even though my pace slows to little more than a brisk walk.

Part of me is tempted to glance behind, check on Ophelia, but I don't dare risk one more second of delay.

I'm *almost* there…

Just across the finish line, Digory's eyes widen. I can't tell what his finger's pointing at.

A glint of light. I look down at a small metal disk camouflaged by weeds.

Digory's hands cup the sides of his mouth. "Lucian! Look out for the—

BLAM!

TWENTY-FOUR

Thousands of hot needles pierce my side. It's as if a giant invisible hand has batted me aside, tossing me at least five feet backward. The miner is wrenched free from my hold, and my tailbone smacks into the dirt with a *thud*. Another jolt rips up my spine. When I try to stand, I can't feel the difference between my right and left legs and I wobble, smacking back down on the hard earth. I try to brace myself with my right hand, but that same cross-wired sensation hits me and my left hand spasms instead. I topple over.

"Nerve scrambler!" Digory cries. "It's jumbled your neural pathways!" His voice sounds like it's coming from the bottom of a well. "The disorientation will pass in a few. Just breathe slowly. Focus on my voice … you can *do* this."

My eyes feel like driftwood, bobbing further and further into an endless horizon. Maybe if I just rest for a few minutes …

"Lucian!" Digory's voice echoes through the depths of my numbness, pulling me back up to the surface. "You *need* to hold it together. There isn't much time."

The urgency in his voice snaps me back. My eyes spring open. There's only one reason his voice would be tinged with fear.

Willing my mixed-up nerves to obey, I take a deep breath and force my head to twist so I can see behind me.

Ophelia's still a distance away. The poor survivor's still wedged a little less than halfway into the debris. Even if she pulled the girl out right now, there's no way Ophelia will be able to carry her and make it back before me.

But Ophelia's given up on trying to pull the girl free. Instead, using one hand, she's stretching out the wriggling girl's arm, the one wearing the beacon.

In her other hand, Ophelia clutches a mangled piece of metal debris that glints in the harsh artificial light. Even from here, I can see its rusted, jagged edges.

Ophelia raises the hand that's holding the makeshift tool high overhead—

"Help me! *Please*, help me!" the girl shrieks, over and over again until her cries are nothing but garbled noise that barely resembles anything human.

"*Don't* stop, keep moving," Digory urges.

But I can't tear my eyes away.

Darkness eclipses the whites of Ophelia's eyes. With a long, guttural wail, she plunges the makeshift blade across the girl's forearm.

I wince.

The screams die out.

The girl's lifeless body slumps over—all except for her right hand. Detached from the rest of her, the appendage is now a grisly stump, clutched by Ophelia and crying bloody tears onto the face of its former owner.

The blinking green of the beacon reflects off Ophelia's eyes and teeth, the only parts of her not covered in gore.

Our eyes meet.

She glares for an instant. Then she's dashing toward me, heading for the safety zone, waving the glistening shiv.

"C'mon, Martino! We gotta go!" Grabbing the miner, I pull us both to our feet and half-carry, half-drag him along.

"You got this, Lucian!" Digory's voice is like a balm to my aching muscles and spirit.

Despite the hammering in my chest and the pain in my starving lungs, I lunge forward.

Digory's holding his hand out just over the line and I reach for it—

Fire blasts into my leg. Digory's eyes bug. Then his fingers, which were barely an inch in front of me, are suddenly moving away. A blurry wind grazes my side. Then I crash to the ground, letting go of the miner's hands.

I feel dizzy, like I'm going to pass out. Was it another taser mine or neural scrambler, so close to the finish line?

My leg continues to burn. I have to get up before Ophelia—where is she? Is she still gaining? But there's no one behind me.

The source of the fire is a chunk of metal lodged in my left thigh.

Ophelia gazes at me from the other side of the finish line. She's giggling, dancing around triumphantly, taunting me with the amputated limb.

Digory shoves her aside. "*What did you do to him?*" he cries. He tries to step over the line but his locator flares bright yellow and his face contorts until he doubles over.

So they rigged the locators with pain inducers, for just such an attempt.

My heart thrashes my rib cage. I drop to my knees. I was so close.

And now Digory's going to die because of me.

"Lucian!" he calls. But his voice sounds like it's miles away instead of just a few feet. "How bad did she hurt you? Damn it! Answer me!"

I slump on my side. I can't bring myself to look at him any longer, afraid I won't be able to hold it together. Instead, I focus on my leg, watching the blood ooze from the edges of the metal but unable to feel a thing.

The thought penetrates my stupor. I grip the shank so hard it slices my fingers. Still I feel nothing. Taking a deep breath, I rip it out and fling it away. If only I could do the same to my heart.

A moan to my left. The miner. He's still alive. Maybe I could do one good thing and get him to safety before I end Digory's life with my choice.

I stumble toward Martino and grip his arms again. But I'm too weak. I close my eyes to get my bearings. Take your time. After all, there's no reason to rush anymore. And the longer I take to cross this line, the longer it'll be before I cross *that* line and give up what's left of my humanity forever.

I drag the miner a couple of more feet and drop. My pant leg is soaked. It reminds me of the wine Cassius spilled back in the Prefect's antechamber, back before… before I realized that the terrible infection had set into him.

My vision doubles. Two bloody legs instead of one. I try to focus. Maybe Ophelia did her job too efficiently and infection is already settling into me as well.

I don't think I can go on. They'll have to carry me across. I chuckle. Hope they don't mind me making my choice from a stretcher. My eyes feel weighted down. Maybe I'll feel better if I can just sleep for a few…

A shadow falls over me.

I look up. A dark shape is holding out a hand to me. Digory? How did he get past the pain sensors?

I open my eyes wider and let them adjust.

It's not Digory. It's Gideon.

How's that possible? Did I pass out without realizing it and wake up on the other side of the barrier? I look past him. Digory, Cypress, and Ophelia are still standing across the finish line with their rescued survivors lying behind them. But then that would mean—

I bolt up and allow Gideon to pull me to my feet. "You haven't gone across yet?" I ask.

He half smiles. "No. Not yet." He nods toward an old woman who's slumped a foot away from the line, her tracker blinking in harmony to his. "After *you*."

Adrenaline surges through me. I grab the miner once

again and start for the finish line. I can still *do* this. I freeze in my tracks and whirl to face Gideon. "*Why?*"

His pulls off his glasses and wipes his eyes. "I'm not sure."

As heartsick as I feel, I heave the miner across the line with me and he drops to the ground.

The audio system crackles to life with Slade's voice.

Gideon Warrick. You are the last Recruit to complete this Trial. Enter the safety zone and prepare for the Culling.

TWENTY-FIVE

Gideon crosses the finish line, carrying the old woman in his arms. He sets her down gently, his face a mask of eerie tenderness. "Sorry I took so long."

Her trembling finger traces his cheek. "Thank you, young man."

Ophelia glares at me and then at Gideon. "You could have *beat* him, Giddy. I expected more from you. I thought we understood each other. You really let me down."

He reaches out for her. "Ophelia—"

But she brushes his hand off and moves away to sulk.

"Lucian!" Digory has run over and gathered me into his arms. "Your leg." He turns. "Cypress! Gimme a hand!"

Cypress joins us. "Got 'im."

The two of them set me down. Cypress clears the tattered fabric from the wounded area on my leg while Digory fixes a strip of cloth he's torn from his own sleeve over it. "Don't you worry. You're going to be okay."

I smile. "Without a disinfectant or any meds I'm not so sure."

The lights in the battle zone dim.

Initiating whitewash procedure.

At Slade's command, a panel opens in the simulated sky. Hundreds of small, steam-powered spherical drones, no more than two feet in diameter, swoosh through the opening like angry hornets. They swarm across the battle zone over the remaining survivors, spewing them with a substance from stinger-like cylinders that jut from their surfaces.

Only their venom isn't some poisonous toxin. Whatever the substance makes contact with begins to sizzle and melt away.

Acid.

The entire chamber fills with the screams of people being melted alive.

Just over the line, a young woman holds out a hand, screaming for her life. A drone flies over and sprays her. She continues to shriek, even as her skin curls and peels and her face and body liquefy into bloody goo that congeals into a puddle and dissolves into nothingness. The lights in that sector go out completely.

There are a few stray screams, then nothing but deafening silence.

A new horror fills my thoughts. I scramble to my feet. "Slade!" I point to the huddle of suffering humanity we've rescued. "These people need medical attention right away!"

BLAM! BLAM! Ratatatatatatatatatatatat!

Instead of more acid, the drones spit gunfire all around us.

"Take cover!" Digory pushes Cypress and me to the ground and shields us with his body.

I can't breathe. The air's filled with thick acrid smoke and the cloying stench of spent weapon casings.

Sterilization is complete.

None of them ever had a chance. Despite the burning in my leg, I crawl out from under Digory. Where the survivors once squirmed, there's nothing left but a pool of crimson soup. Chunks of body parts riddled with ragged punctures bob on the liquid surface. Smoky tendrils of scorched flesh and fresh blood waft into my nostrils, violating them. I choke on the stink.

"Is anyone wounded?" Digory cries behind me.

"We're still in one piece," Gideon answers in a voice that's quiet, hollow. He tries to help Ophelia to her feet but she pushes him away, leaving him standing there with his eyes glued to the red spattered spot that a moment ago was the old woman he rescued.

Cypress brushes against me, staring at what's left of the little girl she rescued. Tears forge a path through the grime coating her cheeks. "She was about my... my *children's* age."

A low rumble drowns out the sound of my breathing. A platform rises out of the ground, containing a darkened glass enclosure the size of a small room. From the rock just beneath it, a series of metal steps slides out.

Recruit Warrick. Approach the podium.

If *my* heart's pumping a million beats per second and I can barely catch my breath, I can't even imagine what Gideon must be feeling when he hears Slade's latest orders.

He stares at the dais. The nub of his throat bobs up and down. Then he moves forward.

As he walks past all of us, Digory squeezes his shoulder. "Stay strong."

When my eyes meet Gideon's, I'm surprised by a fleeting glimpse of satisfaction there. Then it's gone and he's past us, climbing the stairs, his gait as delicate and measured as if he's maneuvering through a mine field.

The moment he's standing in front of the dark chamber, the lights inside it come on, revealing Mr. and Mrs. Warrick.

My breath lodges in my throat.

Stripped of their formalwear, they're clad in filthy rags that dangle from their bodies, barely concealing their dignity. Mrs. Warrick's hair hangs in knotted disarray about her scrawny shoulders, while one of Mr. Warrick's eyes is practically sealed shut and ringed in a swollen patch of dark purple. Bloody slush fills my veins at the thought of what all the other Incentives must be going through, imprisoned in Purgatorium.

But even more disturbing than the Warricks' physical appearance is the fact that they're both sitting on metal chairs on either side of the chamber, strapped down by their wrists and ankles. Just to the side of each of their necks, long metal blades curve toward them like sickles, casting blinding flashes of light.

Recruit Warrick. You have sixty seconds to make your selection.

At Slade's announcement, the digital countdown display above the podium begins hacking away at the seconds.

Mr. Warrick just sits there, his wide eyes glazed.

In contrast, Mrs. Warrick, despite her frail appearance, struggles with her bonds. "Gideon, honey. Please! I'm your *mother*! You have to get me out of here!" Her face contorts into a mask of terror.

Gideon's face frightens me more than anything else I've seen. Tears are flowing like rivers down his cheeks. But his eyes gleam with a twisted fire.

And he's *smiling*.

"How does it *feel*, huh?" His voice is a bitter frost. "Are you scared, *Mommy*? Does it feel like you're all alone and you're never going to live to see the sunrise? The light?"

Mrs. Warrick's scream pierces through me.

"Gideon, *please*," Mr. Warrick begs, his voice drained of any strength it might have once had. "Don't do this to your moth—"

"Shut up!" Gideon spits. "You're always covering for her! How could you *not* know what she was doing to me all those years? You saw the marks, heard the screams. You did nothing. *Nothing*! You're a coward, always have been."

"I was always a good mother to you, Gideon!" Mrs. Warrick wails. "Anything I did was for your own good!"

Gideon pounds the glass. "What kind of a mother beats her child and locks him in the dark for days on end just for crying because he was *hungry*?"

Anger flashes on her face. "You're *weak*. Always have been. And ungrateful. I was trying to toughen you up. It's a harsh world—"

"Harsh world?" He flings the words back at her. "It's not supposed to be a harsh world at home, with the people that are *supposed* to love you." He rips his shirt up and turns, exposing his back to her. "I *can't* forget. I'll *never* forget." He slumps against the enclosure, sobbing. "I hope you're terrified, like I was."

Make your selection.

Gideon raises his head to the sky. "I choose *her*, Sgt. Slade. My *mother*."

The blade springs forward and arcs into Mrs. Warrick's throat, slicing clean through to the other side with a loud *thwack*. For a second she just sits there, her eyes looking confused. Then a red line fades in around her neck and her head topples off, rolling down her body and across the ground until it stops, pressed against the glass at Gideon's feet.

Mr. Warrick's horrified eyes take in the sight of his wife's body, still sitting in the chair, gouts of blood pumping from the severed neck. A deep moan stretches out from his throat and turns into garbled sobs.

"I just wanted to scare her, that's all," Gideon says with an eerie calm. He slides down the panel and traces the glass as if he's trying to caress his mother's face. "How does it feel, Mom? Huh? How does it *feel*? Tell me. How does it *feel*? How does it—?"

He repeats the mantra over and over again, rocking back and forth.

This Trial is now complete. Recruits will now proceed to the next station where you will have a rest period before receiving instructions and proceeding to your next Trial.

Slade's voice fades into nothingness.

None of us move. If the others are feeling anything like I am, they're too stunned to even speak.

A swarm of drones buzzes overhead and hovers over us, their glistening pincers providing the motivation we're lacking. Slowly, we slog single file toward our next horror.

All except one of us.

I look back.

Gideon's still rocking and chanting, even after the chamber's lights have dimmed and faded to black.

TWENTY-SIX

Everything's dark. For a terrified second, I feel like I'm back in the Fleshers' Lair...

"Lucian. Can you hear me? Are you okay?"

Digory's voice buffers the throbbing in my head. *Thwack! Thwack! Thwack!* Each pound reminds me of that sharp blade lopping off Mrs. Warrick's head, over and over again, until it's not just *her* head, but Ophelia's, Cypress's, Gideon's.

Digory's...

"What?" My eyes snap open, burning despite the chill rattling my bones. I try and sit up and I'm overcome with lightheadedness. A firm hand on my back steadies me until I'm able to sit upright on my own.

"It's about time you woke up, sleepyhead." Even though Digory tries to smile, a translucent veil of fear clings to his face. Tiny red veins mar the whites of his eyes.

It doesn't look like he's gotten any sleep. Has he been

awake since we reached this holding station? Watching over me?

He presses his large palm against my forehead. It feels cool, soothing against the heat baking my face. "Fever's worse. You're burning up." His lips curl in. The muscles in his jaw flex.

"H-how l-long have I-I b-been out?" I force the words through chattering teeth.

"It's been about five hours, I guess. Hard to say without a real sky." He glances at the sterile artificial light shining down into the holding station.

I glance around the cramped, concrete dome that reminds me of a beehive. Except in this case it's what's outside that can sting you dead.

Ophelia is pressed against one of the curved walls, doing some kind of stretching exercise. When she sees me, her eyes narrow and a long breath hisses out, as if she's disappointed I've regained consciousness.

It's a good thing the rules say we aren't allowed to kill each other, otherwise I'd never get any rest.

On the opposite wall, Cypress sits cross-legged on the floor next to Gideon. She's murmuring to him, stroking his hair.

Everything after that first Trial is a blur. All I remember is stumbling after the others through the dark metal catacombs of the Skein, trying to escape the horrors of the battle zone.

"You collapsed just after we got here," Digory says. "I figured it was just exhaustion and stress after..." He drops his gaze. "After what happened." His eyes meet mine again. "But I saw you trembling, and when I came over to check on you, I realized it was a fever." His fingers graze the crimson-stained bandage around my thigh. "How does it feel?"

I inhale sharply. Even his light touch sends electric pain rippling through me. "I'm … okay … just a little sore … " Another chill rattles me. I press a fist against my lips to stifle a cough. Now it's my turn to look away from him.

He lifts a corner of the bandage, careful not to touch the swollen skin beneath it. "I tried dressing it as best I could, but there aren't any medical supplies here." He tucks the bandage back. "Actually, there's not much of anything here except a hard floor. No water, no food, not even a damn blanket. How do they expect us to keep going without any provisions?" He yells the last above him, for the benefit of Slade and whoever else is probably eavesdropping. When he looks at me again, his face is flushed, as if he, too, is suffering with fever. "I figured I'd try and keep you warm as best I could."

He pulls the zipper of his jumpsuit up the rest of the way, hiding his bare chest.

All this time he's been lying next to me, sharing his body heat to keep me warm.

Another shiver ripples through me.

"Anyway." He stands. "You need to conserve your strength. I tried to let you get as much rest as possible, but you slept through the Sarge's latest warning announcement." His lips form a thin rigid line. "They're about to cart us off to the next Trial, in the order we finished the last one."

I nod. "Which means you're first."

"Yes." He looks disappointed, despite the advantage.

"Did they say what this next Trial's all about?"

He shakes his head.

The speaker system crackles to life.

"Looks like we're about to find out," he says.

Attention Recruits.

We all gaze above us as if we're trying to pinpoint Slade's whereabouts.

One by one you will pass through the barrier on the other end of this pavilion in the order you completed your first Trial. The goal of your next mission is to simply make your way through a labyrinth until you find the exit.

"Sounds easy enough," Digory grunts. He smiles and squeezes my hand.

Along the way you will find supplies that will aid you through the next Trials. These include food, medicines, tools, and weapons.

I squeeze his fingers. "Guess your speech made an impression after all." My hollow laughter becomes a raspy cough. Digory pats me on the back until it subsides, his eyes worried slits.

You are urged to appropriate as many of these provisions as you can carry, as they will not be made available at any other time and are vital to your continued participation in the Trials.

Digory shoots me a nervous look. "Sounds *too* simple."

But you are cautioned to be as efficient as possible,

balancing your needs with your speed. The locator wristlets you are all still wearing have now been programmed to act as chronometers, monitoring and timing your progress. You will only have fifteen minutes to navigate the labyrinth.

I study my now-flashing wristband.

00:15:00

The Recruit who takes the longest to make it all the way through shall be the next to participate in the Culling. Anyone that does not make it out at all will be immediately shelved, along with their Incentives.

"There's your catch." I sigh.

Recruit Tycho. Prepare to depart for your next Trial in one minute.

He kneels down beside me. "I *can't* go and leave you like this." His head turns toward the others, who seem to be oblivious to us, caught up in their own anxiety no doubt. He nudges his chin toward Ophelia, who's now doing push-ups. "I'm sure *she'd* switch places with me if I can get them to allow it—"

"No." Ignoring the throbbing in my head and leg and the tremors in my muscles, I push myself up, teetering to my feet.

Digory is at my side in an instant, providing me a shoulder to lean on.

I grip him only long enough to steady myself, then let go. "You *have* to go. We both need each other to make it through this. If either one of us comes in last and is forced to choose … " The words hang above us like a threatening storm cloud. "Besides." I swallow the bitterness scorching my throat. "You have someone that's depending on you, and he should be your first priority, not me."

"Lucian…about that…" His eyes fidget and shift away. "You're a priority to me, too…"

Recruit Tycho. Your departure will commence in thirty seconds.

I fight waves of dizziness and nausea. "Looks like you're up."

Our eyes lock.

Digory's are flooded with concern. "I'll be waiting for you on the other end, Lucian. *Please*, be careful." He reaches out and takes both my hands in his. "You just get through as quickly as possible. I'll try and grab enough supplies for both of us."

"Good luck, Digory." I give him a final squeeze and let go.

He lowers his head and turns, walking toward the entrance and pausing in front of the crackling energy barrier. He turns and stares at me again. And this time his eyes are tinged with something else.

Fear.

The sizzling of the field dissipates.

Recruit Tycho. Proceed into the labyrinth and commence your Trial.

He holds my gaze just a moment longer. Then he's gone.

"Don't worry."

Ophelia's voice sends a different type of chill through me.

I whip around, and then have to close my eyes for a few seconds to ward off the dizziness.

She giggles. "You two are *so* cute together." Then she cups a hand around the side of her mouth and whispers, "It should be really interesting to see what happens when the both of you are in a dead heat against *each other*."

I ride out another wave of tremors. "Too bad you won't be around to see it."

Her eyes slither up and down my body. "You're such a big kidder, sweetie." Her lips bow into a pout. "How's that fever? You should really get more rest." She chuckles like it's the funniest thing she's ever heard, then goes back to her calisthenics as if I don't exist anymore.

I limp over to the other side of the dome, where Cypress and Gideon remain huddled.

She's stroking his hair. But he's stone-faced, like he's somewhere far away.

"How's he doing?" I ask her.

"How do you think?"

I crouch down and almost topple over. "I can't even imagine."

"Soon the rest of us won't have to *imagine* anything. It's only a matter of time before we each get our shot." She hugs Gideon close, resting his head against her and rocking him. "You have to be strong."

I can't help but wonder if her words are meant to console not just Gideon.

A feeling of being powerless spreads through me quicker than the infection is spreading through my blood, eating away at what little hope I have left. The dizziness shrouds my brain. I sag.

I don't think I'm going to make it.

Recruit Goslin. Prepare to commence your next Trial in one minute.

"Don't worry, Goslin," Ophelia calls. "I'll be right behind you." Her snickers cut like a knife.

Cypress ignores her. Instead, she kisses Gideon on the forehead and strokes his face with such tenderness that my heart aches.

Then her eyes search out mine. "Can you stay with him until it's your time? I don't think he should be alone."

"You really care about him."

Her lips curve into a smile laced with bitterness. She gently detaches from him. Leaning on one another, we both stand up.

"*Even if* we were away from all this, there wouldn't be a chance for us," she says. "Not now. Not ever."

I know what she's feeling because it hits me like a taser blast. None of us will ever see each other again, after this is all over.

Cypress throws her arms around me, her cheek cool against my burning one. "Don't let it be over without telling Digory how you really feel, or you'll always be sorry," she whispers.

Recruit Goslin. You will now commence your second Trial.

Cypress squeezes me one last time, then approaches the barrier and disappears through it just like Digory did.

I'm left standing there, her last words swirling through my pounding brain.

I'm not sure if it's the fever or all the emotions ricocheting through my mind, but I lose track of how much time passes before Slade's next announcement blares through the pavilion.

Recruit Juniper. Proceed into the labyrinth to commence your Trial.

Ophelia shoves past me, practically knocking me to the floor, and disappears through the barrier without a word.

Three down.

The acid rips through me.

It's my turn next.

"Cypress is right, Lucian."

Gideon's voice startles me.

When I turn he's looking right at me, not through me as before. "You don't want whatever time you have left spent in regret." He buries his forehead in his palms.

"Gideon." Despite the sickness ensnaring me, just hearing his voice—seeing him responsive—is a boost to my spirit. I hobble over to him and squat down despite the searing pain, and pry his hands from his face. "If you could hear us, why didn't you say—"

"I couldn't get too close. You *have* to understand." Desperation soaks Gideon's bloodshot eyes. "To Cypress, I mean. To *anyone* really..." His eyes turn glassy again. "I'm really evil, aren't I?"

My body burns hotter. "Gideon, listen to me. The Establishment... they forced you to do something—"

"They didn't force me to *enjoy* it." The words burst from his quivering lips. "They just gave me the opportunity to do something I've dreamed of ever since I can remember. That's probably why I was recruited—why we were *all* recruited."

"What do you mean?"

His eyes bore deep into me. "We all have it inside us. *The darkness*." He glazes away again.

Recruit Spark. Proceed into the labyrinth to commence your second Trial.

I slowly back away and enter the maze.

TWENTY-SEVEN

The darkness is almost impenetrable. It's like I'm standing in the vastness of space but every star in this false horizon is dead, its light completely snuffed out.

I squint, in the blue glow cast by the chronometer, which feels like it's cutting off the circulation in my wrist.

00:13:15

How can almost two minutes have gone by already? I need to get moving.

I take a tentative, step, then another, and another, until I'm teetering along like a sleepwalker, guided by the gradual adjustment of my burning eyes and the dim light of my timepiece. I can only make out shapes a couple of feet ahead of me, but that's a start at least.

Where are Digory, Cypress, and Ophelia? Can they be so far ahead of me that I haven't seen or heard a trace of them? What if they've already made it to the exit with their supplies in tow?

My pulse careens through my ears.

Even if the others are way ahead of me, Gideon must still be behind me.

Holding out my hand, I graze cold, smooth steel. A wall. Pausing a second, I steady myself against the partition and realize that a row of shelves is facing me. Small pouches are stacked on each shelf. I cast the glow of my timer on the writing on the nearest one.

Penicillin.

I recognize that name. It's one of the medicines we learned about during our med training. Some kind of miracle drug. It occurs to me that it might slow down the infection ravaging me long enough to provide Cole with the one miracle he so desperately needs.

I reach out a shaking hand, but the medicine shrinks away from me.

It feels like I'm falling backward and I tense. It's not the fever or my imagination—the wall's shifting, as is the entire corridor, reconfiguring into an entirely new pattern.

Damn it!

I should have grabbed the medicine while I had the chance. Now it's gone, and once again I face darkness. That's why I haven't seen any of the others. They must be keeping us separated on purpose, shifting this labyrinth every time we get too close, just in case we decide to work together. But besides Digory and me, who else would really go out of their way for each other at this point? Ophelia and Gideon? I can't see it, especially given her anger at him for letting me beat him in that last trial. The Establishment must have another reason for wanting to keep us isolated from each other. And as unsettling as that thought is, I don't have time to ponder it. The next time I come across supplies, I can't hesitate for an instant.

If there *is* a next time.

I check the chronometer again.

00:11:33

Bracing myself against the walls, I push farther along this new corridor, twisting and turning through passage after passage. Even if Digory succeeds in finding enough supplies for both of us, the one thing I need to find right now is a source of illumination, or else I'm never going to get out of here.

Along the way, I stumble across a few stray packs of ration bars. I shove them into my pockets, along with a canteen filled with cold water and a switchblade. I flick the switchblade open, and without thinking I run my fingers over the serrated edge, drawing blood. I wince.

Snapping the blade shut, I tuck it in my belt.

Faster and faster I move, my fingers leaving a trail of blood and cold sweat along the passageways. The farther I go, the more I have to rely on supporting myself against the walls to remain upright. If I'd only taken that medicine.

I stagger around another corner and come to a dead end.

There's a chest propped against the wall. I lurch toward it and fumble with the metal latch, but it's locked. Then the floor vibrates, and once again the walls shift, but not before I grab the chest and drag it to me.

The dead end's gone, replaced by yawning blackness.

That sound. Something's shuffling out of the darkness, headed my way.

I check the watch.

00:09:47

I tug at the latch a couple of times, but it won't budge, and it slips through my already slick fingers.

The pocket knife.

I rip it free, but it my haste it clatters to the floor. I fall to all fours, my hands sweeping over the cold tiles ...

The sound comes again.

I whip my head around, my eyes trying in vain to penetrate the murk.

Something's sliding along the tiles. It's like something heavy being dragged across the floor ... *drag and stop ... drag and stop ...*

It's the fever. I'm delirious ... there's nothing there ... *nothing ...*

A new sound weaves in and out ... wheezing ... as if something's struggling, out of the depths, for air ...

My heart's a battering ram trying to breach the walls of my chest. One of my fingertips brushes against icy steel. I grab the knife and plunge it toward the trunk. It misses the lock, instead digging into the lid. I wrench it free.

The sounds oozing out of the gloom are louder now, and I can't keep denying they're real.

"Lucky..." The sound of my name carried on a labored rasp causes every hair on my body to petrify. Whatever's in here is coming for *me*.

I have to get the lock open before whatever it is reaches me...

I plunge the switchblade into the lock.

Snap!

The lock breaks away and hits the floor with a loud *clank*.

Tucking the knife back into my belt, I dig my fingernails into the thick groove between the lid and trunk, prying it apart and yanking the cover open. I can just make out about half a dozen shiny flashlights.

Stuffing one into my pocket, I whirl, brandishing the other one ahead of me like a weapon. My sweaty finger finds the power button and I press down.

Nothing happens.

"*Lucky... why...?*"

The voice sounds like it's just a few feet away...

I bang the flashlight against my leg to rattle the batteries, realizing an instant too late that it's my wounded side. Pain sears through me. I nearly double over. A blast like the sun itself blinds me with hot light, momentarily making me forget about the pain.

"*Why, Lucky? Why...?*"

The wail's so close, ringing through my ears as if its source's lips are about to touch my earlobes...

My body bolts fully erect. I shine the light ahead of me...
And gasp.
It's Mrs. Bledsoe.

TWENTY-EIGHT

It can't be—I saw her ashes.

Unless ... unless Cassius lied to me. That *has* to be it, because she's standing right here looking at me, her eyes muddy puddles of sadness and accusation. Maybe it's just my distorted senses, wracked by fever, but her skin, though pale as snow, radiates a light of its own, shimmering against the darkness beyond her.

My veins pump joy into my sagging heart, causing it to swell. "You're alive." I move toward her, arms opened wide.

She opens her mouth and coughs. A torrent of blood gushes from it, soaking the dirty smock she's wearing, spilling down her arms, her legs, dripping off her fingers.

I freeze. No one who's lost that much blood can still be standing.

It must be a trick. Some kind of illusion engineered by Cassius to torment me.

But it looks *so* real.

Maybe she *is* dead. And I've finally lost my mind.

The scarlet stream pouring out her cracked lips thins and dissipates. "How could you do this to me, Lucky," she croaks. "How could you let them kill me after everything I've done for you?" Her voice sounds disjointed, as if she's pulling the words from her mind at random and assembling them like a puzzle.

I back away. "I'm so sorry, Mrs. Bledsoe. I never meant for you to get hurt. I *love* you." A tide of pain crashes through me, the worst kind, because no bandage, no antibiotic, no medicine ever invented can ever heal it.

Another chill sweeps my body. I feel like I'm burning up. I squeeze my eyes against the throbbing in my head.

When I open them again, Mrs. Bledsoe seems to flicker like a breeze blowing through a candle, and then she's steady again. Her eyes bore right through me as if I don't exist. "You're a *murderer*, Lucky." Her mouth twists into a sneer that's unlike anything I've ever seen on her face since I've known her. "And you need to be punished."

"Mrs. Bledsoe, please . . ." I almost trip over the chest of flashlights as I continue to retreat from her. My chest heaves with shallow, rapid-fire breaths.

Mrs. Bledsoe shambles toward me.

Drag. Squish. Drag. Squish . . .

She opens her arms wide and smiles, her teeth caked with goops of bloody phlegm. I cringe, expecting to feel the heat of her rotting breath sear my nostrils. But all I can sniff is a cold, cloying antiseptic stench that's suffocating me.

"Don't be afraid, Lucky," she caws through a mouthful of bile. "*Your* pain won't last as long as mine."

She reaches for me—

I stumble backward. "I didn't mean for you to get hurt. It's not my fault. *Please…*"

Drag. Squish. Drag. Squish…

"*Leave. Me. Alone.*" I whirl to get away from her.

There's someone standing at the far end of the corridor, facing me.

I cast a beam of light in that direction, and even though I can't make out a face, I can make out a form. A familiar form. The form of a little boy.

"Cole?" The name quavers in the air. My heart swells. Can it really be?

The figure doesn't respond. Then it darts around the corner.

The aching of my entire being propels my wobbling legs after him. "Cole! Is that you? Don't be afraid! It's *me!*"

"*You can't outrun your past,*" Mrs. Bledsoe's voice yelps after me.

I'm sprinting now, the beam from my flashlight zigzagging ahead of me, my pounding heartbeat trying to drown out my panting breaths. I hug the walls for support against the dizziness that throws me off balance as I chase Cole down winding corridors, darting left, banking right, ignoring any number of supplies along the way, ignoring the shuffling and dragging of Mrs. Bledsoe nipping at my heels. The only thing that matters is Cole. I've got to find him. Make him understand that I didn't leave him... that it's not my fault... that without him, there's nothing left to live for...

"Cole! Wait! Why are you afraid of me?" I rasp the words in between the painful breaths that I squeeze from my lungs. My eyes blur with wet stings, making the pathway ahead a dizzying array of streaking light and swooshing movement spiraling out of control.

Careening around another corner, I almost crash into the figure. He's standing just a few feet away, on a ledge, with nothing but gray sky ahead of him. I brace against the wall to break my momentum so we both don't go over the edge—gasping for air, burning with fever, exhausted. But despite this, I feel better than I have in months. Cool relief douses the fire of my sickness.

It's finally over. I found him at last.

His back is still toward me, but I recognize his shock of fine hair, glistening almost like a halo, the same as Mrs. Bledsoe's skin. It must be the fever distorting my vision. Cole is dressed in the same baggy clothes he was wearing the day I got recruited, right down to the scuffed brown shoe with the tattered laces. They never even got him a change of clothes, after all this time? He's clutching something in his hand. Weathered parchment pages. It's the story of the Lady. I recognize the missing corner on the page. But Cassius torched those pages right in front of our eyes...

Am I so far gone that my memories are now haunting me, intermingling with my reality?

I push the inconsistencies from my head, aching to wrap

my little brother in my arms once again, tell him he's safe at last.

I swallow a sob. "Cole. It's okay, buddy. I'm here." All it takes is just a few steps to finally bridge the once enormous gap that separated us. I reach for his shoulder—

Without uttering a word or even looking at me, he steps off the ledge and plummets away...

"No!" I leap forward even as my heart leaps into my throat, jamming there. My belly smacks the hard floor, knocking the wind from me. I slide the rest of the way, until my torso's hanging over the edge. "Cole!" My eyes search the bleak landscape far below. It's lined with jagged spikes, jutting upward like a gigantic pincushion. My heartbreak turns to confusion.

Where *is* he? His body should be lying there, impaled like one of those beautiful butterflies in one of the science labs at the Instructional Facility.

But there's no trace of him. He's gone, as if he never existed.

Did he ever really?

I can't hold back the sobs any longer. "Please don't go..."

Drag. Squish. Drag. Squish.

"You can't save him," Mrs. Bledsoe's voice rasps behind me.

I'm too numb to be startled.

"And you can't save yourself," she adds. "Just let go, son. Join him. It'll be over a lot quicker than it was for me." Her voice crackles like live wires in my ears. "You're running out of time. Make your choice."

Choice. That's what this whole Recruitment's been about.

I edge a little closer to the brink.

Maybe she's right.

And though I'm not even sure I really *saw* Cole, there was a time I wouldn't have hesitated to follow him into the void. But this is bigger than just us now. I finally understand what Digory had tried to tell me when we met. I'm not really saving Cole if I'm condemning him to live in a world that allows these things to happen—encourages them to happen.

I actually don't really have a choice at all.

The empty vessel of my body is suddenly overflowing with a sense of purpose, even more so than when my face flashed on the jumbotrons on Recruitment Day. I have to keep going not only so I can save my own little brother, but so that no one else will ever have to save anyone they love—their sisters, mothers, fathers, wives, husbands, friends—*anyone*—

Digory's face flashes in my mind's eye.

I pull away from the ledge and climb to my feet.

Cassius and his techs have been preying on my fear and guilt. None of this is real. Not Cole. Not Mrs. Bledsoe.

Taking a deep breath, I turn to face my accuser.

Mrs. Bledsoe continues to stare at me with blank eyes, an occasional trickle of blood oozing from her lips. It's as though she's hovering rather than standing.

"I'm going to make you pay for what happened to me,"

she whispers. She staggers forward, groping for me. But I'm no longer afraid and walk right up to her. I take a deep breath as her gnarled hands ripple like water, passing right through me.

Once I'm past her, I whip my flashlight to the corner of the ceiling. There, on a narrow track, I glimpse a tell-tale pinprick of yellow light beaming down.

The shimmering halos. The static. The truncated speech. It wasn't the byproduct of infection spreading within me, it was holograms. Just like a part of me suspected from the beginning.

I almost laugh aloud. I guess I passed their test by deciding not to off myself.

Mrs. Bledsoe—the projection *masquerading* as her—turns and smiles again. "It doesn't matter. You're too late... son. You'll never find your way back now."

Mrs. Bledsoe flickers and disappears, just like Cole did.

My eyes dart to my chronometer.

00:01:48

Less than two minutes to go.

The holograms were all a trick to derail me from the exit, and I was stupid enough to fall for it.

But they were triggered when I found that one corridor—which probably means it leads to the exit. How can I trace my way back again, with such little time left?

My flashlight illuminates the bloody handprints I left on the walls.

I dash back the way I came, whipping my light back and forth until I find the next crimson marker, and the next, speeding my way back down twisting hallways and sharp corners, allowing my own blood to guide me toward salvation.

I risk a glance at my watch.

00:00:59

A couple of times I have to double back when I miss a print or it's too faded to see clearly. My heart's beating so fast it feels like it's going to rupture. And the intermittently shifting walls aren't helping matters.

I lurch around the next bend. This is it! I recognize this corridor. It's the same one where the image of Mrs. Bledsoe first appeared. It *has* to be the way out.

The walls start to shift again . . .

Springing across the remaining few feet, I smash against the floor and slide the rest of the way, through a gap in the wall, just as a buzzer goes off and the wall slides shut behind me.

I grab my wrist.

00:00:00

Looks like I made it.

I collapse against one of the dark glass walls of a small, octagonal-shaped enclosure. I'm gasping for breath. It almost feels like there isn't any air in the room. My legs splay out in front of me on the hard surface. The glass around me remains opaque. I tense for the inevitable announcement from Slade, but none comes. My pulse twitches in my wrists.

I shove my face into my palms. How am I going to keep going now? Even if somehow I made it through this Trial, I won't make it past the next.

My body curls into itself like coiled twine.

Then I just lie there, eyes closed … and wait, wondering if I'll live to see Cole and Digory again.

Attention Recruits!

Slade's voice blasts through the loudspeakers and jolts my eyes open.

How long was I out?

We are pleased to announce that all five of you have made it through the labyrinth. The time has come to reveal your rankings.

TWENTY-NINE

The screens that have been obscuring the glass of my prison rise with a *whir*. I squint against a blast of light and raise my hand against it. Despite the cramps in my stomach, I steady myself against the wall and slide upward until I'm standing. When my eyes adjust I see Digory and the others surrounding me, in identical chambers.

A rush of relief surges through me.

I press my face against the glass on the side facing Digory, rubbing the pane to get his attention. But he's staring straight ahead, not noticing me. His face is sullen, the blue in his eyes so drained they look almost gray. His upper teeth grind his lower lip. Every few seconds a ripple goes through the hard lines of his jaw.

All around me, his expression is mirrored on the faces of the others. Cypress, who's in the chamber on the other side of me, chews her hair, pacing back and forth, mumbling words only she can hear. Gideon cowers in the chamber to her right; his glasses magnify his glazed eyes, which resemble hollow eggshells. To *his* right, and directly across from me, Ophelia's face is pressed against the glass just like mine, her eyes brimming with fear instead of confidence, as if she's a reflection of what I'm feeling inside.

They all look like old shoes worn well past their prime, having spent years tramping through rough terrain, now whittled down to thin soles. And that's how I must look to them. I think about the holograms of Mrs. Bledsoe and Cole, and can't help wonder what nightmares the other Recruits faced in the labyrinth.

Digory's eyes finally meet mine. *Are you okay?* he mouths.

I nod despite everything, drawing strength from his gaze. *Are you?* I mouth back.

I am now, he says silently.

His lips curve into a sad smile and he presses his hand against the glass, just on the opposite side of mine. I imagine the barrier that separates us isn't there, and I can almost feel the warmth of his skin. For a moment, I'm not alone anymore, and things are a little better.

The whine of motors and grinding gears shatters that illusion into a million pieces.

It feels like someone has poured ice down my back. Not able to stop myself, I turn in the direction of that relentless noise.

Rising from the platform in between all of our chambers is a dark rectangular enclosure—just like the one that housed Gideon's parents.

My rib cage squeezes tight against my organs, crushing them.

Is Cole in there now? Soon to be joined by Digory?

You all did exceptionally well in a Trial designed to test your strength of character and resolve, but in the end, one of you did not prove yourself as capable as the others.

Our glances ricochet around the ring, alternating between curiosity, nervousness, and outright fear, as if we're caged animals. We *are*. And one of us is about to pay a terrible price for his or her failure.

SLAM!

The box-like chamber completes its ascension and locks into place with a piercing screech of metal, which may as well be the thoughts screaming inside my head.

The lights of our paddocks dim, the contrast drawing more attention to the brightly lit rectangle, which looms like a dark crypt. I chew on my tongue, tasting blood. My fingers are a blur as they thrum the glass in front of me with the speed of a woodpecker's bill.

What's taking so long? Why are they prolonging this agony?

Digory and I lock eyes. His jaw clenches. He can't pretend for my benefit any longer. He knows if he's failed he'll be forced to choose my death, destroying Cole in the process—just like my failure will mean the same for him and his husband.

Gideon's just standing there, eyes vacant. In his state, he

must be the loser. I hate myself for the moment of relief that I feel.

The speakers crackle with static.

Your rankings, from best to worst, are as follows:

My throat goes dry.

In first place … Recruit Goslin.

Cypress practically collapses against the glass of her pen. Her body heaves, partly with laughter, partly with a sob.

In second place … Recruit Warrick.

Gideon? But he's barely responsive. How … ?

He remains motionless, without so much as a blink. Maybe his tragedy has actually made him a stronger competitor. Someone who isn't burdened with fear or guilt.

In third place … Recruit Spark.

My moment of delirious relief dies a quick death. Digory's still at risk.

He's facing away from me.

My eyes flit between him and Ophelia … the sound of my breaths piston through my ears …

The Recruit who ranked in fourth place is …

The furious pumping of my heart makes me light-headed—

Digory Tycho.

I can finally swallow. Digory's forehead presses against the glass, and I press my own opposite him. We stare at each other, our eyes only an inch or two apart, conveying more than any words ever could.

Recruit Juniper. You have ranked last in this Trial. You will now step forward and prepare for the Culling.

Ophelia's as pale as a corpse.

Click. The lock on her chamber springs open and the doors slide apart.

She shakes her head. "No. This must be some mistake." Her voice quavers through the speakers. She takes a step forward, freezes, then takes a step back. For the first time in ages, she reminds me of the confused girl who could barely make her way to the dais when this ordeal first began.

And *that* girl, I ache for.

Recruit Juniper. You will approach the podium now or risk forfeiture of the Trials.

Still shaking her head, Ophelia steps forward, and trips on her way out, landing with an audible *splat.*

I spring forward, bumping against the wall of my chamber, wanting to help her despite everything but knowing I can't. No one can.

She scrambles to her feet, blood oozing from a cut on her forehead. She wipes at it absently and staggers past Gideon as if she's intoxicated. She taps the glass of his enclosure, leaving bloody fingerprints. "Giddy, if only you hadn't turned your back on me..."

But he remains motionless, looking right through her as if she isn't even there. As if he isn't there either.

She weaves past him, stumbling by Cypress, then stops between Digory and me. She stares up at us, her face confused. "Why?" she asks us, looking like a little child.

I shake my head, wishing I could offer some kind of answer that could make sense of this horror. But there is none, and there never will be.

Her eyes flutter, then glaze over with frost. She frowns at us. "*You two* did this to me."

Digory and I exchange glances. Even though I'm burning with fever, I feel colder than ever.

Ophelia turns and strides up to the podium.

The lights inside the enclosure brighten.

Inside, her mother and her sister stand with their arms shackled above their heads. Unlike Gideon's parents, they don't seem to be afraid. Mrs. Juniper looks uncomfortable in that position, almost bored. Madeleine, on the other hand, seems fascinated with everything around her, the type of wonder that only the very innocent can have. She smiles at all of us, but when she sees Ophelia, her eyes grow wide and sparkle like twinkling stars.

"Mama! Maddie!" Ophelia bounces up the steps and presses her hands against the enclosure.

Her mother and sister are separated from each other by a thick glass partition, just like the Recruits are. Except for coils of black tubing snaking into each of their sections from below, the enclosure is barren—no furniture, no instruments, nothing. My eyes fix on the ends of each tube, covered by gleaming metal flaps.

Whatever horror the Establishment's thought of this time, *that's* where it'll come from.

Recruit Juniper. You have sixty seconds to make your selection.

Madeleine beams. "Are you going to play, too, Fee-Fee?" She tugs at the shackles like it's all a game.

Ophelia waves to her. "Maddie, sweetie. I'm right here, honey." She claps a hand over her mouth.

Madeline lifts her legs and swings from her chains. "I knew you'd come!"

Mrs. Juniper clears her throat. "I wasn't expecting it to be this soon."

"Oh, Mama! I'm so sorry," Ophelia wails. "I *tried*. I *really* tried, just like you taught me. I hope you're not too disappointed in me."

Mrs. Juniper shakes her head. Her lips purse. "I don't want to hear any of that sniveling, Ophelia. It's unbecoming for a future Imposer." Her expression softens. "And you *will* become an Imposer, darling. I just know it. We've just suffered a minor setback. Nothing you can't course-correct."

Ophelia buries her face in her hands. "I *can't* ... I can't do it ... "

Madeleine stops swinging. "Why are you crying, Feefee?"

"Pull yourself together, Ophelia!" Mrs. Juniper barks. "You can still triumph! You're a good girl. I understand how hard this is, but you'll do the right thing, I *know* it."

Ophelia looks up at her mother, her eyes puffy, tears streaking down her face. "You mean ... ?"

Mrs. Juniper nods. "You'll do exactly what we talked about. Kill your sister."

Ophelia clutches her head with both hands, her face a mask of anguish. "Mama ... "

Mrs. Juniper shakes her head and tsks. "*Look* at her."

She nudges her head toward Maddie, who's now humming to herself. "She'll never even *know*…"

Then Ophelia bolts up and glares at her. "My *mother*!" she shrieks. "I choose *her*!" She bangs a fist against the glass, her eyes cold, defiant.

A moment of shock registers on Mrs. Juniper's face. Then she smiles. "So headstrong. I taught you too well."

The flap covering the tube in Mrs. Juniper's section grinds open. There's the sound of buzzing. A lone bee zips from the tube and circles the room until it settles on her exposed arm. She flinches.

The tube begins to rattle. A loud vibration pierces the sound system, creating grating feedback. Mrs. Juniper's eyes look like they're ready to leap from her skull.

The shackles holding Madeleine's arms above her head spring free, dropping her to the ground.

Ophelia beckons her close. "Maddie, baby. We're going to play a special game. Close your eyes and cover your ears until I say you can look, okay?"

Madeleine giggles. "That's funny!"

Ophelia gets down on her knees. "Just do it for me, pretty please?"

"Okay, Fee-fee!" Madeline squeezes her eyes shut and clamps her hands around her ears.

A dark cloud bursts free from the tube, billowing like smoke, growing, until it practically fills Mrs. Juniper's section. Only this cloud's teeming with life—insects, bees, hundreds upon hundreds. The light strobes as they swarm, settling on the only other living thing, covering every inch of her flesh like a shroud.

Mrs. Juniper screams, but her cries are muffled by a living clump that jams into her mouth, piercing her tongue and throat with poisonous barbs until she's choking, no longer able to get air, flailing helplessly like a fish on a hook.

"Can I look now?" Maddie shouts over the frenzy.

"No, Maddie!" Ophelia shrieks. "*Don't open your eyes!*"

I slump against the glass, unable to peel my eyes away from the horror, sinking to the floor.

In a matter of minutes, it's over.

Swaying from the ceiling is an unrecognizable slab of meat that Ophelia once called Mama.

Only now she's a *thing*, a bloated hunk of purple flesh covered in pustules. Magnified on the speakers is the sound of a constant *plop* as the sickly yellow secretions seep from the wounds and douse the floor, now entirely carpeted with dead bees.

They sacrificed their lives for the will of the Establishment, just like our loved ones.

The lights in the enclosure dim, finally obliterating the gruesome sight.

The locks on our paddocks *click* and the doors slide apart.

This Trial has ended. Follow the markers to the next holding station.

Collecting my things, I hobble out of my pen and collapse into Digory's waiting arms.

"I got something for you," he whispers in my ear. I pull away and stare at his smiling face.

He opens his palm. In it rests a small, familiar pouch.

The antibiotics.

I'm overwhelmed—with relief, gratitude...and so much more.

My hand cups his. "But *you* might—"

"You need them more than I do. Take them. *Please*."

I hug him as tight as I'm able to with my trembling arms. "Thank you."

Behind him, Ophelia stares at the now dark enclosure that houses her sister. "I'll see you soon, Maddie. I promise."

Her eyes find mine and cut right through me. "And *no one's* going to stop me."

THIRTY

After resting several hours at the next holding station, we resume the trek to our third Trial, plodding through the winding corridors of the Skein in near silence. The quiet is broken only by the occasional grunt that barely penetrates the white noise of our wheezing breaths, which lulls me to the brink of exhaustive sleep before the panic of failure jars me back to my senses.

Despite my fatigue, the burning in my eyes settles into a low simmer while the chill in my blood turns lukewarm. Could the medicine be working already? Or am I just so far gone that my body can't feel anything anymore?

The only thing that still burns is my mind, bristling with images of Ophelia's mother, swollen beyond recognition, and the stump of Mrs. Warrick's neck, a broken fountain jetting streams of blood. Every so often the images shimmer like waves of heat baking the horizon, and it's not Mrs. Juniper or Mrs. Warrick I see but Cole and Digory in their places.

My breath catches in my throat.

I look around at Digory trudging along beside me, followed by Cypress and Gideon, with Ophelia bringing up the rear. From their vacant eyes, cradled in dark circles, and the new creases burrowing into the corners of their thin and cracking lips, I have no doubt their brains are infested with similar thoughts.

A geyser of pain shoots up my leg on my next step. I lurch to the side. Digory is beside me in an instant, hooking my arm around his shoulder and holding me upright.

"Gotcha," he says.

I pause for a moment, my hand gripping the back of my knee, riding out the pain like a receding wave. "I'll be okay. Just took a bad step."

He leans in close. "Don't push yourself."

Taking a deep breath, I straighten up, suddenly very conscious of how close our bodies are, how solid he feels against me, his breath hot and tingly against the hollow of my neck. A rush of energy surges through me, invigorating me more than any medicine ever could. A hot stream floods my face. For a panicked second I think I'm having a relapse, that the fever's starting to rage again.

Then I pull away. "I'm fine. *Really*."

He nods. "I'm here if you need me. Always."

I'm trapped by his gaze. "Thanks."

His eyes seem to want to say more, but I look away before they can drown me in their undertow.

Slowing my pace, I let everyone pass me.

Gideon and Cypress have fallen into step. At one point, her hand brushes against his and he clutches it, neither one looking at the other. Their steps synchronize as if their shared experiences have linked them in a tragic symbiosis, each feeding off the other's pain like emotional scavengers.

"Look! Up ahead!" Digory's shout shatters the quiet. "We're here!"

Despite my weariness, I jog to catch up to the others.

Looming ahead is a stone wall about twenty feet high, extending in both directions as far as the eye can see. Embedded in its center is a thick iron gate with a large number emblazoned above it, flashing like a beating heart: **III**.

My pulse accelerates. My eyelids stretch so wide I can almost feel the skin tearing at the corners of my eyes. This is it. The Third Trial. Is this where the ironies of my nickname will finally catch up with me?

We crowd next to each other, Cypress on one side of me, Digory on the other, with Gideon and Ophelia next to him. This time I'm in no hurry to move away from Digory. Instead, I find myself leaning into him, trying to siphon his strength into my veins. What if I can't pull through this time?

A burst of static.

Greetings, Recruits. Unlike with your previous Trial, the order in which you placed will have no bearing on this specific task.

At Slade's words, Cypress's shoulders slump. I understand exactly how she feels. She came in first in the labyrinth, and I was hoping my third-place finish would give me some kind of advantage for this Trial.

I glance at Digory, who's nodding. At least he'll get the chance to pull away from a low-ranking position. I breathe a little easier.

Understandably, Ophelia's eyes spark, faint embers turning into a steady glow. Now she has the chance to overcome her last-place slump and ensure her sister makes it through this round.

But Gideon, who came in second and should be crushed at the news, remains unfazed, his eyes fixed ahead, the blinking numbers reflecting through his glasses onto unblinking eyes.

When the gate opens, you will all commence at the exact same moment. This particular Trial will test strength, endurance, and speed. Once the Trial is underway, you will be required to overcome several obstacles by working together as a deployment team, set down in enemy territory.

I survey my fellow Recruits. After a near-catatonic Gideon came in second place during that last Trial, I can't afford to underestimate *anybody*. A false sense of confidence can turn out to be any of our undoing.

Be warned. Although you will need to cooperate to make it through the obstacles, in the end it will come down to a race to cross back into ally territory. The last one to arrive will be the one to participate in the Culling.

I try to swallow but my mouth's dry.

Good luck, Recruits.

CLANG!

The gate rumbles open with a grinding of gears, and I bolt through it.

THIRTY-ONE

The first thing that surprises me as I dash through the gateway is the fact that we're on a hill. High above, on the ceiling of this artificial landscape, there's a circular opening—a patch of night sky in the form of hundreds of twinkling stars shining down upon the sloping field. After being entombed in the Skein for what seems like a lifetime, I'd lost track of whether it was morning or evening. The sight fills me with dread.

Another solid wall looms in the valley below, its smooth surface brushed with moonlight. The only pathway to it is a thin slice of terrain with a sheer drop into darkness on either side. It looks to be barely wide enough for six people to fit across standing elbow to elbow.

I sprint down the hill, jostling against the others as we reach the strip of narrow grass. They're nothing but a blur in my peripheral vision. My breaths clog in my throat—

it's like the darkness is folding in on itself, suffocating me in a claustrophobic haze. Fueled by pure adrenaline, I pull ahead of them, needing to break free … to breathe …

SPROING!

A cylindrical object sprouts from the ground just to my left, startling me.

WHIRRR!

A gun turret swivels in my direction. I lose my footing and stumble, just as the weapon begins to fire.

RATATATATATAT!

Screams fill the air. I can't tell whose.

"Everyone stay low to the ground!" Digory cries, somewhere to my right.

I roll farther down the slope as bullets whiz past my cheeks. One nicks the tip of my right ear. Digory crashes into me, smothering my body with his weight. All around us the sod explodes, spraying through the air like gritty rain.

"You hit?" Digory yells.

I squirm out from underneath him. "Just a nick."

Ophelia rolls past us without a word.

SPROING!

Another turret juts through the earth in front of her and unleashes a volley of firepower. She flattens herself on the ground about ten feet from us.

"Ophelia! This place is rigged. Hold your position!" Digory tugs my arm, pulling me to my feet. "Any ideas?"

More shots ring through the sky.

"Ah!" This cry comes from behind me. I whip around just in time to see Cypress tumble to the ground.

"Cypress!" I tear out of Digory's grasp and stumble toward her.

Her face is twisted into a grimace. Her right hand is tucked under her left armpit, and even in the dim light I can see the dark trail oozing down.

I wrap her in my arms. "How bad?"

She clutches me tight with her other hand. "Flesh wound."

BLAM! BLAM! BLAM!

More blasts hit the ground beside us. I pull her away, hugging her tight.

Digory darts toward us, dodging a spray of sparks and smoke that nip at his heels like an unrelenting shadow. He swerves to a stop beside us. He jabs a finger toward the base of the hill. "We need to get over that wall *now!*"

I prop Cypress up against my shoulder. "She's been hit. Her *hand.*"

Trying not to hurt her further, I ease her injured hand out. It's covered in blood. Near the center of her palm is a ragged hole outlined by scorched flesh.

"Looks like it went straight through." Digory tears off a piece of her sleeve and wraps it around her hand, ignoring her winces.

A steady hum fills the air, getting stronger and stronger. Ophelia looks up. "Something's coming."

Cypress grabs my collar. "*I'm okay,*" she hisses through gritted teeth. "We have to get out of here. It's not safe in the open." Her body slumps back against mine.

Digory nods. "She's right." Then he moves in close and lifts her into his arms.

"What are you doing?" She makes a fist but it barely glances off his shoulder. "Put me down, Tycho!"

RATATATATATAT!

More bullets zip past our heads.

Close.

"I'll put you down just as soon as we're out of firing range." He turns to me. "C'mon!" He tramps down the remainder of the hill after Ophelia, carrying Cypress in his arms as if she were light as a baby.

My eyes search the dark. I stop dead in my tracks. "*Wait*! Where's Gideon?"

Digory freezes and turns. His eyes dart from me to the blazing turret.

Ophelia shakes her head. "There's no time—*leave him.*" She starts to run, but another blazing turret springs from the ground and fires. She dives onto her stomach and holds still.

"Look! There he is!" Cypress points behind me.

I whirl.

Gideon's sitting down in the grass a few feet up the hill from us. He's completely immobile, eyes opened wide as if he's in some kind of meditative state. He's sitting in the shadow of another turret, right underneath its swerving barrel.

"Gideon?" I take a few steps toward him. The weapon roars to life, flinging death at me in fiery flashes.

I dive to my right, slamming into the ground on my injured leg.

"Lucian!" Digory yells. Still carrying Cypress, he runs a

few steps toward me. Yet another turret springs to the surface and fires at them.

Digory drops to the ground and Cypress rolls away from him, still clutching her bloodied hand. When she attempts to get up, another gun breaks through the ground and swivels her way.

A blast of pain rips through me, and for the longest second in my life, I think I've been hit again.

But it's only the old wound in my leg, squishing open to douse my bandages with the warmth of fresh blood. I roll onto my stomach to take the pressure off.

Dead ahead, the barrel of the second turret faces me, a dark, gaping snake just waiting to spit its lethal poison through me.

And still Gideon sits there, beneath it, staring right past me, past the field, as if he's relaxing under the shade of a tree on a hot summer day.

WHIRRR…

I lift my head and risk a glance behind me. The first turret veers until it's pointing at my back.

They're motion activated, I realize. Its sensors must be tracking our every movement. That's why Gideon hasn't been fired at yet.

And now we're all trapped right along with him, each at the mercy of one of the turrets, unable to move forward or backward without getting ripped apart.

The hum in the air is louder now. From the circle of sky above, five lights zoom toward us like angry wasps in a perfect V formation.

Squawkers.

It's a no-win situation. If we stay still, the turrets won't get us. But we'll be easy targets for these aircraft to take out.

Unless...

I raise my cheek off the ground as far as I dare without entering into the turret's sensor range. "Everybody listen! These guns are motion activated. As long as we stay close to the ground and don't move too fast, they won't fire on us!"

"Great!" Cypress shouts back. She repositions her hand and winces. "You know how long it's going to take to crawl our way down like that?" Her voice barely carries above the approaching craft.

Digory sighs. "We've got bigger problems. Those birds are heading our way. They're almost on top of us. We'll never make it in time."

The Squawkers blaze a path in the sky like shooting stars.

Shooting stars. I glance from one turret to the next, calculating the distances, approximating the angles of the barrels, tracing a mental line from one to another just like I did with the star patterns I showed Digory on top of the Observation Tower.

Picking up a handful of pebbles, I toss them at random turrets.

One...two...

Ratatatatatatatatatatatatat!

"What are you *doing*?" Ophelia shrieks. "You'll kill us all!"

It might just work...

My heart pounds against the grass beneath me. "We can

do this if we work *together*. That's the key, how this Trial was designed."

The wind picks up, rippling through the grass as the Squawkers roar into the simulated valley.

"Whatever you're going to do, do it fast!" Digory shouts.

I clutch fistfuls of damp grass and raise my upper torso. "I've been timing the blasts. It takes just under three seconds for the gun sensors to track their marks and fire. When I give the signal, Gideon and I will run toward each other's turret, while you guys run toward the turrets ahead of each of you—Digory over to Cypress's, Cypress over to Ophelia's, Ophelia to the final turret by the wall."

"Let's just make it easier for them to kill us, why don't we?" Ophelia cries.

"We'll be safe as long as we drop to the ground no later than two seconds in!" I shout back. "The guns will react to our movement and take each other out before they can redirect their course. Then we'll be clear."

BOOM! BOOM! BOOM!

The ground rocks with the force of the Squawker's blasts, which rip out chunks of landscape in bright red fireballs. The air's filled with acrid smoke that clogs my lungs. Burning tears streak down my cheeks.

Digory's eyes meet mine. "I'd rather go down trying than just wait here to die."

"I'm in, too." Cypress chimes in.

Ophelia's eyes are glued to the sight of the Squawkers as they bank back toward us. "Let's do it then," she groans.

I turn to face Gideon. His eyes remain blank, unfocused.

He's the last cog in this carefully constructed machine. If I can't get through to *him*…

"Gideon." I lower my voice. "*Please*. We *need* you."

He blinks, removes his glasses, wipes them with his shirt, then pushes them back on his nose.

"I'm ready," he says.

Thank you, I mouth.

I turn to the others, four sets of desperate eyes, trusting me with their lives. "When I give the signal, we *move*. Remember—drop at two seconds, not a moment later."

The growl of the Squawker engines rips through the sky toward us.

My heart's thundering. My breaths come in quick, shallow bursts.

"Run!" I sprint, heading right for the dark eye of my gun turret, a black hole of unblinking death.

THIRTY-TWO

Everything's a slow-motion blur. I bolt toward Gideon and his turret, ignoring the searing pain in my leg, the piercing shriek of the Squawkers overhead—nothing matters except the cold gleam on the barrel of the gun, blinding me. For a split second I can taste its metal, but it's only the blood of my lower lip as my teeth sink through.

One second . . .

CLICK!

The sounds of the guns locking onto our movements are like gigantic tumblers shifting into place, crushing my brain . . .

Gideon's a blur almost parallel to me . . .

Two seconds . . .

"DIVE!" I shriek at the top of my lungs, half expecting the blast of the gun to rip me apart before the word's last echo fades into nothingness. I drop, slamming against the hard earth. The breath I've been holding bursts free. The flesh on my palms and cheek burns as my momentum slams me into the base of the gun placement...

BAM! BAM! BAM!

I shove my palms against the sides of my head, barely able to suppress the blasts ripping through my eardrums. Then the turret above me bursts apart in a flaming ball, singeing my hair and spraying the air with a geyser of smoldering shrapnel. I clamp an elbow over my eyes to shield them from the onslaught digging into my uniform and roll away from the impact.

My eyes risk a peek over my arm.

One by one, the gun turrets topple over in a haze of smoking, twisted metal until they're all nothing but silent, steaming heaps, casting wispy trails up the hill.

Hot tears sting my eyes.

It *worked*.

I spring to my haunches, ignoring the pain. "Is everyone okay?"

"I-I-I think... so." Cypress calls back. I can make out her silhouette through the smoke as she crawls to her knees.

"Looks like I'm still in one piece!" Ophelia shouts, hands waving from further down the slope. Despite the hard edge in her tone, I can almost hear the giggle hiding just beneath it.

Ahead, Gideon sits up, his face smudged with blood and dirt. His glasses hang askew on his nose. "Still breathing," he mumbles, sounding more cursed than relieved.

But what about—?

I leap to my feet. "Digory!" My heart pistons up my

throat. "Are you hurt?" I stumble down the slope, wiping my eyes against the wet haze obscuring everything.

Smudges of blood and dirt glisten through the sweat on his forehead, contrasting against his noticeably paler face. "Guess I banged myself up a bit." He climbs to his feet and moves his hand to rub his injured shoulder, jerking it back as though he's touched an electric fence.

"Careful!" I hold him steady, gently grazing his exposed shoulder with my palm.

He flinches, squeezing his eyes shut. "You think it's broken?"

I shake my head, studying the angle of his shoulder. "Nope. Looks dislocated to me. We have to reset it."

He shakes his head. "No time. Let's go." His hand grips my arm as he struggles to retain his balance. Another flash of pain on his face.

Touching his good shoulder, I hold him firmly in place and gaze right into his eyes. "I just want to look at it."

"Okay."

Digging my fingers into his shoulder, I yank on his hand. *Pop!*

The snap echoes through the valley. Digory drops to his knees. "Son of a—!" His jaw flexes and his eyes squeeze shut for a moment. Then he looks around at the fallen turrets, turns back to me, and winks. "You did good."

"We *all* did good." Turning, I make eye contact with Gideon and give him a thumbs-up.

He nods and returns the gesture.

The entire valley thunders with the hum of the Squawk-ers' engines.

They'll be on us again any second…

"I'm not waiting around!" Ophelia dashes toward the wall.

The Squawkers are directly above. Tiny black shapes drop from their underbellies and zoom toward us, remind-ing me of the bees that stung Mrs. Juniper to death.

Cypress grabs my arm. "Run!"

Without bothering to answer, I haul Digory to his feet and motion to Gideon.

Then we're all scrambling down the rest of the hill toward the wall.

KABLAM!

Another of the Squawkers' bombs plows into the field behind us, striking with the force of a major earthquake, scattering us like paper dolls in a breeze. Waves of heat ema-nate from the fireball, shoving me forward with fiery hands.

Then the next bomb hits, and the next, rocking the ground with a deafening roar that transforms the entire field where we stood just a moment ago into a raging inferno.

A black cloud covers everything. I choke on the thick, pungent smoke, trying in vain to cough out the gritty intruders lodging in my lungs. I drop to the ground, gasp-ing for air and only succeeding in inhaling more dark death, smothering me with each breath. My eyes water, and I can't help but think how unfair this all is… how close we were… making it past the guns, just to suffocate… I lose focus… as if I'm drifting into a nightmare…

Digory latches onto my arm, rousing me from my stupor, pulling me through the smoke until I can glimpse the small scrap of sky. He half carries, half drags me from the smog. We stagger to the wall a few feet ahead. His strong hand is slapping my back over and over again. I alternate between gulping fresh air and hacking out ash.

My eyes regain focus.

Everyone's crowded around us, staring up at the wall's smooth surface. It must be almost thirty feet high, with no footholds or handholds in sight. Something glistens on its top surface, reflecting the deep oranges and reds of the blazing tongues that lick at our backs.

Bracing against the steel of Digory's arm, I pull myself to my feet for a better look. There's a metal ring embedded at the top of the wall. A metal ring attached to … is that what I think it is?

"Up there!" I shove a finger in the direction of the ring. "It looks like a rope ladder!"

More explosions rock the terrain behind us. The Squawkers fly past. I can already see the angle of their flight pattern arcing in the sky, preparing to zoom in for another run. With the blazing field behind us and the wall blocking the path ahead, we're boxed in.

"What good is a rope going to do us up there?" Cypress shouts over the aircraft's growing buzz. "If we could reach it, we wouldn't need it!"

Ophelia sucks in her cheeks. "Looks like the Establishment has a sense of humor after all."

Digory and I exchange glances. He shakes his head, probably thinking the same thing I am.

There's no way out of this.

But that makes no sense. If the Establishment wanted to murder us outright, it could have done so at any time.

I glance above and then back at the others' faces. "That rope *has* to be there for a reason. It's a test, just like the gun turrets were. Somehow, someway, we *have* to reach it and pull ourselves over."

"Maybe only one of us is meant to reach it."

We all turn to look at Gideon. He takes off his glasses and wipes the sweat from his eyes, focusing on me.

"Gideon's right," I say. "We need to form a human ladder." My eyes bounce from one to the other of them, estimating their different heights, adding them up and figuring the distance between the ground and the top of the wall.

Ophelia's eyes roll. "That'll *never* work!"

The hum of the circling Squawkers gets louder.

"Doesn't look like we've got too many options. Let's go." Cypress holds out her uninjured hand to Gideon. "You coming?" She fixes a tender gaze on him.

He shrugs, and his eyes drop to the ground. But he takes her hand and slips his fingers through hers.

Digory's staring above us. He squeezes his injured shoulder and winces, then turns to me, shame flooding his eyes. "I'm not sure how much weight I can take on this damn shoulder."

I smile at him. "Don't worry. I got you covered."

"What order do we go in?" Cypress asks.

Ophelia steps forward. "I'm the lightest. I'll go *first*—"

Digory bars her way. "Not a chance. The moment you get up there you'll climb over without tossing us the rope and leave the rest of us behind."

Her eyes become angled slits. "How surprisingly self-righteous of you, Tycho." She circles him. "What's to stop *you*"—her gaze burns through the group—"or *any* of you from doing the same thing?"

Gideon swats cinders away from his face. "She does have a point…"

Cypress avoids eye contact with all of us.

I can't blame any of them for having doubts, especially Gideon and Ophelia. They know better than the rest of us what's at stake.

I clear my throat. "We don't have time to debate this. The Squawkers will be here any second. Even though Digory's the strongest, with his shoulder in the shape it's in, he won't be able to support any of our weight. So he'll have to be the one to climb to the top—"

Digory shoots me a shocked look.

"But—" Ophelia interrupts.

"All of you, especially *you*, Ophelia, believe that Digory and I have each other's back. Which is why we're going to be on opposite ends of this task. He'll be at the top of the wall, and I'll be at the base of the ladder. If you truly believe we're working *together*, then you must believe he'll never go over the wall and leave me behind."

For a few seconds, the only sounds are the steady crackling of the flames growing closer and the purr of the returning Squawkers, which soon becomes a steady growl.

"You've convinced me." Cypress breaks our silence at last.

Gideon nods.

I back against the wall. "Ophelia, since you don't trust me, you get to stand directly on *my* shoulders. Then Gideon, so he can lend Cypress a hand because of her injury. Cypress, you're next, so you and Digory can help each other."

Another burst of flame billows our way, narrowing the gap between us and the smooth stone.

Bracing myself against the wall, I hold out my hands to form a cup. "C'mon. Let's move."

Ophelia rushes over, slides her foot in between my hands, and hauls herself onto my shoulders. Gideon's next, teetering slightly before settling on Ophelia's shoulders. Then comes Cypress, who, despite her blood-soaked bandage, darts up me and Ophelia to perch on Gideon's shoulders as easily as a mouse scurrying up a pipe.

I grip Ophelia's ankles, trying to hold her steady against the tremors racking my body. It's already too hazy to see more than a foot ahead of me. Heat bakes my skin. Every inch of me's dripping. My mouth fills with the taste of acrid smoke already clogging my straining lungs.

Digory pauses in front of me and touches my cheek. Unable to pull away, I can only stare at him, quenching my thirst in the blue waters of his eyes.

"See you on the other side," he whispers. Then he steps into my hand and pushes up.

My knees buckle from the added weight, but I force my muscles to lock down despite the agony coursing through me.

The fire's devouring everything in its path, eating away the field we came through, getting closer and closer until the searing heat ripples my vision as if I'm looking through a burning waterfall.

"Hurry," Ophelia groans.

Every bone in my body creaks from trying to hold steady against the constant wobbling of Ophelia's feet on my shoulders. I hear Digory reach the top and grip the end of the rope. Our teetering ladder lurches—

But Digory scrambles up and pulls himself on top of the wall. Free of his weight, our human chain holds steady.

"*Here!*" He tosses the ladder down.

Cypress grabs it and scampers up toward Digory, followed closely by Gideon and Ophelia. One after the other, Digory hauls them onto the ledge. I snake up the wooden planks until I'm standing at the top alongside them.

Below us, the fire's reached the base of the wall, burning through the lower part of the ladder.

Above us, the Squawkers swoop in for the kill.

"Hurry!" I shout. "We have to get down the other side *now!*"

I grab the remainder of the rope and start to reel it back up the parapet. Then it's burning through the flesh of my fingers and palms. I glance behind me at Digory and Gideon, their arms pistoning like the gears of a steam engine as they pull along with me until the ladder's frayed ends reach the top. Cypress slams a foot down on the ladder, trapping it in place before it can skitter off the edge and over the other side.

"It's not long enough anymore. It won't reach the bottom." The incoming craft nearly drown her words in a surge of roaring engines.

I peer down over the other side of the wall. A strong feeling of vertigo nearly overtakes me. My body teeters from the wave of dizziness and I have to grip Digory's arm to steady myself. The distance seems much greater from this vantage point than it did from the ground looking up. Far below, a moat of dark sludge oozes against the wall's base. At least it's not a solid surface, though I shudder to think what could be lurking underneath.

Digory yanks the ladder free from under Cypress's foot. "We only have to drop about ten feet or so. That muck down there should be able to break our fall."

Explosions rock the terrain nearby. The wounded ground shudders as if in pain. There's no more time.

"*Out of my way.*" Ophelia grabs the ladder and swings off the other side without looking back.

Digory flinches as the ropes go taut and tear into his skin, streaking it with glistening darkness. He stumbles and slides halfway over the edge before I grab his leg and drag him back to safety.

Below, Ophelia's half swimming, half crawling through the mire toward solid ground, with a clear, unobstructed path to the finish line.

Adrenaline gushes through my muscles. I grab the slackness of the ladder. "Cypress! Gideon! Let's go!"

First Cypress, then Gideon grab hold of the ladder and leap off the edge, leaving just Digory and me.

KABOOM!

Another Squawker missile strike.

CRACK!

A chink erupts in the stone underneath Digory and me. A tremor ripples through the wall as the chink turns into a ragged gash that rips down the wall between us. Our eyes meet. The sections we're perched on begin to slide away from each other...

Digory grabs me and pulls me over the breach, tight against his chest, just as my side of the wall crumbles away. "You're not getting away *that* easy!"

Even though I catch a glimpse of a smile, I can hear the thunder of his heart raging against me. I grip him tighter. Still tangled in each other, we both grasp the ladder and tumble off the side after the others, just as the loudest explosion of all rips through the air.

The Squawkers have breached the wall at last.

A blast of heat pushes us forward. If not for the ropes of ladder searing through my fingers, I'd swear we were free falling.

I can't look down as we plunge. Then we've literally reached the end of our rope and *are* free falling.

A few seconds later, our bodies slam into marsh. We're rolling through the muck, our arms locked around each other. A foul stench not unlike that of the sewers overpowers my nostrils, suffocating me with noxious ooze. I open my mouth to breathe, but only succeed in gulping a mouthful of pungent sludge. I spit it out and gag.

We've finally stopped spinning.

Digory pulls away to get a better look at me. "Still in one piece?"

I nod, not trusting my mouth to open again.

A terrible rumble fills my ears, and we both look up—

Just in time to see the wall collapsing toward us in a hailstorm of stone.

Digory springs to his feet and yanks me to mine. "Run!"

We slog through the fetid bog as fast as we can, dodging slabs of rock that crash everywhere around us, drenching us with putrid waves.

"*This* way." Digory jerks me to the left just as a stone chunk slams into the ground that I occupied a mere second ago.

"*Watch out!*" I return the favor by pushing him out of the way of another block twice his size.

Ahead of us, Cypress and Gideon are scrambling out of the quagmire, with Ophelia just ahead of them.

I grab Digory's hand and tug him faster, too afraid to risk a glimpse at the destruction behind us that continues to pound the earth.

We clear the marshland at last and let go of hands, sprinting like the wind. Although I have the crushing urge to look into Digory's eyes, I pull away and will myself to go faster and faster, despite the ache of my starving lungs and the wild hammer of my heavy heart.

I look up just in time to see Ophelia cross the finish line. She throws up her hands in triumph and drops to her knees.

My veins are an adrenaline refinery, charging the engine of my heart, which pistons my legs like a well-oiled machine.

Cypress crosses the finish line next. Unlike Ophelia, she collapses onto her back and just lies there... her ordeal over...

Scrounging the last of my energy reserves, I narrow the gap until I'm almost even with Gideon. I glance over and our eyes meet.

There's a desperate hunger there. The first time I've seen it since we were recruited.

He *wants* to win this time. Just as badly as I do.

And every agonizing second he's pulling further and further into the lead...

Digory's a blur as he swoops past on my other side and catches up to Gideon. They race neck and neck, leaving me trailing in last place.

My lungs chug like a steam engine. They're almost at the finish line. No way I can catch them, much less win—

Gideon stumbles into Digory, whether on purpose or accidentally, I can't be sure. The two tumble to the ground just shy of their goal. I leap over their bodies and sail across the finish line. My chest heaving, I whirl.

Gideon's crawling over Digory's body, inches from the finish line. "I'm ... *sorry*," he sobs.

Digory's eyes meet mine. "I'm sorry too."

He lifts his torso up, thick chords bulging from the sides of his neck. Gideon's eyes stretch wide. Then Digory twists around, grabs Gideon by the throat, and tosses him backward.

Gideon lands with a loud thud on his back.

And Digory crawls over the finish line and into my arms, burying his face against my chest.

I'm too stunned to speak and can only hold him, rocking him back and forth even as tears stream from my eyes and into his golden hair.

A few feet away, Gideon rises to a sitting position. The life that had returned to his eyes is gone again and he just stares, his lips moving soundlessly.

Recruit Warrick. You have ranked last in this Trial. You will now step forward onto the podium as there is still a selection to be made.

THIRTY-THREE

Still a selection? What the hell is Slade talking about? What *else* could he possibly choose? I thought that once you lost your second Incentive, it was just a matter of watching them be executed before you were condemned to the work camps. What new level of depravity are they sinking to now?

The familiar hum of a platform rising to the surface fills the quiet. It lifts all the way, then is as silent as it's dark.

Gideon trudges across the finish line like a sleepwalker.

A long sigh hisses from Ophelia's lips. "Oh, well. *One* down..." She shakes her head and turns away.

Digory steps forward. "Gideon. I had no choice."

"I forgive you." He shrugs. "It doesn't matter anymore anyway."

His tone... the look in his eyes... sadden and terrify me.

Cypress wraps her arms around him.

He kisses her on the forehead and traces a tear down her cheek. "You're supposed to be the tough one, remember?"

Her face contorts. "Y-yes, *S-Sir*."

He smiles at her and pulls away.

Then he turns to me and takes off his glasses, placing them in my palm, and closes my fingers over them. "Can you hold these for me?"

A lump wedges in my throat. "Aren't you going to need them?" My voice cracks.

He squeezes my hand. Then he walks past all of us and up the stairs until he's standing right next to the chamber.

The lights in the enclosure grow bright.

Mr. Warrick is standing on one side of the structure separated by a partition from the other, darkened side. His arms are strapped to the wall behind him. He looks even more haggard, his hair scraggly threads, his eyes sunken and hollow. It's as if he's already died inside.

The outer door to the chamber hisses open.

Recruit Warrick. You will now step inside and make your selection.

Gideon walks past the threshold. He stumbles and braces himself against the glass, staring at his father.

The door hisses shut behind him and the lock engages with a sharp *click*.

Cypress's bandaged hand trembles against mine. "What are they going to do now?"

I can only shake my head, terrified at what's to come, unable to tear myself away.

Recruit Warrick. The time has now come for your

second Incentive to be shelved. But you still have a choice in the matter.

The other half of the chamber lights up at last. My insides turn to liquid.

The entire side is jammed with rodents—large rats, larger than any I've ever seen in the Parish, at least three feet in length not counting their sickening pink serrated tails. They've obviously been bred as weapons, just like the bees that devoured Mrs. Juniper. Glowing orange eyes glare at us. The mutant rodents snap at each other with bared teeth, some chomping into the bodies of the others with razor-sharp fangs that drip with drool, greenish against the dark crimson wounds. Claws that are more like talons scratch against the glass of their prison. And to make things worse, the sound of their screeching, now amplified through the sound system, makes every hair on my body prickle...

Recruit Warrick. Either you allow your Incentive to be shelved in the manner prescribed...or, should you elect, you have the option of shelving your Incentive in a more sedate manner. One which you must carry out personally.

A pedestal rises from the floor.

On it lies a solitary object, reflecting the bright light in its smooth silver finish.

A gun.

Be warned. The weapon's firepower will not penetrate the reinforced glass surrounding the chamber. You now have sixty seconds to make your decision, Recruit Warrick.

Gideon walks up to his father's side of the tank and splays his fingers against it.

"I'm sorry, Dad," he says. "I guess I *am* a real loser, just like everyone says." He shrugs and drops his gaze, his shoulders heaving.

Mr. Warrick's eyes stream wetness down the concaves of his cheeks. "I'm the one that's sorry, son. For not protecting you, keeping you safe. I don't expect you to forgive me. But please, son, I *beg* you. Show me mercy."

He nudges his head toward the rats without looking at them, his face flinching against the sounds of scratching and screeching. "I don't want to go *that* way."

Gideon lumbers toward the pedestal and stares at the gun. He face is a mask of indecision and anguish as he traces a finger over the barrel.

"You're a better person than your mother and I ever were." Mr. Warrick's words quaver.

One of the rats screeches so loudly I fight not to cover my ears.

Recruit Warrick, carry out the sentence.

He grasps the gun in a trembling hand and slogs back toward Mr. Warrick. When the glass separating them slides into the floor, Gideon runs to his father, throwing his arms around him.

"I'm so sorry, Dad. I wish things could be different ... "

Mr. Warrick closes his eyes. "So do I, son."

BAM!

Gideon kisses his father's cheek and moves away. Blood gushes from a wound right over Mr. Warrick's heart. For the first time since I laid eyes on him at the Graduation Ceremony, Mr. Warrick looks serene, as if he's merely taking a well-deserved nap.

The suffering's over for him.

Recruit Warrick. You have accomplished your task. Now return the weapon to its proper location and prepare to be transported to the work camps.

But Gideon doesn't seem to be paying attention. Instead, he staggers from his father's lifeless body and presses against the glass that's overlooking us.

We all rush up to face him, even Ophelia.

Recruit Warrick. Return the weapon at once. This is an order. Failure to do so will subject you to immediate shelving protocol.

My heart's running an obstacle course of its own at Slade's warning. I'm pressed against the glass trying to will myself to melt through it somehow. I need to touch Gideon. *Now ... before ...*

"Gideon. *Please.* Listen to them. Put *down* the gun." I try to sound calm, but I can hear the panicked edge creeping into my own voice. "You can go to the camps. At least you'll still have a *chance*."

He shakes his head. "Thank you." His eyes sweep the four of us. "Thank you all for trying. But I'm so tired ... I just need to rest ... yeah ... that's it ... just rest. It's gone on way too long." He smiles despite the stream leaking down his cheeks, onto the bridge of his nose.

Recruit Warrick. You are in violation of a direct order. Under the military code, you must now be shelved.

The enclosure holding the rats begins to vibrate as it prepares to slide open and let them loose—

My fist clenches Gideon's glasses so tightly I can feel the frames cutting into my skin. "Don't be stupid. Things can *change*."

"*Listen to him, Gideon.*" Digory bangs on the glass himself. Cypress's bloodied hand is cupped over her mouth.

Gideon slides down the transparent wall and I mimic him from my side, nose to nose, separated by the reinforced glass, so thin, but impenetrable.

He shakes his head. "There's *nothing* for me now." He cocks his head as if he could whisper through the barrier. "I *wanted* to be a *good* person. Make a *difference*...But I...I mean...after my mom...my dad..." He shrugs and his eyes connect with mine. "Am I unforgivable, Lucian?"

The panel holding back the writhing rodents rises an inch...

I pound as hard as I can. But the glass doesn't shatter. The only thing that does is my heart.

"You *are* a good person, Gideon. You *are*," I sob.

"Thanks for everything." He smiles at me. "I wish we could have gotten to know each other better in school."

He lifts the gun to his temple and looks right at me.

I can't breathe.

"*Don't do it!*" Cypress shrieks. She grabs onto me, her fingers digging into my arm.

Gideon squeezes the trigger—

CLICK.

It's empty. The gun drops from his hand and clatters on the floor.

I sag against Digory. Of course they'd only load it with one bullet.

Gideon's face is a mixture of regret and fear. "That's what I figured." He reaches into his pocket and pulls out something that flashes in the light…something familiar…

I open my hand, staring at his glasses—and at the empty socket on one side, where the lens has been removed.

He shrugs. "I hope it's not *too* dark…"

"Gideon, *no!*" I shout.

He jabs the small shard into his throat, tearing a ragged smile all the way across it, choking and gurgling as a dark river flows down his neck.

His head slumps over.

And then I can't hear the rats' claws, the screeches, my heartbeat…nothing but my wails, which drown out everything else.

———

Far above, in that opening that let the Squawkers through, the sun tears through the dark veil of night and into a cloudy morning.

We've been at it for hours. The four of us pause in our labors and lean against the mound of sticks to gaze at it, no one saying a word. The muted light casts a creeping grayish brown pall over us. For a moment we're frozen in time, like an old sepia-toned photograph.

But time's fleeting. No matter how hard we try to capture it, it always trickles away through our fingers like fine sand, gone forever.

As the soft light deepens to a fiery orange, I can't help but think how cold the sunrise is despite its radiant warmth, how indifferent to the fact that one less pair of eyes will ever be in awe of its majesty.

"It's time." Digory's voice breaks the silence, plaintive notes whistling through a hollow reed. In his hand, he holds a makeshift torch which he's lit by using one of the matches he found in the labyrinth. It flickers across his face in the deep orange and red hues of autumn, highlighting the circles under his eyes and infusing his pale cheeks with color.

I finally move, wiping the sweat from my brow, and place the last naked branch atop the others, careful not to disturb *him*. He looks so peaceful lying on the pyre, hands folded across his stomach, almost as if he's stretched out in sleep. I run my fingers through his hair, and pull his collar closed, covering the long dark scar on his neck that shatters the illusion.

Cypress steps up to the pyre. Her face is ashen, eyes red and swollen. She bows her head, her lips moving in silence.

Ophelia stands a few feet away, her arms crossed, her eyes empty wells. "Why do we have to do *this*?" she mutters, her voice drained of any emotion. "We could get a penalty for this. If we had just left him *there*—"

I whirl on her. "They would have just dumped him in some unmarked grave, buried him as if he were *trash*—as if he…" The words catch in my throat. "As if he didn't mean *anything.*" I bury my face in my hand, letting my fingers slide upward until they're knotted in my hair. I bite into my lip to hold it together. But I'm powerless against the tremors rocking my body, making my shoulders heave.

I expect her to say something snide, to fight back. I don't care. But she doesn't, just continues to stare at Gideon. And then I think of her own mother, how horrible she looked at the end, how Ophelia never got the chance to lay her to rest, and I can *feel* her anguish. My grief is compounded with guilt for lashing out at her, and I reach out and clasp her hand.

Cypress sidles next to me, resting her head in the crook of my neck, not bothering to fight the tears running down her cheeks. Digory pats me on the back and lowers the torch to the kindling.

The branches sputter and sizzle as the fire catches, growing stronger and stronger, consuming the rest of the branches until it swaddles Gideon's body in a blinding blanket of blazing light. Cypress's sobs harmonize against the steady crackle of the flames.

"Anyone want to say anything?" Digory asks.

Ophelia can only shake her head, her eyes glazed with firelight.

I step forward and take the torch from Digory, a sudden rush of strength coursing through me.

I have to do this. I *need* to.

My eyes challenge the brightness of the fire, now raging like a miniature sun. But I don't blink. Instead I let its heat seep into my pores as if I'm absorbing a part of Gideon that will forever be seared into my soul.

"Goodbye Gideon," I say. "We'll miss you. You will always be remembered for the kind, brave person that you were. A *good* son. And a *true* friend. May you find the peace at last that eluded you for so long."

I hold the torch high.

The tendrils of flame look like fingers that reach up to the sky and merge with the risen sun, now bursting free of its cloudy prison, brilliant rays beaming down upon us.

The warmth finally penetrates my heart. I smile. Tears fill my eyes, trapping them in prisms of glistening color. "Rest in the light, Gideon, and never fear the darkness again."

THIRTY-FOUR

Hours later, after a sleepless rest at the holding station and a wordless breakfast of ration bars and water, we're trekking past the end of the field and through the metallic arteries of the Skein once more. The only sounds are the drag and shuffle of our boots against the steel floor. Along the way, I pop a few more of the antibiotics into my mouth. But instead of swallowing, I swish them around my mouth from side to side and grind the pills with my teeth, concentrating on each bitter particle as it dissolves against my tongue.

With each chew, one thought echoes in my brain.

There are only four of us now.

We finally reach the end of the corridor.

I force the last of the gritty medicine down my throat.

Before us looms a silver bunker lined with five metal doors, four with names stenciled on them that correspond to each of our own:

The surface of the fifth door is blank and marred by a series of scratches, as if someone hastily removed the name that recently appeared there. I glance behind us. A needle stitches through my heart.

The speakers above the doors crackle with static.

Greetings, Recruits. Congratulations on making it this far in your Trials.

If Slade's announcement is intended to bolster our moods, one look at the sullen expressions plastered on our faces is confirmation of the utter failure of that attempt.

When you're given the signal, you will each enter the chamber that is marked with your name.

We shamble past each other like sleepwalkers and line up outside our individual doors.

This Trial will involve two phases. In Phase One, you will race to disable the explosive mechanism you will find in your chamber. Whoever accomplishes this task first shall emerge victorious. However, if none of you disarms the explosive, it will detonate and all of you, as well as your Incentives, will be shelved.

It takes a moment for the words to penetrate the shock.

A *bomb*?

Slade said we'd *all* be shelved. Recruits and Incentives alike. What if Cole's just beyond that door, only a few feet away, closer to me than he's been since this whole ordeal began? A blast at such close range would kill him. And he'd never even know I fought for him. He'd die thinking I abandoned him. The thought terrifies me so much I can't even move.

The bomb could kill us *all*. And given my track record with disarming explosives . . . only it's not a Sim this time. And if I'm the one to screw up and set it off, it'll be like I murdered everyone myself.

My eyes flit to Digory. The lines etched into the stone of his face tell me he's struggling with the same anguish.

Should one of you succeed in preventing the explosion from triggering, then that Recruit shall proceed to Phase Two and await further instructions.

My eyes fix on the iron door with my name on it, examining every inch of its shiny surface, every circular bolt screwed into its perimeter, including the flecks of paint that have withered away like dead skin, exposing patches of red rust like mottled wounds.

"I can't do this," I whisper to Digory.

He reaches out and squeezes my hand. "You can and you *will* do this."

CLANG! CLANG! CLANG! CLANG!

The locks on each of our doors disengage. They spring open in a chorus of drawn-out creaks, exposing slices of darkness within.

Proceed inside your chambers and begin weapons diffusion.

Ophelia's halfway through her door before Slade's voice finishes echoing through the speakers. I practically leap through my own door, catching a blurred glimpse of Digory entering his to my left.

It suddenly occurs to me this may be the last time I ever see him—

SLAM!

The door crashes shut behind me, blocking out the light and leaving me in total suffocating darkness.

I freeze in my tracks, afraid to touch anything that I might accidentally set off. Try as I might, my eyes can't penetrate the black veil. I take a tentative step and my foot's blocked by a hard surface. Reaching out my arms, I find I can't stretch them out fully before they, too, are blocked by cold, sturdy metal. Panic sets in. My mouth dries up. I can't suck in air.

It feels like I've been buried alive inside a vertical coffin.

Thoughts crank through my head on well-oiled gears. What if my chamber's been sabotaged? Cassius has obviously been keeping tabs on Digory and me. It wouldn't be beneath him at this point to rig it so the explosive detonates, killing both of us.

"Something's wrong!" I yell at the top of my lungs. "*I can't see!*"

But there's no response. Thick silence seeps into my ears, clogging them until I feel a pressure in my brain that grinds my thoughts into anxious grit. I bang a fist against the cold metal barring my way before I can stop myself. The impact rattles the bones in my fingers. Pain jolts through my hand, echoing into a throb. I bring my hand to my lips, sucking on the sore knuckles.

Is that my heartbeat rippling through the sound vacuum in my head?

No … it's too high in pitch and not nearly as fast as the throbbing in my chest and temples.

It's a steady, measured sound, *blip … blip … blip …*

Like the sound a timer makes … or a countdown clock …

What if I've set off some kind of timer when I struck the panel?

But how the hell am I supposed to disarm a weapon I can't even *see*?

I still have my flashlight. I thrust my hands into my pockets, not caring how many ration bars and penicillin tablets spill onto the ground, and pull out the flashlight, flicking it on.

There's a circuit board to my right, and a vent right above it.

I wonder what's supposed to come out of *there*?

My eyes lock onto the circuit board instead, studying the configuration, trying to commit every facet to memory.

I recognize the basic setup from the schematics during our explosives training and Sims. It's a standard detonation device composed of three elements: Primer. Reactor. Ignition timer.

The flashlight flickers and dims, even as my heartbeat kicks it up several notches.

"C'mon! Not *now!*"

I hunch closer to the board and scan it with the ebbing light, trying to see the digital readout so I can figure out just how much time I have left before—

But the beam fades away and dies before I can get a good look, drowning me once again in pitch black.

I shake the flashlight a couple more times, but it's no use. At least I have an idea of what I'm dealing with now.

I reach a trembling hand down to the circuit board, trying to dredge up from my memory as many of the details as I can picture. I make contact with one of the three thin wires, gripping it between two fingertips. It's cold, like the bloodless vein of a corpse. I relax my grip, afraid that my trembling fingers are going to pull it free. Unless I splice the wires in the correct sequence, everything that I've gone through until now will have been for nothing.

I strain the threads of my memory until they're taut. "Cut the wire leading into the primer *first*. Then the reactor wire. And *finally* the wire that feeds the ignition timer." I speak the words aloud, as if that'll somehow lend accuracy to my sketchy recall.

Letting go, I brush my fingers across the rest of the board, past the other two wires, until they come to rest on a square shape.

It's *got* to be the primer.

I can feel one of the leads jutting from it. This is the first one I have to cut.

I think.

No pair of wire cutters either. Reaching into my pocket, I pull out my knife and position it just above where the icy tendril feeds into the metal cube.

My blade rubs right against the wire . . .

I pause.

What if I'm wrong?

Inhaling deeply, I slice through and brace myself for the explosion—

Nothing happens.

I parole the breath I've been holding and unclench all my muscles, which ache with relief.

Just two more wires to go.

Unless someone else blows us all to bits first...

Once again, I reach down and grope my way across the panel until I trace a rectangular piece with a protruding filament. My knife hesitates above it.

Is this the reactor wire?

RING!

The sound of an alarm pierces my ears. I tumble back and smash against the wall.

Attention Recruits! Attention! One of you has just clipped the incorrect wire and activated the detonation sequence. Unless someone correctly deactivates the explosive within the next thirty seconds, it will be automatically triggered and all of you will be shelved, along with your Incentives.

Blip ... Blip ... Blip ...

I reach out my arms, fumbling until I make contact with the control panel once more, my fingers retracing the path to the reactor wire. Along the way, I come across a smaller box.

Is *this* the reactor wire instead? Or is it the ignition timer?

Sweat trickles into my useless eyes and I don't bother to blink it away.

This is exactly where I screwed up during the Sim. And I could actually *see* what I was doing then.

My sweaty hand runs between the two possibilities one last time before settling on my original choice.

Blip… Blip… Blip…

Gritting my teeth, I hack through the wire—

Nothing happens. No loud explosion.

I was *right* this time.

I'm running on pure adrenaline now. No time to fear. My palm engulfs the remaining box and hacks off the lead feeding into the ignition timer.

BEEP!

The sound screeches through my ears.

I messed up—

Searing light engulfs the room, blinding me.

Then it feels like the room's moving. And I'm still in one piece.

Congratulations, Recruit Spark. You have successfully deactivated the explosive and emerged victorious in this Trial.

I sag against the circuit board, too fried to feel anything remotely resembling joy.

The vibrating motion ceases abruptly and the room cants left and right before coming to a stop. My eyes adjust to the brightness at last and I take in the cramped chamber.

It really does seem almost like a coffin, with barely enough room for me to stand. I spy my supplies strewn across the floor and hunch down on creaking knees to stuff them back into my pockets.

Woosh!

A slot above the control panel slides open, letting in more

light. Bracing myself against the wall, I push myself back up to my feet and peer through the glass.

Digory, Cypress, and Ophelia peer out of identical oblong rooms arranged in a diamond pattern. Digory is directly across from me, Cypress is to my left, and Ophelia is to my right.

Digory presses a hand against his window as if he's greeting me. Despite the mics embedded in the glass, neither one of us says a word. His cheeks are drawn, his eyes somber. I mimic his gesture with my own hand and try to smile, but the muscles in my face feel numb. My eyes dart from Cypress to Ophelia. Both looking exhausted—

And *afraid*...

A terrifying thought oozes through my skull.

If *I* won, and no one else was able to disable the bomb in time, how are they going to determine who will have to endure the Culling?

What is Phase Two?

Recruit Spark. As the victor, it now falls upon you in Phase Two to decide which of the other Recruits must choose between their Incentives.

My gaze lingers on each of them. And then I tear away. "I *won't* do it—I *can't*."

But even as the thought escapes my lips, I know I have no choice.

A panel rises from the circuit board containing round buttons numbered one through three. All are lit in vivid green.

Recruit Spark. Before you are three numbered buttons. When you are given the prompt, you must simply press any one of these buttons within ten seconds, blindly choosing one of your comrades as the losing Recruit. The losing Recruit will, in turn, make a blind choice between their own Incentives. If you should choose Recruit Juniper, she will be selecting the manner of her remaining Incentive's shelving, just as Recruit Warrick did. But be warned that the wrong selection will make *you* susceptible to shelving, despite your victory.

A blind choice. Someone else's life will be shattered by my whim.

And if I should select Digory's button, then he in turn might end up blindly selecting *me*—and therefore my Incentives—for execution.

There's no choosing correctly.

Recruit Spark. Make your selection now.

Everything in the room seems to shrink around me, everything except for the three green buttons which grow larger, pulsating like noxious slugs.

My hand hovers over them, wavering.

I slam a fist down onto button *One*.

My chin slumps to my chest. I don't care what happens to me.

What if I've not only condemned myself, but murdered Cole and Digory as well?

DING! DING! DING!

I take a deep breath and look up.

Nothing's changed. Digory's looking at me, just the same way he was a moment ago.

Then he smiles wide.

I almost laugh out loud.

Cole's safe. And I guess *I* am, too ... for now.

My joy evaporates. There's a green light blinking in my peripheral vision ... to my left.

I whip my gaze in that direction.

The light's flashing right above the window of Cypress's chamber.

I've chosen her.

After Digory, Cypress was the last person remaining I'd ever want to put through such horror. To my right, Ophelia's jumping up and down, clapping her hands, giggling.

Recruit Goslin. You have been chosen by Recruit Spark to make your selection. The panel that has just opened in your chamber will trigger the release of toxic gas into your Incentives' chambers. By selecting either the key marked Incentive A or Incentive B, you will decide into which chamber the poison shall be dispersed. However, the identity of the recipient shall not be revealed until after your decision has been made. Prepare to select at once.

Just as before, there's the whir of motors and a darkened glass chamber rises from the floor between us like a behemoth from the depths of the underworld. The lights come on, revealing the little girl and boy I saw at the Graduation Ceremony sitting on identical cots, divided by a partition of thin glass. I can see the metal vents in each of their sections, just like the one in my own chamber, gleaming like teeth. The girl's playing with a torn stuffed doll, while the boy's jumping up and down on his cot, both totally unaware of what's in store for one of them.

I collapse against the glass.

I'm responsible for murdering one of them.

Recruit Goslin. Make your selection. Press button A or button B.

Cypress looks at me with empty eyes. Then she turns and stares at her children, together for the very last time. Even from here, I can see her fingers digging into her cheeks, drawing blood.

Make your decision now, Recruit.

"*I can't.*" She cups a hand over her mouth.

My heart's breaking, especially knowing that I'm the cause of all her agony.

Your time for making a selection has expired, Recruit Goslin. You have forfeited your position in the Trials, and as a result, you, as well as both your Incentives, shall be shelved immediately.

I pound the window over and over again until I finally slump against it. Weak. Empty. "I'm *so* sorry, Cypress. Please forgive me."

She looks at me, her green eyes glazed into icy lakes. Then she shakes her head. "There's nothing to forgive, Lucian." Her voice sounds tinny over the speakers. "You've done nothing except what they made you do."

I make a decision. "Your brother never abandoned you, Cypress," I say. My voice quavers. "You have to believe that he loved you and would have been there if he could." Even now I can't bring myself to tell her everything.

She smiles. "I choose to believe that."

Woosh!

The door to Cypress's chamber slides open.

Recruit Goslin. You will now enter your Incentives' chambers.

"Don't do it, Cypress," Digory calls.

Her face contorts into a mask of anguish. "You know it'll be worse for them if I don't."

The divider between the children sinks into the floor.

Cypress steps out of her chamber on tentative legs and weaves like a drunk over to the children's chamber. It's so unlike her determined walk up to the dais on Recruitment Day. The door to the children's prison slides open. Cypress wipes her eyes, takes a deep breath, and grips the edges of the threshold, pulling herself inside. The door slides shut again, sealing all three of them inside.

"Hello again," Cypress says to the children. Her voice sounds hoarse through the speaker system, as if she's been screaming.

The boy stops jumping and bounces over to sit next to his sister. "You're the soldier lady."

The girl elbows her brother. "What's she doing here?"

The boy stares at Cypress, then cups his mouth to whisper something in his sister's ear.

"Sssh!" The girl nudges him. "You'll make her upset again." She turns to Cypress. "Do you wanna play?"

Cypress wipes her eyes and smiles. "I'd like that very much." She sits on the cot beside them.

A round slot in the panel before me opens up, and a sleek, dark lever, like a small dagger, rises from it.

Recruit Spark. In a few seconds, a pack of starving Canids will be set loose in Recruit Goslin's Incentive Chamber. As victor of this Trial, you can choose to override this method of shelving by pulling the lever yourself and releasing a painless toxin into the air vents instead. As always, the choice is yours.

Memories of blood-curdling screams and tearing flesh coming from that alley back in the Parish drown out Slade's voice and my throbbing heartbeat. The idea of those vicious, horrible beasts pouncing on Cypress and these innocent little ones is too much to bear.

My shaking, sweaty hand grips the ice-cold lever and pulls it. "Forgive me," I whisper, collapsing against the panel.

A faint hissing comes through the speakers.

The boy shifts on the bed, moving next to Cypress. "Do you have any children?"

I bite into my lip.

Cypress's eyes glisten. She shakes her head. "I...I never...did...but I always wanted to." Her lips curve into the saddest smile I've ever seen. "Maybe you two can be my children now."

My fingers scrape the glass. I can't bear to look anymore, but I can't tear my eyes away.

Cypress pulls the children close. "I think you're both

pretty special," she whispers. She kisses each of them on the forehead.

Both children yawn and huddle closer to her.

Then Cypress starts to sing.

Her voice is melodic, echoing softly through the speakers. A bittersweet song of love lost and found again. Each lyric tugs at my heart, sometimes gentle, sometimes wrenching through my chest. I think of my mom, my dad, Mrs. Bledsoe—all the warm memories of them, carved out of me by the Establishment, leaving me hollow inside except for the single flame that still burns.

I'm hugging myself, rocking back and forth.

Through a blur of tears, I can see Digory, glassy-eyed, as if staring at another life.

Even Ophelia seems touched, her cheeks like dewy leaves.

By the time the song comes to an end, neither child is stirring.

Cypress pulls them closer and kisses them again. "Sleep well and have wonderful dreams." Serenity washes over her face.

She smiles and closes her eyes.

THIRTY-FIVE

I wake up curled into a ball on the floor of the next holding station. Digory's sitting cross-legged beside me, his hand stroking my hair. I barely remember half-walking, half-stumbling here after that last Trial.

After Cypress was—

The memory of Cypress and her children lying there with closed eyes, perfectly still, jolts me fully awake. I replay the scene in my mind—the entire pen containing the bodies sinking into the ground as it were being swallowed by quicksand. My hands are still sore from pounding on the window, my throat raw from crying out. When our pens were unlocked, Digory wrapped his arms around me, but I broke away and staggered toward the next holding station. As soon as I reached it I collapsed into a fetal position, and exhaustion gave way to sleep.

Cypress and her children had just vanished, as if they'd never existed. And once again, I did nothing to stop it.

Unlike with Gideon, the Establishment robbed us of our chance to say goodbye to Cypress in our own way, just like they've robbed us of everything else. Grieving is a weakness—too human, too mired in compassion, and we can't repeat that mistake, can we?

My eyes finally wander. Ophelia's lying on the ground a few feet away, sound asleep. A soft, rhythmic purr bleeds through her parted lips, which look curved into a smile. I can just make out her eyeballs rolling beneath their sheaths before she turns on her side, away from me.

A shudder penetrates the numbness.

How can she actually nap, after what happened? What's *still* happening?

But even more disturbing is the thought of what dreams lie coiled in that mind, hidden deep, waiting to spring.

Digory stops stroking my hair. He holds out a ration bar.

"Lucian, you really should eat something. You don't look well. You need your strength."

My eyes finally connect with his. A shard of anger stabs me. Why does he care what happens to me? Why keep pretending when he already has someone?

I sit up. "I'm not hungry."

Instead, I swallow the sour clump lodged in my throat. My fingers dig out the crud from the corners of my eyes. There aren't any tears left to spill, nothing left to feel except the longing to see Cole, to hold him one last time, make sure he's okay before I, too, take my last breath. I'm so tired of fighting, tired of surviving.

I think of that empty space where Cypress and her children disappeared into the ground and stifle a cynical laugh. Instead of grieving for Gideon and Cypress, there's a part of me that actually envies them.

Digory wraps a hand around my arm. "I'm gonna have to insist—"

"*Let go of me!*" I'm barely able to wrench my arm free of his grip and knock the ration bar away.

He recoils as if I struck him. A film of hurt coats his eyes. "Sorry. I'm just ... worried about you. It's getting down to the wire and ... and I know how hard this must be for you ... with your brother and all ... " He looks down, his fingers fidgeting, tugging on the thumb of one hand with the thumb and index finger of the other.

My anger dulls. I rest a hand on his knee and give it a squeeze. "Look, I didn't mean to snap at you. It's just ... with everything that's happened ... I ... " I remember that empty space again. "I can't believe Cypress is *gone*. And Gideon ... " I look back to find Digory's eyes waiting for mine. "Besides, you have your own troubles, someone else to worry about."

I state it as a fact, but the masochist in me is grasping for confirmation or denial of something I don't want to be true.

Digory's gaze is so intense I forget to breathe. "Yes," he says at last, looking away.

Is that disgust? Regret? I can't be sure. And it really makes no difference. Nothing will change, regardless.

He engulfs my hand in his warm palm. It feels so comforting, yet painful at the same time. His face kaleidoscopes with emotion: sadness, regret, anger, longing, all facets of the blue gems fixed on me. "Just because I have a commitment…a *duty*…to someone else…doesn't mean I don't…*care*…about you."

As hard as I try to resist, I slide my hand out from underneath the shelter of his. "I appreciate everything you've done for me, Digory, all your support. But as you said, we're getting down to the wire and you need to focus on your priorities."

I stuff my hand into my pocket, trying to rub away that lingering feel of his skin against mine, which short circuits the few remaining synapses in my brain. I try to remain nonchalant, but I'm doing all that I can to hold it together, and I'm angry at myself for feeling this way.

Digory and me—it doesn't matter.

Cole's my priority.

But that doesn't make it hurt any less.

I shrug. "As noble as your intentions may be, I don't need you feeling sorry for me. You need to do what's in your own best interest from this point on, Digory." I pause and draw strength to spit out the rest. "That's what *I'll* be doing."

Digory purses his lips and nods. "Fair enough. But there's one thing you need to believe." His eyes pin me to the spot. I can't move. "What I feel for you. It's not pity, Lucian. Far from it."

My heart thunders through my chest. No. I can't let him pull me in again. Not at this juncture. He and I…it's just not possible…never was. I compose myself as best I can and clear my throat. "I wish I could believe you. But I don't really believe in much of anything anymore."

His smile overflows with sadness. "Then I guess I'll just have to prove to you how I really feel."

The hiss of static through the speakers shatters the moment.

Attention Recruits!

Nervous energy courses through me at the sound of Slade's voice. I spring to my feet, brimming with anxiety and fear.

Ophelia rolls onto her back and yawns, stretching her arms out. Her eyes flutter open. "Darn! I was just having the most amazing dream—"

Her words stick when she spies Digory and me. She frowns. "Oh. You two are still here." She sighs and climbs to her feet, rubbing the sleep from her eyes.

Stand by. Your next Trial shall commence momentarily.

Digory hops to his feet. I can tell he wants to say something but I look away, focusing on the image of Cypress and her kids sinking into the ground...buried...gone forever...

I shrink from the memory, reeling with vertigo as if I'm poised on the brink of a great precipice staring down at my own doom.

With so few of us remaining, this ordeal will be over soon.

My eyes flit to Digory, then back.

A thought jabs me in the gut. There's a good chance only one of us is going to make it through this next round.

Ahead of us, a panel *wooshes* open, revealing a solitary metal door flanked by two small alcoves inlaid in the wall. A sign above the door says,

BIOGENETICS LABORATORY # 4

Both alcoves are empty, except for gaping holes about eight inches in diameter, ringed by tiny chasing lights trying to devour each other. The interior of each fissure gives way to unsettling darkness.

I force a swallow. What *are* those things?

And why are there only *two* of them instead of *three*?

Ophelia kicks dirt over the spot where Cypress and the children disappeared. I flinch. Then she cups a hand over the side of her mouth and leans in toward me.

"I hope you were able to get some sleep," she says. "I'm feeling *so* rested and refreshed. I feel like I can take on anything—or *anyone*." She chuckles.

Recruits Spark and Tycho. Before we begin this penultimate Trial, you will both approach the inoculation tubes flashing on either side of the gateway.

Digory and I exchange glances infested with worry. "*Inoculation?*" he asks the invisible Slade.

Now, Recruits.

We both shuffle ahead until we're each standing in front of the strange openings.

I glimpse the shadow of satisfaction creeping across Ophelia's face. There's only one reason I can think of that Digory and I are standing where we are and she's been left out.

This next step must be tied to the fact that the two of us are each other's Incentives, and she isn't.

Recruits Tycho and Spark. Both of you roll up a sleeve and place an arm inside the inoculation tubes immediately.

My entire body stiffens. The thought of placing a fingertip, let alone one of my limbs, through that impenetrable darkness terrifies me. But what choice do we really have? If we refuse, they'll kill us on the spot. One look at Digory tells me he's thinking the same thing.

We jam our exposed arms into the Inoculation tubes simultaneously.

Our eyes lock. I struggle to ignore the fear pressing down on my head, on my chest, trying to crush them.

Instead, I focus on the calming blue staring back at me and drowning out everything else—the cacophony of my racing heart, my ragged breaths, the tingling in my fingers. My thoughts settle into manageable anxiety. If I can just hold on a little longer, maybe it won't be as bad as I imagined. Maybe—

Prick!

A sharp pain digs into my inner arm. Digory's eyes flinch at that exact moment, breaking the spell.

Then the pain's gone and we both wrench ourselves free.

Digory walks over to me. His eyes dart from the mark on my arm back to the identical one on his own, then up at me. "You good?"

I flex my biceps a couple of times, then let my arm drop to my side. "Think so. How 'bout you?"

He shrugs. "Can't feel much of a difference."

Ophelia scowls. "You don't *look* hurt."

I ignore her. "Maybe it's just some kind of vaccination."

Digory traces the pinkish patch on his own flesh. "I don't think so."

Recruits Tycho and Spark, you are now in compliance with regulations.

Peals of nervous laughter erupt from me, then sputter out just as quickly. "*Compliance*. I'm not sure that's a good thing."

Digory shakes his head. "I don't think so either..."

Viral Infection is complete. You are now ready to commence this Trial.

THIRTY-SIX

Viral infection?

But deliberately making us sick is just the kind of thing the Establishment specializes in. I close my eyes against a wave of dizziness.

The vent in my chamber during that last trial. Digory said there was one in his, too. They were meant to gas either one of us, as each other's Incentives.

Which means if we've both been infected with some disease prior to starting *this* Trial, then—

"Cole!" I shout at the speakers. "What've you done to him, Slade?"

All of the Incentives have been infected with a mutated form of the Reaper virus, including Recruits Tycho and Spark. The virus has an extremely short incubation period.

Images of Mrs. Bledsoe hacking up blood bubble to

the surface. Except her face changes to Cole's. My knees buckle. Stark desperation rips through me.

When the gateway opens, your task is to retrieve the vials of antivirus and deposit them in the marked cryogenic chamber at the top of the stairs corresponding to your respective Incentives. In the case of Tycho and Spark, should you each procure an additional vial, you're allowed to inject yourselves or each other with the antidote. But be cautioned that there are only four vials total.

Despite the increasing thudding in my head, my thoughts spin through a cloak of fog, calculating the different scenarios based on the amount of remedies versus the number of Incentives. The results of my calculations knife through my Reaper-dulled senses.

Ophelia doesn't need the cure, so all she needs is one vial for Maddie.

I'll need a vial for Cole—that makes two vials claimed. Then another one for Digory. That's three.

That leaves Digory with only one vial, the *final* one, with either his husband or me as its recipient.

Which means I'm a dead man if he's forced to choose.

Once you have deposited the antivirus in your respective Incentive's chamber, they will be transported via pneumatic tubes to their final location and you must immediately proceed to your final Trial. Prepare to enter the gateway, Recruits.

The mechanisms on the door to the Biogenetics Laboratory grind and creak. The sound hurts my ears, which ache with a dull throbbing. Digory and Ophelia crowd against me, each of us facing our potential doom.

The gears of the door stop crunching and the locks spring free.

Even if I were to use my second vial on myself instead of Digory, then he'd be left to choose between the life of his husband and his own.

A quick glance at Digory's pained expression tells me he's been doing some arithmetic of his own.

The door arcs inward with a high-pitched squeak, exposing a flight of stairs. I fight the urge to push through.

The only way both Digory and I can both survive, with both of our other Incentives intact, is if we find all four vials—including the one intended for Ophelia's sister. Effectively *murdering* Maddie.

The door swings open all the way with a deafening *clank*.

Already a fever's baking my brain. Cold sweat weaves down my face. A vise squeezes my chest and I cough into my palm.

"How're you holding up?" Digory whispers into my ear. A red trickle's threading its way down his left nostril and teetering on the edge of his lip.

I shake my head. It's already started.

"You poor dears," Ophelia clucks in mock sorrow. "See you on the other side." She eyes us both up and down and tsks. "Well, *one* of you at least. Maybe."

A broad grin tears across her face, growing wider and wider until I realize I'm seeing double. I grind the base of my palms into my eyes, then let my hands drop back to my sides. I blink a couple of times. Ophelia goes from a total blur to slightly out of focus.

Panic chews on my heart. I have to be quick if I'm going to find those antidotes before the virus takes hold. If I should go blind…

Cross the threshold and begin antivirus retrieval, Slade's voice booms.

Ophelia shoves me into Digory and disappears through the gateway.

I almost topple to the floor, but Digory's arms engulf me and his hands lock against my stomach, propping me upright against him. My eyes finally tighten their focus on the blood streaking through his interlaced fingers.

"You *have* to keep it together," he says. "We can't let her get this, Lucian. Do whatever you have to—*she* will. Understand?"

I nod.

Then he releases me and dashes through after her. I seize a painful breath and lurch through behind him.

The gateway slams shut, with a terrible echo that penetrates my throbbing brain like shards of jagged glass.

"*Careful!*"

Digory's warning startles me. I expected him and Ophelia to be way ahead of me. But they're both standing close by, eyes riveted ahead.

I follow their gazes…

And gasp.

The wide steps that dominate the dimly lit compartment are no ordinary steps. For a horrified second I think that the virus has seriously impaired my faculties, to the point where I'm severely hallucinating.

"What *is* that?" Ophelia asks, all traces of bravado leeched from her voice.

The stairs are not so much hewn from the earth as growing from it, each step pulsating with slimy moisture. Translucent membranes separate each rise. Pressed against these are writhing shapes, twisted bodies with misshapen fingers trying to claw their way out.

"The sign on the door," I croak. "*Biogenetics*. It must be where the Establishment experiments with genetic manipulation…" I stifle a cough with my fist. "And biological weapons, like the virus."

Throbbing red and dark purple tendrils cling to the surface of each step like an arterial system, squirting random jets of a sickening yellow pus-like substance that coats the chamber floor in a gooey mess. With the door closed, cutting off any fresh air, the confined space reeks—a mixture of excrement and vomit…and something else…

Rotting meat.

I double over and cough up a dark wad that looks like tar.

But I know it's not.

Digory rubs my back. "Lucian…"

I shoo him away and straighten up.

Groans all around us, getting louder and louder.

It's those shapes, trapped behind the stairs. Their moans rise and swell in intensity until a crescendo of doom vibrates through the air.

Above, on the landing of this organic nightmare, are three circular steel tubes, each large enough to fit a grown man. Even from down here I can make out the designations stenciled on each one.

Tycho Incentive Storage
Juniper Incentive Storage
Spark Incentive Storage

Ophelia pushes past us. "*Maddie's up there!*" She bounds up the first two steps. One of the undulating tendrils wraps around her ankle and slams her down.

Splat! She hits the viscous rise headfirst.

Without missing a beat, Ophelia pulls her torso up with her arms. Blood trickles from her forehead, mixing with strands of gelatinous slime that sticks to her cheek. The slime gives way with a sharp *rip* the more she pulls her way upright, tearing flesh from her face until she's free.

"Ophelia!" I pitch forward.

But Digory's arm shoots out and barricades the way. "*Look for the vials.*"

His eyes plead through the glaze that encases them. More blood oozes from his nose, as if it's a spigot. Heat radiates from his body like a furnace.

I half nod to him and manage a grunt of agreement. When I swivel my head from left to right to pan the room, it feels like it's going to slip free of the creaky bearings barely attaching it to my neck. I take in the solid walls, which ripple in the heat of my burning vision.

Digory wipes his nose and runs his palms over the walls as if searching for something—a hidden panel or concealed door, maybe? Soon the metal finish is streaked with his blood, and it looks like he's trying to claw his way out his own tomb.

He turns. "*Nothing!*" Anger flashes in his eyes. He kicks the wall. The impact causes him to flinch and slump against it. I can tell by the effort on his face that he's trying to keep himself upright and not slide the rest of the way down to the floor.

The *floor*.

I try to focus on the ground. "Maybe the vials are hidden inside the gunk *underneath* us?"

He weaves toward me. "But we'd have stepped on them by now ... " He sloshes his boot through the goop and almost slips. He looks back up at me. "Wouldn't we have?"

I shake my head, making myself more dizzy. I search the room again, until my gaze lands on Ophelia ... still tangled on the stairs, trying to pry herself free of the tentacle gripping her leg. "Unless the vials are somewhere we haven't stepped *yet*."

Despite the waves of pain and nausea, I squat, careful to avoid the flailing tendrils, searching through the opaque membranes between each rise of the stairs, past the silhouettes of disease-riddled victims, their glowing eyes blinking at me ...

Those aren't eyes.

I dig my fingers through the clammy diaphanous skin coating the stairs and tear a portion away.

The blinking is actually the green flashing of a miniature

beacon. It's attached to a transparent packet, which contains a hypodermic needle and a small bottle of clear fluid. The packet's half-wedged into the muck.

I point at it. "That's gotta be one of the four vials," I whisper so Ophelia doesn't hear. Considering both our handicaps, we need every advantage we can get.

Digory leans in, his lips grazing my cheek on their way to my earlobe, penetrating my fever with shivers that tingle through every nerve-ending. "You get that one and then keep looking," he whispers back. He smiles at me despite the weariness in his eyes. "You're going to make it, Lucian."

Something about his tone saddens and frightens me. I clutch his hand. "We *both* are."

His smile ebbs. "Of course. Keep moving." He squeezes my shoulder then moves away, searching through another part of the membrane.

When I look back, Ophelia's eyes are glued on me. The tendril that gripped her lies torn in her gore-streaked hands, leaking a dark pool by her feet.

She may not have heard us, but she's *seen*... she *knows*...

Our eyes hold one more second. Then she whips around and plunges her hands through the membrane nearest her.

I shove my own hand through the gash.

Sharp fingernails dig into my flesh—

THIRTY-SEVEN

I try to jerk my arm away, but it's held tightly by an infected man with splotchy, yellow-gray skin and bloodshot eyes. His cheeks are gaunt. Blood vessels underlie his face like a road map.

To make these innocent infected people, whose minds are as scrambled as rabid Canids, protect the very antidote that could save their own lives is truly sickening. Revulsion and pity fuse in the pit of my stomach.

The man opens his mouth wide, releasing a jet of blood and teeth that douses my jumpsuit. That pungent, rotting odor wafts past his cavernous throat, suffocating me. It's as if his insides have already putrefied.

This is what's going to happen to Cole, to Digory, to *me* if I don't get the vials in time.

Still in the diseased man's grasp, I stretch my fingers until they're grazing the packet of precious antidote, pulling it out by my fingertips … slowly … a fraction of an inch at a time … until I'm able to grasp it firmly.

The man senses what I'm doing and leans forward, his mouth opened wide—

I shove my other hand through and grip his scraggly hair, yanking his head back just before he can sink what's left of his teeth into me.

And then we're deadlocked, the infected man still grasping my arm, preventing me from pulling out the cure.

Somewhere nearby, Digory shouts something unintelligible even while Ophelia lets out a savage battle cry that pierces through the grotesque chorus of groans.

But I can only focus on holding my attacker's foaming mouth at bay with the last remnants of my strength. I'm losing the struggle. Strands of his hair rip from his skull and through my fingers.

His mouth hovers above my arm—

My fingernails dig through the packet and grasp the empty hypodermic by the plunger, just as his craggy lips graze my flesh. I jab the plunger through his eye, feeling it sink into the mushy tissue. Warm pulp seeps through my fingers as I rip my hand away, snatching the packet free.

Digory's perched on a rise above me, the upper half of his body buried inside another membrane. I can tell by the way his body's thrashing that he's struggling with someone, just like I was.

"Lucian!" His voice sounds muffled. "I *almost* have one! Don't stop! *Keep going!*"

I'm torn. I don't want to leave him. I *can't*. But already

I can feel the sickness overwhelming me, wringing the energy from me, fogging my brain and vision to the point where I can barely distinguish shapes a few feet away. I cough up another wad of bloodied phlegm.

If this is what it's doing to *me*, I'm heartsick at the thought of what it must be doing to little Cole. But I can't chance taking the antidote now—not until I've secured another one.

My breath comes in horrible rasps.

"*Got it!*" Ophelia's shriek sounds like a battle cry. She's little more than a blur, holding up an equally distorted reddish object.

The second packet.

That means Digory and I *have* to compete against each other for the remaining two packets of the antidote...and he's practically got one already...

One of us isn't going to make it.

Something grabs at Ophelia's ankle. "*Don't touch me!*" she shrieks. I can just make out the toe of her boot mashing against the thing, over and over. Loud splintering noises assault my sensitive ears.

CRACK!

She stops kicking. That can't be a head slumping over at her feet, can it? But, as hazy as my eyesight is, I can tell that's exactly what it is, or was, until she caved in its skull with her unrelenting fury. She flicks a clump off the end of her boot. Then she stoops and rips away more of the membrane, which comes loose with a *plop*.

Her head swivels in my direction. "I wouldn't want the two of you to get lonely." She giggles and sprints up the stairs.

"Ungh!" Digory grunts. He's climbing the stairs, teetering up them, more like it. His hand clutches blinking green.

It's official. Only one dose of antivirus left.

My wobbling legs give way and I sink to my knees, bracing myself against the rise above me. Then I'm pulling myself up to the next step, then the next, crawling, squirming like a slug even as I push my face into the slick-coated membranes searching for the final packet.

A choir of growls oozes out of the gap where Ophelia retrieved her vials, freezing me in place. A tangle of limbs pushes through, clawing at the air. Dark forms slink into the outer room with us.

That's what Ophelia did by ripping out the membrane. She opened up the gap so that—

"*They're getting through!*" The fear propels me up the next stair.

And there, flashing through the crystalline layer between rises, is the last of the packets, tempting me to my potential doom.

I plunge my hand through, heedless of the possibility that ravenous jaws are waiting to snap at my fingers and chew them off. But nothing stops me as I grasp the packet and pull it back through.

A shadow falls over me.

The infected are busy creeping through the opening Ophelia made for them and heading my way.

I tear the packet open with my mouth, leaving bloody teeth marks on it. Then I'm fumbling with the vial. My heart tries to lurch out my throat when the cure almost tumbles from my grasp. But I seize it at the last moment and shove the hypodermic inside it, letting it gulp up the precious fluid.

Digory kicks a snarling contaminated man in the gut and sends him reeling against two others, buying us valuable seconds. But just beyond them, more dark shapes loom, hissing, reaching for us.

I graze the skin above my vein with the hypodermic. I hate myself for being so selfish and for what this will mean to Digory. He's going to have to choose between his husband's life or his own. But if I don't take the antivirus now, I'll pass out before I can outrun this diseased mob and make it up to Cole with *his* vial.

Digory sees what I'm about to do and nods.

Then I can't bear the pain of looking at him anymore and I turn away, plunging the antivirus into my vein.

It starts off like a small sting, then spreads like wildfire through my blood. I feel like I'm burning both inside and out. The needle clatters to the ground. I grip my stomach against the pain. My eyes dim even further. My head feels like it's going to cave in and my brains are going to pop through my eyes and ears.

Just when the pain gets the most intolerable, it suddenly washes away like a quick-moving tide. The fever dissipates and the clouds over my eyes disperse. I still feel like a Squawker has plowed into me, but its more weariness than infection now.

I swipe at the cold sweat coating my face with my forearm just in time to see two of the sick grappling with Digory. If he weren't ill, he'd be able to hold his own. But in his weakened state, they're steadily gaining the upper hand. My eyes widen, now able to take in every terrifying detail.

One of them's about to bite into the wrist holding Digory's hypodermic packet.

"*Watch out!*" I lunge and shove the man away before he can sink his teeth into Digory's flesh. The man falls to the ground and grabs my ankle, but I kick it away.

I spin around. Digory punches the second one in the jaw and he topples backward, sprawling down the stairs.

"*Th-thanks...*" Digory rasps, trying to smile.

But my relief's short-lived. Half a dozen more of the infected drones are scrambling up the stairs, trampling the two on the ground in their effort to reach us.

Crunch!

One of our pursuers grinds a heel into the jaw of the man I just pushed, and shatters it.

"*Let's go!*" I grab Digory's arm and sling it over my shoulder, running on pure adrenaline now. It's awkward going. I'm too weak, and he's too heavy. But I manage to haul him up the stairs, dogged every step of the way by the unrelenting pack.

Just a few more steps to go and we'll be at the top, and I can get the remedy to Cole.

Recruit Juniper. Your Incentive has received the antivirus. Proceed immediately through the next gateway to your final Trial.

There's the *woosh* of a door sliding open just as Digory and I stagger over the last step. Digory leans against the tube marked *Tycho Incentive Storage.*

Aside from the three steel capsules, one of which is now blinking green, there's an open door with nothing but darkness beyond. Ophelia must be halfway to the next Trial by now.

I rip out my second packet and am about to shove it into the receiving slot of Cole's tube when Ophelia steps out from behind the capsule and tears it away from my hand.

My breath crystallizes in my lungs. "What the *hell* are you—?"

"Now *you* can get a taste of what it feels like to lose someone *you* love, Spark." A smile rips across her face, from one of her ears to the other. She draws back the hand clutching Cole's salvation.

I stumble forward on liquid legs, my hands flailing for the packet.

Her face twists into a snarl. She hurls the cure back down the stairs...

I drop to my knees, watching, stunned, as the packet twirls end over end, the vial of antivirus glinting in the light, moving farther and farther away from my brother, taking his life with it in the process.

It shatters against the far wall, exploding into a million gleaming shards, just as my entire universe implodes in on itself.

As my cheek slams into the cold floor, I see Ophelia's boot withdrawing. Then she runs through the door and disappears.

I punch my fist into the base of Cole's storage tube—his *coffin*—feeling as if my soul's been ripped out, and I squeeze my eyes shut for what will probably be the last time.

Recruit Spark. Your Incentive has received the anti-virus. Proceed immediately through the next gateway to your final Trial.

My eyes flutter open.

I bolt upright.

Arms lock around me from behind and drag me away from the looming infected bodies, toward the gateway that Ophelia disappeared through.

I manage to turn around.

It's Digory. He looks paler than I've ever seen him. Trails of dried blood cake his nostrils. A grayish film coats his once brilliant blue eyes.

But he still smiles at me. "*Lucian ...*" he croaks. "*You ... gotta ... go ... now ...*"

Behind him, Cole's tube is blinking green, just like Maddie's.

How is that possible? I *saw* Ophelia destroy Cole's cure with my own eyes.

And that's when it hits me. Digory sacrificed not only his husband's life but his own, so that Cole might live.

I grip his forearms. "What about *you*? What about your husband?" My eyes flit toward the tube still pulsing red.

He shakes his head. "F-forget ... about ... *me* ... save ... your ... *brother ...*"

He collapses. I don't have the strength to hold him up so I slide down with him.

Beyond us, the horde's making its way onto the landing and lumbering toward us.

I seize Digory's wrists. "*I'm not leaving you here!*"

I pull with every fiber of strength I have left, dragging him across the floor toward the doorway. One of the infected springs from the ground, gripping his ankle.

I pull Digory through the doorway and hit the button on the panel on the other side, praying it's the locking mechanism.

For a split second, nothing happens.

The sickly woman opens her mouth right above Digory's ankle...

Then the door *wooshes* closed again. There's a sharp snap as it severs the infected woman's hand and slams shut at last. The hand's still gripping Digory's foot, jetting out gobs of dark blood from the jagged end with each twitch.

Kneeling beside him, I pry it off and hurl it away from us. "It's going to be okay now, Digory."

His eyes are closed, his chest bobbing up and down with each raspy breath. I touch my palm to his forehead. It's like touching fire.

Recruit Tycho, your actions have caused you to forfeit your participation. You must remain behind and await collection. Recruit Spark, continue now or face forfeiture as well.

I can see a light, down the sloping path Ophelia took.

What am I going to do? She's going to reach Maddie before I reach Cole.

"Lucky," a voice whispers in the dark behind me.

Even before I whirl to see the figure emerging from the

shadows, I know who it is. That voice is branded into me forever.

Cassius.

THIRTY-EIGHT

I spring to my feet.

He's the cause of all of this. All the pain, the suffering.

I'm so overwhelmed by rage, I'm paralyzed. I can only watch as Cassius slinks into the light. Behind him, I can see the outlines of two Imps holding weapons. Styles and Renquist. Of course the coward wouldn't come to see me alone.

He looks at me with shock and pity, holding out his arms. "*Oh, Lucky*... look at you ... I ... I never wanted things to be like *this*... " He takes a step forward.

I shrink from his disgusting hands. "What do you want, Cassius, huh? Killing Mrs. Bledsoe wasn't enough for you? You need to make sure you destroy *everyone* I care about?" My fingernails pierce my palms.

It doesn't matter about the Imps protecting him. I'm going to kill him right now.

He shakes his head, dislodging tears from those hateful

eyes. "You have to listen to me, Lucky. I feel terrible about what's happened. I've come to set things right between us."

A hollow laugh bursts from my lips. "Set things *right*?"

His eyes pierce mine. "I can make *sure* you get Cole back."

The words stop me cold. "What're you talking about?"

He steps aside. A side door in the tunnel opens, letting in a stream of harsh artificial light that knifes through the dimness, causing me to squint against it. Beyond the door I can see a gangway leading to a Squawker.

"That's my private transport," Cassius says in hushed tones. "Right now, Recruit Juniper is traversing the sea to get to the final Trial. I can *fly* you instead. You'll get there ahead of her and be reunited with Cole *before* she even arrives."

His words are like hypnosis. I walk past him to the threshold, staring at the Squawker that could mean Cole's salvation.

"You want me to cheat," I mutter. I search the ceiling for cameras. "Aren't you afraid your fellow officials will find out about this?"

He shakes his head. "I've risked making sure all the surveillance in this sector has been disabled, just so I could give you this chance."

After everything the five of us went through—all our hard work training at Infiernos, the horrors we endured. That's what it all comes down to. Rigging the final Trial.

He sidles up to me, but I'm too deep in thought to move. "It could all be over in a few minutes. Your brother will be safe. And all this will be over and behind us." He rests his forehead against my shoulder. "Aren't you tired, Lucky? Don't you want to rest at last?"

Everything I've dreamed since this whole ordeal began is right at my fingertips. How many times have I thought to myself that I'd do *anything* to rescue Cole from this nightmare?

And now here's my chance.

If I kill Cassius now...

I press my fingers into my throbbing temple. "Yes," I mutter. "So tired... I can't do this anymore..."

But what about—

I run over to Digory. "I can't leave you."

He's sitting up, his eyes barely open and coated in a gray film. "There's nothing you can do for me now," he says, patting my hand. "Besides... I've gotten out of worse scrapes." He tries to laugh but it devolves into a choking fit that takes a minute to subside. "Listen to him, Lucian. Do what he says. Your brother *needs* you."

Cassius wraps his hand around my arm and gently tugs. "For once, Tycho's right. If you're to beat Juniper, we have to go *now*."

As much as I've hated Cassius up to this point, I hate him even more now.

Hate him for being right.

Digory's hand grips my shoulder and squeezes. "I'll... be... okay. Don't... worry." We hold each other's gaze for what seems like forever.

I feel shell-shocked. I can only nod as Cassius pulls me away.

The next few minutes are a haze. Cassius leads me through the doorway and across the gangway, leaving Digory further and further behind us with every step.

When we reach the entrance to the Squawker, Styles and Renquist position themselves to flank the hatchway as Cassius takes a step inside.

I freeze, gripping the handrails.

Cassius turns to me. He smiles again and holds out his hand. "It'll all be over soon, Lucky, you'll see. You'll have Cole back and we can be a family, just like we used to be."

The gangplank whirs to life.

I turn to watch it slide away from the tunnel, leaving Digory cut off from everyone ... awaiting death ...

Alone.

Our eyes meet.

Once I step into this Squawker and the hatch seals, I'll never see him again.

Cassius takes my hand. "I was just so angry before, Lucky, but it's all over now. In time, you'll forgive me, just like I've already forgiven you. And now that Tycho's no longer between us, things will be different. I *promise*."

He pulls me through the Squawker's hatch—

Digory saved Cole's life at a terrible cost. And here I am, wallowing in the empty promises of a liar and a murderer, leaving Digory to die all alone.

I never even told him that I—

The hatch starts to slide shut—

"I *can't*." I wrench myself free of Cassius and his treachery and squeeze out what's left of the opening, tumbling onto the rapidly shrinking gangplank.

"*What are you doing?*" Cassius yells after me.

Then I'm dashing across the dwindling walkway, my heart thundering, away from Cassius and his toxic life of endless lies and enslavement to the depravities of the Establishment.

I leap off the edge of the gangway, across the subterranean depths of the Skein, and crash against the tunnel door, dangling from its threshold by my fingers. I squirm upward and through the doorway—

Into Digory's waiting arms.

It's the first time I've seen him so utterly vulnerable. He sobs against my cheek, his massive shoulders heaving. He teeters from weakness, and I slide down to the floor with him, cradling him in my arms.

"I couldn't leave you, Digory. And after what you did for Cole ... what it *cost* you ... your *husband* ... "

He shakes his head. "Husband in name only. Rafé was a friend and fellow resistance fighter. We married as part of our cover, should either of us ever get recruited. We knew what we were getting into, what the risks were ... but Cole's just an innocent child with his whole life ahead of him."

My heart thunders against my chest, and fresh tears stream down Digory's face. His eyes are opaque from the virus, almost every hint of blue gone. I can tell he can't see me anymore, and I'm dying inside.

He clutches my hand to his lips. "I couldn't bear your

heartbreak if you lost him. It was killing me more than this virus could."

"Shh. Don't think about any of that. You're gonna be fine … " My voice chokes.

His words are tumbling out now. "Back at school … all those times I ignored you, was never your friend … I couldn't risk getting close to you because I was afraid one day you'd be *my* Incentive and I never wanted you to go through this hell." He reaches up and caresses my cheek. "I *love* you, Lucky."

"I love you too."

And then we're kissing each other, and it's like I've never lived before. Warm fire feeds my entire body, growing until it's a blaze of emotion that empowers me, gives me the strength that I need to do what I have to do.

When we finally break free, I can barely breathe. But this time, I welcome the feeling more than anything in the world.

Warning. The tunnel leading to the final Trial will seal in approximately one minute.

Sirens blare.

I look back down the passageway.

I may already be too late to save Cole. But I have to go on.

"Digory, I … "

"I know. *Here* … " He pulls his ID tag from around his neck and tucks it in my palm. "Carry me with you."

We draw close and kiss again, a deep hunger that can never be satisfied. I finally force myself to pull away. It literally hurts my flesh, as if somehow our skin's bonded together by the most powerful adhesive of all.

"I'll come back for you Digory. I *promise.*"

"Don't worry about me." He kisses my forehead. "Find Cole. *Never give up.*"

I tear myself away and race down the passageway, sobbing, feeling like a knife's ripping through my innards. Red warning lights twirl from the ceiling in a blurry wet haze, disorienting me, making me dizzy. Up ahead, the sliver of light coming through the opened door at the end narrows faster and faster...

I slip through just as the door *clangs* shut.

The elevator zooms upward at high speed, curling my stomach. Then it jolts to a stop and its doors swoosh open.

I'm free of the Skein at last.

I step out onto a small, rocky landing in the middle of the sea.

The sky's heavy with black clouds, like the shroud over my heart. The deep rumbling of thunder fills my ears. Before me, a dark ocean looms. White caps churn through its turbulent ripples—

I gasp.

Staring down at me, across those choppy waters, is the Lady. The Lady that sparked the stories I would tell Cole every night.

The Lady of his dreams ... and mine.

She's *real* and larger than life—at least one hundred feet tall.

I hug myself. It's too much. Emotional overload. Grief

over Digory. Shock at this latest surprise. The sound of my own laughter startles me. It's soft at first. But in moments, it's roaring from my lips as freely as the tears cascading down my cheeks and into my open mouth, filling it with salty freshness.

The Lady still brandishes her torch high, about one hundred and fifty feet into the sky. But there's something different about her that shakes me out of my momentary insanity. No longer standing on a pedestal, she's partially submerged in the waters that lap against the lower part of her gown. Her towering form lists to one side, as if standing has become a great burden. The spires of her crown are missing parts or are broken off. Her entire body's riddled with welts and holes in the stone, like gaping wounds.

My eyes track her gaze across the sea. There are no sparkling lights, no shimmering buildings for her to stand sentinel over. Only a thick mist that hovers over mounds of crumpled ruins.

Despite her battered state, and everything she must have been through, the Lady still endures ... standing strong, regal, and fearless, clutching her book, daring anyone to try and take it from her.

Never give up.

A tiny figure crawls out of the water and scales a stone fold of the Lady's gown, disappearing inside one of the craggy openings.

Ophelia.

She may have gotten a head start. But she's not as fast a swimmer as I am. I can narrow the gap.

Attention!

Slade's voice cuts through the wail of the wind and echoes across the sea.

Congratulations Recruit Spark. You have made it to your final Trial. Your task is simple. The first Recruit to find his or her respective Incentive in the ruin shall earn a place as a trainee in the Imposer Task Force. All previous restrictions, regarding the infliction of lethal force against your fellow Recruits, have been rescinded. You are free to use any means at your disposal to accomplish this task. Good luck.

Even though the Lady's torch is unlit, it's a beacon that lights the way to my brother, at long last. A soothing calm comes over me. I can do this. Without Cassius's interference, without cheating. I can *do* this.

For Cole.

For Digory.

I dive into the cold water and swim toward whatever fate awaits me.

THIRTY-NINE

I can't feel my body.

It's as if I'm a spirit, gliding through the ice-cold waters. But not feeling anything is freeing. It allows me to concentrate on staying afloat, and freezes out every other thought except for my immediate goals.

Reach the Lady. Rescue Cole.

My arms hack their way through the water. In minutes, I'm bobbing on the surface and clinging to one of the giant stone shackles broken open at the Lady's feet.

Guess she doesn't take too kindly to being anyone's slave either.

I spit out a mouthful of freezing water. My breath comes in short, quick bursts. I can barely feel the stone links as I grasp them and haul myself out of the sea, rolling onto my back.

Goal One accomplished.

But there's no time to rest. Ophelia's still in the lead in a trial where mere seconds will mean the difference between Cole's life or death.

Hauling myself to my feet, I grope the huge crumbling manacles, trying to find purchase so I can climb. A couple of times my feet dislodge weak rock and I almost topple back into the ocean. But I clutch the stone with an iron grip, wincing as it tears through the flesh of my palms.

Just a foot or two above me looms one of the jagged holes in the stone I spotted when I exited the Skein. Trying to balance myself against a layer of the statue's robes, I lift a trembling arm and hook it over the bottom edge, dragging myself upward until I'm scuttling through it.

I find myself wedged in a narrow steel staircase that spirals upward like a twisted spine to dizzying heights. Handrails coil up this spine, resembling thin nerve fibers. Steel girders crisscross all around; some are torn and curled, trapping me inside a huge fractured rib cage. Everything seems held together by enormous bolts and rivets, like the ballbearings and joints of a giant. Stale dust wafts through the dimness, clogging my nostrils with dank decay.

I cup my hands around my mouth. "Cole, can you hear me? *Where are you?* It's me, Lucky!"

My only response is the clatter of booted heels echoing from the top of the stairs.

Ophelia.

Squirming out of the cramped space, I dash up the narrow, rickety stairs feeling more claustrophobic the higher I go.

Below me, the hole I first crawled through is already half-submerged in the swirling waters created by the incoming storm.

Don't give up.

I take a few slow, deep breaths and continue my climb.

Creak!

The staircase shudders. My fingers dig into the rails.

No need to panic. These stairs have stood for hundreds of years and will probably be around for hundreds more.

Pop! Pop! Pop!

Several of the steel pins holding the staircase in place rip free with a terrible clang that ricochets like the sound of gunfire. The entire column of steps lists sharply. I'm thrown against the rails. My upper body sails over the edge and I dig my booted toes into the skeletal framework to prevent myself from toppling completely over.

A nut and bolt the size of my head crash through the handrail, inches from my head.

I glance at the obliterated railing, now a clump of twisted metal.

That was no accident.

"*Stay away, Spark!*" Ophelia's shrill cry reverberates through the Lady's innards.

Trying to hold my balance on the tilted stairs, I stretch my neck out and over the remaining part of the banister, centimeter by centimeter, and peer up.

There she is, maybe seventy-five feet above me, awash in flashes of lightning that dissect her body into slivers of light and shadow.

"There's no way you can beat me," she trills. "And I'll hurt you if you try."

A blast of thunder rattles the staircase.

Anger flares through me. "You mean like you tried to hurt me back at the lab by destroying Cole's antivirus?"

Ophelia slithers away from the railing and out of sight.

My eyes dart from the railing to the stairs' supports.

Time to do a little destabilizing of my own.

Gripping the stairs above me, I leap onto the railing. A deep groan reverberates through the murk, as if the Lady's in pain. I rock back and forth as hard as I can, gaining speed and momentum. Years of exposure to the elements has rendered the structure unsound. Ophelia and I are probably the first people to put weight on these steps in ages.

"Spark!" Ophelia shrieks from somewhere above. "What are you doing? *You'll kill us both!*"

The entire staircase teeters for a moment—

Crack!

The whole structure lurches forward, collapsing into the dangling network of steel support girders.

A dense haze of dislodged grit veils everything.

The impact sends violent shudders through my body as I struggle to hold on. But these are minor compared to the spasms that rock the Lady to her very foundations. A cacophony of screeching metal, buckling walls, and exploding bolts fills the air.

I lose my grip and dangle from the twisted metal railing by one hand. Below me, a fresh surge of seawater crashes through a new gash in the thin copper of the Lady's skin, chilling my flesh with its icy spray.

My slick hand slips—

I plunge, regaining my grip on the gnarled handrail at the last moment and stopping myself from being impaled on a protruding rivet. Then I'm penduluming back and forth on protesting metal, one second over freezing ocean, the next over jagged steel, over and over, as if it's fate that's lost *its* Trial and now has to decide which manner of death I deserve.

At least I've bought some time, and maybe even narrowed the gap between Ophelia and myself.

Snap!

The bar I'm clinging to breaks free of its fasteners.

As I drop, I swing, arcing into the latticework opposite the collapsed staircase.

Then I'm tangled in its metal strands, which resemble a huge web. I look up. The crossed metal beams run parallel to where the staircase used to be, extending all the way to the top of the Lady's head. The open space between each diagonal strip is only a few feet wide, well-suited for hand and foot holds.

This *could* work. But it's not like I have a real choice.

Wasting no more time, I spider up its length. Even though I tug at each bar before I pull on it or trust it with my entire weight, I try to move fast and not linger too long on any one section, just in case.

As I skitter the rest of the way up the makeshift ladder, two thoughts tussle in my brain.

The higher I climb, the closer I'm getting to Cole...

And Ophelia's even more unsettling when she's *nowhere* to be seen…

I reach the top and slide onto the platform that used to connect to the spiral staircase.

My heart drumrolls in my chest.

Gasping breaths burst from my lips.

"Cole! I'm *here*! I've come for you, buddy!"

Only the sound of my own voice replies, its echoes distorted by the mocking wind.

Before me, there's a series of panoramic windows spanning maybe fifteen feet. If there once was glass, it's long gone now. The row of windows looks like a crescent moon collapsed on its side, the ends pointing downward like a frown. Black clouds like billowing smoke stream past these open frames, along with the chilly wind that whips through my hair and weeps into my ears.

Based on the size and shape of the room, this must be the Lady's crown I'm standing in. Whoever built this place must have designed it so that its people could come up here and gaze at the wonder of the city.

My fingers latch onto one of the curved support beams and I pull myself to my feet, staggering toward the center window.

There's nothing to be seen outside now except an all-consuming darkness that's plucked the stars out of the sky and swallowed them whole. Lightning flickers in the sky, reflecting on the choppy sea below. Then there's a low rumble, as if the night's growling a warning. The air up here feels like icy teeth biting into my skin.

Another flash of lightning turns the dark into brief day. A deafening clatter of thunder rattles my body. I back away from the window frames. As much as I rub my shoulders, I can't shake the tremors.

As soon as the rumble subsides, I can hear the sound of breathing directly behind me and I spin—

Crack!

"Ah!" A volcano erupts against my ribs. The impact sends me reeling across the room. It's as if my side's on fire. I clutch the wound, fresh waves of pain slicing through me. I feel like I'm going to be sick. Every breath I take is torture. When I'm finally able to open my eyes, it's like looking through a rain-soaked pane.

Ophelia's wielding a broken pipe—which she just used to shattered my ribs—like a club.

Another lash of thunder. I flinch.

She steps closer.

There's a blur of metal. I try to roll out of the way—

Whack!

My kneecap explodes in agony.

Lightning and thunder struggle to overtake each other, striking faster and louder.

Somehow, I'm able to use my arms to drag my body backward, never taking my blurry eyes off her. Soon, the cold steel of rivets digs into my back. I'm backed into a corner with nowhere to run... even if I *could*.

Rain pelts the window frames like bullets, spraying the interior of the crown with an icy mist.

Ophelia's shadow drapes over me like a burial cloth.

She raises the pipe high overhead—in direct trajectory to my skull.

I raise my palm. "Ophelia... *please*..."

She snarls. Drool seeps from her parted lips, scalding my frosted cheek. She slams the pipe down like a mallet, but before it connects, I smash the toe of my boot into her shin as hard as I can.

She shrieks and drops the pipe, falling to her knees. It starts to roll and I lunge for it, my fingers grazing the tip. But she pounces on top of me, her weight grinding my fractured ribs against the hard floor as she knots her fingers in my hair and whips my head back.

"*I... hate... you*," she growls into my ear.

Then she slams my face against the floor, pulls it back, and slams it again. Warmth trickles down my forehead... the room spins...

She pulls my head back a third time—

My fingers wrap around the rain-spattered pipe.

Clutching it as tight as I'm able, I swing it backward, jabbing it into whatever part of her I can reach.

Her body spasms against mine, crushing me harder against the floor. I squirm out from underneath her.

Pressing against another support column, I grab it and haul myself to my feet, teeth grinding into my lips against the throbbing pain. I stagger to the far corner of the room, away from Ophelia and toward the farthest window, hoping that the torrential rains and frigid air will help revive me.

But Ophelia's unrelenting. Hands twisted into claws,

teeth bared, she charges. The collision sends me reeling backward—through the open window.

My stomach lurches into my throat. Instinctively, I grab onto her and pull her with me—

Then we both free-fall into space.

FORTY

My body slams into ridges of hard stone, much sooner than I would have imagined.

The jolt sends currents of pain sizzling into my knee and ribs, made worse by the deadweight of Ophelia's body, still straddling mine.

Our fall was broken by the crook between the Lady's neck and right shoulder. Through the pall of rain, I can make out the stone robes draping halfway down her upraised arm, which rises about forty feet above us, clutching the torch.

The wind is fierce, buffeting my body with sharp blows, and the rain stings like a lash. If it weren't for Ophelia's weight anchoring me to the spot, I'd have toppled over to my death.

The sheer terror numbs my pain. I'm petrified, unable to move a fraction of an inch and risk rolling over.

There's nowhere to go …

Ophelia's eyes flutter open. She looks dazed at first, as if she's woken up from a dream and isn't sure where she slept. She lifts her head. Rain spatters her cheeks and she rubs it away. "Where—"

A gasp bursts from her lips.

Her eyes open wide and flit about. When they settle on me, it's like flint igniting fuel.

"*You're trying to kill me too!*" The sound of her voice barely carries over the roaring storm. Her face contorts into a hateful mask. Hands clamp around my throat, squeezing.

My own hands lock onto her forearms, trying to rip her grip loose.

She squeezes even tighter...

Everything grows impossibly darker... and then the stars finally appear... bleeding through the sky... but I know it's really the lack of oxygen... shutting me down... killing me...

No.

Releasing her arms, I ball my hands into fists and pummel her face with as much strength as I can muster.

When she lets go of me to shield herself, her body rolls halfway off me and I squeeze out from under her. She gropes for me but slips on the slick stone, hooking her hands around one of the robe's folds. The powerful air currents rock her body.

For a second it looks like she's going to topple over.

But she regains her balance and crawls back over. "I should have finished you off earlier. Tycho, too." She leers at me. "But *he* wanted me to watch you, keep you two alive so you could feel the pain of losing each other in the end. And now that Tycho's gone, there's no reason to keep you around any longer."

"What are you talking about? Who wanted you to spy—?"

Her eyes are glass. "Prefect Thorn. He wanted to teach you two a lesson ... make you suffer ... he made a bargain with my mother and me ... "

I nod numbly. "He'd help you win in exchange for you being his spy, making sure nothing happened to us during training. Planting a camera on us so he'd have his little footage for the Graduation Ceremony."

She smirks. "All I care about is my sister. And my Mama. She'd still be alive if you and Tycho hadn't plotted—"

"Don't you see?" I burst out. "He's manipulating *you*. Just like he tried to do with Digory and me. Right after our last Trial, he showed up and offered me a free pass to get here first and beat *you*. Since I didn't take it, he's using you to get his revenge. He doesn't care about any of us. We're all just pawns in his own sick games."

She shakes her head. "You're lying!"

She pounces—

Instinct blots out the fear. I kick out, booting her in the face. She slams back against one of the stone ripples. Blood seeps from her nostrils.

She glares at me and keeps on coming ...

Ignoring the agony in my side, I move the only way I can ... away from her ... forward.

When I drop to a crawling position, my knees hit the stone and I scream out in anguish, my voice blending with the moaning wind that's determined to drag me away to my doom. Hand over hand, I haul myself up the steep incline of the Lady's arm, using the stone mounds of gathered cloth as steep stairs. Rain stings my eyes, making it almost impossible to see, which probably keeps me from focusing too much on just how high up I really am.

Through the howling winds, I can swear I hear her breaths... the sounds of her boots digging into the stone... getting closer... *closer*...

I climb the last ridge, now hugging the bare stone arm, clinging to its slick, smooth surface for dear life.

Dead end. I'm trapped.

My face presses against the thin flesh of the Lady's inner elbow, inhaling the pungent aroma of copper and mossy stone.

All those nights I told Cole the story of the Lady, I never realized I was describing the place I would die.

Then, I notice a thin slit of light visible between the panels of skin. I press on one of them, and it buckles.

The rotted panel crashes inward—

I lose my balance and my upper body wedges through the twisted metal, into the statue's arm. As startled as I am, it doesn't compare to the shock of what I see.

Hidden inside is a rusted ladder, extending up the entire length of the arm.

Up toward the torch.

That's where Cole is.

My upper body squeezes through. Pain rips through my

fractured rib. I bite down against the tears and seize the near-est ladder rung with both hands.

Ophelia's hand clamps around my ankle. Her giggles turn into a howl that rivals the storm winds. The sound of splinter-ing stone pierces through the horrific yowl. Her eyes bulge.

I turn just in time to see the stone ledge she's perched on disappear beneath her. More lightning flashes, providing me with a clear view of it tumbling down the dizzying abyss toward the foamy sea.

Still clutching my foot, Ophelia drops, yanking me downward and jamming my rib cage against the warped panel.

"*Ah!*" The pain's like a thousand knives carving into my flesh. I can't breathe…

"Please, Spark! Please!" Ophelia whimpers. "Don't let me fall! I *can't* die! Maddie needs me! *Help me!*"

"Hold still!" I yell at her over the pounding fury. Only my tenuous hold on the ladder is keeping us alive. The wind bats us from side to side. With each swaying move-ment, the metal saws at my ribs.

I grip the ladder tighter. "*Hang on and work with me, Ophelia!*"

It feels like my shoulders are tearing from their sockets. But I pull with all my might until I lift her high enough that she can crawl through herself.

Then we're finally perched on the ladder, her on the rung opposite me, both gasping for breath.

But there's no time to rest.

Our eyes lock through the crossbars.

We both grab the rung above at the same time and begin the most important race of our lives.

I scramble upward as fast as I can, ignoring the searing ache in my side with each strain of my arms, the flashes of anguish that burst through my lower body with every *pop* of my mangled knee. As much as I struggle to outpace her, Ophelia's eyes are a constant on the other side of the ladder like my dark shadow, a reflection of what I might so easily become if I let my guard down.

With every clang of our boots against the rungs, the ladder shudders and creaks. Just above us, there's a semi-circular landing leading to a short, curved staircase that twists its way up to a door.

The door that leads to the torch.

Ophelia's on the side of the ladder that dead ends underneath the half-moon slab of steel, giving me the edge I so desperately need.

One glance into her wide eyes tells me she knows it, too.

Gritting my teeth against the relentless aching tearing through me, I reach up and grab the next rung to haul myself onto the platform—

Rip!

The ladder breaks apart from its moorings and cants away from the landing, tilting me backward—

Ophelia whips around me and leaps, grabbing hold of one of the steps of the smaller staircase.

She twists her body around until she's facing the rusted crosspieces composing the steps——

I spring after her just as the ladder topples beneath me, leaving nothing but a fifty foot drop into darkness.

Ophelia skitters up the remaining six steps of the smaller staircase. She lunges for the handle on the door—

I tackle her, pinning her down before she can open it. Her elbow slams me in my ribs. The pain's excruciating and I roll off her, curling into a ball, writhing in misery.

She springs to her feet and stares at me with her emotionless eyes. The toe of her boot mashes into my ribs, and I let loose an agonized scream that echoes down into darkness.

When her boot draws back to kick me down the shaft, I somehow grab it, twisting with what I have left.

Crack!

She drops and tumbles over the edge of the platform, grabbing the end of the ladder, her body flailing like a hooked fish. Then she starts to climb up again, ignoring the moans of the metal as it tries to twist loose and topple into the chasm.

Without looking back, I drag myself up the corroding steps, clutching my side, which feels like it's on fire. I grip the door handle and fling it open.

I've reached the torch at last.

I dash out of the spherical base from which the flame must have once burned, onto a circular dais surrounded by a thin railing. The cloud cover's dissipated, and I can see the gray waves crashing against the statue far below.

I grip the railing to ward off the dizziness and skirt the base, my heart thudding in my head and throat.

"*Cole!*" I shriek.

And there above me, embedded in two tongues of

opaque, synthetic flame protruding from the torch, are two figures.

The outline of a young girl ...

And a little boy.

My heart almost bursts.

"Cole! It's Lucky! I'm here!"

Congratulations, Recruit Spark. Select the button to release your Incentive from cryogenic stasis and claim your victory in the Trials.

There are two buttons—marked *Juniper* and *Spark*—implanted in the wall.

I reach a trembling finger toward the button that will release Cole and finally end this nightmare—

Ophelia grabs my hand before I can press it. She tries to push her own button instead, but I grip her hand with my free one.

Then we're locked in a dead heat, each trying to overpower the other. She snarls and jabs her knee into my ribs. I drop to the floor, my eyes fixated on the button that would free Cole, just behind her shoulder, gleaming, taunting me—

Ophelia reaches for her own button—

I kick her as hard as I can, slamming her into the panel—into the button marked *Spark*.

A green glow surrounds the synthetic flame encapsulating Cole, while the other one—the one with Maddie inside—glows red, despite how many times Ophelia now jabs her button.

Stark realization dawns in her eyes.

Congratulations, Recruit Spark. Your Incentive has been reprieved. You have bested your fellow Recruits.

It feels like I've just been reborn into a new world.

Ophelia's shaking her head, as if in the throes of a nightmare. She reaches up, clawing at the shell encasing her sister. "Maddie! Maddie, sweetie! It's *me*! It's Fee-Fee! I've come for you! I'm *here*! Maddie! Maddie!" she bellows.

Another panel slides open underneath Maddie's flame.

Recruit Juniper. You have failed the Trials and will be sentenced to the work camps. Your Incentive will now be shelved. In ten seconds, a stream of hydrochloric acid will be released into her enclosure. However, if you choose, you can activate the override instead, releasing an electrical charge that will instantly stop your Incentive's heart. As always, the choice is yours.

Despite everything she's done, I feel icy claws ripping through my heart, shredding it.

Anybody that's capable of love can't be *all* bad.

"I'm sorry, Maddie ... I tried ... I ... *really* ... tried ... " Ophelia bows her head, weeping.

I limp over to her. "Ophelia. I'm so sorry." I reach out to touch her shoulder—

"*Don't touch me!*" she shrieks.

Make your selection now, Recruit Juniper.

"Goodbye, Maddie," she whispers, pressing the button.

There's a quick spark inside Maddie's chamber. Then it goes dark.

The glow inside Cole's chamber intensifies. Then the torch flame slides open.

I crowd in front of it. A cloud of frosty smoke billows out, obscuring the opening. Then a set of steps unfolds from the capsule, leading to my feet.

I step closer, arms held wide to hug him and never let him go—

Ophelia shoves me out of the way and starts to dash up the stairs toward Cole.

I leap on her and we crash into the railing. The thin metal gives, sending us both over the edge. My nails dig into the rusty metal of the rim to keep from going over as Ophelia dangles from my boot, which starts to slip off.

She stares up at me. "They made me kill my Maddie." Her eyes turn to slits. "*Take them down.*"

She lets go, her body somersaulting once before slamming into one of the spires from the Lady's crown.

Blood gushes from the wound, dripping down onto the Lady's eyes, where it mixes with the drizzling rain and streams down her stone cheeks.

Pulling myself back over the edge, I collapse, a mangled heap of emotions.

The rain's all but stopped now. Dawn seeps through the clouds, the fledgling rays warm against my ice-cold skin.

I look up and gasp.

It's Cole.

He steps through the last wisps of the fading cloud of cryogenic frost like a beautiful angel from the old tales, coming down from the clouds. He's rubbing his eyes as if he just woke up from one of his nightmares.

He sees me ... and stops.

I can't move.

All this time, I imagined running to him if I ever saw him again, scooping him up in my arms.

But now that he's standing just a few feet away, I can only stare, paralyzed with emotion, overpowered by watching a wish I dared dream becoming a reality before my eyes.

My mind races. There are a million things I want to say. When I open my mouth, all my thoughts logjam in my throat.

"Hi," is the only thing that comes out.

"Hi," he says back, staring at me with those big brown eyes.

Just hearing his voice again is like the first spring day after a long, hard winter. I bask in his brightness, taking him all in. "You've gotten *taller*," I finally say. As I clear my throat, I feel my eyes growing moist.

His lower lip quivers. "Lucky, why are you sad?"

The words send a pang through my heart. "I was so afraid you'd think I wasn't coming for you."

He looks confused. "But you always take care'a me." His eyes grow sheepish.

The dam breaks. I can't contain the flood any longer. I bury my face in my hands. So much has happened . . . so many have suffered . . . and died. Yet I endure. And so does my brother. And we have each other. And as fleeting as that may be, it makes everything just a little less dark.

I feel his warm hands around my neck and I open my eyes.

"Are you okay, Lucky?"

Laughter bursts from my lips, from deep within a well I thought had dried up ages ago. "Yes, buddy. I'm okay ... *now*."

Somehow, I find the strength to lift him up.

Two Squawkers appear in the distance, our transport back to Infiernos no doubt.

Hugging Cole tight, we both stare out across the brilliant waters, watching as the strong current creates ripples that spread across the horizon as far as the eye can see.

FORTY-ONE

I press my face against the window of our tenement.

You can never really pull together the threads of an old life after they've unraveled.

It's not like our neighborhood in the Parish is any different. In fact, it's still exactly the same as the last time Cole and I saw it—the cobblestone streets filled with potholes, garbage littering the alleys, plumes of smoke from the factories draping the horizon in a cloud of smog... the haunted faces of the passersby, hustling to get indoors before curfew. Nothing's changed.

Yet everything has.

I sensed it the moment Cole and I disembarked from the transport that brought us home from Infiernos several days ago. We decided to walk home hand in hand rather than have a military escort.

It was in the way people sneaked looks at us, awe and fear

crowding their faces. The way they averted their gaze rather than make eye contact.

We're not part of them anymore. We're not an *Us*. We're a *Them*.

And the truth is, the Lucky who once played Dodge Piss in these streets and rummaged through Dumpsters ... the same one that accepted living in squalor and an early death ... *that* Lucky died during the Trials, along with the others.

I stare, for a moment, at the small wooden number 1 I plucked from above Mrs. Bledsoe's door, then toss it into the hearth and watch as it smolders into ash.

We could have stayed at the Citadel these last few days, but as the victorious Recruit, I was granted permission to return here. The place we've always called home.

This is where it began. It seems fitting that this is where it should end.

Cole and I haven't spoken about what our lives were like during the time we were apart. Maybe it's for the best. And now, on this, our last night together, why spoil it with talk of terrible things?

Tomorrow morning, I ship out to parts unknown to begin my new life as an Imposer trainee. I glance at my neatly pressed uniform hanging from one of the rafters, sporting the shiny silver Imposer pin I was awarded for being the last Recruit left standing—

Just like Cassius.

But so different in every way.

Gideon was wrong when he told me we'd all been selected

as Recruits because of the darkness within us. I was never supposed to be selected. I don't fit the profile. Neither did Digory. Cassius made a critical error in trying to get his revenge. I'll wear their uniform, say what they want to hear—even as I use every skill, every tactic, that they teach me to plot against them.

What better way to slay the monster than from within?

I reach into my nightshirt and clasp Digory's ID tag to my heart.

I won't *ever* give up until I bring them down.

Somewhere out there is a group of freedom fighters that I'm going to make contact with. And then there's the Fleshers. I need to find out what they are, and why they terrify the Establishment so. In the meantime, I'll do what I can on my own—sabotage munitions depots, penetrate defense grids, destroy supply lines—*anything* I can to hasten the day when people can be free and dare to dream.

Cole's feet pad on the creaky floorboards.

I smile. "You ready for bed?"

"Yup." The springs of his mattress squeak as he sinks into his cot and I tuck him in.

The light from the gas lamp flickers across his face.

I kiss his forehead. "G'night, buddy."

I'm about to turn out the light when his hand stops mine.

"Lucky. What happened to the Magic City? Did it disappear when the Lady's fire went away?"

I clasp his hand in mine. "Her fire didn't go away Cole. It's still around. Inside all of us." I tap his chest. "Right *here*."

His laughter's like soothing music. "Can you tell me more stories about the Lady?"

"Don't worry. I will. And I'll also tell you stories about her friends."

"What are their names?"

"There's Gideon, and Cypress, and ... " My eyes well and I turn my head so he can't see. I tweak his nose instead.

He tweaks my nose back.

I clear my throat. "And then there's a very special little girl named Maddie, and her poor big sister Ophelia who got lost in the dark, but found her way back again by the light of the Lady's torch."

"I think I'm gonna like that story."

My throat tightens. "The last friend is *very* special. He helps the others along on their adventures. And he brought me to you."

"What's his name?" Cole asks.

I swipe my eyes. "His name's ... *Digory*."

He smiles. "He sounds nice."

I smile back. "He is."

Cole's eyes cloud over. He cups my cheeks in his hands. "I don't want to keep the stories a secret anymore," he whispers.

I nod. "You don't have to. We're going to pass on the stories to others—as many people as we can—so that no one will ever forget the Lady and her friends."

Cole claps his hands. "Oh, I *like* that!"

I ruffle his hair.

My nose touches his. "I love you, Cole. Always have. Always will."

His face breaks out into a broad grin. "I love you, too."

Then we're hugging each other.

"There once were five friends who went to visit the Lady," I begin.

The stories go on long into the night, and don't stop even after the flame goes out and the first rays of a new day filter through the window.

THE END

Acknowledgments

This novel is the synthesis of amazing support from so many different people.

Thank you Ginger Knowlton, my wonderful agent and cheerleader at Curtis Brown, Ltd., for getting me and believing in my work, even during those dark days when I was convinced no one else was going to ever get the chance to read my words and visit the shadowy places in my head.

Much appreciation to Brian Farrey, my fantastic editor at Flux Books, who helped cure my protagonist of his severe gastric condition and co-dependency issues, even while teaching me a thing or two about pesky ticking clocks. Tick Tock, Brian. I'd also like to commend Sandy Sullivan, my production editor at Flux, for her keen eye and catching the little details that have helped enrich the story, as well as Mallory Hayes, my publicist; Alisha Bjorkland, from marketing; and the rest of the staff at Flux Books. You guys rock!

None of this would have been possible without the SCBWI Aventura Critique Group, who embraced me from day one when I showed up with my telephone-book-sized first novel and had no idea what I was doing. Big hugs to members Dr. Stacy B. Davids, Norma Davids, Angela Padron, Pascale Mackey, Ellen Slane, Jennifer Hill, Julie Edelstein,

Martin Goldman, and Ty Shiver. Props to Mariolga Locklin and the students in the Writers Café at Palmetto High School for making my first speaking engagement as a writer so awesome! Special thanks to Medeia Sharif, for all her invaluable pointers about social media and marketing, and to my fantastic Beta Readers, including Amanda Coppedge Bosky and Marjetta Geerling, for their great feedback. Big shout-out to my sit-com writing partner David Case and his wife, Michelle Visage, for their moral support and efforts in spreading the word, and to Lori Tanner for her wonderful postcard design and giving me the swag hook-up.

Extra special thanks to Joyce Sweeney, my friend and writing mentor, who is always there to console me on this roller-coaster ride to publication and beyond, and her Thursday writing workshop for listening to me ramble and offering insightful critiques. Thank you Linda Rodriguez Bernfeld, SCBWI Florida Regional Advisor, for your tireless efforts in putting on the conferences that allowed me to connect with my agent and editor. Stacie Ramey, you are my writing rock, a true friend, confidante, and daily support that gets me through the dark days. Muah!

And to my adoring partner, Jeffrey Cadorette, *my* Digory, who is always there to answer endless questions about the technical stuff and puts up with my late-night writing sessions, as well as my utter silence as I toil away in front of the computer, virtually ignoring him for hours on end: your patience means the world.

About the Author

Steven dos Santos was born in New York City and moved to Florida at the tender age of five. He wrote his first book, *The Enchanted Prince*, when he was in second grade.

Steven has a BS in Communications but spent most of his career in law, even going to law school before realizing he wanted to be a writer. *The Culling* is his debut novel with Flux.

Visit the author at www.stevendossantos.com.